EVERYTHING WE COULD DO

ALSO BY DAVID MCGLYNN

One Day You'll Thank Me: Lessons from an Unexpected Fatherhood

A Door in the Ocean: A Memoir

The End of the Straight and Narrow: Stories

David McGlynn

Everything We Could Do

A NOVEL

TRIQUARTERLY BOOKS / NORTHWESTERN UNIVERSITY PRESS
EVANSTON, ILLINOIS

TriQuarterly Books
Northwestern University Press
www.nupress.northwestern.edu

The Author's Note appeared, in a slightly different form, as "Look Back in Wonder," in *The American Scholar.*

Chapter 20 was first published, in a slightly different form, as "Heron Lane," in *Story*.

Printed in the United States of America

10 9 8 7 6 5 4 3 2 1

Library of Congress Cataloging-in-Publication Data

Names: McGlynn, David, 1976– author
Title: Everything we could do : a novel / David McGlynn.
Description: Evanston, Illinois : TriQuarterly Books/Northwestern University Press, 2025.
Identifiers: LCCN 2025019113 | ISBN 9780810149175 paperback | ISBN 9780810149182 ebook
Subjects: LCGFT: Fiction | Novels
Classification: LCC PS3613.C485 E94 2025 | DDC 813/.6—dc23/eng/20250527
LC record available at https://lccn.loc.gov/2025019113

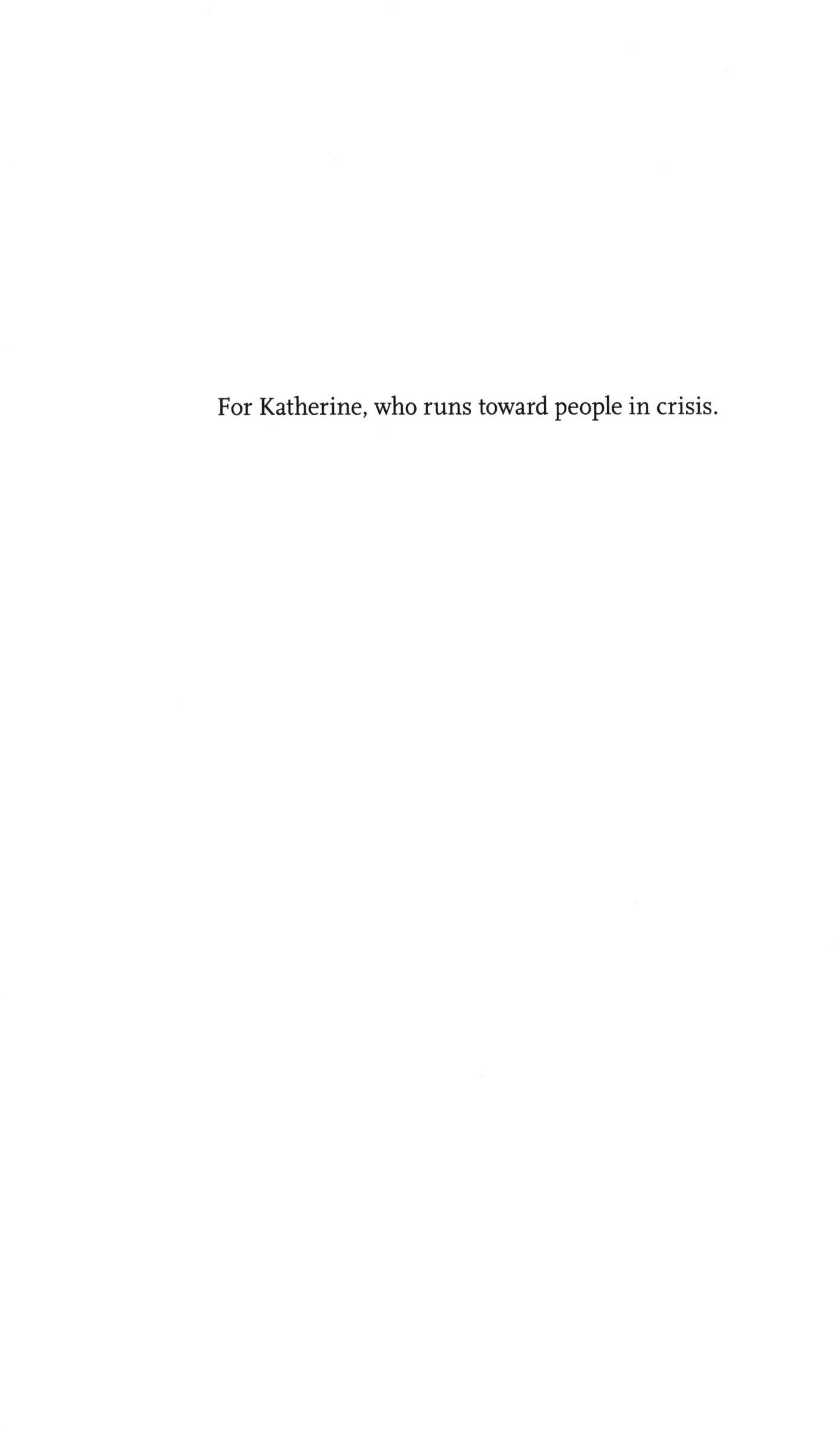

For Katherine, who runs toward people in crisis.

It is correct to love even at the wrong time.

—SPENCER REECE

EVERYTHING WE COULD DO

Part One

1

The words didn't fit. Babies. Children. *Hers.*

In their see-through boxes, buried among the wires and tubing, their tawny skin wrapped in plastic and crosshatched with wrinkled tape, their fused eyes blindfolded, their ears muffled, Opal and Emery Jensen—all of sixty-hours old, born just twenty-three weeks after taking root inside Brooke's body—looked more like globs of organic matter in a science experiment than human beings. That they were alive at all seemed impossible except for the fact that they were. Their names were printed on the bands around their ankles. The lines flowing across the monitors testified to their beating hearts, their breathing lungs.

The nurses had done some on-the-fly redecorating, wheeling the medical supply carts to one end of the bed space and shoving two glider chairs to the center so Brooke and Harper could sit between the Isolettes. Opal was to their right, Emery to their left, in the alcove behind the welcome desk. The incubators glowed an ultraviolet blue, like aquariums. Emery's was bluer than Opal's. The babies reminded Brooke of fish lying on beds of ice, though she didn't dare share that with anyone.

The nurses moved in and out of the bed space with such frequency that they never pulled the curtain shut. When she wasn't watching the babies, Brooke stared at the receptionist's back, her fine white hair so thin the pink orb of her scalp was visible beneath it. Past the front desk was the rest of the neonatal intensive care unit, the NICU, nine bed spaces circumferencing a mission control lined with computers. From time to time, Brooke stared at the moms and dads huddled around the other Isolettes; she registered the shock on their faces and wondered if she looked the same way. Mostly, though, she watched the lines undulate across the monitor.

Harper said he and Brooke looked like a couple in an ad for boner pills. Ma and Pa in rocking chairs on the front porch, waiting for Pa to get it up.

"Stop it," Brooke said, a hand to her flaccid stomach. "Don't make me laugh." The incision from her emergency C-section was raw beneath the gauze. The Maternity nurse had pulled the catheter only that morning, and any involuntary movement sent a jolt of pain straight to her crotch. Opal and Emery, along with Pearl and Ruby, their sister and brother, had been delivered in the emergency room after Brooke's placenta detached from her uterus and began to hemorrhage. A placental abruption, a sudden and lethal problem. The ER doctor told Brooke she was lucky. Not so long ago, women died from abruptions. In many parts of the world, they still did.

Harper gazed up at the ceiling vent. His neck and jaw were dotted with red bumps from the cheap razor the nurses had given him. Even in cargo shorts and a polo, he looked like a news anchor, which he was: Front and Center on WHNR, weeknights at five, six, and ten. On occasion, he conducted interviews at Lambeau Field or down in Madison when the legislature was in session, but most of the time he wore dark suits and sat with his back straight behind the desk in the studio. "Do you know why hospitals have such good air conditioning?" he asked.

"It feels warm in here to me."

"I mean in general."

Brooke shrugged.

"To keep the vegetables fresh."

"God, Harper."

"Sorry," he said, and dragged his eyes to the nurses' station. "It's a lot to take in."

"It is for me, too." Brooke leaned closer, to breathe him in. Barbasol and Dial weren't his brands, and on him they smelled astringent. They were better than the NICU's odor of baby formula and liquified plastic, which made her want to gag.

Harper had a talent for looking on the bright side. For as long as she'd known him, since she was twenty-one, a senior in college, she'd known him as an optimist, a purveyor of silver linings. Late-winter blizzards meant longer skiing and better fishing. Dismal Packers seasons resulted in stronger draft picks. People's lives were hard enough, he said, without everything always sounding like a tragedy. He kept on his bedroom dresser a jar of coins he'd found on the street. Mostly filthy pennies though also a few filthy nickels and filthy dimes. When the jar filled to the point that new coins fell to the dresser, he carried it to the Pick 'n Save and emptied it into the CoinStar machine, then blew the cash on something frivolous, ice cream or an avocado peeler. Every August, he did a story on the Lake Hanover Edsel, the classic car resting on a bed of stones in ten feet of water in a wooded cove. The car had been in the lake for so long that no one knew who it belonged to or how it came to be there. People assumed it had fallen through the ice, though no one could say when. A conservation group claimed the Edsel was leeching toxic fluids into the lake; fishermen said it was a habitat for the prehistoric sturgeon that roamed the lake's bottom. Each summer pictures surfaced of daring swimmers sitting behind the wheel, their eyes bulging and their cheeks puffed. Downtown boutiques sold postcards of the car, the water encasing it blue and clear, practically Caribbean.

Hanover, the city for which the lake was named, lay a hundred miles north of the capital, almost smack in the center of Wisconsin. Home to an ivy-covered liberal-arts college with a famous music conservatory where, years ago, Brooke had started as a cellist before hopscotching through majors on her way to her eventual degree in history and psychology. Nearly a quarter of a million people were scattered across Harper's viewing area, twice that if you added in Green Bay. Once the paper capital of America, Hanover's downtown neighborhoods showcased wide avenues of well-kept Victorian homes, wood-railed porches displaying—depending on the season—flag bunting or tangerine mums or strands of garland. Red barns stood among the cornfields, the tall rows following the contours of the land with geometrical precision. North of the city, the lake crossed the forty-fifth parallel, straddling the hemisphere's midsection like an eyelet on a belt. There the farms turned to forest and grew dense with pine and spruce, paper birch and sugar maples. Two-lane highways meandered all the way to the Michigan border and the infinite, wind-scythed shore of Lake Superior.

The first time Brooke miscarried, Harper said it would be better to have a baby when they were ready, in their own good timing. After his divorce had come through and they'd found a better place to live than Harper's dilapidated one-bedroom above the BrewHaha Café. A few months from graduation, Brooke had at first despaired the image of herself as a pregnant college student, a person who'd let such a thing happen. She didn't even think of the pregnancy as a baby, a would-be person, until she lost it. At which point the blood clots and tissue masses that had filled one pad, then another, and then a third became exactly that—a *person*, a tiny girl or a tiny boy whom Brooke pictured splashing in a bathtub or riding its bike on the driveway. Except now it, she or he, was gone. "In our own good timing," Harper said again, stroking her back. Of course, he wanted to have a family with her. He'd told her already: they *were* a family now.

Every pregnancy loss that followed, and over the next ten years there were many, Harper found some way to turn toward the positive. There was the money they'd save, the freedom they maintained to travel, the stress they'd avoided now that Oliver, Harper's son, was starting school. Brooke had wanted a baby while Ollie was still small, so they'd grow up together. Harper's son, her baby. Harper said Mother Nature kept the score. "Miscarriages are nature's way of making sure human beings are compatible with life," he'd said. He'd meant to sound reassuring. Her last pregnancy, she'd made it to seventeen weeks, past the first trimester. Just yesterday—even, of all days, *yesterday*—he said that a stint in the NICU would give them time to get the house ready, pick the paint colors they wanted for the nursery. How lucky they were to live at a time when modern medicine could save babies this small.

Harper stayed upbeat so long as he didn't look inside the boxes. Staring too long could make anyone, no matter how sanguine, pass into shadow. An endotracheal tube the size of a cocktail straw and held in place with a basket weave of white surgical tape ran from the ring of Emery's mouth to the ventilator. And the breathing tube wasn't half as bad as the needle piercing and disappearing into his fontanel. Emery's pulse throbbed between the unfused bones of his skull like something boiling beneath a swamp. The neonatologist had explained that cranial veins could better tolerate the central line. Once Emery got a little bigger, they'd move the line to some place lower down.

Brooke patted Harper's wrist. "Don't be scared." Though she was scared, too.

The windows along the far side of the unit overlooked a walled courtyard, the tops of three birch trees fluttering in the downdrafts from the roofs. Across the small garden was another hospital wing, its red brick façade going purple in the shadows. It was early September and the birch leaves had started to yellow. In Wisconsin, seasons changed with the flip of a switch. The babies stationed along the windows did baby-like things such as cry and eat and sit in motorized swings. Their bed spaces were crowded with stuffed animals and homemade cards instead of machines. A nurse told Brooke her babies would move bed spaces as they grew bigger. When they made it to Bed One, it would be almost time to go home. Bed Nine, their space, was the starting line.

Their nurses, Dash and Fran, jostled around each other in the tight space. Their sneakers moved like they were dancing, anticipating where the other one needed to be before she got there and moving out of the way. Fran wore her hair short and spiky, like she'd stood in front of a fan, and Dash's was tied back in a braid. She had a bruise on her face that looked like a map of South America, purple and black around her eye socket, yellow as it tapered toward her mouth.

"Clowns to the left of me, jokers to the right," Harper said, wiggling the chair. He used a lot of corny one-liners on TV. People seemed to like them.

Dr. Fackelman, the neonatologist, stood with her glasses halfway down her nose, peering at Emery's ventilator. Her sleeves were unbuttoned and rolled above her wrists. She'd been tweaking the settings all morning. "I think this is officially a watched pot," she said.

"Are we in the way?" Brooke asked her. "Do you need us to move?" Most of the time Brooke had no idea what was going on, even with everything they'd been told. Blood was drawn, a syringe was injected into a hanging sack of fluid, the machines beeped and toned. The nurses' voices fired at twice the normal speed even when they whispered, like a radio stuck between stations.

"You're fine," the doctor said.

What Brooke did understand was that, for the first time, two human lives had survived her body. Opal and Emery were small and sick but they were, by God, alive. The words *son* and *daughter*, like every other name for them, sounded as triumphant and impossible as *astronaut*, which wasn't far from how she thought of them: wired into their glowing capsules and floating through space. They'd orbit here for a while, aboard this intergalactic vessel, turning somersaults and breathing filtered oxygen, and then return to Earth to meet their adoring fans. When Brooke imagined their homecoming—something she tried not to do, but it was hard, the babies were right in front of her—she pictured riding on the back of a convertible with her feet on the back seat, the way beauty queens and mayors do in parades, Opal in one arm and Emery in the other, a marching band and flag corps setting the pace up ahead. Hanover still had parades for everything, even holidays nobody cared about, like Flag Day and the National Day of Honor. Harper had been grand marshal on several occasions. He could make a parade happen, if he wanted to.

Harper had been ready to stop trying, they'd even agreed to stop trying, when Brooke's obstetrician invited her to participate in a clinical trial of a new fertility drug, one intended to help thicken the uterine lining while also stimulating ovulation. Early results were promising, though the chance of multiples was high. Brooke had to pinky-swear to discuss options if she conceived more than triplets. Getting pregnant with a single fetus had consumed the entirety of Brooke's twenties, the first year of her thirties, and more than a hundred thousand dollars. All for nothing. Conceiving multiple babies at once sounded as far-fetched as an asteroid exploding over the Great Lakes and wiping out all life on Earth.

When the ultrasound revealed four babies elbowing one another for room in her uterus, the obstetrician scheduled a consultation with a perinatologist, a specialist in high-risk pregnancy. Dr. Assefa was an elderly Ethiopian man with warm hands the color of potatoes. He touched Brooke's abdomen near her diaphragm and said the most prudent option would be to reduce the fetuses from four down to two. Carrying four babies would be difficult; statistically, they'd have a better shot with twins. Harper liked Dr. Assefa. He'd never heard of perinatology before, but he admired anyone who made a career of going toward danger instead of away from it. He wanted to follow the expert's advice, even if it meant losing two of the babies. Harper was already forty-three, twelve years older than Brooke. The babies would be in first grade when he turned fifty. They'd be paying for college, for four, until he was almost seventy, when he and Brooke should be visiting Europe and watching *Masterpiece Theater.* One child was all they'd ever wanted, he said. Twins would be a blessing, more than they'd ever hoped for.

By then, however, Brooke had named them. Pearl, Ruby, Opal, and Emerald. Emery for short. They weren't *fetuses*—they were *babies.* Her four little jewels. Brooke harbored suspicions a woman of her education and upbringing ought not to have held. An avowed agnostic who only ever set foot inside a church for her stepson's choir concerts, she believed the spirits of her lost children hovered in the ether around her, inside her. Not their souls, exactly, but some irreducible essence of them: the electrical signals pullulating from the squishy gray matter of their neural folds, the very beat she could now see in the soft spot in Emery's head. The electricity of every baby that had ever lived inside her had been absorbed into Brooke's brain like a sprite flashing in the ionosphere. If a lightning strike in Japan could move in a needle in Rhode Island, it seemed no less impossible that the energy of a life that had come into and out of existence entirely within the casing of its mother's body could be conserved. In the synapses between her dendrites, perhaps, or in the spaces between her cells. Driven deep within her most secret corners, they waited for a new body to form.

Lying in bed, or alone in the car, she saw all the contradictions, the double-talk, the rabbit's-foot bullshit of it all. Everyone had their private faiths in the unseen mechanics of the universe. Harper swore that sitting in the right chair on Sundays gave the Packers extra luck, though when they lost he never blamed himself or the chair. That's the thing about superstitions: they're there to save us, not convict us.

In the end, Harper had been the one to ask the doctor to save them. Brooke had been unconscious and bleeding, and the decision had fallen to him. At twenty-three weeks, the babies were premature enough that he could have let them go. Instead he told the doctors to do everything they could. Three doctors—an emergency specialist, a trauma surgeon, a neonatologist—as well as a respiratory therapist worked for half an hour but hadn't been able to get Pearl or Ruby to score any higher than a one on the Apgar. Opal came out pink and vigorous, making crying noises and even trying to breathe, and Emery had required multiple doses of epinephrine and a tube down his lungs before the doctors could bring him to the NICU with his sister. Ruby and Pearl were gone, but Opal and Emery belonged to Harper now, as surely as to her.

Harper's face was inscrutable after years in front of the camera, but from the side Brooke could detect what she took to be his truer feelings, the subtle subcurrents of doubt that had grown around their marriage the way a vine coils around a tree. Or maybe the doubts were Brooke's alone. She had loved him for a decade, a third of her life, and when she considered the sacrifices they'd made, both of them, though arguably him more than her, it seemed impossible she could love anyone but him. Despite what people thought, the terrible things they'd whispered or simply come right out and said to her, she hadn't been helpless, a naive girl warped by too many rom-coms. That she and Harper had made it this far Brooke took as evidence that they really did belong together. And yet, deeper down she wondered—how could she not?—whether their beginning was to blame for her body's failures, and would one day bring about their end.

Harper caught her staring. "What?"

"Just wondering what you're thinking about."

"Ollie," he said. "If he's scared, too."

"He's with his grandparents," Brooke said. "I'm sure he's okay."

"I'm also looking at those brownies." He gestured at the unit, the nurses leaning around a foil tray at the central station.

"You want one?"

"God, no. I'm wondering if we're in the right place here. Hanover's fine for easy stuff, like hearing aids and getting your appendix out, but if we needed a bigger surgery, you know, something serious, we'd go to Milwaukee or Madison. Maybe even Chicago." He leaned closer. "Wouldn't we?"

"We didn't have much choice." The abruption had occurred while they were on their boat, in the middle of the lake, a pool of blood in the vinyl chair. Harper had thrust the throttle forward, rocketing across the water to Hanover

Medical Center, its modern new wing, mirrored and curved like an enormous glass cube, rising up from the shore. That much Brooke remembered: the bow lifted, the growl of the engine, her weight pressed to the boat's sodden floor. What happened after—the medics who helped get Brooke inside, the ER nurses inserting needles into her veins, whether Oliver had been abandoned in the boat—she could not recall. Her memory started again when she woke up in Maternity, her window overlooking the lake, a gossamer fog over the water, the trees orange with sunlight. For more than an hour she'd lain alone, watching the water shimmer, wondering what had happened to her babies, whether any of them had survived.

"Wouldn't it look bad for you if we transferred them?" she asked. "The news anchor who has lost faith in his own city?"

"I don't know. I'm mostly thinking aloud."

"Better than staring off into space."

Nurse Dash came to the bedside, drinking from a bottle of water. The nurses were always drinking something. Coffee, Mountain Dew, God knows what from huge travel mugs. Dash took a swig and poured the rest of the bottle into the reservoir at the foot of Opal's Isolette. Brooke watched the water leave the bottle and wondered if it was sanitary. Would her daughter breathe the nurse's cooties? And that bruise on her face. Whatever happened must have hurt.

"Are you hungry?" Harper asked Brooke. It sounded like a leading question. Dash stepped between the Isolettes, peeling off one pair of gloves and snapping on another. "Do you want me to find you something to eat?" Harper said.

"Maybe a Diet Coke," Brooke said. "But don't get up right now."

"Only water is allowed at the bedside," Dash said without looking up.

Harper cleared his throat. "You'll give yourself kidney stones if all you drink is coffee and Diet Coke," he said. "You need real food."

"I haven't been very hungry."

"I could go for coconut curry, with shrimp. Or Bolognese over polenta." He sat back in the glider. "Mmmm."

"You can go home, if you want." Brooke said. "Maybe it would help to cook."

"I don't want to leave you."

"Sounds like quite a meal," Dash said, interjecting again.

Harper turned his face toward her, pleased she'd asked. "I'm a cook. Cooking relaxes me."

"How do you stay so lean?"

"I run. Not very fast, but I'm out there."

"He also has the metabolism of a sixteen-year-old boy," Brooke said. "It's so annoying."

"Brooke's a better cook than I am," Harper said, gesturing. "She can make anything. Seriously, Julia Child."

Dash shrugged. "I'm a meat-and-potatoes gal. I wouldn't know a braise from a broaster."

"What about brownies?"

"What?"

"You like brownies?" Harper's eyes swung toward the central station. There was a ring of crumbs on the counter and wads of napkins in the trash.

"Another nurse brought them in. We all eat too much sugar around here."

"You're on your feet a lot," Brooke said.

Dash nodded and opened the porthole windows of Opal's Isolette. Opal's diapers were the size of a shirt pocket and still the nurse had to fold down the top to make them fit. Opal's face was masked by crisscrossing felt straps that held in place a clear plastic valve, a CPAP, that forced pressurized air through her nose. The nurse's hands worked swiftly, as though working to diffuse a bomb, her purple gloves glowing beneath the ultraviolet light. "I have never in my life seen a baby born this early *not* on a ventilator," she said.

"What's the earliest baby you've cared for?" Harper asked. Another of his talents: making experts sound smarter about their own subjects.

"I've seen a twenty-one weeker once." Dash looked up from the Isolette, pausing in mid-task. She caught what Harper was asking and her eyes narrowed. "I've seen my share. I've been in this unit for seventeen years. Dr. Fackelman came to us from a massive Level IV unit in San Diego. She's seen it all. The fact that she put Opal on CPAP means her lungs are going gangbusters."

The nurse's gloves hovered in mid-air. Purple, almost phosphorescent, they spanned the length of Opal's body. Her daughter disappeared beneath them, like a dove in a magic trick.

A red light flashed on the monitor. An alarm toned, *honk, honk, honk*. "Oh, hush," Dash said, jabbing at a button. She peeled a foil sticker away from Opal's chest so she could reattach it. The line on the screen briefly went flat before resuming its jagged wave.

2

The intercom at the door crackled and her mother-in-law's voice broke through the murmuring silence. The panes in the NICU door and the window beside the receptionist's desk were an inch thick and muffled nearly every outside noise—the steady river of people streaming toward Maternity with balloons and flowers and stuffed animals, toddlers in *I'm the Big Brother!* T-shirts. The NICU was next door to the one wing of the hospital where people expected only good things to happen.

Harper asked if his parents and son could come inside, but Penny, the white-haired receptionist, shot him down cold. Every visitor needed a wristband, and each family only got two. Kids under twelve weren't allowed, period, and it mattered not one bit that Oliver was eleven and tall for his age. Penny appeared pleased to inform Harper of these facts. One of her incisors was capped in silver. Brooke noticed the vein rising in Harper's neck, the same one that bubbled up whenever he had sex. Anger and lust weren't so different from each other. They're both ways of feeling desperate and vulnerable.

Harper forced a smile and said he wasn't trying to make waves. He only wanted his son to meet his little brother and sister.

"Let's go out to them," Brooke said, hoisting herself from the glider. Standing up hurt worse than using the toilet. "There's no room in here anyway."

"Use the Family Room," Penny said. She hit a button and the heavy doors to Maternity swung open. It was possible Penny controlled the entire hospital from her desk behind the window. With her silver fang and framed photograph of her corgi, she reminded Brooke of Roz, the white-haired slug in *Monsters, Inc.* She'd watched that movie with Oliver at least a thousand times.

Kleenex boxes occupied the end tables and three more stood on the coffee table, the tissues rising from the cubes like frozen white flames. Brooke's father-in-law, Mel, led her to an armchair and held her hands to help her sit. She'd rather have stayed standing to avoid having to stand back up again, but she followed his lead. Harper's mom and sister, Susan and Elizabeth, settled in together on the loveseat while Oliver, clutching an iPad, turned a chair around to face the flat screen mounted to the wall. He scrolled the channels until he found cartoons.

"Do you need anything?" Susan asked her. "Can we get you anything?" She wore a sleeveless blouse, her arms tanned and lean from playing tennis twice a week, though she was past seventy. Mel, standing beside Harper in front of the door, wore navy shorts and a Tommy Bahama shirt and was as catalog handsome as his wife. All the Jensens were. Elizabeth cultivated enough gray in her curly dark hair to look corporate sexy even in jeans and rubber sandals. She ran an educational policy firm, whatever that meant.

Brooke shifted in the chair. "It hurts no matter how I sit."

"I remember that pain," Elizabeth said. Her daughters were sixteen and fourteen, already glamorous. "I thought I was going to die. I had to pack bags of frozen peas between my legs."

"Witch hazel," Susan said. "Nothing better for a sore business than witch hazel."

"I had a C-section," Brooke said. "My business isn't half as sore as my stomach."

"Mel, ask the nurse for a pillow," Susan said.

It felt strange to have Harper's parents fuss over her. Throughout her marriage, Mel and Susan had been cordial but wary, always a little wary. In their presence Brooke felt that they registered every word she said. They hadn't been supportive of their relationship, of course they hadn't, not at first. Harper was thirty-three and had a baby at home. They didn't know what had gone wrong in his marriage and they didn't need to. Harper had let his pecker lead him down a bad road; he needed to kiss his coed goodbye and hightail it back to the real world. As if Brooke had no say in the matter. As if she moved through her still-nascent life like a drunk girl at a fraternity party, fantasizing about married news anchors. "Happiness is something you get to think about *before* you tie the knot," Mel had said. "Once you're hitched, your bed is made and you have to sleep in it. That bed and no other." Brooke sat beside Harper on the couch the night his father called; she could hear Mel's voice as Harper held the phone to his ear. Nine weeks pregnant, she'd yet to meet anyone connected to Harper, even Ollie, and the disapproval—Harper's parents, her own mother in Oak Park—had only fueled her desire, her certainty the universe had conspired to bring them together. Harper said he felt the same way. Fate was a force too powerful and mysterious to fight, and what did other people know of what went on between the two of them? His old man could take a long walk off his own short dock. He could go fuck himself in his own icy lake.

Now Mel was sliding a pillow behind her back. At least their being here gave Brooke a reason to tell her own mother not to drive up from Chicago. "Tell us," he said, patting her shoulder. "How are my grandchildren?"

"So far, so good," Harper said. He sat on the edge of the sofa, both feet planted, refusing to lean back. He had news to report. Emery was on a ventilator, he explained, but Opal was on the CPAP. He made a claw with his hand to demonstrate how the CPAP forced pressurized air through her nasal passage while leaving her mouth and throat unobstructed. "She's got good lungs," Harper said. Brooke waited for him to say "gangbusters."

"She's a Jensen," Mel said proudly. "Ahead of the curve."

"Can she eat?" Susan asked. She looked directly at Brooke. "Are you able to nurse her?"

Brooke shook her head and Harper interjected. "She's way too small, Mom. Doctor said the suck and swallow reflex doesn't develop until, like, thirty-two weeks. Opal and Emery get their calories through an injection. White goop in a syringe."

"Yuck," Elizabeth said. "Then again, I've tasted baby formula. Talk about nasty."

"I'm supposed to pump and freeze my milk for later," Brooke said. "Once it comes in."

"There's no substitute for breastmilk," Susan said. "Don't let the people here try to tell you any different."

"I used formula once the girls started daycare," Elizabeth said. "They're plenty healthy."

"The babies are two days old. It's not something we have to worry about quite yet," Brooke said. The things they did have to worry about were almost too many to digest at once. The nurses seemed to speak only in letters: Brooke had heard Dash ask another nurse to fetch a UVC and not to fuss with the SIMV, and then whisper to Dr. Fackelman that once the babies got a little bigger they'd do a POS to rule out CCHD. Brooke didn't know what any of it meant, though she had figured out that both Opal and Emery had holes in their hearts.

The ductus arteriosus joined the aorta to the pulmonary artery while in utero, allowing blood from the right ventricle to bypass a fetus's fluid-filled, nonfunctioning lungs. Under ordinary circumstances, the ductus closed on its own after birth, but in premature infants, it stayed open. The condition was called a PDA, short for patent ductus arteriosus. If the holes didn't close on their own, certain medicines could help and surgery was an invasive but effective last resort. Retinal damage was also common among micro-preemies. Of more immediate concern were their hematocrit numbers. Levels dropped during the first week of life until they hit the nadir, jumpstarting the bone marrow into producing red-blood cells. If Opal and Emery didn't get there soon, they'd need a transfusion.

"My word," Susan said. Elizabeth, too, held her hand over her mouth.

"The doctor's optimistic," Brooke said. Through the cross-hatched windowpane the lake glimmered in the morning sunlight. A sailboat leaned to one side, though it appeared still. A white gull dropped over the surface, chased by its shadow, and disappeared.

Harper turned to Oliver, still staring at the TV. "What do you think about all this, Stone?" It was one of Harper's nicknames for his son, along with Twist, Holmes, North, Platt, and Hardy—all famous Olivers. As if his son would forever command the world's attention. "Pretty scary stuff?"

Oliver watched with his mouth open and his jaw slack. At eleven, he still sat crisscross applesauce on the living room floor. Some nights he slept with his thumb in his mouth. His mom thought it was time for him to get a cell phone, but Harper wanted him to wait another year, until junior high. Brooke knew well enough to stay out of it.

Oliver shrugged. "How long do we have to stay here?"

"I wanted you to meet your brother and sister, but Nurse Ratched said no."

"Is that really her name?" Mel wanted to know.

"She's not even a nurse," Brooke said. "She just controls the door."

"Couldn't they have made an exception?" Susan asked. "Just long enough for us to take a peek? Could you say you're going to do a story on them? People love to be on TV."

"I don't want to be on TV," Brooke said, looking down at her slippered feet. She was glad Penny had taken the hard line. She didn't want Harper's parents and sister arguing about witch hazel while they crowded around the Isolettes.

"I don't want to be on TV, either," Elizabeth said. "You can blur me out."

"No one's going to be on TV," Harper said.

"We've come all this way," Susan said. "You told them we're from out of state?"

"Another time, Mom. Okay?"

"I'm bored," Oliver said. "It's boring here."

"We should go," Susan said. "It's not fair to make poor Ollie sit around with nothing to do."

Poor Ollie. Destined to a life of suffering because his father had let his pecker lead him down a bad road with a coed. Poor, poor Ollie, who had two birthdays every year, two Christmases, who made double the cash on every lost tooth, who one year went to Disney World twice—once with Harper and Brooke and a second time with Sara and her husband. When Ollie was a baby, Brooke and Harper spent hours crisscrossing Wisconsin in pursuit of apple orchards and harvest festivals, story times at small-town libraries where a life-sized Cat in the Hat was scheduled to appear, all to prove that they could somehow form a family even if Ollie was theirs only half the time. Time divided, Brooke understood, was time multiplied.

Elizabeth squeezed Brooke's hand. "Text me later. I can bring you a latte." Brooke could see that her sister-in-law meant it. Elizabeth saw herself as a person who came through for others, who showed up with lattes or bottles of wine in the nick of time, a real lifesaver who penned little handwritten notes that said just the right things. Again Brooke thought, gratefully, of Penny behind her desk, her extra chins glowing in the papery white aura of her reading lamp. The impenetrable lock on the door. "Thank you," she said, hoping it didn't sound fake.

"I get the policy when it comes to grandparents and aunts," Harper said. "But Ollie is immediate family." Grains of sand drained from an hourglass timer on the washbasin. They were supposed to scrub until all the sand ran out, and they were supposed to do this every time they entered the NICU, even if they only stepped out for a moment. "Ollie could have scrubbed in, too. He's not sick. None of us are."

"The babies are," Brooke said. "They don't even have red blood cells."

Harper dried his hands while Brooke read the titles of the books along the shelf above the sink: *Goodnight, Moon, The Very Hungry Caterpillar, Welcome Little One,* at least a dozen more. She pictured herself reading to Opal and Emery. Dr. Fackelman had told her to expect Opal and Emery to stay here until their original due dates. Brooke looked at her fingers and counted out the months till January. A month for every finger except her thumb. If everything went perfectly, they might make it home by Christmas. It was a comforting image: the fire going, snow piling on the windowsill, the babies lying together on a blanket spread across the living room carpet. Even Halloween felt remote when visitors arrived at the hospital in shorts and Tommy Bahama shirts.

Jenny Ramirez, the unit social worker, told Brooke that a lot of moms went back to work while their babies were here, to preserve their maternity leave. "All the fun stuff happens after you go home." Brooke was a project manager in a local marketing firm, and the thought of sitting at her desk while Opal and Emery were here, breathing through tubes with their eyelids still fused, as close to the beginning edge of life as two humans could be, their bones from her bones, their flesh from her flesh—she couldn't fathom it. She'd called human resources that morning to say she'd be going on family medical leave and didn't know when she'd be back.

Dash had chocolate smeared on her scrub top. Harper focused on it, as if to divine its Rorschach shape. "I like your name," he said to her. "It's unique, for a woman."

"My real name is Dolores. I'm an Irish twin. My sister Dorothy is only eleven months older than me. We're the youngest of seven, and in family pictures we're hard to tell apart. To keep us straight, my mother put a little dot beneath my sister and a dash beneath me. Dorothy became Dottie and I became Dash."

"It fits you," Brooke said. "Dolores is more old-fashioned."

"Can I ask you something else?" Harper said.

Dash touched her cheek below her eye, her continent-shaped, multi-colored bruise. "You're wondering if I'm married to a wife beater?"

"That's none of my business," Harper said. "But it looks painful."

"I was playing catch with my son and missed. It looks worse than it is."

"I was actually going to ask about these lights." Harper pointed at the ultraviolet panels angled over the Isolettes. Emery's was slim and modern and attached to an adjustable arm; Opal's was boxy and on a wheeled stand. Beneath them, the babies glowed slightly different shades of blue, their veined skin like an alien reptile's. "How come the one over Emery's bed is a different color than the one above Opal's?"

"Emery's bilirubin light is newer," Dash said. "Uses more efficient bulbs."

Harper sat tall in the chair, like he was about to go on the air. "Opal's is old? Why don't they have the same one?"

"Not old, just older," Dash said. "We're replacing them gradually. We only have a few of the slick new ones."

"I hate to ask, but shouldn't there be a protocol for things like that? I mean, if our babies are so small and sick my son can't come inside, shouldn't they have the most advanced equipment?"

"They're nothing but bili lights," Dash said. "A desk lamp could almost do the job. In the old days, nurses put jaundiced babies by the windows. The older ones work the same."

Harper stood and craned his neck to survey the unit. "There's a newer light right over there. Think we could switch them out? That other baby looks healthier."

"You don't know that," Brooke said.

Harper held up his hands. "I don't, you're right. I don't mean to gripe, but I can't help feeling like something isn't right. We've had two babies die and they can't give us both good lights?"

The door buzzed and Dr. Fackelman came inside. She stopped to talk to Penny before coming toward them. "I understand you're concerned about the bili lights."

"Well, yeah, if I'm being honest," Harper said. He set his hand on the back of Brooke's chair. "I am concerned. I'd really like my daughter to use one of the newer lights."

"Phototherapy is a noninvasive treatment," the doctor said. "At this stage it's a precaution."

"In that case, she should have the best *precaution* available," Harper said. He forced a smile now, his news anchor face. “I was telling your colleague here that there should be a protocol for doling out the equipment. Surely our insurance covers the higher-end technology.”

“We have a policy against switching equipment between patients,” Dr. Fackelman said. “Especially because a parent demands it.” She looked down at Brooke, as if to enlist her aid. “Trust me, your babies are receiving the best possible care.”

“I’m not demanding anything,” Harper said. “I’m only asking. We’ve had a tough few days and I’m starting to have some doubts. You hear these kinds of stories, you know? Other affiliates in our network have run them. The hospital that kills all its patients and no one can explain why. Scary stuff.”

“Harper,” Brooke said. She laid her hand atop his, across her shoulder. She felt the knobs of his knuckles against the lifelines of her palm.

“That’s not going to happen,” Dr. Fackelman said. “Maybe it would help you to talk to our unit staff manager?”

“I’d honestly rather huddle with the hospital president,” Harper said. “The person actually running the show.”

“A man, you mean,” Dr. Fackelman said.

“I’m not trying to make it about any of that stuff. But since we’re talking, I have some real concerns. I’d like to talk to someone who can address them.” His hands went up again. “That’s all I’m saying.”

Harper often talked about the news as a service to the community. It not only shed light on the facts, it also *made things right.* Some people were selfish and lazy unless they had their arms twisted. Other people were downright cheats. Showing up on TV kept people accountable. In most cases, it was enough for people to recognize him. Once they did, they went the extra mile without saying a word. Their restaurant tables moved nearer the windows and the waiter checked in more often. Harper only grew irate when he needed to protect his people, like the time a neighborhood kid blew a stop sign on his moped and came a breath away from hitting Ollie on his bike. Harper chased the kid in his car, cornered him in the marina parking lot, and kept him there until his parents arrived. Now, though, watching Dr. Fackelman stomp away, Brooke felt pulled to defend the nurses and doctor, as if she needed to stay on their good side, as if her babies' lives depended on the staff seeing her and Harper as good, kind people who deserved to escape suffering.

Half an hour later, the hospital president, Leif Gunnarson, in a crisp white shirt and tie, buzzed into the NICU. His shirt was hardly wrinkled though it was after four o'clock in the afternoon. "My wife and I watch your newscast," he said to Harper. "I'm sorry to hear we may have dropped the ball here."

"No," Dr. Fackelman interrupted. "There was no mistake. A minor confusion is all."

Emery's monitor toned. Dash pressed her index finger to her lips.

Leif said, "Let's give the staff here space to do their work."

Harper followed him and Dr. Fackelman to the open space in front of Penny's desk. The doctor stood with her arms crossed and her sleeves rolled above her elbows. Harper's thumbs were hooked inside the belt loops of his shorts. Brooke's embarrassment washed out of her and was replaced by a flood of pride. She remembered Harper flying after the reckless punk on the moped, his clenched jaw behind the wheel when he shifted from reverse to drive at the bottom of the driveway. It pleased Brooke, and soothed her, to see her husband fighting for *her* babies, the lives they'd made together. She'd been waiting ten years for a day like this.

The first time—and maybe, also the last—she'd felt so aligned with him, as though they were one flesh, was the first time she'd ever told Harper she was pregnant. Their affair—though at twenty-one the word felt too old to her, too middle-aged and bougie—had been going for three months. A winter of beautiful, desperate madness. At times it was the danger itself she enjoyed, sneaking into friends' apartments, the sound of his hard shoes in the corridor of her dorm, the dizzying adrenaline of skiing toward a blind hill or speeding in a car through the fog. Up until then, their secret had felt abstract: because no one knew about them, the only lasting damage would be to Harper's conscience, if such a thing were even real. She planned to graduate in June and move to New York for an internship at Ogilvy. Harper would try to save his marriage for the sake of his son. But a pregnancy test filched from the student health center had come up pink. Their secret was now a physical thing, one she was sure she could feel when she lay silently in the dark.

Harper picked her up from the dorms a little after two; it was a soggy February afternoon, the rain turning to slush and gumming up the wiper blades. All their usual places were crime scenes, and Brooke sat quietly as Harper headed first west and then north, into the woods. The trees sagged with wet, new snow and leaned across the empty highway. The shadows between the trees were abyssal pockets of blackness. They listened to the radio until the reception gave out. Brooke switched it off and they drove for an hour without talking or passing another car until they made it to Solberg Lake, where Harper's in-laws had a cabin. They had to walk the last half mile. The road wasn't paved and no one plowed it; even if someone figured out where they were, Harper said, they'd be hard to reach. He knew which window to jimmy open and where his father-in-law stored the firewood. The pipes had been flushed, but the propane stove worked, and there was plenty of snow around to melt. For three nights they ate bean dip and pretzels from the gas station and lay beneath a pile of musty blankets, their phones powered down and wedged inside the toes of their shoes. She didn't ask him what he'd told his wife or boss about where he was going, or whether he'd said anything at all. Harper didn't mention Oliver or Sara or even the life growing inside her. His mouth on her breasts, her belly, between her legs, was ravenous, more desperate than ever, as if each time they touched each other could be the last. She wanted to stay there forever. She wanted to die there.

Harper hadn't told anyone he was leaving, and when they returned to Hanover on Sunday evening the police were waiting at his house, along with Sara's parents. Brooke confessed everything, first to the dean of students and then, later, to her mother, coughing and weeping. Her mother told her to delete Harper's number from her phone. Harper needed to figure himself out without her interference, and Brooke had her own decisions to make. The best thing she could do was to walk away before she made things worse. "And trust me," her mother said, "they can get a lot worse."

Brooke deleted him from her contacts, deleted his texts, emptied the folder where she'd saved his emails. She wiped her phone clean. But when he called the next day, she recognized the number, the Hanover area code, the string of digits behind it. She knew her mother would say not to answer it, but she did anyway. Harper said he was sorry for all the hurt he'd caused—caused her and the other people in his life. He said he'd never wanted to be a person who hurt others, especially not the people he loved. He wasn't that kind of man. Brooke started to say it wasn't *all* his fault, she'd obviously played her part. Maybe it would help if he blamed everything on her. She was graduating in a few months anyway, and perhaps she could figure out how to leave campus sooner rather than later. Harper said that as much as their little Houdini act had made things worse for him, it had also made things clearer. The prospect of losing her was worse than any other regret. His marriage was over either way, but if he lost Brooke he'd never get over it. He'd turn into one of those crazy old guys who ate at restaurants every night because he couldn't face going home without her.

"You mean that?" Brooke asked.

"Every word."

Within a week he'd moved into the apartment above the BrewHaha. By the time she miscarried a month later, he'd consented to supervised visits with Ollie until custody could be worked out.

Leif Gunnarson and Dr. Fackelman came back to the bed space while Harper left the unit, his phone in his hand. "When one of the newer lights becomes available, let's switch it out," Leif said. He offered a political smile. "No rush. Whenever it's no longer needed elsewhere."

Nurse Fran frowned. "They work exactly the same."

Dash interrupted. "Yes, sir. We'll move it over." Fran scowled. Dash's face, despite her acquiescence, had turned stern. Harper had breached a line Brooke hadn't known existed until they crossed it.

"And let's keep food in the nurses' lounge. The NICU should be as sterile and sanitary an environment as possible."

Dr. Fackelman bit down on her lip. An alarm sounded across the unit, and she appeared relieved by the opportunity to rush toward it.

Fran covered Opal's bed with a fleece blanket and carried her laptop back to the central desk to finish her charting. Dash adjusted the dials on the pump and switched out

Emery's IV. Emery lay inside his Plexiglas chamber like a specimen pinned to a board.

Dash sat down on the stool beside the cart and set her hands on her knees. "I don't mean to nose in, but this is a long haul. A trip to Mars and back. A lot can happen. The bili lights are nothing to get worked up about."

"Harper means well," Brooke said. "He goes into Mike Wallace mode when he's scared."

"The doctor is right. You need to trust us."

"It's a lot to take in," Brooke said. She waved at the unit. "All of this."

"Every parent feels that way," Dash said. "I felt that way, and I'm a nurse."

"You had a baby in here?" Brooke asked. "In this unit?"

"Back then the NICU was a single room down one of the Maternity hallways," Dash said. "Four beds, three nurses. I didn't start working here until after my son was discharged. Landon was born at twenty-eight weeks. That's a cake walk today, but back then we weren't sure if he'd survive. He was here eighty-six days."

"How old is he now?"

"Seventeen," Dash said. "Eighteen this March." She lifted the ID badge slung around her neck and flipped it over. From inside the plastic sleeve she extracted a family photograph. Dash sat beside a smiling balding man, a graying beard at his chin. A teenage boy and younger girl stood behind them, their hands on their parents' shoulders. The studio's logo was embossed in the corner.

Brooke stared at the photograph of Dash's son. His chest and shoulders stretched the T-shirt tucked into his jeans. The faint wisp of a mustache shadowed his lip, and his eyes were wide-set and slightly off center. A creature as small as Opal or Emery growing to such a size, all that height and girth, the awkward body of a teenager—it was like looking at a picture of a tropical island, a palm tree crooked over the sand. She could scarcely believe it, even as she hoped it was real.

"Handsome," she said.

"Landon's the sweetest boy on the planet," Dash said. "My pride and joy."

"He looks like it," Brooke said. "A fine young man."

3

Landon sat on the living room carpet, his legs crossed and a crescent of skin peeking over the waistband of his shorts. He gazed at the television with his jaw slack and his tongue shelved on his bottom lip. He was watching one of those dragon movies he liked, from *The Golden Lance* series. Dash had no idea what number. There were so many and more came out every year.

Until two years ago, Dash had prescreened everything Landon watched, charting each occurrence of violence and sex in the same five-subject spiral notebook she used for Landon's therapy. She weighed and measured her son's movies and TV shows like they were medications for her patients. *Harry Potter and the Sorcerer's Stone*: Voldemort drinks blood from a dead unicorn; *Spiderman*: Mary Jane attacked in the rain, nipples visible through wet T-shirt. Since the paper mill had closed and Dash had started picking up extra shifts to make ends meet, she'd had to rely on the opinions of others. Common Sense Media gave *The Golden Lance* three stars and rated it safe for kids ten and older. Over on AutisMom.com, everydayablessing78, who always had smart things to say, said the movies were harmless except that the women wore tight leather corsets that made their breasts bounce like beach balls at a Jimmy Buffet concert. "Who can fight a dragon that way? I mean, seriously. I'd worry about the fire spit going down my cleavage. Why even wear the armor if it's not going to cover the important stuff?" As far as Dash could tell, the movies didn't contain any actual nudity. If they had, she doubted Landon would notice.

"Dad and I are going to take Kasey around to sell her popcorn for school," she said. "Can you hang out for a little bit?"

"Volleyball, not school," Landon said, without turning to look at her.

"She's on the school team, honey."

"Volleyball sells popcorn. Soccer sells candy and cross country sells cookie dough. Football and basketball both sell coupon books because they're in different seasons of the year."

"Okay," Dash said. "Volleyball popcorn."

"Do you have all the flavors?"

"Got them."

"Do you have the cheddar and the caramel?"

"Yes."

"Garlic lime?"

"We got them all, Landon. Can you watch your movie and relax? We'll be right outside." When Landon was fourteen, he'd developed a sudden fear of being left alone. If Mike left the house while Dash was in the basement, he'd wail and hammer his fists against the walls. Neither of Landon's therapists—back then they could still afford both occupational and behavioral specialists—could pinpoint what had caused the panic, and for several months Dash roamed the house with one of Mike's hunting walkie-talkies clipped to her waist. One day the fear stopped, with no more explanation than when it started.

"You'll be able to see us everywhere we go," she said. "We won't leave our block."

Landon's eyes stayed glued to the screen as he rested his weight on his right hand, the hand he'd punched her with nine days ago. Seeing it prompted Dash to reach up and touch her cheek. The swelling had gone down but the pain was still exquisite. Landon hadn't knocked into her during one of his stims; he'd cocked his arm and driven it like a piston into her face. Until the moment it happened, until she was lying on the front lawn watching the clouds pass over the maple, she hadn't thought him capable of it.

Mike and Kasey waited for her at the bottom of the front walk, their old Radio Flyer wagon loaded with cardboard boxes. Mike wore his Cabela's cap. He was boxy through the chest and gut, the source of their son's girth but not his height. His once peppery beard was now fully gray, a change that still caught Dash off guard. They'd been together since high school.

Kasey's volleyball coach had told the girls to wear their uniforms when they knocked on doors, to help connect their customers to the team they were supporting, but seeing her daughter in dinky spandex shorts made Dash wonder if the coach had other things in mind. He was young, drove a hybrid car, called his live-in girlfriend his "partner." You never knew with someone like that.

"Are you wearing a sports bra?" Dash asked.

"Gross, Mom," Kasey said. "Stop checking out my rack." She'd been mouthy since she was little. She was the one to teach her brother to swear, prodding him to yell "shit" and "ass" on the school bus when she was seven. Seven! Turning thirteen had only made things worse, as though the gun used to implant the gold studs in her earlobes had also injected a booster shot of sass.

"Young lady."

"My mammary glands," Kasey said. "My chesticles."

Mike glanced at his daughter's chest, then stared off toward the end of the street, trying to look as far away as possible.

"That's enough," Dash said. She'd come off a twelve-hour shift and was in no mood for back talk. "Maybe you should go back inside."

"Why do I have to sell this crap anyway? It's all MSG and artificial dyes. Like anyone wants that. Izzy's mom wrote a check."

"Too bad you're not in her family," Dash said.

"Selling is good for you," Mike said. "I had to sell chocolate bars for wrestling when I was in school. Do you know how hard it is to make weight when you're lugging around a big box of chocolate? But I tell you what, I was sure proud of myself when I stepped on that scale." Dash remembered Mike at seventeen, sitting down with only an apple for lunch and eating the entire thing, core and all. His every rib defined, countable, as he took the mat in his singlet, the bulge in the crotch that seemed to her the epicenter of her unfathomable, inevitable future.

Mike nudged the wagon over a crack in the sidewalk. "This way we can talk to people about what happened."

"Why do I have to come for that?"

"Two birds, one stone."

He'd been the one to insist on talking to the neighbors. They'd lived on the street for twenty years, and everyone, even the folks they didn't much talk to, knew who they were. They'd seen Landon riding his bike and shoveling snow, and if they hadn't been there the day the police came, they'd surely heard about it. They owed people an explanation. Dash wasn't so sure, but she'd won every other battle so far. Mike had wanted to take her and Landon both to the emergency room after he punched her, but she'd said no way in hell. When it came to their son, Dash had always been in charge. She'd been the one to make sure his IEP was in place when he started school, the one who fought to add behavioral and sensory intervention plans, the one the school nurse called whenever Landon had a hard day. Dash was the nurse, the expert, and in most cases, Mike deferred to her. This little house-to-house apology tour was a concession, a bone tossed to a dog.

A pack of cigarettes swelled Charlie Weyenberg's breast pocket, and a stale odor flooded out his front door. He'd lived next door to Dash and Mike for as long as they'd lived on the street, but the smoking had kept them from being closer friends, even when Charlie's wife, Sonja, was dying of kidney cancer. Dash had left food on their step or passed the dishes across the threshold. He and Mike drank beer in the garage some nights, but Dash had never been all the way inside his house.

Their street of small clapboard boxes had been built in the years following World War II, when the mills were hiring as fast as soldiers were being discharged. Some houses had three-season porches or extra bedrooms squeezed into the attics and basements, but almost none had fences. Their early years here, before the kids came along, their block parties had lasted till two in the morning. Dru Heineman would set his stereo on milk crates and the string lights in the oaks would join one yard to the other in a long, dotted chain. Not so much had changed in twenty years, other than the children getting older, learning to drive, leaving for college or the military, their parents dying. On summer nights, Dash could stand in the backyard and see the firepits glowing, one after another, all the way to the end of the block, the lingering dusk light hazy with smoke. Enough beer open at once for her to smell it in the wind. Not all the men worked in the mills, but a lot of them did. Paper was supposed to be recession-proof. No matter how bad the economy got, babies needed diapers and wipes, women needed tampons and pads, old people needed Depends, all of which were made in Hanover, along with carbon paper, coated freesheets, and corrugated cardboard. The mill had hung on through the worst years of the recession, but right when things were getting back on track, when shops were reopening and Obama was running ads about how much better things were than when he took office, the paper company announced that production would be consolidated to the Georgia facility and the mill in Hanover, the city where the company started in 1875, would close. By that time, Mike had advanced to shift supervisor and was bringing home thirty-six an hour. Now Mike worked part-time at Lowe's, driving the forklift and assembling patio furniture, and was halfway through a certification program in tax accounting at Hanover Valley Tech. Five years earlier, he'd installed a French drain in their basement, hung drywall, and wired in both canister and recessed lights, and the summer before last he'd hauled in a forty-eight-inch Muskie, so big it took two hands to lift it for the camera. It was hard for Dash to picture her husband, good with his hands and temperamentally taciturn, sitting in a cubicle at Jackson Hewitt, in khaki trousers and a tie, punching other people's receipts into a computer.

"Hey there," Charlie said, nodding at Mike. "This is your new gig, huh?"

"Very funny," Mike said. He nudged Kasey. "Go on."

This whole thing was a bad idea. At least Mike had agreed to let Landon stay home instead of parading him from door to door. She'd put her foot down about that.

Kasey unfolded a sheet of paper and began to read in a flat, robotic voice. Dash couldn't tell whether she was being ironic or just thirteen. "I'm selling popcorn to raise money for my school volleyball team. Popcorn is the perfect fall treat. We have caramel, cheddar, and garlic lime. We also have cherry and bubble gum."

"Bubble gum popcorn?" Charlie asked.

"It's blue," Kasey said. The pointed ends of the ribbon tied around her ponytail floated in the breeze. Colored leaves blew out of the trees.

Charlie reached into his shorts' pocket and produced a roll of bills. Who sat around with a money roll? "I think I'll stick with the cheddar. How much will this set me back?"

"Twenty for the small and thirty for the large," Kasey said.

Charlie whistled through the gap in his teeth. "Highway robbery." He glanced over his shoulder at the football game moving across the gigantic TV mounted to the wall. The heavy curtains blocked the glare, and the living room was cast in funereal amber light that deepened inside the empty bottles on the coffee table. Sonja had been gone five years. "What the hell, go ahead and give me the large." He pulled a twenty and a ten from the roll and handed them over. "You don't have any beer in that wagon of yours, do you?"

Kasey looked at her dad. "We have some in the fridge. I could run home."

"I was kidding," Charlie said, grinning. Dash noticed how his big calves swelled and his skin was splotched with white striations. He was smoking too much and not walking enough. Charlie took the popcorn canister and set it on the floor by his feet. "How's the big guy doing?"

"That's actually something I wanted to talk to you about," Mike said. He lifted the brim of his cap, snugged it back down. "It was probably alarming to see the police in front of our house."

Dash curled her toes against her flip-flops. She'd seen Charlie standing at the end of his driveway while the firefighter attended to her, asking her to follow his pen with her eyes and palpating her occipital bone. Mike had talked to the police while Landon sat in the grass, his face in his hands. Dash wondered which of her neighbors had called 911. It could have been Charlie.

"Landon don't always know how to handle his emotions," Mike said.

Charlie slid his hands inside the pockets of his shorts. "Who does?"

"Right. Well," Mike said. "It's a little worse for him, see. He's got issues we've been working on. He sometimes lashes out when he don't mean to. We're sorry about all the commotion."

Charlie shrugged. "Aw, heck, Mike. I know Landon's a good kid. Too bad the boys in blue had to show up. My older brother clocked me square in the nose when I was fourteen. My dad reset the joint on his workbench and tanned Wally's butt with his belt. No police required. No doctor neither." He pinched the bridge of his nose. "Maybe that's why I look this way."

"I was wondering," Dash said. She'd meant it to be funny, but Charlie squinted and dropped his hand. Mike pressed the toe of his shoe over her bare foot.

"How about you, Dash?" he asked. "How's that shiner?"

"Healing," she said. "I've had worse."

"We appreciate your understanding," Mike said. "We'll let you get back to the game."

"You have everything you need?" Dash asked, eyeing his calves again. "You eating healthy?"

Charlie picked up the tin of popcorn and drummed on its lid. "Well enough." His face was sallow; he wasn't well. Charlie patted his breast pocket. "Too many of these, but that's no secret."

"You should try to walk more," Dash said. "It'll do you good."

"Maybe later," Charlie said, and retreated inside his smoky cloud.

"See?" Mike said to Dash as they pulled the wagon along the sidewalk. "Not so hard."

"He doesn't get it," Dash said.

"He doesn't have to. He only needs to know that we do. Our problem won't become his."

"I don't like that Kasey's dragged into all this, too," Dash said. "Like Landon's *her* problem."

"You can sell my popcorn for me," Kasey said. "I'll be happy to go home."

Mike stopped walking but held the wagon handle tight in his fist. "You're not going anywhere except to the next house," he said to Kasey. Then to Dash, "She should see us tackle the problem head on. We're doing the right thing."

"I'll trust you on this," Dash said. "But for the record—"

"I'm well aware of the record," Mike said. The wagon rattled behind him.

Near the corner lived a younger man who rode a Japanese motorcycle and across from him was an old woman, Noreen something, who didn't come out except to yell at dogs. Both shrugged at Mike's explanation about Landon. The motorcyclist bought a small can of caramel from Kasey. Noreen bought nothing. Eventually they knocked on the Heinemans', across the street from where they'd begun. Dash turned to look at her house. The sun through the maple leaves appeared to highlight the work they'd been putting off, the peeling siding and the crumbling front stoop. She worried that the fissures and flakes somehow amounted to evidence that she'd lost the ability to manage her family.

Georgina Heineman wore a purple T-shirt that read JESUS LIVES! She'd grown plump when she was pregnant with Leo and had never lost the weight. If Dash had ever resented her long hours, or the throb in her shins at the end of a shift, she was thankful that the job kept her active. When Landon and Robbie were babies, she and Georgina had pushed strollers together, all the way to the park if the sun was out. The developmental gaps between the boys hadn't seemed so great then. Both boys squealed and cried and eventually needed food or to be changed or put to bed.

Dash could hear Georgina's sons somewhere inside, the clatter of wood knocking against concrete. "We wait all winter for the snow to melt and then they spend the summer in the basement, slapping that puck against the wall." Georgina rolled her eyes in feigned annoyance. Robbie had been offered a hockey scholarship in Minnesota after he played a year of juniors. Rumor had it Andrew and Leo had even more talent.

Georgina smiled at Kasey. "So, what are we selling today?"

"Popcorn," Kasey said. "The perfect fall treat. We have caramel, cheddar, and garlic lime. We also have cherry and bubblegum for dessert."

"Dessert popcorn?"

"It's colored kettle corn," Dash said, tired of the incredulity. How many raffle tickets for four-wheelers and deer blinds had she bought from the Heineman kids? What fundraiser sold anything of real value, anything other than the reassurance that we're good and decent people who support our neighbors' children? It was the unspoken compact of their street. You bought from the neighbor kid to be nice. Because you *were* nice. The stuff itself was beside the point.

Boy voices echoed through the floor vent. "Eat my puck!"

"How about you floss your teeth with my stick!"

Georgina set her hands on her knees and bent toward the vent. "Cool it! We have company." Straightening her back, she asked. "How much for the big can? The variety pack?"

"That one's forty," Kasey said. "Comes with all five flavors."

"Can you take a check?"

"Sure," Mike said. "Maybe make it out to us and we'll see it gets turned in."

Georgina separated the paper from its perforated edge and handed it to Kasey. She took a long look at Dash's sunglasses, trying to see through them. Dash felt grateful for the dark lenses.

"It was so frightening, seeing Landon lose control like that," Georgina said. "My Bible study had been discussing the stoning of Stephen, when Saul held the Pharisees' coats. I knew I couldn't do nothing."

"So you're the one," Dash said. "We were wondering who called the police."

"I saw him hit you."

"Landon doesn't always have a good sense of himself," Mike said. "He didn't mean to hurt his mom."

"He doesn't know his own strength," Dash said.

"My boys don't, either." Georgina hiccupped a laugh. "I've threatened to call the police on them a time or two."

"But you didn't," Dash said. "Just on mine."

Georgina's smile evaporated. Mike said, "We're grateful to you. The police scared Landon, in the right way. He knows better now that actions have consequences."

"He's not dangerous," Dash said. "He's not like that." Footsteps thudded up from the basement and Robbie appeared in the living room behind his mother, sweaty and still panting from whatever had been going on in the basement. His biceps stretched the cuff of his T-shirt and his eyes traveled the length of Kasey's body, the bare skin of her thighs and knee-high socks, her breasts budding beneath her jersey. Dash felt Kasey notice Robbie, the subtle rise in her barometer, and again regretted letting her wear the uniform.

"Home by eleven," Georgina said.

Robbie slipped past his mother, pausing in the doorway to let Mike pat his shoulder.

"Hi, Mr. Coenen," Robbie said. Even without touching him, Dash could feel Robbie's indestructible vigor, the confidence that comes from being seventeen, the certain immunity to weakness and failure and certainly to death. That made her think of the Jensen babies, Ruby and Pearl, as she slid them one at a time into the arms of the funeral director.

Robbie crossed the lawn to his pickup, parked against the curb in front of the house. Landon had come outside and stood on the grass, squinting against the sun. Robbie waved to him as he opened the door to his truck. Landon sat down and began pulling at the grass. He began rocking and flicking his fingers, motions Dash had long ago recognized as stims—little ticks that came out whenever Landon felt nervous or afraid. He usually couldn't say what was bothering him, only that he was bothered. Could he hear his name being spoken from across the street? The need to protect him—even if it meant standing in the way of his fist, absorbing his blows—rose up in Dash's throat, as fierce as a sickness.

Georgina touched Kasey's elbow. "If anything like that happens again, you should come here. I'll leave the door unlocked whenever I'm home. Just come on inside." She lifted her eyes to Dash and Mike. "Just in case."

Kasey shifted away from Georgina's hand. "Landon's such a spaz."

"He's not a monster," Dash said. "He's intellectually delayed."

"He's on the autism spectrum," Mike said, though that term was also imprecise. Mike used it because autism was a word people knew. Landon's diagnosis had changed a dozen times over the years. One pediatrician surmised he had cerebral palsy; another said it was attention deficit disorder. A neurologist in Madison said the best summation of their son's condition was PDD-NOS: pervasive developmental disorder, not otherwise specified. Of all the diagnoses, Dash liked it best because it sounded honest: There were problems but they were hard to pin down. Fran quipped that PDD stood for Physician Didn't Decide. To Dash it meant a long struggle without a clear cause or treatment, though in Landon's case the cause was obvious: the bilateral intracranial hemorrhage he'd suffered during his time in the NICU. PDD-NOS had been reclassified as an autism spectrum disorder, a too-broad catch-all that encompassed everything from math prodigies to institutionalized invalids who never uttered a word. Mike said it made Landon's struggle easier to explain. Dash said it only told people what their son was not.

Georgina said, "I heard on the radio about a doctor in Florida treating autism with a vitamin regiment. It's galling how few nutrients are in food these days. Our microwaves zap them right out. This man sounded very knowledgeable. And he loves the Lord."

"Landon has a doctor," Dash said. "He's seen many." Until the mill closed, they'd had insurance through both of their jobs, enough to cover almost half of Landon's occupational therapy and applied behavior analysis sessions. The rest they'd paid out of pocket, along with his speech therapist, which insurance didn't cover at all. But now Mike didn't work enough at Lowe's to qualify for benefits and Dash's plan paid for only nine sessions a year.

She felt Mike's shoe against her toes again. "We'd be happy to read about it," he said.

"I'll see if I can find the link," Georgina said. "Have you considered other arrangements? Like a group home with a staff trained in this sort of thing?"

“He belongs with us,” Dash said. “We’re as trained as any staff would be.”

“We’re discussing Landon’s future,” Mike said. “He’s doing some jobs around the neighborhood, assembling shelves and furniture. He’s a whiz with those Chinese picture directions, and it’s teaching him responsibility. Living somewhere else is an option down the line, but we’re not ready yet. He’s still in school.”

“Not ready?” Dash glared at her husband. “It’s not anything we’re working toward.”

“We can talk more later,” he said.

“My God.” Dash stepped backward quickly, stumbling down the stoop. Her calves bumped against the wagon and she nearly fell over. She righted herself and turned toward her house. Landon had stood up from the lawn and was watching her. “I’m going home.”

“I didn’t mean to upset you,” Georgina said. “Dru tells me I should keep my big mouth shut. I’m only concerned.”

“We’re grateful,” Mike said, touching his brim, though Dash was already across the street.

She sat on the edge of her bed with her hands on her knees, breathing. An old labor nurse’s trick for calming the nerves during contractions: focus on a small object, a figurine or a soda can, and force it to bear your agony. The hospital had once hung crucifixes on the wall so laboring mothers could train their eyes on Jesus as they bore down against the pain. The crosses had all come down during the renovations, when Our Lady of Perpetual Help Hospital became Hanover Medical Center. But the crucifixes seemed to make NICU parents feel better, so they’d stayed up. God knew what it was like to watch a child suffer. Dash stared at her scrubs in the pile beside the dresser, wrinkled and rank from last night's shift, the dingy white soles of her sneakers.

She missed her family. All her brothers and sisters and parents had once lived within a few hours' drive. Having so much family nearby had allowed her to believe that friends and neighbors were extraneous. Nice to have, but not necessary. Her uncle Verlyn had damaged his brain when his snowmobile hit a tree; the accident had blinded one eye and impaired his speech to the point that it became incomprehensible after a single beer. He'd lived with Dash's grandparents until they died and then he'd moved between his brothers and sisters, including a year with Dash's family. The notion that he'd live anywhere but with family was unthinkable, and Verlyn seemed to rest assured in the knowledge that he'd never be turned out. Verlyn was gone, and so were her parents, and Dash's own brothers and sisters had scattered to different states, to Florida and Arizona and Georgia, where Dottie and her husband Jan had gone so Jan could stay with the paper company.

The wagon's wheels rattled over the uneven driveway concrete. The top of Kasey's head moved past the window. Mike leaned his shoulder against the refrigerator, waiting for her. "You two have been friends a long time," he said. "You can't fault her for speaking her mind."

"We've been neighbors a long time. We haven't been friends in years."

"You've known her twenty years in any case." He set his cap on the counter.

"That gives her the right to tell us to send him away? Ship him off to some home where they can tie him to his bed at night?" Dash balled her hands into fists. "Kasey was right there."

"How many babies have you seen whose parents couldn't admit their kid would have problems?" Mike said, bending inside the fridge for a beer. The fridge light shone on the top of his head. He cupped his hand around the cap and the bottle released a small hiss. "You've said it yourself. It's hard to imagine when it's your child."

"These words bother me. Problems, special needs. Like we can't just say who he is."

"We know very well who he is." Mike sipped from the bottle. "He's going to finish high school this spring. It's not like we can sign him up for the Navy. We need to talk about his future."

"He's in the next room," Dash whispered through her teeth. "He hears every word we say. If I heard my mother and father talking about sending me away, I'd get upset, too." She squeezed her eyes and nose inside her palm. "I'm tempted to march back over there and let her have it."

"What good would that do?" Mike said. "Let's talk about this later, when you're calmer."

"I don't have time to be calmer. I need to make dinner." Her T-shirt was damp, the armpits briny. "Then I need a shower."

Dash set the chicken on the board and pulled a knife from the block. She cut the breasts into shorter strips, rolled them into the breading, and set them in the fryer. Cutting the breasts this way could make two feel like four, a trick from the early days of her marriage, when she was in nursing school. How easily the old cost-cutting habits came back to her. She chopped lettuce and tomatoes and tossed them in a bowl, added the second half of her morning grapefruit and blue cheese. She could have asked Kasey to help, but she was happier working alone. She cracked the ice trays and cubes tumbled into the bowl. She dropped four in each glass and ran them under the tap.

She washed her hands again and carried the towel around the corner to the living room. Mike sat beside Kasey on the sofa, working together on a sudoku, Kasey's elbow on her dad's shoulder, her thighs crossed. Landon sat on the floor, engrossed in his movie, a rosacea of acne falling from his temple. He'd sat in the same spot since he was a toddler and had discovered television. He took to the area so habitually, in fact, that Mike had laid down a square remnant for Landon to sit on, to keep him from wearing out the carpet beneath. Cross-legged with his weight on his hands, his seventeen-year-old body took up nearly all of the square. His sacral dimple above the waistband of his shorts was dark with hair. Despite his age and size, she could still see in his shoulders and face, the folds of skin where his wrist met his arm, the small boy who once knocked against his bedroom wall when he needed her help. The child patient enough to stare at the night sky for a meteor to streak across, who howled with delight every time he caught sight of one. He was older now, but also not. Dash kissed her fingertips and touched them, gently, to the shoulder of Landon's T-shirt, thankful that when the Robbie Heinemans of the world had moved away and women like Georgina were alone inside their houses, Landon would still be with her, right here, right where he'd always been.

4

In college it had been exciting, turning her back on her friends. Brooke had been exiled from her freshmen posse when she'd quit the cello studio, and the girls she'd pooled in with had all come out of similarly disastrous first years. Regan was a refugee from the music conservatory; Lily, an anorexic who'd had to miss the winter term after she dropped to eighty-six pounds and her hair began to fall out. Janet, Brooke's roommate, had started college with a boyfriend at UW–Milwaukee who promised to break up with her if she danced with other guys, and once she summoned the courage to dump *him*, showed up at her dorm with a bottle of sleeping pills and threatened to down them all if she didn't take him back. Janet declared their quad a "drama-free zone," which meant no overnight guests, and on Fridays the four girls would change into their pajamas and watch movies until midnight. There was a comfort, even a pleasure, in vegging out while her classmates stumbled between the College Avenue bars, chased by a hoard of lacrosse bros from Evanston and Lake Bluff. Yet even then Brooke understood they were thrown together more by the things they'd missed than by any common passion, and she often felt she was biding her time. She fixated on going to New York after college—Lower Manhattan still smoldering with the wreckage of the fallen towers—because her friends, timid Midwesterners all of them, feared it.

She met Harper at a charity spelling bee for the Hanover Literacy Council, two weeks after landing the internship at Ogilvy. Brooke had organized the team from the college's Mortar Board society and Harper was the emcee. She'd never seen his broadcast, but talking with him during the intermission, she could envision him behind the desk in the studio, his voice fluid and confident. Hanover was his first anchor job. He planned to move in a few years to a mid-sized city like Nashville or Portland before trying for one of the major markets or auditioning for a network. In his navy suit and buckskin loafers, he seemed connected to her soon-to-be adulthood in New York: twenty-dollar martinis, expos and openings, men with tattoos and ponytails who talked about Foucault and Kurosawa. She noticed a smudge of camera makeup on Harper's neck, as if she'd been afforded a view of him no one else got to see. One of the best parts of the affair, the afternoons she skipped class to meet him, the mornings she showed up at breakfast in yesterday's clothes, were the looks she received from the other girls. They seemed to fear *her.*

But first, they met for an innocent cup of coffee at the Brew-Haha. At Brooke's invitation, in fact: she'd been networking with alumni and area professionals since junior year, taking informational interviews, asking for advice. She wore her houndstooth blazer and picked a table near the front window, where anyone walking by on the street could see them. The people in the café who didn't recognize Harper's face spun toward him when they heard his voice. He said it happened a lot; people told him he looked familiar or asked if he had a brother before they realized who he was. He was a voice in their kitchen and living rooms—in a weird way, a part of their families.

Harper said it wasn't what you hoped, being recognized in public all the time. It wasn't like running into a friend. You were a puzzle for people to solve, then a brush with someone on TV, like that was anything special. But when an older lady approached their table, Harper stood to greet her. He shook her hand by setting his second hand on top of hers, and he used the woman's name when he introduced her to Brooke. Brooke assumed he knew her, but Harper said he didn't. Not before right then. He said you never knew who you were talking to, and if someone made the effort to come say hi to him, the least he could do was be cordial. He said there were good and interesting people everywhere you went, if you took the time to meet them. It was what he liked best about being a news broadcaster, meeting people who did interesting things. People who volunteered their time to help kids and old people, a guy in town who taught the blind how to hunt and a community that taught traditional basket weaving, simply to keep the craft alive. There was even a Michelin-trained chef in a tiny town up north who cooked gourmet meals exclusively in an open hearth, in cast-iron kettles and skillets. Unbelievable flavors. Meeting him had inspired Harper to start cooking. He'd tried to talk his wife into taking some classes with him, but she wasn't interested. He'd tried a few things on his own, including building a wood-fired pizza oven from bricks and pavers he bought at the hardware store. Brooke asked what kind of pizza he liked to make. He said, "No one has ever asked me that before. Isn't that funny? People always want to tell me what they *don't* like on pizza, what they think is gross. Like I'm going to force it on them."

"Anything that melts is probably pretty good," Brooke said. She'd made a s'mores pizza at camp when she was a kid and thought it was delicious.

"Exactly! I've fried an egg on a pizza and it blew my mind. And my squash-and-apple pie has become a staple." He stared into his mug. "People look at news anchors and think we're shallow. Ken dolls or whatever. Maybe we are. But I'm also trying to be happy."

Brooke wasn't sure what he meant but she saw he was sad in a way he wanted to hide. She sipped from her coffee—it was bitter, over-roasted—and told him he made his job sound more adventurous than she'd have guessed. He asked if she wanted to blow off classes that afternoon and come with him to the station. It was a Wednesday, and her classes that semester were all Tuesday/Thursday, so it was an easy yes.

Harper used Brooke's first and last name when he introduced her to his producer and news director. He said she was a student at the college, exploring career opportunities. Nothing he said was a lie, not even when he called his wife and said he might be late getting home that night because he was showing a student from the college the ropes of the news. Brooke stood behind the cameras in the studio during the broadcast and felt that Harper was speaking directly to her, that he wanted to impress her, which touched her. The ten o'clock show was smoother than the six o'clock, though she couldn't pinpoint what changes he'd made.

Afterward, they sat in his car in the station's parking lot. They'd been together for nearly twelve hours and hadn't touched beyond a handshake. The day was nearly over, and she wished it wasn't. As if reading her thoughts, Harper said, "Thank you for a really great day. I needed it. I didn't even realize how much I needed it."

"I didn't do anything."

"You were interested. That means more than you think."

"I had fun, seeing you work," she said, and meant it. Standing in the studio during the broadcast, sitting in on the meeting during which the news director and Harper and researchers planned the show, the two field reporters chiming in through a conference speaker—it was all more real than anything she'd done in college. Sitting beside him in the darkened car while the November wind drummed against the windows, the boys from school seemed to her exactly that, *boys*, hairy children with headphones around their necks who wore sweatpants to class and smelled of unchanged bed sheets. And the New Yorkers she'd fantasized about, all the intellectual conversations about literature and film struck her not as pretentious but boring, nothing she really cared about. If Harper had right then offered to drive her to the Canadian border, she would have taken him up on it, simply for the adventure, to say she *did something*.

Harper had yet to start the engine. Their breaths fogged in the cold interior. A crescent of moisture formed on the windshield. "I don't want to go home," Harper said in the dark. He'd never admitted that to anyone before, afraid of what it would mean if he said it out loud. He often felt as though he'd been living in a glass canister, like the tubes the banks used at the drive-up, shooting from one part of his day to another without ever truly coming into contact with anyone. He heard Brooke exhale beside him, and watched the faint smoke of her breath dissipate. The band of dampness widened on the windshield. He'd known her for less than a day and she seemed to understand him better than anyone else, including his parents and his wife. He wanted to cry. Harper squeezed the bridge of his nose to stop it. "My son is my whole world," he said. "We moved here to be closer to my wife's parents. Help with the baby and all that. I hoped she'd be happy here. Happier, at least."

He let a sigh escape and his chest seemed to deflate. He sank into his seat. It was the second time that day he'd mentioned happiness. Brooke knew for certain now he wasn't happy, no matter how many wood-fired pizzas he ate. She wanted to ease his pain. They'd later tell each other—for they talked about this often—that happiness wasn't something that just happened, but was something to work for, something to make. They were happy when they were together, even if the odds were stacked against them. Who could say when, or if, they'd ever feel happy again?

Brooke returned from her vanished weekend at Solberg Lake under a cloud of scandal. Rumors spread quickly across campus, accelerated by the fact that they were true. Yes, she was banging the news anchor. Yes, he was married and had a kid. Yes, she was knocked up. Whatever fear her suitemates had once felt turned into disdain. People she'd never spoken to stared at her from across the commons. Standing in line for coffee, she heard a guy behind her cough, then mutter, "Hey, weather girl, how many inches you get last night?"

Even her mother, a federal district court judge, joined the piling on. "If you're really the feminist you claim, you'll give up the baby and send him away," she said on the phone. "His wife shouldn't become another woman cast to the dogs. The world isn't so kind to single moms, despite the gains we've made."

"*You* were a single mom," Brooke said in disbelief. Her father was a half-Chinese British citizen from Hong Kong, an ethnic heritage all but invisible in Brooke's face and chestnut hair. He'd returned there after her parents divorced, married a Cantonese woman, and had two daughters. Brooke's half sisters, though she'd never met either of them. Or her stepmother.

"I was a lawyer in a big city," her mother said. "I finished my education before I had children. By the time your father and I separated, I'd established myself in a profession. I had privileges." Papers shuffled on the line, and then Brooke heard her mother's voice again, all the background noise removed. "In case I wasn't clear before, you should give him up. It'll hurt, but one day you'll have a family of your own. You'll see you did the right thing."

What Brooke remembered most from that conversation, the words she carried with her for years, was the argument she *didn't* make to her mother. The vow she buried in her heart, where, fed by silence and secrecy, it felt like the truth. *If I can have Harper, I'll never need another person ever again.*

She didn't call home when she miscarried. She didn't talk to her mom at all, in fact, until her mother and Brooke's brother, Ian, came for graduation. After the ceremony, Ian and Harper moved Brooke's clothes and books and computer from the dorms into the apartment above the BrewHaha. It was June and humid, the white sky thick with river flies and the acrid smell of the coffee roaster. Harper and Ian went back for more boxes. For the first time that weekend, she found herself alone with her mother. Brooke began arranging her books on the small shelf, the way she had whenever she'd moved into a new room at the start of the school year. The books were textbooks, and she knew she'd never read any of them again, but she wasn't ready to give them away. Her cello, too, in its burgundy thermoplastic case, lay on its side against the wall. She'd backed out of the internship in New York, and in the divorce, Harper had agreed not to move more than eighty miles away from Hanover until Oliver finished high school. Whatever ambition they'd had for their careers, to become citizens of larger, more exciting cities, was dead. Once Brooke and Harper signed the papers at the courthouse and exchanged vows, she'd officially be a stepmother and permanent resident of Hanover, Wisconsin. Officially no longer a child.

Her mother knelt beside her to help, reading the spines as she moved the books to the shelves. After a while, she asked, "Have you seen a doctor? Are you taking prenatal vitamins?"

Brooke said, without looking up, "I lost the baby."

"You're young," her mother said, nodding as though she'd already suspected. "You'll be pregnant again. You'll have all the babies you want."

Other people had said as much, as though miscarriage were a lesson she needed to learn.

Through the open window, a car door slammed. Harper's voice rose up to meet them, floating on a cloud of heat. Brooke could hear him laughing. "Great day to fly a kite!" she heard him say. The coffee grinder echoed through the floor. Her mother went to the window and looked down at the street, the main thoroughfare of the town where Brooke would, for better or worse, make a life. She wiped her eyes and pulled Brooke close. "I guess you're here now."

Harper swore he and Sara had problems that went back to college. They'd fight and break up, drink too much, hook up, get back together. They were in an upswing when they graduated, so they got engaged, but it didn't take long for Sara to resent the moves he needed to make for his career. Hating Fargo made sense, but Greensboro was a huge improvement and Jacksonville he actually liked. Having Oliver made their problems worse, not better. No, he didn't regret his choices and hoped Brooke didn't either; he and Sara were heading for a cliff one way or another. "She dreamed of becoming a young widow," he said. "I swear to God, she used to ask me about our life insurance all the time. I'm lucky I never got into a car accident. She'd have pulled the plug for sure."

If all that was true, what had he seen in her in the first place? "I was young and horny," he said. "She had boobs."

"Great boobs?"

"At nineteen, all boobs are great."

"I was twenty-one when we met," she said, cupping her hands over her breasts. They were smaller than Sara's. "Was that what you wanted when you met me?"

"Give me a break. *You* were twenty-one. I wasn't."

Yet there was something between Harper and his ex-wife, even still. Brooke couldn't quite name it, but she saw it whenever they were together, the transfer of heat between them. Maybe it was history, the body remembering the disobedient thrill of freshman year, of a real-life person taking their clothes off and lying down naked in your bed, their skin and hair in the very sheets where you'd fantasized about exactly this. Except when Brooke recalled Evan Desroches or Spencer McHenry, she didn't feel anything special. Their names were like her old phone numbers: locked in her memory but no longer connected to anyone she wanted to talk to. Watching TV could make her think about New York. She didn't know how to ask Harper if he had similar thoughts about what might have been, and she wondered how well she really knew him. Two years together felt like a lifetime. And also, no time at all.

One Sunday evening in May, Sara parked her minivan in their driveway. Oliver was asleep with his thumb in his mouth, harnessed into his car seat. Harper unbuckled him while Sara handed Brooke the diaper bag with an efficiency just short of rude. Oliver opened his eyes when Harper tried to lift him and started kicking his feet, demanding to climb out by himself. "All weekend he's been like this," Sara said. "Wouldn't let me help him with anything, including the bathroom."

"So he's potty-trained now?" Harper asked. He stood barefoot on the driveway. Next door, Jerry Stark was walking behind his lawn mower, a beer bottle in his hand. The mower sounded like a swarm of bees growing angrier as it zeroed in on them.

"Not exactly. You might want to invest in a mop and a pair of rubber gloves."

Ollie had one arm wrapped around his mother's leg. He reached for his dad with the other. Harper took a shuffle step forward to accommodate him. Let no demand go unmet. "Using the toilet is like riding a bike," Harper said. "Takes a few spills to master."

Sara laid her hand atop her son's head. Brooke felt a current zap across the wire between her husband and his ex-wife, an electrostatic charge that made the hair on the back of her neck stand up. There *was* something between Harper and Sara. That thing was Oliver, his arms winching his father and mother ever closer until the space between their bodies was less than a foot. Having a baby may not have been enough to save their marriage, but Oliver was enough to bind Harper and Sara together forever. Fifty years from now, Oliver would still join them in a way that was indestructible, chromosomal, and ultimately exclusive of everyone but them. Standing on her driveway with her stepson's miniature embroidered backpack slung over her shoulder, Brooke saw the trio in exactly that way—as *them*. She was twenty-three years old, intimately acquainted with her stepson's bowels and bladder, his propensity to vomit in his sleep. But no matter how many nights she answered Oliver's call or foraged the house for turds, he'd always belong to Harper and Sara. Them and not her.

Her focus on motherhood became singular, lasered. She noticed babies in strollers in the mall, at Pick 'n Save, at the

YMCA, in the stick-family decals affixed to the rear window of every minivan. Babies were all she saw. It shamed her to think this way. In college, she'd volunteered at Planned Parenthood and marched around the capital in Madison to protest a bill that would have restricted access to abortion.

Some pregnancies lasted weeks before her body rejected it in a tide of blood and pain. Others were revealed during the ultrasound to be blighted ova, pregnancies without embryos but all the same requiring a dilation and curettage. The blogs said the best way to get pregnant was to stop trying, to enjoy sex for its own sake. She reminded herself to linger on Harper's nipples, the patch of hair on his sternum, her tongue on his abdomen until the muscles begin to convulse. But as soon as she felt him inside her, his DNA rushing toward her cervix, she thought, *maybe*. And then, involuntarily, *please*.

By 2011, they were coming up on nine years of marriage and decided to try IVF. Multiple rounds of tests had revealed no identifiable cause for her recurrent miscarriages. Her cervix was strong, her antiphospholipid antibodies within normal range. On paper, she *should* have been able to get and stay pregnant. After four weeks of Lupron injections, another two of Follistim and Repronex, and a final shot of human chorionic gonadotropin to trigger ovulation, a trio of Brooke's eggs were aspirated from her ovary, fertilized with Harper's pornography-activated sperm, and implanted inside her uterus. Two of the zygotic embryos passed from her body almost immediately, but the third stayed. At twelve weeks a sonographer slid a lubricated transducer inside her vagina, and there it was on the screen: in grainy black and white, distorted by fluid, but there. She could see its spinal column and head, the mellifluous opening of its heart. Everything looked fine, the obstetrician said. Prenatal testing revealed no chromosomal abnormalities. She was due in May.

Through Christmas and New Year's she watched the snow drift around Ollie's abandoned play set in the backyard (at ten, he'd declared himself too old for it and Harper hadn't gotten around to taking it down) and imagined her own child one day descending the slide, sitting in the swing.

One Tuesday in early January, Brooke woke up nauseous. Her lower back spasmed and the computer made her temples throb. The nurses in the obstetrician's office suspected she'd caught the flu that was going around, nothing to worry about, but if she felt unwell, she should go home. She was ahead of schedule designing a mailer for a local boutique; she still had to tune the kerning, but that she could do on her laptop on the couch. Her car's windshield was glazed in hoarfrost and the frozen lake was dotted with fishing shanties. She gripped the wheel with both hands and sweated through her pants.

Inside her bedroom she peeled her slacks away, the wool like cellophane, and pulled her blouse over her head. The heat was turning to chills. She called the doctor's office again and said she was running a fever. The nurse suggested a bath and a cold compress. Brooke opened the tap and felt the torque in her spine release some when the water crested her breasts. She reached between her knees to shut off the water. She had her hand on the knob when a tidal jolt of pain passed from her diaphragm to her thighs, so fierce and unexpected that she clenched her eyes shut and cried out. The water turned crimson. Between her legs she felt the baby's head and shoulders. Its body slid quickly out when she cupped its head. The umbilical cord was as thin as dental floss, and the placenta, emerging in a second burst of pain, was globular and red. Its heart beat feebly against her hand, though it never opened its mouth, never tried to breathe, and within moments the faint percussion disappeared.

Brooke grew very calm. She stood from the bathtub and used her toe to free the drain. She pulled the towel from the rack and let it pile in a heap on the floor. She laid the baby there while she went naked into the nursery, not yet containing a crib but with a chest of drawers, the few clothes and blankets she'd allowed herself to buy, and the ones she'd received as gifts. She found the green plush blanket she'd set aside for bringing the baby home from the hospital. She wrapped the baby in it and carried the bundle to the bed. She called for an ambulance before getting dressed, then carried the baby through the front door to wait.

Discarded Christmas trees lay against the curb. The temperature had come up and was only a few degrees below freezing, warm enough for her not to need a hat. Linda Stark backed her Buick out of her driveway and waved as she shifted into drive. Then Brooke was alone among the bare trees and the snow and the echo of the wind. She folded back the blanket and slid the nail of her pinky finger beneath the baby's hand. Its fingers were fused but she could see where they would have separated. The bones of its skull were splayed beneath the skin like a fractured jigsaw. Its chest and belly and legs were perfect, just small. She couldn't tell whether the whorls of skin between its legs were the beginnings of a penis or a vagina, though she knew the baby's sex had been inscribed from the moment Harper's sperm had been injected into her egg. Before, even, it was transferred to her body. She decided it was—that her baby had been—a girl.

For sixteen minutes she stood in the cold and examined her daughter's body, the weight of her hand against her fingernail and the mushy bump of her nose, certain that once she let go she'd never see her again. This was as close as they were going to come to knowing each other. Brooke pressed her fingertip to the baby's chest and a piece of her daughter's skin clung to it. It was still there when the ambulance turned the corner. She closed the blanket, covering the baby's face and head. The paramedic who opened the back door was young, Asian, his hair cropped close. He had a small pot belly and rubber bracelets around his wrist. Brooke moved the blanket into his arms. It weighed almost nothing.

Brooke told the nurse and social worker at the hospital that she wanted to be the one to tell her husband what had happened. By law they had to respect her wishes, and her wish was for the twenty minutes she'd spent on the driveway to remain a secret, hers and hers alone. The social worker held up both hands, her pen squeezed between her index and middle fingers. "Fine by me."

Harper came into her room with a bouquet of daisies and gladiolas, bought in the downstairs gift shop. "I'm so sorry," he said. He bent to kiss the top of her head. He lingered, his face close, for her lips to turn toward his. "Oh, Brookie, I'm so sorry."

She thought of the vow she'd once made. *If I can have Harper, I'll never need another person ever again.* Maybe the universe meant to hold her to her word.

"I lost the baby," she said. The phrase by then had become a code. The baby was gone; what more was there to talk about? The one thing she could not stand right then was the possibility of a bright side. She wanted to keep this sadness, the tender sorrow of holding her daughter in the wind, all to herself. Depriving Harper of the chance to hold the baby, to know what had happened, felt more like a kindness than a cruelty. Though, she knew, it was also cruel.

At home, recuperating on the couch, she told Harper she was ready to consider other options. The social worker at the hospital had given her the name of a foster care placement agency. Fostering wouldn't cost them much in the short run, and if they did decide to adopt, grant programs could help them recoup expenses. Harper gathered her feet into his lap and began kneading her arches with his thumbs. She could feel his relief in his fingers. "We can rent-to-own," he said. "Test-drive the kid for a few months to see how he does."

"That's not nice."

"I'm kidding." He let his head rest against the couch cushion. "It's a good idea. We can't keep going the way we've been. Too much heartache."

The application paperwork was more extensive than any she'd completed in a doctor's office. Under *Check the boxes that best characterize your childhood relationship with your mother,* Brooke carefully inked "respectful, "distant," and "idolized." Under *Have you or your spouse/partner ever experienced any of the following?* she checked "miscarriage" and "infertility" but not "death of a child." Under *Have any of the issues listed below ever presented a problem for you or your spouse/partner?* she left everything blank, including "sex," "work," and "infidelity." She and Harper would welcome a baby from any ethnic group. The only medical conditions they couldn't accept were congenital heart defects, microcephalus, and those with limited life expectancies. They submitted detailed histories of Harper's divorce and custody agreement for Oliver, verifications of their home and car insurance, fingerprints and background checks, letters from their doctors, a drawn floorplan of their house. She and Harper attended foster parent training classes at the YMCA, and on three separate occasions Brooke led an agency social worker on a tour of her bedrooms and bathrooms, opened her kitchen cupboards, set out tea to occupy her hands while she answered questions. When her obstetrician called to offer her a place in a clinical trial for Ovomid, a new fertility medication showing better results with follicle stimulation and uterine implantation, Brooke considered saying no. Their foster care licensing was complete and the social worker said a placement could come as early as the summer. Brooke had cleansed the house of every reminder of her blundered pregnancies, every test result and ovulation calculator, every pill bottle beneath her sink. The red-inked box around May 10, her original due date, in her checkbook calendar, drawn months ago while she waited in the drive-through, seemed to signal the end of a misbegotten journey she should have quit long ago. A newfangled experimental drug wouldn't change that. If anything, she expected it would only make her moodier, more nauseous. She agreed to try it only because her doctor said it wouldn't cost her a dime. She had nothing to lose.

As she knelt over the toilet a few minutes after midnight on May 10, Brooke thought one more time of her bygone due date, and of the baby she'd held in the cold.

A blood test had confirmed what three at-home pregnancy tests had failed to convince her was true. Based the amount of HCG in her blood, her obstetrician suspected she was carrying at least twins, possibly more.

Harper brought her a glass of water and a towel. "We'll have our own basketball team. Or we can start a band. The Jensen Five."

"Oh, Harper."

"I can't wait," he said. "I can't wait, I can't wait."

5

Another buzz at the door and a young mother pushed a stroller inside. The baby, a toddler, was sitting up, gnawing on a graham cracker. Brown slime ringed his lips and coated his chin. "We had an appointment for Brucie's one-year follow-up. We wanted to come say hello."

"Welcome back!" Penny said. She turned to Dash in the alcove behind her. "Look who's here to pay us a visit."

Dash closed the drawer in the supply cart and trotted around Penny's desk, her braid swinging behind her. "Hey there!" she said, opening her arms to embrace the mother. Brucie's mom wore jeans with rhinestones on the seat pockets and a fuzzy pink fleece. She bent to unbuckle the baby from the stroller.

"Who names a baby Bruce?" Harper whispered to Brooke.

Dash bounced the baby—plump, pink, almost completely bald—on her hip. She carried him to the wall of photographs beside the cubbies where parents stowed their bags and jackets. "Can you find yourself, Brucie Smoochie? How about you, Mom?"

Harper leaned toward Brooke again. "Dash doesn't remember him. Look."

"You think so?" Brooke asked.

"One hundred percent."

Brucie's mom pointed to his picture on the wall. She knew right where it was. "Some days I get in the car, and I start driving here," Brooke heard her say. "On autopilot."

"Girl, don't I know it," Fran said. She'd come over from the central station.

Emery's monitor toned and Dash handed the baby to her.

"How long did it take you to figure out who he was?" Harper asked her, once she was back inside the alcove.

Dash's face tightened. Since the dustup about the bili lights, Harper's presence in the unit had set the nurses and the doctor on edge. She stared at the monitor screen for a moment before she said, "We see a lot of babies. Once they leave, they grow like weeds. The picture on the wall jogged my memory."

"I thought so," Harper said. "Must not have been here super long."

"You'd guess that to look at him, but little Brucie was here several months. He was a twenty-five weeker." Dash stepped closer and tilted her head toward the gliders. "Here's another thing I remember. He was born without an anus. Had to go to Madison for surgery."

Harper's eyes grew wide. "You're saying he had to go all the way to Madison so the doctors could tear him a new one?"

Dash stifled a laugh, like she'd never heard that one before. "Simple procedure. His bowels took a little time to get working, but everything got going eventually."

"I can't imagine not having a butthole," Brooke said.

"The little things we take for granted," Dash said. "In here, though, that's nothing. It's what I keep telling you—give it time. The monitor you keep staring at, think of it like your car's dashboard. Good to keep an eye on numbers, but if you stare for too long, you'll miss the road."

"It's sort of addicting," Brooke said. During their first uncharted days in the unit, she sat in the glider and tried to make herself invisible, to concentrate on the colored lines flowing across the monitors. She learned the peaks and troughs, and to separate one wave from another: green for heart rate, yellow for respiration, red for blood pressure, blue for pulse oxygenation. The nurse and doctor studied the blue wave the longest, so it was that one Brooke focused on the most. She lost hours watching the monitors, hours in batches of four and six, like packs of soda. Opal's pulse ox levels were solidly above ninety, but Emery's languished in the seventies. Brooke willed them higher and sometimes they obeyed: from seventy-four to seventy-six, seventy-six to seventy-eight, enough for her to almost believe her vigilance—along with the surfactant and antibiotics—was working. She whispered, "Make eighty and we'll call this a good day. Make eighty and I'll go use the bathroom. Make eighty and when you get out of here, I'll buy you whatever you want."

When Dr. El Sadda, the pulmonologist, arrived from Madison, as she did every other week, she said that Opal's lungs were very strong. Her hematocrit was on the rise and her low hypertension meant they could start lowering the oxygen level.

"Doesn't she need it?" Harper asked. "The oxygen? She's barely two weeks old."

"There's a fine line between not having enough oxygen and getting too much." Dr. El Sadda slid her stethoscope beneath the flaps of her hijab and paused to listen. "Too little hurts the brain. Too much hurts the eyes and lungs. The more baby breathes on her own, the better."

The pulmonologist frowned when she moved on to Emery. His skin was yellow-brown and his arms lay limp at his sides. He was already on 100 percent oxygen. Dr. El Sadda pulled her chair close to the Isolette and leaned close to his mouth, her hijab tucked behind her ear. She chewed her bottom lip. Dash had turned off the volume on the alarm, but the numbers on the screen continued to blink.

Dr. El Sadda pulled the curtain around the bed space when she went to consult with Dr. Fackelman. Fackelman was the one who came back to them. "Emery is very sick," she said.

"Sick, like pneumonia?" Harper asked.

"Thank God, no," Dr. Fackelman said. "It's the prematurity. His lungs are struggling to keep up." She concentrated on the monitor. "I'm becoming concerned about his heart and kidneys."

Brooke sensed the tension in the doctor's voice, her effort to keep the situation calm. Dr. El Sadda watched them from across the unit. "The next week will be crucial."

"Go to work," Brooke told Harper. "You should go to work. Get your mind off all this."

"You're sure? What about you?"

"I'm not going anywhere. I'll call you if anything happens."

The mood in the unit lifted once Harper left. Dash circled away from the babies to talk to Fran while Dr. Fackelman moved between the bed spaces with her stethoscope around her neck. Brooke slid around the welcome desk to the picture board at the front of the unit. She couldn't say for certain which baby was Bruce, but every image on the board was a cousin of every other: wrinkled faces with their eyes closed, some with oxygen tubing pronging their noses but most without, wreathed with blankets, binkies, toy animals. She touched the empty paper in the board's corner, the place where Opal's, and Emery's, pictures would go.

Jazzed on hope and too much coffee, Brooke told Dash she needed to pee, then pushed through the locked door and buzzed at the entrance to Maternity. The doors swung open for her without a word from the speaker. Most of the rooms were open, the moms propped up in bed, watching TV or holding their babies, hair tied in ponytails. One mother had a bouquet of flowers on her nightstand, autumnal oranges and reds in a beveled green vase. Brooke could smell the flowers, the pollen pungent and dense. Flowers weren't allowed in the NICU for fear of contaminants. She pumped the hand sanitizer from the wall and told herself that one day all the ordinary joys of motherhood would be hers, too. A year from now, the nurses will have forgotten she was ever here.

A nurse came around the corner, wheeling a baby in an open bassinet. A simple clean box, lidless and unmechanized, the baby inside swaddled like a burrito. The nurse was a bosomy black woman Brooke recognized as Latria, the nurse who'd cared for her after her C-section. Latria had been the one to pull the catheter from her ureter before helping her use the toilet and take a shower. Brooke stopped and waited for her. The baby in the bassinet was massive, with eyelashes and hair, its mouth gripped around a pacifier. To think that something so large could fit through a woman's body. "That's a roly-poly thing," she said.

Latria regarded her quizzically. "Do you need help finding your room?"

Apparently, she'd been forgotten already.

"I'm looking for a bathroom," Brooke said.

"Are you visiting someone?" Latria asked suspiciously. "Who you here to see?"

She showed Latria her wristband. "My babies are in the NICU," she said. "You took care of me after my C-section."

"Of course," Latria said. Her unchanged expression said she didn't remember. "We've been up to our ears lately. There's a bathroom close to the NICU. Want me to show you where it is?"

"I needed to stretch my legs," Brooke said. "I'll head back that way."

Once out of Latria's sight, Brooke turned right instead of left and followed a sign that pointed toward Pediatrics. She passed through an unoccupied hallway, the lights dim and the beds inside the open doors all squarely made and empty. A maintenance worker on a stepladder was changing out a bulb in the ceiling where the hallway intersected with another set of locking doors. Past the junction, the wood laminate floors gave way to older scuffed linoleum; the hotel-like earth tones mutated into floral wallpaper and green cinder block. Instead of beds, these rooms held cribs on casters, gun-metal gray, wide and solid and too tall for a toddler to scale. The rooms were empty, except for the last one. A child, maybe two or three years old, lay with her left arm protruding between the bars. Oxygen tubing threaded through the rails and connected to a canister on the wall. The little girl's face was sallow, her hair sweaty and matted against her forehead. Oddest of all, she lay beside what looked like a tremendous patchwork quilt. An open purse sat on the nightstand beside a yellow grocery sack darkened with magazines. The quilt stirred and a woman lifted her head. Brooke hadn't noticed the pair of knees curled against the railing, the purple-socked feet. The woman's hair was dark and straight. She glared at Brooke through the bars. Brooke wasn't supposed to be here. "Sorry," Brooke said softly, backing away. "I'm sorry."

Joanne, a square-bodied nurse who wore wire-rimmed glasses like an army colonel, came to sit with the babies so Dash could take her lunch. Brooke mentioned that she hadn't eaten all day, and when Dash and Fran disappeared inside the nurses' lounge she lingered in the hallway before ambling toward the elevator. If she could join the nurses for a meal, maybe she could ask a few questions about the other babies, other Brucie Smoochies, who'd grown and healed and gone home. Maybe she could ask Dash about her own son, that big boy in the photograph Dash carried around her neck. She heard Fran's voice coming down the hall, the nurses' shoes squeaking. When the elevator arrived, she held the doors open with her foot.

Dash and Fran were quiet in the elevator. Brooke stepped aside to let them out, then followed a pace or two behind. The hospital lobby featured a tall stone wall with water cascading into a wishing fountain, vinyl chairs facing the water and the windows where elderly volunteers in blue vests ate sandwiches. In the center of the atrium, the black and ivory keys of a self-playing piano moved up and down, as though played by a ghost. Around the corner and down a short hallway was the cafeteria, an open food court with glass refrigerator cases and a long salad bar shielded by plastic guards, a hot line with a whiteboard listing the menu. On offer for that day: Thanksgiving Dinner. Turkey, mashed potatoes, stuffing, canned cranberry sauce, a sliver of pumpkin pie for dessert. Brooke checked her phone: September 20.

Two male surgeons in scrubs and paper hairnets stepped directly to the front of the line and no one said a word. Dash and Fran, when their turn came, pointed to the steaming trays of turkey, potatoes, stuffing, and green bean casserole. Brooke ordered a salad and a cup of minestrone.

It was Dash who turned and looked back, her mouth pinched. Brooke smiled and felt foolish for thinking that the nurses might welcome her company. She'd never been very good at distinguishing politeness from actual friendship, or the point at which one became the other. She found an empty table along the wall, where she crushed crackers into her soup and opened her Diet Coke.

She was blowing across her spoon when a tray landed on her table. Brooke looked up and saw the patchwork quilt she'd seen upstairs—though now, she realized, it was a sweater. "Would you mind?" the woman asked. Her hair fell down her right shoulder. "All the other tables are full."

Brooke put down her spoon. "No problem."

"I know you," the woman said, sitting. "I saw you upstairs."

"I didn't mean to invade your privacy."

"I didn't recognize you is all. I thought we were the only ones on the unit."

"Mine are in the NICU," Brooke said. "My son and daughter."

"How long has it been?" the woman asked. "Two weeks? Three?"

"A little more than two. How did you know?"

"You were strolling," the woman said. "It's one of the stages you go through when you're here for a long time. After a few weeks of riding the rocking chair, you need something else to look at, even if it's the same thing in another part of the building."

"I could see the lake from my Maternity room," Brooke said. "The windows in the NICU face a brick wall."

The woman cut into her slab of turkey breast and fed a bite into her mouth. "Peds isn't much better. All you've got is the roof and the rear parking lot. They save the million-dollar views for the new mommies and the old fogies getting their knees replaced." She seemed annoyed by this fact. "Next, you'll find yourself running errands for, like, a really long time. You take forever at the store, you know, really weighing the pros and cons of the low-sodium Wheat Thins. You won't even realize you're avoiding the hospital until you catch yourself." She chewed, swallowed. "Like everything, you get used to it."

"Even the food?" Brooke wasn't ready to admit what she felt right then, the knowledge settling into her stomach. *This was her life now.*

The woman lifted her fork. "Maybe not this holiday spread. But some days it's not so bad. You'll know you've really hit your limit when you start dreaming about running away."

Brooke couldn't imagine. It felt strange not to be sitting beside Emery and Opal at that moment. She'd sleep in the unit if only the staff would let her. "How old is your daughter?"

"She's three. But what you really want to know is what she has. She has cystic fibrosis."

"Her lungs," Brooke said. Her mind flashed on Emery, the ventilator.

"As well as her pancreas, liver, and kidneys."

"What's her name?"

"My daughter? Anna. I'm Ingrid."

"Brooke."

"The other thing you're wondering about, Brooke, is my sweater." Ingrid looked down at herself and extended her baggy sleeves. "My Amazing Technicolor Dreamcoat."

"It's hard to miss."

"I used to be in a quilting circle," Ingrid said. "The group made this for me, and it's become a kind of security blanket. Anna sleeps with it when she's in the hospital."

The noise in the dining room had grown louder, a suddenly clamorous din. A voice was speaking overhead. "I like it," she said, pointing her spoon at Ingrid's sweater. "It looks cozy."

Ingrid turned toward the room, frowning. Brooke worried she'd said something offensive. "You said, your name was Brooke, right?" Ingrid asked.

"Yes."

"Is your last name Jensen? Brooke Jensen? I think I just heard your name called over the page."

Brooke looked toward the table where Dash and Fran had been sitting. Their trays were there, but the nurses were gone. Crumpled napkins lay piled on their plates. Soda bottles stood uncapped. The speakers crackled and the voice came on again. This time, Brooke heard it.

6

Brooke closed her eyes and tried to pretend the noise belonged to a different machine, the washer on spin or her car's engine with the hood propped. Dr. Fackelman had switched Emery to an oscillating ventilator, a box that looked like an old stereo, with ugly square red numbers—the kind where the ones look like sevens and the nines like lowercase g's. Instead of filling Emery's lungs with oxygen, the oscillator rifled out micro-puffs of air, more than nine hundred per minute. Beneath the warming light, Emery's chest and belly pulsed, seizure-like, too rapid to appear rhythmic. The sight of it made Brooke sick to her stomach.

He'd crashed like a bird shot out of the sky. It had happened that fast, his heart rate plummeting below forty beats per minute. Dr. Fackelman described it as a cascade: his kidneys weren't making urine, causing waste fluid to back up into his chest cavity, which only added to the strain on his already weak heart and lungs. His organs were starting to fail, one by one. The oscillator was a rescue device, a last resort. Brooke overheard Fran say that Emery was circling the drain.

"We need to talk about stopping," Dr. Fackelman told them, her face grim. She led Brooke and Harper to the conference room down the hall from the NICU. "It's time to talk about that."

"Stopping what?" Harper asked. He'd raced over from the station in his suit, a dull tie the color of a turned leaf and a matching square in the breast pocket. Beneath the fluorescent tubes in the ceiling, his powdered foundation looked like a spray-on tan.

"Stopping treatment," the doctor said. "We'd take him off the vent and let nature take its course. We'd give him Versed to make him comfortable, and oxygen through a nasal cannula, and you could hold him till the end. We can even take pictures, if you'd like."

Not the kind of picture Brooke had imagined, not one for the wall. Once the end came, she'd never hold Emery again. "Do we have any options?" she asked, softly.

"We've got him on diuretics and 100 percent oxygen. We can't push the vent any higher. Steroids would likely result in neurological problems. Possibly severe problems."

Brooke wiped her eyes with the back of her hand. "They could help? The steroids?"

"In the short run, maybe. Boost his lungs enough to keep going a little longer. His quality of life, though, will likely be seriously diminished."

"But it's not a guarantee? I mean, there's a chance the steroids *won't* hurt his brain?"

"Nothing's a guarantee," the doctor said. "But I've seen a lot of babies in this situation. *A lot* of babies. Their bodies can only take so much."

"I'd like to try it," Brooke said.

Dr. Fackelman looked at Brooke, then at Harper, as if asking for his help. He took Brooke's hand beneath the table. "Maybe the doctor is right. We don't want Emery to suffer. That's no way to live."

"We're the ones who're suffering," Brooke said. "It's harder on us than it is on him."

"I don't think that's true," Harper said. "I think he is suffering. He's small, but he's still a person." His shoulders slumped and his suit jacket hung loosely across his chest, as though it were suddenly a size too large. He pinched his nose as he began to cry. "God! This is all so much."

"It's a lot," Dr. Fackelman agreed. Brooke waited for the doctor to react to Harper's emotions, but she didn't. Despite his clothes, his daily television presence, he was just another NICU parent on the verge of a horror the doctor knew only too well. "I know it's a hard decision," she said. "A hard thing to endure."

"How do people go through things like this?" he said, digging a knuckle into his eye socket.

"The ones who go through this"—she paused to search for the words—"they don't have much choice."

"We do, though," Harper said. "Right now we can choose to let him go. That's what you're saying?"

The doctor nodded. "That's my recommendation, yes."

Harper cried some more. "I knew this would be hard. The perinatologist told us the babies would go to the NICU, but I never thought it would be this hard. I never thought we'd lose them."

Brooke squeezed Harper's hand. "That's why we can't quit. We can't."

"I want to do the right thing," Harper said. "I don't want to keep the poor guy going just to end up with a kid who's a vegetable. Those jokes I made, I didn't mean them."

"I'm sure you didn't," Brooke said, though less softly than she should have.

Harper stared away from Dr. Fackelman, away from Brooke, into the corner of the conference room, as though he could see his future projected there: a son he would never truly know kept alive by machines, the hospital's hisses and beeps haunting the rest of his days. "I don't know if I'm the kind of person who can care for a baby like that. I don't think

I am. We have Ollie to think about, too. His life is already hard enough."

A flare inside her sparked and sizzled. Before she could stop herself, Brooke said, "*You* have Ollie to think about. Not me." She hadn't meant to say that, but now that she had, she knew she meant it. Ollie wasn't hers and never had been. Later, she'd tell herself Harper shouldn't have brought him into the discussion.

Harper snatched his hand away, his eyes full of hurt. "How can you say that? Ollie's our son. We're a family."

Because I want you to know how it feels, she thought. "I'm not his mother," she said. "I'm Emery's. I'm not ready to let him go. He deserves every chance."

"We've done everything we could," the doctor said. "His organs are failing."

"We haven't tried the steroids," Brooke said. She turned toward the doctor. "Can we try them?"

"You understand the risks they carry?" Dr. Fackelman said. "What could happen?"

"I do," Brooke said.

"I'll put in the orders," the doctor said. "We can try and see what happens."

Harper stood, his chair sliding against the wall beneath the whiteboard. "I guess that's it then?" He buttoned his jacket. It once again fit him perfectly. "Just so we're clear, Brooke. This is one of those times when the things you say and the decisions you make, you can't take them back."

"Got it," Brooke said.

Harper gripped the handle of the door. He stood at the far edge of Brooke's peripheral vision. She could only see his profile, his dark shape, but his expression was one she could feel in her bones: hurt, and more than a little resentful, with the conviction he deserved something Brooke refused to give. "When we're stuck with a kid that can't walk or talk, that doesn't know who we are, you'll have to remember who insisted on this path." He turned and walked out, and the door swung shut behind him.

Dash rotated to nights and Fran to the feeder-growers by the windows. Brooke's nurses now were Joanne, who always seemed in the doctor's pocket, and Ting, whose teeth were small and sharp, like a cat's. If Emery were to crash again, Brooke worried the nurses might respond slowly—to allow nature to take its course. She couldn't stop picturing a lion with its jaws clenched around an antelope. Nature's course was brutal and bloodthirsty and heartless. She watched Emery's chest quake as the hydrocortisone dripped from the IV pole, cupped her elbows in her hands, and whispered a two-word chant: *Stay alive.*

The day's light crawled across the courtyard, the birch leaves going from gray to green to orange in a continuous arc. Brooke measured time by the people who came to the unit. Environmental Services emptied the trash cans after rounds. Then came the physical, occupational, and speech therapists, along with the dietician, who wore clogs and striped tights and a skirt sewn from old T-shirts. Dr. El Sadda, the pulmonologist, wasn't due back till next week. Jenny Ramirez, the social worker, was in and out all day, the pager on her hip buzzing constantly. In the afternoon, parents of window babies slumped down from Maternity, in no great hurry. One was an overweight teenage girl with impressive breasts and stringy hair, another a Hmong couple, Laotian and small, barely five feet tall. They said little to each other or the nurses.

The only other man in the unit was a lanky doofus who shuffled down from his wife's Maternity suite in plaid pajama bottoms and slippers, his hair peacocked from the pillow. He stared at his baby in Bed Three with a slack-jawed stupor of amazement. The nurses called him "honey." "Did you sleep well, honey?" "Anything we can get for you, honey?" Each morning he selected a new book from the shelf above the sink to read aloud, cooing and burbling and oblivious.

Fran noticed her glaring and crossed the unit to whisper to her, "Don't worry about Honey. One day that baby he's reading to will hate his guts."

Brooke laughed and caught herself. Honey was irrelevant. So were the other babies in the unit. All that mattered was that Emery continued to breathe, to live.

Stay alive, Emery. Stay alive.

The one bit of good news was that Opal was off the CPAP. It was nice to see her face without all the tubing in the way, and once her O_2 saturation dropped a little more, they'd start gavage feedings of breastmilk. Brooke had been pumping every few hours, closing the curtain around the bed space while she filled a Lansinoh bag, which she stored in an assigned rack in the NICU freezer. At last the packets would get some use. Once Opal could suck and swallow, she could nurse, even if only a little. Brooke closed her eyes and tried to picture her daughter's gums around her nipple, her warm breath against her skin. When it happened it would happen here, in the very chair where she sat. Brooke felt the glider beneath her move back and forth, like a raft in a pool. The monitor toned and went quiet. The NICU felt expansive, suddenly.

Ting touched her shoulder. "You can't sleep here, Mrs. Jensen. It's a rule."

"I'm sorry," Brooke said, blinking and kneading her eye sockets. "Won't happen again."

"You're here more than I am," Ting said. "You should go home. Get some rest and come back later."

"It's too far away," she said. "It's at least forty minutes without traffic. I don't want to go all the way there for a nap and then have to drive all the way back."

"I mean you should go home and stay home," Ting said. "Get a few good nights of sleep. Eat dinner with your family. Take care of yourself."

Brooke remembered what Ingrid had said, in the cafeteria, about wanting to run away. There was no way she was going anywhere. Emery needed her. "I'll stay awake," she said.

"We have the Hibbert House," Jenny Ramirez said, spinning in her chair at the nurses' station. She wore a knit scarf around her slender neck and her black hair tied in a ponytail. "It's our version of the Ronald McDonald House. Just across the street."

"What does it cost?" Brooke asked.

"It's a charity. It's free."

Ting said, "If it were me, I'd want to sleep in my own bed."

"Do they have room?" Brooke asked.

"It shouldn't be a problem," Jenny said. "Let me make a call."

She rode the gilder until eleven, no longer sleepy. Ting and Joanne and Fran had left for the day and Barb, the night nurse, had come on. In her mid-fifties, Barb had the rasp of a longtime smoker, though Brooke had never smelled cigarettes on her. When it was time to go, Barb called security for her and the guard said he'd meet her by the entrance to Emergency.

The security guard was a teenager, or looked like one. The ID badge pinned to his breast pocket said his name was Denny. His bangs covered his eyebrows and his buttoned shirt collar hung loosely enough to reveal the T-shirt beneath it. A long nylon lanyard hung from his key chain. The commercial playing over the radio when he put the truck in drive was still going when he parked in front of the Hibbert House, a dark green Victorian with wedding cake siding and metal storm windows. Denny told her it had once been the rectory for the priests who worked at the hospital. The sisters used to live inside the building, but the padres had bunked here. There were no shrubs or flowers in front, just the venting pipes for the furnace, stark and white in the moonlight.

Denny said, cranking up the parking brake, "I was supposed to ask if you had any luggage."

"Not tonight," Brooke said. She slid her purse over her shoulder. "I'll run home tomorrow and grab a few things."

The wind off the lake smelled of pine and wood smoke. The hospital rose from the shore like the prow of a ship, each window containing a person either healing or dying, as though the building were an ark of human frailty. White exhaust rose from its stacks. In the distant fog, a horn bellowed. A small, irrational part of Brooke feared she'd wake up in the morning and find the place unmoored from the shore, floating and unreachable.

A coffee can of discarded cigarette butts sat to the left of the door. On the right side of the door was a small ceramic plate, like a dish left out for a cat, also littered with crushed filters. Denny fished around in his pocket and produced a single key, unattached to a ring. He gripped the knob with one hand and the key with the other and pressed his shoulder against the wood. The key rattled but wouldn't turn. The lanyard hanging down the hip of his pants swung back and forth. Brooke could smell his body spray, the icy menthol marketed to college kids and teenagers. Janet, her roommate, used to call it Eau de Horny. Brooke tried to remember college, that faraway place and time, though her alma mater was only two miles away, at the other end of the city. Janet now worked for a software developer in Minneapolis, a city Brooke had once dismissed as quaint and boring when she seemed destined for New York. The last time she'd checked Facebook, Janet had posted pictures from a girls' weekend in Toronto: four women in sunglasses standing outside the St. Lawrence Market, toasting pints, holding a wheel of cheddar like it was a sandwich. She wasn't married, probably hadn't dreamed of having a baby. Like Brooke, Janet was only thirty-one, still in her prime.

"Jesus, finally," Denny said as the door gave. Musty air wafted out into the cooler night. Denny collected the plate and carried it inside, flipping on the lights as he moved through the rooms, the darkness giving away to flowered wallpaper and wide wooden doorways. The front parlor was decorated with the same industrial wood-and-fabric furniture found in the hospital's waiting rooms, and a TV sat in a corner. Beyond the staircase was the kitchen.

Denny set the plate in the sink. "The coffee can's there for a reason," he said, shaking his head. He opened cupboards to show Brooke the dishes, boxes of Oreos, Wonder Bread. He turned on the faucet and then harshly pulled the lever down. "Please keep the front door locked. We've received calls of homeless people sleeping on the sofas and stealing food."

"How many other people are staying here?" Brooke asked.

"A few, I think," he said, heading for the stairs. "I'm not in charge of this place. But whoever's here is probably sleeping, so, you know, shhh."

She could feel the scar tissue and sutures from her cesarean, and had to pause on the staircase to wait for the pain to pass. Denny waited for her at the top, his foot tapping. Brooke pressed her palm to her abdomen and remembered, happily, that she was in this strange house because of this pain. Because she shared a world with her children.

Stay alive, Emery, she thought. *Hang in there, kid.*

They passed a series of closed doors. Denny stopped in front of the third on the left and used the same key he'd used on the front door. Here was a room that could only have housed a priest: eight feet by ten, furnished with a twin bed, a small dresser and desk, a pedestal sink in the corner. The toilet and shower were down the hall. A thin white towel sat folded on the bed, along with a disposable toothbrush and miniature tube of toothpaste, a hotel-sized bar of soap. Brooke had given no thought to brushing her teeth or washing her face, and the provisions on the bed, the toothbrush laid diagonally across the soap by a human hand that had expected her to arrive with nothing—it felt like a small kindness.

Denny gave her the key. "This works both doors. Hang on to it. Some of the older guys say there's a tunnel that connects this place with the hospital. The druids used it, back in the day."

"I'll use the sidewalk," Brooke said. "Thanks for showing me around."

"Anything else you need?"

"A good night's sleep," she said. "Got any Valium?"

Denny pushed the door partway closed and stepped closer. Brooke smelled his body spray again, and now noticed the acne bubbling up beneath the stubble on his chin. "You looking?"

"I was joking."

"Right." He shuffled away. "So was I. But if you don't want to joke, let me know."

She listened to his footsteps growing fainter on the stairs, the front door clicking shut. She sat on the edge of the bed and laid her hand on the pillow. She wanted to lie back in her jeans and shoes and close her eyes, but her breasts were heavy, overdue for pumping. Brooke didn't have a toothbrush, but since the births she'd carried a breast pump in her purse, a small funneled cup that attached to a squeeze ball. She fit the cup against her nipple, and when the bottle was full, she poured it down the sink. The milk swirled around the flange. *Circling the drain.* She plugged in her phone and called the unit. "We hoped you'd give yourself the night off yet," Barb said. "Given how late you left."

"I'm settled in now," Brooke said. "If you need me I'm right across the parking lot."

"Sounds like a plan, Stan," Barb said. "We'll call you if we need you."

"You have this number?" Brooke asked. "My cell? I'm not at home."

"Yes." Barb rasped, stifling a laugh. "We have it."

"What were Emery's last blood gases?"

"Same as last time," Barb said.

"Opal's okay?"

"Opal's going to ride her bike out of here."

"Well then, goodnight."

She draped her jeans and blouse over the back of the chair, balled up her socks and stuffed them in the heels of her shoes. She added her bra to the pile, pulled on her fleece, and folded back the blankets. The sheets were white and stiff, like hospital linens, and in the sudden silence she could hear people moving inside the house. A floorboard creaked and water sluiced through the pipes. Shadows traced across the walls in patterns she didn't recognize. An ambulance siren howled. Her scar was throbbing and she felt the pulse in her back.

Harper's apartment above the BrewHaha, she remembered, was small and smelled of paint and cigarette smoke, but it came furnished, sort of, with a mattress on the floor in the bedroom and a futon in the living room. The first night he brought only a single box of clothes, his dress shirts and ties in their plastic sleeves from the dry cleaners, a duffel full of shoes and socks. He was several glasses into a bottle of Dewar's when Brooke arrived after her Mortar Board society meeting. Ollie had been napping when he'd left, he'd said, and Sara hadn't let him wake him up to say goodbye. The thought of his son waking up with him gone—gone officially, gone for good—was almost more than he could bear, even if he knew in his heart he was doing the right thing. Sara, for all her spurned victimhood, almost seemed relieved that Harper had been the one to put the end in motion. Save her from having to do it. She'd keep the house and savings, the furniture, her reputation. "What do you keep?" Brooke asked.

"I get to keep you," he said, pulling her toward the futon. "I'll live in Hanover forever if I get to live here with you."

"No Portland?" she asked. "No Nashville?"

"Portland's too wet. Nashville's too hot." He nuzzled his face against her belly, ran his hands up the backs of her legs. "I'm where I want to be."

She led him to the bedroom. The new sheets on his bed smelled of the plastic wrapping they'd come in. He watched her undress, his eyes cloudy and sharp, at once focused and not, and when she slid in beside him, he spooned in close and for a moment began to weep. "Oh, Ollie," he whispered, and Brooke had to fight off the jealousy. His palm on her belly was broad and warm and she moved it down to her underwear, pressing his fingers into the cotton. His breath was peaty and his skin was clammy and cool, as if he'd emerged from somewhere deep underground. She slid her hands down his spine and took hold of his ass, the muscles flexing as he worked, the spongy tip of his nose pressed against hers. His eyes shot open and she felt a tear, like a droplet of Visine, fall into her eye. He started to cry again and the vein rose in his neck. It seemed to Brooke she could feel every emotion at once, as though she had come to the center of a funhouse maze and could see her reflection repeating into infinity in every direction. She gripped Harper's face and held it until he gasped and collapsed beside her.

She shifted beneath the sheets in the Hibbert House, the rough cotton against her thighs. She missed Harper, his weight against her, but also his warm feet at the bottom of the bed, his slow breaths in the night when she got up to pee. She texted him to say she'd be spending the night near the hospital, likely the next several nights, until they knew whether the steroids were working. She typed, *I love you*, but not that she was sorry for what she'd said about Ollie. If he called her she'd say it then. Her phone said it was 11:30; Harper would be home from work by now. She watched the message turn from Sent to Delivered to Read, and she stared at the screen, waiting for him to respond. After a while, she returned the phone to the desk and lay breathing in the dark until the room came into focus. She could see through her window the faint pulse of the blinking traffic lights at the corner, and beyond it, the steadfast glow of the hospital. The amber light settled over her room like a blanket. She could almost hear her babies' hearts beating in the night, the *whir* of their breathing machines. They were close. Nothing else mattered.

7

Kasey talked like words had expiration dates. They'd go bad if they didn't get used in time. Dash knew she ought to be grateful—before long her daughter would want nothing to do with her—but when Kasey met her in the driveway, yammering away before Dash had even shifted into park, she felt nothing but irritated. She'd worked five nights in a row and had picked up a sub shift in the Peds clinic for time and a half. After twenty-plus hours on her feet, she was a walking zombie. She'd put her good sheets into the dryer before leaving for work, and throughout the day she'd thought of them tumbling around with a sheet of Bounce, the crisp snap of the edges when she fit the bottom sheet over the corners. She wanted to make Hamburger Helper for dinner, take a hot shower, and collapse into bed. Kasey's prattling wasn't on the agenda.

"I need some things for school," Kasey said. "Can we go to Target?"

Dash shut off the engine and unfolded her legs from the car. Her knees and ankles ached like she'd run a marathon. Kasey smelled like peanut butter; a wad of neon gum rolled around the back of her mouth. "I went to the grocery store yesterday," Dash said. "What do you need?"

"Listen, Mom, okay? I need a flash drive, one with, like, a lot of storage on it. My group in World Cultures is doing a project on the Three Gorges Dam, you know, the one in

China that flooded like two hundred and fifty square miles. We're going to make a video showing all the villages that went under. All those people, like, *Help! Help! My house is floating away!*" Kasey looked up at the sky, mouth agape. The gum rolled from one side of her mouth to another. "Can you imagine your whole town going underwater? You think all those people live in houseboats now? That would be kinda fun. You could tool around and see your neighbors."

"I think the people displaced by the dam live somewhere else," Dash said. "They were relocated."

"That's exactly why I need the flash drive, Mom. So we can show where everyone went. If we go to Target, I also need new volleyball socks because I ripped a hole in my good pair, and more ankle tape. Coach says that junk you bought at Walgreens is no good. I also need some tampons."

"I bought you a new box of pads last month. Did you go through them that fast?"

"I have some, but I don't want to use them anymore. Tampons are the way to go, the ones with the plastic applicators. Izzy says they're easier to use."

Dash set her purse on the kitchen counter and lifted the handle on the faucet to wash her hands. The maple in the backyard was at its zenith, like a brush dipped in paint, the lawn skirting the trunk pixelated with fallen leaves. The late sunlight seared through the branches. Dash took it in for a moment, its heartbreaking autumn splendor, before reaching for the dish towel. "You think you're ready for tampons?"

"Duh, obviously. Lexi Klein's already on the pill. She and Micah Wagner have been doing it since the summer."

"Doing what?"

"*It,* Mom. The nasty. Getting their stank on." Kasey pumped her fists beside her waist and thrust her hips back and forth. "Uh huh, uh huh, the skanky stank."

"Lexi's thirteen! So are you." Though she'd had a few moms that age in the NICU. Girls who got pregnant that young had all sorts of problems, besides the obvious. Calcium deficiencies, eclampsia, fistulas causing chronic infections. "Does her mother know about that?"

Kasey shrugged. "No idea. Lexi's jugs are the size of grapefruit. Maybe she was ready."

"Can we please use the proper names for body parts? And, for the record, growing breasts doesn't mean you're ready for sex." The mail was on the table. Dash preheated the oven and slumped into one of the metal chairs and began to sort the junk from the bills. The basement door was ajar and she could hear the furious slap of Landon's keyboard echoing up the staircase.

Kasey pulled her sweatshirt away from her chest and peered down inside the collar. "I wouldn't know."

"Breasts don't pop out overnight," Dash said. "Give it time." She worked her pinky nail inside the corner of her MasterCard statement and tore it open.

"I'd rather have itty-bitty titties than a big old bedonkadonk booty," Kasey said.

Dash dropped the envelope. "All this language! People will think you were raised by wolves."

"Cool. Like Romulus and Remus."

"Who?"

"The founders of Rome, Mom. Duh. They were twins and their dad was the god Mars but they were raised by a she-wolf in the woods. They drank wolf milk, like, straight from her wolf tits. They each built their own city, and when Remus tried to jump over his brother's wall, Romulus chucked a spear at his head. Then Romulus went to this other city and kidnapped all their women so the men of Rome could marry them."

“We’re more civilized now, thank God,” Dash said. She pressed her fingers against her temples. She could feel her pulse in her skull. If Kasey told her one more thing, she might scream. “You think I could look at the mail before I start cooking? Why don’t you go relax for a bit?”

“I know, I know. The birth of Western civilization, whatever,” Kasey said. She slumped off toward the living room, muttering, “Blah, blah, blah.”

Dash loved her daughter, and she often felt guilty—as she did now—about her irritation. That was the hardest part: the domino effect of negative emotions, worry causing fatigue causing annoyance causing guilt, which only led to more worry. A never-ending spiral. On some level, Landon was the easier kid because his needs were straightforward and predictable. His endless questions about the *Golden Lance* movies or *Hadean Eon*, his favorite video game, were so familiar she could recite them. They were easy to indulge while she chopped carrots or folded the laundry. Kasey, on the other hand, was constantly changing, landing on subjects like bees crossing a meadow. And like a bee, Kasey never stopped demanding attention.

Dash hadn’t been trying for another baby when she discovered she was pregnant again. Landon was nearly four and already taking up so much time, shuttling between therapy and Birth-to-Three appointments while she and Mike both worked full-time. The thought of adding another to the mix made her weary, and in bed at night she worried about what problems Kasey’s birth might cause. Three years as a NICU nurse had shown her the horrors that could occur during the short journey from womb to world, even for an otherwise healthy fetus. Cerebral palsy, cognitive impairments, facial paralysis, brachial palsy, subconjunctival hemorrhage, brain bleeds, jaundice, broken clavicles, separated shoulders, fractured skulls. Even after Kasey arrived a week late, eight pounds and as pink as a peony, Dash watched for delayed speech, floppy motor control, crossed eyes and cataracts, an unwillingness to smile or laugh or point or wave. But Kasey passed every milestone right on time—rolling over by four months, walking by eleven, talking by nineteen—as though checking the requirements for normalcy off a list. By the time she started first grade, she seemed like Landon's older sister, correcting his mistakes, even laughing at him. Amplifying the speed at which the world was leaving Dash's firstborn behind.

Dash slid her MasterCard statement out of the envelope and spread the bill on the table. Since the mill had closed, she'd kept a tight rein on the finances, glancing at the checkbook at least once a day and holding back a portion of her paycheck in cash to cover the utilities, which she paid in person at the city offices downtown, counting out the bills at the cashier's window and returning the dimes and nickels to the bank. The interest on sixty cents wasn't much, but it was better than a bunch of coins floating around the bottom of her purse or disappearing inside a vending machine. The credit card they reserved for emergencies.

The amount owed was close to what she expected, but then she saw she was looking at it wrong. *That* number was for the minimum payment. The total balance was $1,922.59. The acid in her stomach rose to her pharynx before nosediving through her intestines. The number had to be a mistake. Their identities had been stolen. The MasterCard people should have called her to verify before letting things get so out of hand. She scanned the page, squinting to decipher the coded charges: gas at MotoMart, Ken's Goodyear after Mike found a nail in his tire, Kasey's volleyball uniform and pads. Farther down, stretching to the twentieth of the month when the billing cycle cut off, were the truncated words she'd been hoping to find—*MtlStrm, BldHnd, HdnEn*—each one absurdly foreign, the work of a hacker on the other side of the world. But when she read them aloud, restoring the missing vowels to the algebra of consonants, she recognized them. *Metal Storm. Bloodhound. Hadean Eon.*

The phone system directed her to log into her online account, something she'd never done before. Paper, she'd long assumed, was safer. After pecking at the keypad on her phone to create a suitably complicated password, she used her thumb and index finger to enlarge the list of charges. Current balance, as of that day: $2,286.37. Interspersed with the games were charges she didn't have to sound out: *XXX, LvePssy, AvatrSluts.* $19.99, $29.99, $69.99. The list went on and on.

The bulbs in the ceiling fan throbbed. The motionless blades had thickened with soft gray cotton balls of dust. Evening light was sliding across the yard now, casting the lawn in blue-green shadow, the maple tinted a deep violet. Landon's bike leaned against the garage wall. A Harley *blub-blubbed* down the street. *Calm down, Dolores.* She widened the basement door and called for Landon.

"I'm busy," he called back.

"I need to talk to you."

"Busy."

"Pause your game, honey," she said. "I need you to come talk to me."

"No."

The third refusal kicked in the anger she'd been trying to suppress. "Don't make me ask you again," she called. "Don't make me ask you even one more time."

The chair creaked. Landon appeared at the bottom of the stairs. He ascended without looking up at her, hunched and lurching, his arms dangling. His eyes were red and sunken into their sockets. The stubble on his face and neck made him look gaunt. He slid a hand down the front of his sweatpants as his eyes skittered away.

"How long have you been down there?" she asked. Mike had worked all weekend, too, on day shift.

Dash backed up and returned to her chair at the table. One of Landon's behavioral therapists had encouraged Dash to sit while talking to him, and to allow him room to pace. Allowing Landon to stand taller than her and Mike would help him feel in control, which might encourage him to take responsibility for his actions. She slid the statement across the table. "Did you download some games? A whole bunch of games?"

"Evolution boosters for *Hadean Eon*. And viral immunity."

"Those are part of the games, right?"

"Kwan's now a Paleo-Jurassic Master."

"What about dirty pictures?" she asked. "You buy some of those?"

He turned his back to her. "Shut up." His T-shirt was wrinkled between his shoulder blades. He hadn't showered in days. "Shut up!" he said again, louder.

"We owe more than two thousand dollars." Dash pressed the air between her teeth to amplify the sound. She still couldn't quite believe it. "That's a lot of money. Do you know how much money that is?"

"I make money," he said. "I build stuff for people."

"Do you make *that* much?"

He was staring at the ground, his hands close to his chest. Had he been facing her, Dash might have seen him about to stim, the way his face was twisting. From where she sat, she could only see his broad back, the scruffy hairs at his collar. The number on the credit card statement.

"Not very quickly," Dash said. "Not before we have to pay the bill." She breathed in and out until her heart rate slowed some. "Don't worry," she said. "We'll work it out. You can give us what you've earned so far and pay the rest over time."

Landon whipped around as if stung by a wasp. Dash realized too late the mistake she'd made. She'd forgotten how little it had taken to set him off the last time. Her hair dryer had tripped a fuse that had crashed the computer in the middle of his game and her efforts to calm him had given her a black eye. She should have canceled the credit card and waited for Mike.

"You can't have my money!" Landon yelled. He leaned forward and bit at the air.

Dash raised her palms, careful not to touch him. "Let's talk more when Dad gets home."

"It's my money!" he screamed. "You can't have any of it!" His fingers splayed wide and then knotted into claws.

"Can we try to calm down?"

"It's my money!" He shuffled backward and turned toward the sink. His shoulders and back pulled tight and fell slack. His sweatpants were saggy and bunched around his ankles. The drawer rattled, and Landon turned and came toward her with a steak knife in his hand, the short, serrated blade pointed at the tip. He pressed his shins to Dash's knees and leaned his weight against the table, the tip of the knife to her throat. Dash felt the prick of the point, her trachea rigid beneath it, and when she moved her eyes down Landon's trembling arm, she could see only his thumb and wrist, not the blade. The knife had disappeared into the narrow space between the end of her son's hand and the start of her neck. It seemed incongruent to the moment: a kitchen utensil in a kitchen, but not in the right part of the room or put to the right use. Like the time she found her glasses, after hours of looking, nested among the butter sticks in the fridge. Landon's sclera were bloodshot and the knot in his throat bulged.

"Please stop, honey," she said. It took more effort than she expected to keep her voice level. She looked Landon in the eyes, as if eye contact might jar something in him. His lids were heavy and his pupils were tiny. She'd studied his face, awake and asleep, for all of his life, had pinched his tongue between her fingers to help him pronounce the letter G. She'd held his chin in her palm. Even after eighteen years there were vast parts of him that remained unknown to her, locked rooms in his mind, and she wondered if he'd ever seen her the way she'd seen him—with something like hope or want or simply love. Studying his eyes now, she doubted it. If he didn't see her, did he see anyone? It made her sad to think he'd always been so alone.

"You're hurting Mom," she said quietly.

"I'll kill you dead if you touch one cent of my money," he said.

"Mom?" Kasey called. She appeared in the doorway. "Oh, God!"

If Landon turned toward his sister, Dash wouldn't be able to get around him. She needed Landon to stay right where he was. She closed her eyes and said as calmly as she could manage, "Kasey, would you please go across to the Heinemans'?" She swallowed, softly. Her neck moved against the knifepoint. She knew the exact place where the blade would go in. "Go now, please," Dash said. "Go on and see Mrs. Heineman, okay?"

Kasey's eyes were wide, fixed on her brother, even as she backed away. Dash waited until she heard the storm door banging against the latch. "I won't touch your money, Landon." Saying his name was a deliberate choice. "You worked for it. It's yours."

"I'll kill you," he said.

"Then you won't have a mom," she said. "You'll lose the one person who loves you more than anyone else."

"It's my money." He let go of the table and straightened his back. Dash felt the pressure release. "Touch it and you're gone."

Landon set the knife on the counter by the sink. It looked again like a utensil. Dash didn't pick it up or try to move it. She was terrified in a different way than she expected. It occurred to her that these silent, petrified moments before whatever happened next were the last minutes of her old life, the final grains of sand through the hourglass. When the glass turned over and time started again, the first grains would have the farthest to fall. She braced for impact.

The police arrived in separate cruisers, one with its siren lights flashing, the other dark and silent. Dash opened the door so they wouldn't ring the bell. Landon was still in the kitchen, the knife behind the coffee maker. She hadn't known what else to do with it, or with the other knives still in the drawer and in the wood block on the counter. The officers came up the front walkway with their hands on their belts. The second, a woman, held her index finger to the radio receiver on her shoulder.

The male officer's thinning black hair triangulated into a widow's peak, and his upper lip was framed by a thin, department-issued mustache. "Do you need an ambulance?" he asked.

"I'm fine," she said. She stared at his name badge. Officer Buenconsejo. She memorized it, vowing to destroy his career, picket the mayor's office with his name inked on a sign, if he so much as laid an errant finger on her son. "My son's disabled," she said. The word had never sounded more misapplied. "He doesn't always know what he's doing."

"You're bleeding," Officer Buenconsejo said.

She touched her throat and her finger came away red. "It's nothing. I don't even feel it."

"What happened?" asked the woman, stepping in front of her partner, a conduit between the two parties. Officer Allen. Her blond hair was pulled into a tight ponytail and she wore neither makeup nor earrings. The vest beneath her uniform blouse added volume to her chest and shoulders. She opened a pouch on her belt and handed Dash a gauze square. Dash's eye went to her belt, the yellow-handled Taser in the black holster, the pistol on her other hip. Officer Buenconsejo carried both weapons, too.

Dash wanted to lie but Kasey had witnessed everything. She explained about the argument, the knife to her throat—everything but the porn and Landon's threat to kill her. "The funny thing is, this all came about because he's been earning his own money," she said, as if there were humor in all this, a misunderstanding they'd one day laugh about. "He was afraid I'd take it from him."

"He give you that bruise, too?" Officer Allen asked.

"That was an accident. Weeks ago."

"Log shows the department came out then."

Dash nodded. There was nothing she could say.

"We're going to talk to him," Officer Buenconsejo said, stepping across the threshold. His elbows touched both sides of the doorframe. He pointed toward the kitchen. "He's in there?"

"His name is Landon," Dash said. "I'll come with you."

"You need to wait here."

Officer Allen put her hand on Dash's shoulder. "We'll do our best."

"Don't do that," Dash said. "To him, I mean. Don't touch Landon. He doesn't like it."

Officer Allen nodded and turned to watch a car pull into the driveway. Dash already knew the sound. "My husband," she said.

"Talk to him," Officer Allen said. "We'll talk to your son."

Officer Allen followed her partner down the hallway. Dash heard Officer Buenconsejo say Landon's name but she couldn't hear his reply.

Dash shut the front door to hold in the heat and waited beneath the porch light as Mike cut the engine and climbed down from the truck. A spider web stretched between the fixture and the eave, dotted with black insects, one still alive and struggling to free itself, its hairfine legs grappling. Mike eyes beneath his Lowe's cap were wide; Kasey's expressions and gestures all came from him. "Can we go in?"

"They told me to wait."

He cupped his hands around her face. "He hurt you? Where's Kasey?"

She dabbed at her neck with the gauze. "She's at the Heinemans'. Georgina must have called the police. They got here fast."

"What set him off?" He was still wearing his red vest from work.

"He charged two grand on the MasterCard," Dash said. "Downloading games and porn."

"Porn?"

"I thought the same thing."

"He's seventeen, I suppose," Mike said. He lifted his hat and snugged it back down again.

"I tried to talk to him about it, and he pulled a steak knife from the drawer and came at me." She turned to face the front door. The cops were with Landon in her kitchen, their hands on their Batman belts, their cuffs and guns. The siren lights on the first cruiser were still whirling. "They're going to take him," she said. "I can't stand it."

"You don't know that yet," Mike said.

"We had to talk them out of it the last time." She cupped her hands to her mouth and breathed into them. "How long was he in the basement? Didn't you make him go to school?"

"I heard the bus come," Mike said. "I thought he got on it."

"He's been down in that dungeon for God knows how long."

Mike slid his hands from his jacket pockets and held them out. "I didn't realize."

Dash was starting to shiver. She breathed into her hands again. "I didn't either."

The front door opened and Officer Buenconsejo was in the doorway, his right arm extended behind him, gripping Landon's shoulder. Officer Allen was last in line, her hand around Landon's bicep. She told them not to touch him. Landon walked with his head down, meeting neither Dash's eyes nor Mike's. He didn't look violent or even sick, just vulnerable. His hands were cuffed behind his back. Dash felt the loop-de-loop in her gut that had started this whole mess, not even an hour ago. Had she ignored it the first time, she and Mike would be inside together, talking to Landon.

"We're going to have him sit in the car while we figure some things out," Officer Buenconsejo said. "For his own protection."

"Are you taking him to jail?" Mike asked.

"The hospital," Buenconsejo said. "They'll evaluate him and likely admit him."

"Okay," Mike said. He seemed to regard this as good news.

Officer Allen opened the back door of the front cruiser, the one with the lights going, and Buenconsejo palmed the back of Landon's head to guide him inside. He shut the door, walked around the trunk, and sat down behind the wheel. His forehead and eyes and thin mustache glowed in the light of his computer screen. Officer Allen meanwhile crossed the street to talk to Georgina Heineman, who stood waiting inside her own storm door, the glass fogging in front of her. Kasey wasn't there, thank God, and Dash hoped her daughter was in another room, on another floor, too far to overhear the conversation. "Georgina's telling her about the last time," Dash said to Mike. "She's telling the police Landon's a monster."

"They already know about it," Mike said. "It's in their computer system." He toed a maple leaf that had blown across the walkway, careful not to crumble it. "I don't like it either."

Dash ducked inside the house for a jacket, pulling the first one her hand landed on in the front closet, which turned out to be Mike's wrestling jacket from high school, with the blue wool body and white leather arms, cracked and worn but still warm. She buttoned it to the neck.

"There's room for him at Hanover Medical," Officer Buenconsejo said when he came back to them. "A bed on the psych unit."

"Could you take him somewhere else?" Dash asked. "I work there. I'd rather keep my coworkers out of my private business."

"We'd have to go all the way to Green Bay for another inpatient unit," he said. "HMC is big for a reason."

"At least he'll be close," Mike said.

"Could you at least turn off the flashing lights?" Dash said. "You've got him in the car now. There's no more danger."

Buenconsejo said that'd be fine but made no move to return to the car. His partner was inside the Heinemans' house now, the door closed behind her. Other neighbors had come out onto the sidewalk and stood across the street, their faces obscured by the darkness.

"We're coming, too," Dash said.

"We'll take him to the ER and they'll send him up once he's been evaluated. That could take time. Maybe you want to wait."

"We're going," Dash said. "End of story."

She told Mike which way to drive, as if he didn't know the way. The police cruiser had double-parked beneath the emergency overhang, the back seat already empty. Mike pulled into a parking spot and Dash reached up to remove the HMC parking tag from the neck of the rearview. "Employees aren't supposed to park this close," she said.

"You're not here as an employee."

"Security knows the car. I don't want to have to explain it later."

She forced herself not to run. Landon stood at the admitting window, flanked by the officers with his hands cuffed behind his back. Officer Allen's ponytail bobbed as she leaned forward to sign the paperwork. Buenconsejo nodded at Dash as the sliding doors parted for her. Scattered among the chairs she recognized a bearded homeless man who'd been an ER frequent flyer for years, and tried to guess the afflictions of the others. The boy cradling his wrist in his hand beside his mother had obviously broken a bone. The overweight woman in the too-big hoodie was slapping her toddler's back because he had croup. The desiccated old people, liver-spotted and hunched, with fevers or pains that wouldn't let them sleep or who were simply lonely, abandoned by children who lived far away. They all stared at the cuffed boy escorted by the police. Dash wanted to scream.

The heavy steel doors to the emergency unit were wide enough to drive a car through but thick enough to stop one if someone tried to ram the building. Fully opened they revealed the unit's frantic, fluorescent hustle, the corridor crowded with staff, a vacated gurney piled with used linens, shoved against a wall. Landon's heels dragged on the carpet, then squeaked across the linoleum.

Dash had her name badge in her purse and was prepared to scan herself through if the police told her not to follow. Cops didn't have carte blanche in Emergency. They couldn't give orders to the doctors and nurses, especially when the patient was a minor. Neither officer protested when she fell in behind them, following the procession to a room with a sliding glass door. Officer Allen told Landon to sit on the bed. The tech knelt to remove Landon's shoes.

The door slid open again, this time producing Denny, the security guard, and Dr. Griebler, the attending physician. Denny walked Dash to her car whenever she got off late at night, scanning the rows of cars with his long-handled flashlight, his only weapon. Dr. Griebler had been on the day the Jensen quads came in and had helped Dr. Fackelman with the deliveries. Dash remembered him wiping his forehead on his sleeve as he fought, and failed, to get one of the babies to breathe.

Officer Buenconsejo pointed to the other side of the bed, and Denny stepped around to that side. The officer reached behind Landon's back and in one motion, so fluid and swift Dash hardly saw it happen, the cuffs around Landon's wrists were removed and he was lying on his back, his wrists secured in the restraints. By the time Dash caught up, they were doing his ankles. Landon's eyes darted and his breath was short. "Mom," he said. "*Mom.*"

"Don't restrain him," Dash said. "It only makes it worse."

"We'll give him something," Dr. Griebler said. "Does he have any allergies?"

"No," Dash said. She took a step forward and felt Mike's hand on her arm. "No allergies. Please dose him quickly. This is very hard for him."

"Let them do their job," Mike said. Like this wasn't hers. She stared at him again and he moved to the wall where there was an empty chair.

The doctor and guard and police officers filed out and a nurse returned with a bag of saline and a syringe. "Dash," the nurse said, surprised. Her name was Jessica; Dash had known her for years. She double-checked the room number with the sheet in her hand.

"This is my son," Dash said. "What are you giving him?"

"Five milligrams of Haldol."

"Mom," Landon said, gritting his teeth. "These are tight."

"Give it to him, please," Dash said. She waited, watching, as Jessica—a nurse she considered a friend, to whom she'd once confessed over two-for-one margaritas that she could get Mike to do almost anything, including run to the store in the middle of the night, by promising him a blowjob, and who, in response, had cupped her hand around her mouth and admitted she'd once lost her bullet vibrator inside her husband's ass—pierced Landon's arm with a needle, adjusted the position, and drove the plunger home. Landon's eyelids drooped almost instantly and Jessica taped the cannula to the back of his hand to secure it. She hung the saline on the rack and wound the tubing around the stalk. Dash brushed the hair away from her son's forehead. His skin was clammy and hot. "It's okay," she whispered. "You can let yourself fall asleep."

She left Mike in Landon's room and followed Jessica into the hallway, hoping to get her alone for a moment. Jenny Ramirez sat at the desk, squinting at the computer. She looked up at Dash. "What's going on?" Jenny asked. "I didn't see anything about a neonate."

Now everyone upstairs will know, Dash thought.

"My son," Dash said. She struggled for the word. *Hurt? Sick? Crazy?* "He had an episode and the police brought him in." She leaned toward Jessica. "Someone coming down from Psych?"

Jenny interrupted. "I'll do the eval here. I'll speak to the doctor when I'm finished, before he goes up." She eyed the Band-Aid on Dash's neck. "Can you tell me what happened?"

Dash told Jenny about the bill and the knife at her throat, but left out any mention of the porn. She added, at the end, "I think he's out of sorts more than anything. He hasn't slept much."

"How long has it been?"

"A few days, maybe. I've been here a lot and my husband's been working, too. Our schedules were different. I assumed Landon had slept at night. I just assumed he'd had some sleep."

"Insomnia is a psychiatric symptom," Jenny said. "It's something to pay attention to."

"What's going to happen now?"

"We'll admit him and the psychiatrist will determine. Since the police brought him in, he'll need to appear in family court in a few days. Once he's stable, we can address next steps."

Dash wanted the next steps to be going home, going back to normal, Landon building shelves and managing the equipment for the football team. Going to the inpatient unit would mean a full workup and diagnosis. There was no way the psychiatrist could tell them to hang in there, keep doing what you're doing. You go to a muffler shop, you get a muffler. Nowhere was this truer than in a hospital.

"How long will he need to stay?"

"Seventy-two hours to start. Likely longer."

"How much longer?"

A week, maybe two," Jenny said. Her eyes were soft, a little sad. Relaying this news gave her no pleasure. "The doc will make a recommendation when Landon appears in family court."

The officers clopped down the central corridor carrying Styrofoam cups of coffee. They stopped outside Landon's door to talk with Denny. The guard seemed to swell in their presence, his flashlight on his hip like a gun. The cops and guard were congratulating themselves for subduing a knife-wielding perp, though the perp was really a scared teenage kid. Their heavy shoes were loud on the floors. Jenny went over to them. "We've got it from here, guys. He's sedated and restrained. You can hit the trail." That she didn't address them as "officer" shocked Dash and pleased her. "I'm sure we'll see you later," Jenny said.

Only after the officers left did Dash realize she'd neglected to thank them for not hurting Landon. He was scared, but uninjured.

"Can I get you anything?" Jenny asked.

"How about a stiff drink?" Dash said, dragging her fingers across her forehead.

"Ha," Jessica said. "Me, too. And a week in Jamaica with a Spanish underwear model."

Dash pictured the vibrator sliding inside Phil's anus, disappearing inside his rectum. Did Jessica look at Mike and picture Dash bent over his lap? She was glad Mike had stayed put in Landon's room.

"I was at a conference in Las Vegas last summer," Jenny said. "I saw this woman eating dinner at the buffet. She had a paper bib clipped around her neck, the kind you get at the dentist. Who travels with something like that?"

"Did she have a big pile of crab legs?" Dash asked.

"That's the thing," Jenny said. "She was eating a salad."

"Maybe she was hygienist," Jessica said. "Maybe she had lockjaw."

"It was like she was announcing to the world that she couldn't manage a plate of food without spilling it on herself," Jenny said.

"People are so weird," Jessica said. "Good Christ." Dash was grateful for their jokes, regardless of whether they were trying to lighten the mood for her benefit or had forgotten that Dash was there as a mother instead of as a nurse. People were weird. There was no telling what people might do. The weird, though, didn't come to the hospital in handcuffs. That put you in a different category.

Two techs in gray scrubs came down from Psych to move Landon upstairs. Both men had strong, round arms tattooed with looping curlicues of blue and gray, words she couldn't read. They didn't ask Landon to get up. They released the brakes and wheeled the entire bed through the door, Landon's wrists and ankles bound to the frame.

Dash had been to Five North, the locked psych unit, only a few times in her career. Now and then postpartum depression turned severe enough that a mom had to go up from Maternity. Psych was almost a hospital unto itself, in the old wing, un-remodeled and out of date, the walls built of green blocks and the small windows crosshatched with metal wiring. Long fluorescent tubes tracked along the ceiling. Dash could recall when most of the hospital looked this way, paint colors and mood lighting an afterthought. The old units seemed even more forlorn and prison-like given the modern spaces that surrounded them, on the floors above and below.

Dash and Mike waited in a classroom with a circle of chairs and no windows to the outside. A list of promises—*I wont smoke more than 2 packs a day, I wont use inappropriate language or gestures in group*—went top to bottom on the white board. The cabinets were secured with chunky padlocks. The psychiatrist wore a purple shirt beneath his white coat and hair long enough to cover his ears; his soft voice struck Dash as condescending. Along with the Haldol, he'd ordered Seroquel to calm some of Landon's aggression. He'd have a better idea of what to recommend in a few days. He scrolled down the page on his laptop. "Looks like he's had quite a bit of therapy," Dr. Baese said. "Not so much in the last year."

"My employment situation changed," Mike said. "Our insurance don't cover what it used to, and we don't have as much disposable cash. We've tried to make do."

"Well, the good news is that Landon will be eligible for more services now," Dr. Baese said.

"I suppose," Dash said.

"You should call his therapist in the morning. Chances are they'll work with you to set up a payment plan, maybe do a few pro bono sessions."

"His pediatrician has been a big help over the years. You know Jeff Wu?"

The psychiatrist shook his head. "This is an adult unit. The kids' facility is off-site."

"Then why is Landon here?"

"Because of the emergent nature of the problem. Because the police brought him in. And he's seventeen and a half." Dr. Baese capped his pen and looked at Dash directly, singling her out. "Landon's in a legal gray area. Since he's a minor, you still have the ability to make decisions for him. But if his problems continue to escalate, a judge could decide to treat him as an adult. Once he's eighteen, he'll have to consent on his own to therapies and programs, and that gets a whole lot trickier. Intervention now is important, and in his best interest."

That much Dash could agree with: Landon would never choose to do anything proactive on his own.

"Does he need a lawyer?" Mike asked.

"He'll get a public defender when he appears," Dr. Baese said. "You can hire your own if you like, but I don't expect anything other than a straightforward hearing. At some point, a county caseworker might want to do an in-home evaluation."

"Someone will come to our house?" Dash asked. "Poke around in our rooms?"

"Whatever we need to do," Mike said.

"Right now, you can go home and let us treat him," Dr. Baese said. "You're a nurse here, Mrs. Coenen?"

"I am. In the NICU."

"Be a nurse down there but be a mom up here. That's the best thing. And be honest with the CPS caseworker. The resources are there to help."

"Can we see him?" Dash asked, fearing the doctor would tell her no simply to assert control. She'd seen the neos say as much. "We just want to say goodnight."

"For a minute or two," Dr. Baese said. "Then let him rest."

The doors on the unit were locked and each one had a rectangular window above the handle. One woman stood with her nose pressed to the glass, a strand of gray hair between her eyes. The nurses' station was protected by heavy glass panes all the way to the ceiling. Through them Dash could see a row of computer monitors with cameras into the rooms. She leaned close to the speaker. "We're Landon Coenen's parents." She pulled from her purse Landon's iPod and headphones, as well as the scrap of blankie he still slept with. She held them to the window. "We brought him some things."

"He can't have them right now," the nurse said.

"He listens to music when he goes to sleep," Dash said. "He sleeps with this cloth."

"I can hang on to them for you," she said. "But he can't have them yet."

"We'll bring them back later," Mike said.

Landon's room was bare except for a small nightstand beside the bed. The TV and clock were recessed in the wall and protected by a sheet of scuffed Plexiglas. Landon lay on his back in a gown, the fabric dingy and beige against the white linens. His chest and belly were as round as a barrel. The sheets only came as high as his waist. His wrists were still restrained and the IV hung from the stand, connected by a coil of tubing to Landon's hand. Dash prayed Dr. Baese was right. Rest and medicine would help. Twelve hours of drug-induced sleep, a hot meal, and a shower, and he'd feel better. She'd said as much to new moms and NICU parents at least a thousand times.

"Hey, bud," Mike said.

Dash rubbed Landon's arm, from his elbow to the coarse fabric of the restraints. He opened his eyes as if he'd been yanked back to the surface from deep underwater. His eyes helicoptered around the room. "It's okay, honey," she said. "Mom and Dad are here."

He swallowed, and his chest rose and fell. "I'm sorry."

"I know you are," she said. "You're going to feel better soon."

"You stay?"

"If you want me to," she said.

"The doctor said—" Mike said.

Dash turned to Mike, then back to Landon. "How about you sleep here and I'll sleep at home, and I'll come back in the morning? Neither of us've had a good night of sleep in a while."

"When will you come back?"

"I'll be here when you wake up. That sound okay?"

She remembered all the nights Landon couldn't sleep—years when he was four, five, six, when she'd hear him knocking his heel against his bedroom wall at two in the morning. Kasey was a baby, and between the feedings and work and Landon's insomnia she felt she never slept, ever. Only if Dash lay in bed with him would his eyes eventually grow heavy. Back then she believed time and attention, mothering in great abundance, could mitigate every problem.

Saline fluid dripped through the IV. She leaned down to kiss him. As her lips touched his forehead, she felt Landon squeeze her hand and his eyelashes flutter against her cheek. She felt his warm breath against her neck, against the Band-Aid. For an instant she felt terrified all over again. Then, in the next breath, ashamed.

Part Two

8

Fran met her at the unit door. "A baby's in distress," she said, her hand on the crash bar, blocking the entrance. "You need to wait outside until the situation is under control."

"What situation?" Brooke's gut clenched. She'd been staying at the Hibbert House for nearly two weeks, darting home every few days to switch out her clothes after Harper had left for the station. It had been a relief not to face him, or Ollie, after what she'd said at the meeting with Dr. Fackelman, and Brooke was glad for the chance to focus solely on Emery and Opal. If she didn't wash her hair, she could make from it from the NICU to the Hibbert House, shower, and be back at the bedside within a half hour. The next time something went wrong, she'd be there.

Beyond Fran's shoulder, Brooke could see the ceiling lights shining down over one of the beds, the space fenced off by a red cart and a white cart. The white cart held the defibrillator paddles. Dr. Fackelman had come close to using them on Emery once already. The doctor's head was down, her chest and arms draped in a yellow smock. The fax machine shrieked.

"Why didn't you call me?" She'd use her shoulder to get inside, if she needed to. She'd knock Fran to the ground.

Fran registered her panic. "Not one of yours. We got a new admission."

"Opal and Emery are okay?"

"Nothing to worry about."

The torque in her abdomen released by half. "The baby who came in might not live?"

"He's in crisis," Fran said, pulling shut the door. "In here, there's only one kind."

Brooke avoided her reflection in the elevator doors, afraid to acknowledge what she was feeling. She felt lighter than she had in weeks, maybe since the births, and her happiness was the result of someone else's anguish. The world, she believed, contained a fixed amount of joy and despair and one had to be offset by the other. For every miraculous recovery, someone had to die in agony. For once, it was another baby's life teetering on the crumbling precipice; for once, she was the one shooed away from the unit. The floor dropped away beneath her feet and the numbers dinged on the display. If the other baby died, hers might live. A distasteful thought, but a fact she knew about herself.

October sun flooded the lobby's windows. Glimmering water cascaded down the rock wall into a pool of coins. The player piano was into an up-tempo rendition of "The Surrey with the Fringe on Top," the keys moving while the blue-vested volunteers seated together near Registration tapped their feet and sang along. Even the patients appeared renewed in the morning glow, like airport travelers en route to a foreign city. For the first time she saw the hospital the way the building's architects had envisioned it, modern and healing, and knew the baby dying upstairs was the reason why. Yet here she was. Brooke bought a coffee at the Starbucks and crossed to an empty chair in the center of the great room, where she took her time thumbing through a back issue of *Healthy Mom & Baby*. At last she had the right to consider the magazine's advice.

Emery had been moved down to Bed Eight and Opal to Seven. The new baby in the alcove was connected to a machine Brooke had never seen before: a hive of colored hoses and wires feeding what she could only liken to a portable copier and printer. Two of the plastic tubes ran dark with blood—a long spiral through the machine and back to the baby's neck. "ECMO," Fran whispered, when she caught Brooke staring. "Heart and lung bypass. Until he recovers from the injury."

"Injury," Brooke repeated. The baby was enormous, a watermelon with limbs. She'd expected a preemie, not a full termer.

Fran leaned in close and whispered, "I shouldn't say too much, but it was pretty hairy in here for a while. Took three doses of Narcan to bring him around, and that was before his lungs started to bleed." Fran glanced over her shoulder, to see who might be listening. "Enough narcotics in his system to put down a horse. We almost lost him."

Her thoughts swirled: a baby born in withdrawal, his mother an addict, her own babies steadily improving. It was fair, a just tipping of the scales. She hoped the baby would die quickly, while she was away from the unit, so she wouldn't have to witness karma's machine. Guiltily, she asked Fran, "Are you back with Opal and Emery? Are you taking care of them again?"

"I'm not even supposed to be here," Fran said. "I was off at seven, but we caught the admission at five thirty."

"Where's Dash been? She hasn't worked in days."

"Taking time off," Fran said. "Personal reasons."

After more than a month in the unit, Brooke had begun to think of Dash as *her* nurse. Fran was funnier but Dash had the faster, more capable hands. Brooke felt she knew Dash better than she knew the other nurses or the doctor, certainly better than the other parents in the unit. But

Fran's tone reminded Brooke that, for all her proximity to the nurses, she wasn't privy to their lives beyond the hospital. The wall between work and home for the nurses, as for most people, was as thick as the door between the NICU and the hospital corridor. She'd be wise to remember that.

The door buzzed and Brooke turned to watch a man and a woman, both in their twenties, shuffle inside. The woman's hair was dishwater blond and stringy, strands of it matted against her forehead. She wore a hospital-issued bathrobe and had a pointed nose and narrow, protuberant teeth. She looked like she'd once been pretty but had lost her hold on it. Or, Brooke thought, the drugs that had nearly killed her child had stolen her prettiness. The man's shirt, made from a shiny, iridescent fabric, changed from magenta to black beneath the canister lights. A gold-link chain hung inside his open collar, as though he'd come from a nightclub. Patchy, dark stubble covered his cheeks and throat. As they settled into the chairs, mom in the glider and dad in the nurse's high-back, the man caught Brooke's eye across the bed space. He offered a small, knowing smile, as if he knew what she was thinking.

From the osmosis of their close quarters, Brooke learned their names were Shantel and Justus. The baby was Cannon. Shantel had the same last name as the car dealerships along the highway, and Justus had charges pending against him—or had at some point—related to false imprisonment of his girlfriend. Jenny told Ting she didn't trust him any farther than she could throw him. The tox report showed that Cannon had opiates in his bloodstream—not that that was much of a secret. Shantel stared vacantly from her chair while globs of saliva swelled the corners of her lips, as though her stupor had amassed there and needed to be managed like a runny nose. Every few minutes, she wiped her mouth on her sleeve.

Yet after only three days, Cannon came off the ECMO. Dr. Fackelman planned to treat him cautiously over the coming weeks.

"Weeks?" Justus asked. "How many weeks?"

"He's detoxing," Jenny said. "Low and slow is the way to go."

Justus's foot bounced. "Maybe the food people can learn how to cook before we go," he said.

Shantel's slippers were pink but ratty, the faux fur gone black around the edges. Her voice squeaked. "I like the fruit cups."

It wasn't fair, Brooke thought. Their kid shouldn't heal that fast.

Jenny widened her stance. "Now that your son's prognosis has improved, you're going to need to move out of your room."

"You're kicking us out?" Justus asked. "You're going to put us on the curb?"

"Shantel's been discharged," Jenny said. She tapped her pen on her clipboard. "We need her room for other patients."

"Where're we supposed to go?" Justus asked. "We live up in Papasay." He had, like Barb the night nurse, a smoker's wheeze. "An hour each way. You going to pay for our gas?

"I wish I could," Jenny said, trying to sound friendly. "I know it's a long way."

"I know you can," Justus said. "I know the hospital gives out vouchers for cabs and gas. I've seen them do it. I bet you have a whole drawer full of free shit."

"The gift cards we do have are for emergencies," Jenny replied. "For when patients get transferred and their families have no other way to get home."

"We don't count?" Justus asked. "Our baby almost died."

"Fine," Jenny said. Her voice had climbed half an octave and turned clipped. "I'll give you one gift card, good for one fill-up." She held up her index finger. "But we need your room today."

"Where do we go? We'll use a whole tank of gas in one trip here and back."

"The hospital isn't a hotel," Jenny said. "It's up to the families to make their own arrangements. People come here from all over the state."

"Can't you shake your magic drawer for a few nights at the Radisson?"

"You can stay in the Hibbert House," Jenny said. "It's across the parking lot."

"It have a TV?" Justus asked.

"You're in luck," Jenny said. "It's got everything you need. Just bring your toothbrush."

"Is the TV in the bedroom?"

"In the living room."

"Is it old?" Justus said. "The TV? Will it fit my Xbox?"

"I have no idea," Jenny said. "It's just a TV."

"I don't know," Justus said. "Sounds sketch. A hotel would be better."

"We have the Hibbert House for a reason," Jenny said firmly. "Take it or leave it."

"We'll take it, I guess."

Jenny stepped away, swinging the curtain flap shut behind her. She shook her head and her sturdy heels thudded on the carpet. Fran eased up behind Brooke and bent close to her ear. "There goes your neighborhood."

Brooke was still awake when she heard them come in, sometime after eleven. She felt the Hibbert House exhale when the front door opened. Their voices moved up the stairs. Brooke recognized Justus's first. "This place is old as fuck."

"It's pretty," Shantel said. "My grandmother lived in a house like this."

Their key grated inside the lock. Of course they were next door. In a certain way, they belonged together. Brooke could hear them through the wall beside her bed, a mere six inches of plaster and lathe between their two rooms in a house built for priests, without any expectation of privacy. Shoes tumbled. A belt clamored to the floor. In the vacuum-sealed echo chamber of the night, every sound was stereophonic. Their bed frame creaked as they lay down, and quickly began to creak more, and louder, in rhythm with the bodies moving it. They were so close that Brooke could hear Shantel gasp when Justus moved inside her. She'd had a baby—a full-term baby with bleeding lungs—two days ago, yet she seemed to be enjoying herself. Brooke tried not to picture their bodies, but the sound was too loud, too close, and the longer it went on, the more she felt she understood what their fucking meant. They were young; they fucked because they could. Because their bodies were made for it.

She'd once felt that way, hooking a leg over Harper's waist so she could roll him into his back and slide on top without losing contact with his mouth: that her body was made to do this, and that the clandestine places where they hooked up—the Days Inn, her dorm, a friend's sailboat in dry dock, another friend's RV in a storage locker—were there to facilitate her desires. Years of trying to have a baby had changed all of that. At some point, sex metamorphosed from desire to desperation. Sex became production, no longer accompanied by lingerie and candles and wine but reduced to its mammalian origins, a blank-eyed mating. There were nights they didn't bother to remove their shirts, when Harper entered her from behind while she lay on her side, his palm on her shoulder their only contact apart from his penis inside her, his labored breath against her hair.

Brooke missed sex, the old way. Harper's bottom lip going slack and the way her fingers fit between his ribs, the noises they'd made. The kind of sex she now heard through the wall. Brooke doubted that Justus and Shantel had been trying to get pregnant. They'd simply, blithely, added one and one together, over and over, until it equaled three. The prospect of their son's death, even now, couldn't stop them, which meant his death wouldn't either. They'd go right on fucking because fucking was the one thing they could do.

But Cannon was improving. He would not die. His recovery scared Brooke more than she wanted it to.

Downstairs the next morning she found Justus asleep on the couch, his elbow tented over his eyes. He wore his jeans but not his shirt. His chest was nearly hairless and surprisingly slight. He couldn't have been older than twenty-five, an age Harper had never been. A tattoo of a wolf snarled across his left pectoral and a tortoise shell covered the knob of the opposite shoulder, appended to a curlicue of leaves along his clavicle. Down the length of his breastbone, from his heart to his diaphragm, was a coffin, painted purple and green. His mouth gaped open enough for Brooke to see the black valleys of his molars. He looked homeless, but then again weren't they all? Holed up here, waiting for whatever came next.

Justus slid his arm from his face. "Am I in your way?" he asked. He sat up and plucked his T-shirt from the floor. "I didn't know who else was here."

"You're fine," she said. "I didn't want to wake you up. I was going to make some coffee."

"You got any extra? I can't say I slept very good."

"I have plenty."

Justus came to the kitchen doorway while the kettle was heating and leaned against the jamb. His jeans sagged against his narrow hips, exposing the band of his underwear. He nodded at Brooke's French press. "I've seen those things but I've never known how to work them," he said. "Not that I've tried."

"They're easy. Coffee and hot water. But they're a pain to clean."

"I know you," he said. "The twins."

"There were four originally," she said, not sure why she felt the need to clarify. Perhaps because she'd herself begun thinking of Opal and Emery the same way. "They were quadruplets."

His eyes widened. "Next you'll tell me they were mermaids or some shit."

The only funny thing was the way he said it. "No, they were babies. But two didn't make it."

"I bet that hurt four times as much. Squeezing out four."

"They were very small. And I didn't squeeze anything." She didn't know when she'd stopped feeling the pain in her abdomen, only that she didn't feel it right then.

"How long have they been in the NICU?"

"A little more than a month. Thirty-four days, to be exact."

"Long time."

"I'm getting used to it."

"Does that doctor know what she's doing? I'm not always so sure."

"Men seem to worry about that," she said. "Because a woman's in charge."

"That's not it."

"What then?"

He yawned and scratched his belly beneath the hem of his shirt. "Just a vibe I get."

"That's exactly what I mean." Though she recalled Dr. Fackelman urging her to let Emery die. Had Brooke bowed to her authority then, her son would be gone.

"How do you take your coffee?" she asked.

"The way you drink it."

She found two mugs in the cupboard, emptied Equal packets two at a time into each one and poured the creamer. The coffee went in last. Justus accepted the mug without breaking eye contact, and Brooke remorsefully recalled the elation she felt when it was his son, not hers, who was in crisis. "The NICU can feel overwhelming in the beginning," she said. "People who haven't had a baby in there don't know what it's like. Let me know if there's anything you need. Shantel, too."

He set the mug on the counter and leaned against the jamb again. "Well, since you mention it, there is one thing. Shantel's in a lot of pain. Like, a fuck ton of pain. But the doctor won't prescribe anything good because of her past issues. I guess I'm wondering if you have anything, maybe something left over. I'll buy them from you. I ain't looking for charity."

"She didn't sound like she was hurting last night," Brooke said, and quickly regretted it.

"Yeah, well," Justus smirked. "I guess it comes and goes. Sorry if we kept you up."

"That was rude of me to say."

Justus shook his head and waited.

"I don't have any," she said. "I had some Percocet in the beginning, but I didn't like the way they made me feel. I'd wake up and not know how long I'd been out."

"That's the best part," Justus said. He sipped from his mug. "So, what did you do with the Percs you didn't take? Where'd they go?"

She had maybe ten pills left, in the bottle at the back of her drawer. One refill left on the prescription. But if she helped Justus now, then surely her fate, the fates of her babies, would be forever linked with his. She couldn't take any chances. "I got rid of them," she said. "I flushed them down the toilet."

Justus wrinkled his lips. Brooke could tell her didn't believe her. "That's a shame. You could've made a dime on each one."

9

Dash carried Landon's khakis and oxford on a wire hanger. Mike's blazer was short on Landon's arms, but the shoulders fit him fine. In Landon's room on Five North, father and son stood face to face, Landon with his chin lifted to give Mike room to work the knot of his necktie. Landon's cheeks and neck were prickled with stubble, though beneath his temples his skin was still infant pink. Dash wished she'd brought a razor before remembering that blades weren't allowed.

Landon caught her staring and clenched his fists under his chin, like a boxer squaring up. "Hold tight, bud," Mike said, unraveling the knot. "I'm working here." He slid the tie up and down on Landon's neck a few times before starting over.

"I'll give you two some room," she said, and stepped into the hallway, leaving the door cracked enough for her to hear. "Remember to look the judge in the eye," Mike said. "All those times we've talked about eye contact? This is when you want to put it to use. Keep your hands in your pockets, too. Try not to stim."

"Kwan carries a biometer in his pocket," Landon said. Kwan was Landon's avatar in *Hadean Eon*. "He uses it to tell if a predator has an evolutionary advantage he can steal. Kwan can echolocate, like bats can. Good for fighting in caves." It seemed to Dash at once impossible and perfectly logical that he'd be thinking of his game right now.

"Hey," Mike said. "Don't put your hands in your pockets quite yet."

A bench hugged the wall opposite the nurses' station, its legs bolted to the floor. Everything on Five North was screwed down or encased in Plexiglas. Dash could see the monitors through the window to the station, the cameras peering into every room. On one screen a patient paced between the wall and the bed; on another, a formless lump lay beneath a mound of blankets on the narrow mattress. She couldn't see Mike and Landon, but knew the nurses could. Someone, right now, was watching her husband tie her son's tie so he could make his court appearance. She didn't know what to hope for. It seemed counterproductive and unfair, especially if she factored in all the money and time they'd spent on therapists, for a judge to declare Landon incapable of adulthood. Yet if the court treated him like one, he could be charged with aggravated assault. She only wanted him to come home. The prospect of him spending the next forty years playing video games wasn't so bad, in light of the alternatives. The alternatives were beyond anything she cared to think about.

She glanced up at the sound of footsteps around the corner. Two decades of nursing had trained her ear to the peculiar vibrations of the hospital's echoes. She could differentiate between the footsteps of a man and a woman, as well as between doctors and nurses, visitors and staff. The advancing clops belonged to a man, the soles too hard for a physician or a nurse. He was coming for Landon.

He had a thick neck and an impressive trucker's gut stretching the buttons of his white shirt front. The star on his breast gleamed and his belt of weapons looked freshly oiled. Dash headed him off before he could knock on the nurses' window. "You're here for Landon Coenen, aren't you?"

"That's right," he said. He introduced himself as Deputy Garb.

"I'm his mother."

The deputy smiled and said, "How's our boy this morning?" which immediately grated on her. As if Deputy Garb had any stake in what happened to *her* boy.

"He's afraid of police," she said. "He came here in a police cruiser and it scared him."

"I'm only his ride," the deputy said, raising his palms. "Nothing to be afraid of."

"He doesn't know that," Dash said. She itched to brush Deputy Garb back, the way Jenny Ramirez had shooed away the cops in the ER. Wipe that fake sweetness right off his pink lip.

Deputy Garb pointed at Landon's door. "He's in here?" Without waiting for her answer, he knocked and pushed open the door. "Hey there, Landon," he said, his voice so genial it verged on farcical. "How's it going, buddy?"

Landon, neck-tied and shabbily hirsute, stepped backward, knocking the canister from his dresser. Water flowed over the edge and down the contours of the drawers to the floor.

"It's okay," Mike said. He gripped Landon's shoulder to steady him. "It's only water." It was one of the many things Dash would never fully understand: why Mike could touch Landon so freely when neither she nor anyone else could. Mike leaned toward Landon's ear. "Don't be scared. Stand up straight, like we talked about. Say hello."

"Aw, that's all right," Deputy Garb said. "You know why I'm here, Landon? I'm here to do your mom and dad a favor. It's my job to make sure you get to the judge in one piece. Nothing safer than a police car, right?"

“Fire truck,” Landon said. “Ambulance. Armored car. Tank.”

“Ho, ho, well, you’ve got me there.” His belly bounced. “All of our fire trucks are busy at the moment and our tanks are over in Afghanistan defending our freedom. Think you can ride with me this time around?”

“Are you going to cuff me?” Landon asked. Moisture shone in the creases of his forehead.

“Of course not. Like I said, buddy, I’m only your ride. When the hearing’s finished, I’ll run you right back. How about you and me head to the car and you can tell me about your favorite sports. Big tall guy like you must like basketball.”

“He’s the manager of his high school team,” Mike said. “He does football in the fall and basketball in the winter.”

“There you go,” the deputy said. “I bet you know a lot about hoops, then.”

“Andrew Bogut was the Bucks’ number one pick in 2005,” Landon said. “He was the first Australian to ever go number one. He played in all eighty-two regular season games his rookie year, and averaged 9.4 points and seven rebounds.”

“Man, you’re a walking computer,” Deputy Garb said, smiling widely. He sidled up and set his hand on Landon’s shoulder. Dash swallowed. She hated this. “You ever hear of Kareem Abdul-Jabbar? He was Lew Alcindor when he started playing for us, before he went and declared himself an A-rab. That guy could play.” Still smiling, nothing but smiles, the deputy moved Landon toward the door.

The courthouse was an imposing white building with narrow slotted windows that gave little indication of what went on inside. Mike steered down College Avenue in search of a parking spot, the courthouse looming over the colored awnings and tavern signs. Dash could remember when downtown Hanover had been the region's shopping hub, the avenue busy with jewelry and furniture stores, men's and women's clothes, a store that specialized in fine stationery made from a select grade of paper produced at one of the mills. Her sister Vanessa had once worked behind the counter there and had bragged about how she'd processed orders from as far away as Japan and South Africa. The presence of a store on the avenue, the boxed cards and writing tablets displayed in the front window, had made Hanover seem important, indispensable to the world economy. The stationery store now sold magazines and tobacco, Wilson's Jewelry had a sign in the window that said WE BUY GOLD, and Frederick's Fine Clothes was a Loan Max.

Mike pulled to the curb in front of the furniture gallery. The name had changed, and as Mike fed quarters into the meter, Dash peeked through the window. Instead of the elegant displays of couches and loveseats, wooden tables outfitted with china and linen napkins, she saw a line of rusted bicycles, racks of used clothing, shelves of wrinkled paperback books. A thrift store.

"I put in an hour's worth," Mike said. He hiked up his khakis and smoothed down his thin hair with his hand. "Think that's enough?"

"Hard to know."

Dash had been inside the courthouse on exactly two occasions: to apply for her marriage license and, many years later, to pay a parking ticket. She laid her purse on the conveyor belt scanner and the uniformed officer waved her through the metal detector before passing an electronic wand across her waist and pockets. The central lobby, blank and institutional, lacked any decorations save for a framed American flag. A glass case listed offices and courtrooms. Family court was one floor up. An officer led an inmate down the hall, his wrists cuffed to a black belt around his waist. The brown-shirted court officers leaning against the wall didn't even look up as the man moved past, and it struck Dash that the cops in this building were a lot like nurses: menacing from a distance, the keepers of the buildings' secrets, but up close they merely plodded along. Like the sick, once you got used to criminals, you saw them everywhere, all around you, until you hardly noticed them at all.

Landon sat on a bench outside the courtroom. He held his hands in his pockets, as instructed, his knuckles visible through the taut fabric of his pants. He was trying not to stim. He was flanked by two women, one compact and blond, and the other with dark spiral curls hanging past her shoulders. She wore black pants and introduced herself as Maggie Caras, the county social worker. Dash frowned at the stud in her nostril. The blond woman was Hope Wilmar, Landon's public defender and guardian ad litem. She looked much too young to be a lawyer, too young even for law school, and Dash prayed she knew what she was doing. Hope said the cases were heard one at a time, in closed session. Dash and Mike could come inside, but they'd need to stay behind the rail. She and Maggie would sit with Landon. "If the judge asks you a question," Hope said to Dash, "be ready to answer. Pay attention."

"Could they take him from us?" Dash asked. It was the only thing she wanted to know.

"Family court prefers to keep kids with their families." Hope paused. "If they can."

Dash recalled the horribly unfit mothers she'd encountered in the NICU as well as on Maternity. Chain smokers, drunks, addicts, the deranged and depressed, women who had no idea who their baby's father was. There'd been stretches when Child Protective Services practically lived on her floor. Unless you pulled a bank heist while your baby was in the unit, the county almost never took custody. The fact that Landon's removal was even a possibility set her teeth on edge.

They were still waiting when Landon's therapist arrived. Abdul Mogherbi wore a manicured goatee and black wayfarer eyeglasses, new since Dash had last seen him, in March. Abdul had taken over Landon's care after his longtime therapist had moved to an out-of-network practice, and Dash had at first doubted his ability to help her son. He was polite in a way Dash found cold, as if deliberately holding himself apart. She'd been nervous about calling him, expecting him to blame her for discontinuing Landon's treatment when her insurance ran out. Instead, Abdul had said, "Oh dear, oh my dear," and promised to attend the hearing. The sight of him striding toward her, a white folder under his arm, made her want to weep. "Thank you for coming," she said.

"I hope I can help," he said. He wore a plaid shirt that smelled like a fresh load of laundry. When he opened his arms to embrace her, Dash wanted to sink into it. Hot tears rushed out of her.

Abdul patted her back. "It'll be okay."

"Thank God you're here," Dash said. Abdul's shoulder was wet from her eyes. He extended his hand to Mike. "Mr. Coenen," he said, returning to his mannered stiffness.

Mike nodded but stayed silent as he shook Abdul's hand. The courtroom door opened and Deputy Garb flashed his saccharine smile. "You ready, pal? It's your turn."

The courtroom was a small, windowless room with a large wooden desk at the front. The judge sat in the center of the dais, a woman in her sixties with heavy earrings stretching her sagging lobes. A woman in a gray cardigan sat to the side of the judge's desk, typing on a machine, and a young man in a blue suit stood behind the prosecutor's desk. It all felt too much like a trial.

Mike and Dash sidled into their seats, Abdul beside them. Small bottles of water had been placed in front of each chair at the desk where Hope and Landon and Maggie sat. Dash felt her mouth turn chalky and she opened her purse to look for gum. Mike leaned over the rail to squeeze Landon's shoulder. "You can do this, bud," he whispered.

"Landon Coenen," Deputy Garb said.

The prosecutor stood and began to speak. "Your Honor, Landon Coenen was admitted to Hanover Medical Center on a seventy-two-hour hold following a domestic disturbance. He brandished a kitchen knife and held it to his mother's throat."

"Ms. Wilmar?" the judge asked.

"Judge," Hope said. Rising from her chair, she looked even younger than when seated. She held a sheaf of papers. "Landon has severe intellectual impairments. He's been diagnosed with pervasive developmental disorder. The condition is considered part of the autism spectrum."

"Has Mr. Coenen been declared incompetent?"

"No assessment has been done to formally determine," Hope said.

The judge looked at Landon, her earrings swinging. Dash prayed she was a mother, and that she knew the agony of worrying over children. "Mr. Coenen, do you understand the charges against you? Why you're here?"

Landon was staring down at his lap. Maggie leaned toward his ear, and Landon nodded.

"You need to speak your answer," the judge said. Her voice was stern, but then she added, "The court reporter can't record nods. I need you to answer."

Maggie leaned in again. She rose to stand, her fingertips on Landon's elbows. His chair screeched across the floor. Dash watched him rise. Mike's blazer was bunched around the waist of his khakis. He'd missed a belt loop. "Yes, Your Honor," he said. "I won't never do it again."

"That's good to know," the judge said. Her mouth wrinkled around a tight smile. "But do you know what got you here in the first place?"

"I can't control my feelings," he said. A good answer, Dash thought. Canned and rehearsed, but solid. A small, hopeful bloom opened in her chest. She watched Landon's jaw move in its socket, his hands fiddling in his pockets. This performance was taking everything he had.

"That's something to work on," the judge said. "Can we agree to that?"

"Yes, Your Honor," Landon said. "I work. I assemble things."

"Good," the judge said, and told him to go ahead and sit. "Are Landon's parents present?"

Hope turned and looked at Dash, her eyebrows raised. Dash and Mike stood quickly, in unison. "Yes," Dash said. "Yes, Your Honor."

"Can you tell me what happened?"

"Landon's been earning money," Dash said. "He puts furniture together and does odd jobs around our neighborhood. He did so well that I allowed him to buy a new game for the computer."

"An evolution booster," Landon corrected. Dash clenched and Maggie leaned into his ear.

"Excuse me?" the judge asked.

"I allowed Landon to buy an upgrade to his video game. The computer retained my credit card information and Landon was able to download other things, some of which were very expensive." She couldn't bring herself to say *pornography.* "He got upset when I told him he'd need to help pay the bill. He was afraid I'd take his money away."

"Has he done this before?"

"He's had meltdowns," Dash said, and forbade herself from touching her face or the scab on her neck. "This was more severe."

"Does he abuse substances?" the judge asked. "Or anyone in the household?"

"No, Your Honor. Sodas are his special treat."

"That's fine. Is he currently receiving services?"

"Our insurance covers nine therapy visits per year," she said. "We've had some financial issues recently, so we try to use them only when we need them." Mike stiffened beside her and coughed into his hand.

"Landon's therapist, Abdul Mogherbi, is here today on his behalf," Hope Wilmar said.

The judge looked at Abdul, as if recognizing him. "Do you have anything to add?"

Abdul rose and smoothed the front of his shirt. He was trim, his black hair streaked with white. His fingernails were neatly trimmed. "Your Honor," he said. "I worked with Landon for approximately eighteen months before the lapse in his insurance coverage. I believe applied behavior analysis therapy was working. It's been a stressful year for his family and it's no surprise that Landon's faced some difficulties. I spoke with his pediatrician before coming here this morning. He agrees that resuming treatment would be the best course of action."

It's no surprise that Landon's faced some difficulties. So ordinary, so expected, like growing facial hair or refusing to take out the trash. Dash felt an upwelling of love for Abdul.

"Do you feel the family can care for him at home?" the judge asked.

"I do," Abdul said. "I believe returning home is in his best interest."

"Mr. and Mrs. Coenen, how about you?"

"Yes, Your Honor," Dash said. "Home is where he belongs."

The judge then asked Maggie Caras to recap Landon's treatment progress. Maggie said the parents had not resisted the Juvenile in Need of Protective Services petition and were willing to cooperate with county services. The judge asked about other children in the home and Maggie said the Coenens also had a daughter, who was thirteen. The judge frowned and Dash felt her stomach drop. That's all she needs, she thought. Kasey's all the judge needs to steal Landon from us.

The judge asked Hope Wilmar what course she wished to pursue. Hope replied, "Your Honor, Landon's psychiatrist at the hospital recommends extended inpatient medical treatment, followed by outpatient therapy."

The judge turned to the prosecutor. "Any objections?"

"No, Your Honor," he said. He shuffled his papers into the manila file, ready to move on.

The judge nodded, wrote something down. She peered over her reading glasses. "I'm going to agree with the psychiatrist's recommendation. Landon will remain in his current placement for a period not to exceed fourteen days, after which he'll be discharged to his parents' custody. I'm also going to recommend a day treatment program in conjunction with outpatient therapy. Landon will need to sign an agreement to comply with his program and to avoid future episodes for ninety days. After that, his record will be cleared."

"Thank you, Your Honor," Hope said. She turned and smiled at Landon. They'd won something, even if it didn't feel like it. Landon wasn't coming home yet. Two weeks was a long time, but she could make it. It would feel like Landon was at camp. Lots of kids went to camp.

Across the courtroom, Deputy Garb smiled, too, and what Dash had read as fake a few minutes ago now seemed more genuinely kind. She wanted to hug him for his jowly, beer-bellied optimism, as though he'd had a hand in the judge's decision.

The judge banged her gavel. Maggie and Hope stood. They led Landon away from the desk, toward Deputy Garb. "You did great," Dash said as he walked past them. Mike gave him a thumbs up. The deputy slid his hand around Landon's arm, near the armpit, and ushered him out.

"Do you think he understands?" Dash whispered to Mike. "Does he get it?"

"He seemed to," Mike said. "I hope he does."

Abdul followed them out of the courtroom. "I'll check my calendar and find an opening," he said. "We can do a few sessions without payment and continue with a reduced rate after that."

"I'm not much for charity," Mike said, looking down. "I may be underemployed but I'm no bum. We pay our bills. With the holidays coming, maybe I can pick up extra shifts."

"We work too much as it is," Dash said. "That's what got us into this jam."

"It's not charity," Abdul said. "A sliding scale based on income. It's too bad insurance doesn't cover more sessions. Insurers still see applied behavior analysis as experimental even though the data shows it works. It should cover a lot more than it does."

"If insurance covered everything, our premiums would go through the roof," Mike said.

"The best option, of course, would be comprehensive Medicaid," Abdul said. "But the politics of that are difficult."

Mike shook his head. "There's no free lunch."

Abdul smoothed the front of his shirt again. "We'll work something out."

Deputy Garb and Landon waited in the hallway. Hope shifted her briefcase under her arm. "I have another case, so I'm off," she said, shaking Dash's hand before Mike's. She nodded at Deputy Garb but avoided eye contact with Landon. "Good luck."

Maggie Caras patted Landon's bicep, lightly. "You did great today, Landon," she said, and set off beside Hope Wilmar, their strides in cadence.

Dash and Mike followed Landon and Deputy Garb to the parking lot. Pockets of blue poked through the clouds and gulls circled over the trees and lake. The deputy opened the back door of his cruiser and cupped his hand over Landon's head, as the officers who'd taken him from the house had, only the motion seemed gentler now, protective.

"We're outta here, my man," Deputy Garb said. He set his hand on Landon's shoulder and again Landon seemed not to notice. Maybe it was an effect of the medications; maybe Landon was resigned to the fact that his body was no longer his own. Or maybe Landon had seen Deputy Garb's sincerity and goodness before Dash had, and actually liked him. "Now you can go back to the hospital and get better," the deputy said. "You'll be home in no time."

Dash liked how that sounded: Get better, go home. Step by step, things would get better. The worst, she felt certain, was behind them.

10

The valets at the hospital recognized Harper as he came through the sliding doors. He wore a gray suit and a white shirt, the collar crisp inside the jacket lapels though unbuttoned at the neck. He'd add his tie and pocket square before going on the air. From her chair in the center of the lobby atrium, Brooke watched the young valets at the station elbow each other and point at her husband. For most of their marriage, Brooke had taken a certain pride in being married to a man other men measured themselves against. In a larger city filled with successful professionals, Harper likely would have disappeared, but in Hanover he stood out, a quality that helped Brooke believe her life wasn't as small as it sometimes felt. Yet coming toward her, Harper looked small—smaller, in any case, and afraid—like a fisherman crossing the ice in early spring, half expecting the floor to collapse beneath him. She could tell by the way his pants had lost their creases that they were overdue for dry cleaning. She hadn't thought about her husband's laundry, or the state of the bathrooms at home, in weeks.

"Hey there," he said, leaning to kiss her. He smelled of Tom Ford aftershave. She was glad he'd offered to come here, to her. "The temperature's really come down," he said. He kneaded his hands together. They were red, as were his cheeks and nose. "I had to close the window last night."

Brooke looked toward the lobby windows. Checkered clouds quilted the sky and the faint scent of wood smoke wafted through the doors. She thought of her bed at home, her eiderdown comforter and the flannel sheets they'd bought specifically for autumn because Harper liked to leave the window cracked until ice crystals webbed the glass and they could see their breath at night.

"It's colder without you," he said. "Lonelier."

Brooke noticed the creases around his eyes and the pointillist dots of capillaries in his cheeks, which the camera makeup would later hide. She wondered if Harper had come to apologize—or expecting her to. They'd never gone this long without making up. But Harper had spent a week in Madison covering the legislative session, the first since the governor survived the recall, and then a long weekend at Fall Harvest Fest. Brooke had swapped out her duffel for a larger suitcase, enough clean clothes to last a week between washes. She hadn't thought at all about loneliness, her own or Harper's. Loneliness was a wave the monitors in the NICU couldn't measure.

"Are you eating okay?" she asked. She didn't want him to suffer, but she wasn't ready to go home yet. "Have you been cooking?"

"I would, but the neighbors have been bringing over food. We have enough casseroles to feed a hockey team. I'm not sure what to do with it all, to be honest."

"Nice of them."

"How Midwesterners show love," Harper said. "They drop food on your doorstep and turn tail. I did grill some eggplant and dress it with basil and dried cherries."

"Yum."

"I should have brought you some. I could make more."

"It's fine," Brooke said. "I'm fine."

The piano in the center of the lobby atrium began playing. Brooke didn't recognize the song. She and Harper watched the keys go up and down. "That thing is so weird," Harper said. "It's like the Ghost of Christmas Past."

"Something wicked this way comes."

"Does it play 'Witchy Woman'?"

"I heard it play 'Desperado' once. Some melodies are easy to hear."

"Should we go up to the unit?" Harper asked. His leg bounced in a way that reminded Brooke of Justus. Again she wondered why Harper was here, what he needed to say in person that he couldn't say over the phone.

"How about a coffee first?"

"You don't want me to see them?"

"Of course I do." She'd worked too hard to keep the babies' bed spaces calm, to win back the nurses. "I just thought."

Harper forced a smile. "You're right. A coffee sounds nice. Give us a chance to talk."

The cashier at the Starbucks recognized Harper, too. "Hey," she said, when Harper and Brooke stepped up to the register to place their orders. "You're on TV."

"Yes, that's right," Harper said, handing over his card. For the first time in her memory, her husband looked uncomfortable being recognized. He hadn't been here in a few weeks and had forgotten the hospital's noise, the whipsaw pace, the smell. She felt a wave of pity for him. In some ways, it was easier to stay under siege all the time. At least you could count on it.

Harper set his hand on her back, at the curve of her hip. His touch felt at once familiar and formal, a reminder of their early coffee dates. Before there was sex there was this kind of touching: elbows and shoulders, the backs of hands brushing as they crossed through doorways or stood in lines.

She hadn't thought of those touches as a prologue to what was to come, their bodies entangled, every cell on a knife's edge, though that's exactly what they were. Brooke recalled the rush of that contact, lust stiffening her every joint. What she felt now was different. *Determined* was the word that came to mind.

Harper wiped down an empty table with a wad of napkins. He emptied a packet of stevia into his coffee and crumbled the wrapper into a tight ball. "Your mom keeps calling," he said. "She wants to drive up."

"She's left me voice messages, too," Brooke said.

"I wish you'd come home," he said.

"Is that why you're here?"

"Yes. Well, not exactly. I just wanted to see you. I was hoping you'd be ready to come back."

Brooke patted his hand. "I will. But this is working, me being here."

Opal was down to 40 percent oxygen on a nasal cannula, which, according to Fran, was about as much air as standing upwind in a stiff breeze. She was gavaging close to 40 cc's of fortified breast milk every three hours, nearly as fast as Brooke could pump it, and Dr. Fackelman said she was almost ready to try nursing. The steroids had kept Emery alive long enough for him to produce some urine, but his kidneys were still lagging. To make matters worse, the high ventilator pressures had punctured a hole in his right lung, causing a pneumothorax. In addition to the tubes in his throat and umbilical cord, he now had a catheter in his chest, right below his nipple, from which the nurses periodically drew out syringes of yellowish fluid. Dr. Fackelman assured Brooke the pneumo, like all of Emery's issues, could be managed so long as his lungs kept gaining strength. His lungs were the most important factor in the complicated equation that was his life. He was a long way from discharge, and a lot could still go wrong. But he and Opal banged on, breath by breath.

"Ollie asks about you, you know," Harper said. "He misses you."

It would be a lie to say she hadn't meant what she'd said, even if it had hurt Harper. Ollie was only eleven, but still. She owed him an apology, though it seemed too late now. If Harper brought it up, she'd talk about it. She'd apologize if Harper asked her to. "Ollie doing okay?" she asked.

Harper leaned back in his chair. His knees slid forward, and his small belly pooled in his lap. "He got an A on his science project. He did weather maps, and made a video on the green screen at the studio. Arno helped him cut it. Came out great."

"I bet."

"He's still going on about getting a cell phone. I swear, it's every other word. I think there's a girl in his class he likes, but he won't tell me her name." This made Harper smile.

"It's good for him to have a secret."

"Breaks my heart," Harper said. "He used to tell me everything."

"I doubt that."

"Well, at least I hoped he did. Now I know he doesn't." In his voice Brooke heard, once again, why she'd said what she'd said that day. Oliver was the love Harper banked on to outlast every other. Oliver was who Harper had when he had no one else. Who did Brooke have? She was supposed to have Harper.

The PA crackled and the announcer's voice boomed through the atrium. "Code Blue: ICU. Code Blue: ICU." The café and lobby froze. Every ear turned toward the ceiling.

Harper sat up. He touched his neck, the tie that wasn't there. "What's happening? Do we need to go?"

“It’s not for us,” Brooke said. She sipped through the hole in the lid of her latte. “ICU is for adults. Not the NICU.”

Harper’s chest sank again. The noise of the atrium returned to normal. The whir of the blender behind the coffee counter, the water cascading down the rock wall, the chatter throughout the airy room—it all came back on at once. Harper tried leaning back again, but his head continued to swivel in search of the next crisis. In the center of the room, the piano flowed into its next song without pausing, this time with a melody so recognizable it was hard not to hum along. *Tomorrow! Tomorrow! I love ya, tomorrow! You’re always a day away!*

That afternoon, after Harper had gone, Penny refused to let Justus inside the NICU. The second chair beside Cannon’s Isolette was now occupied by a woman Brooke had never seen before. Platinum hair coiffed under her ears, weapons-grade diamond on her finger, slacks that maintained their sharp crease no matter how she crossed her legs. All the plumage of a matriarch. Brooke guessed the woman was Shantel’s mother before she even heard Shantel call her Mom.

“Don’t let that man inside,” the woman said, craning her elegant neck toward Penny’s desk. Her teardrop earrings matched her necklace. “He has no right to be here.”

“He’s Cannon’s dad,” Shantel protested, though Brooke had overheard the social worker explain that since he and Shantel weren’t married, Justus would need to get a genetic test before he could claim parental rights. Until then, Shantel was the only party legally empowered to make decisions for her child, and that included who got to visit him in the unit. Justus had been here by Shantel’s permission, and apparently, obviously, Shantel had taken that permission away.

Sometimes, at night, Brooke heard Shantel moaning and other times she sounded like she was crying. She was missing a chunk of hair from the side of her head, which she tried to conceal by combing her hair over it, but she kept pressing her fingers to the spot, exposing a patch of inflamed scalp, the follicles red and raw. She picked and scratched at the sores dotting her forearms until they bled. Her mother swatted at her hand. "Pay attention to your baby," the older woman said.

Justus buzzed again. "Let me talk to her. Just for a minute."

"Absolutely not," Shantel's mother said. The wrinkles around her mouth were accentuated by her lipstick. The nurses liked her immensely.

"He's my son," Justus said. Brooke leaned away from Emery's Isolette so she could get a look at the window. Justus's eyes had collapsed inside the sockets and the skin around them was a shade between pink and purple.

"I can't let you in," Penny said. "I'm sorry."

"Bullshit!" he yelled, and drove his fist into the window. The thick glass hardly wobbled at all. Brooke wondered just how much force it could withstand.

"You have no right to keep me out!" A burst of spittle splattered the glass.

Penny turned her back to the window. She smiled, nervously, her silver tooth gleaming behind her lip. "Code, please," she said. "Please call the code."

Fran picked up the phone at the nurses' desk and spoke quickly into it. She replaced the receiver in the cradle, and came to the mixing table to stand with Nurse Joanne. The windows were shadowed with a cool, gray light. The birch leaves shimmied in the downdrafts from the roof.

"Let me in, you fucking bitch!" Justus yelled.

The speakers in the ceiling crackled and a static filled the air before the announcer came on. "Code Green: NICU," the voice said. "Code Green: NICU." Green meant violence, someone out of control. Brooke heard it called at least a few times a week.

The nurses at the mixing table nodded.

Security arrived within a minute, two men in blue hospital polos and cargo pants. Brooke recognized Denny, the skinny guard who'd driven her to the Hibbert House. She couldn't hear their voices but could see their lips move. Justus spun to face them, his fist still raised. Denny rushed first, hammering Justus into the window, pressing the back of his head until his cheek flattened against the glass and the tip of his nose turned white. Justus wriggled and bucked, but Denny had him pinned.

"Way to go, Denny!" Fran said. "I didn't know the kid had it in him."

"Stronger than he looks," Joanne said. Her army glasses glinted beneath the overhead lights.

The second guard levered Justus's arms behind his back and pulled him from the window. Justus's bottom lip disappeared inside his mouth and he spat a thick glob of phlegm against the glass. It hovered in the center of the smear where his face had been. The guards yanked him around the corner.

"What a dildo," Fran said, loud enough for Shantel and her mother to hear.

Joanne's hand shot to cover her mouth. "Don't let the doctor hear you."

"It's a good thing she's in her office at the moment," Fran said.

"My husband and I have different words for him," Shantel's mother said, coming toward the mixing table. She stood with the nurses, looking toward the door, the smear of Justus's spittle and skin clouding the glass. "I think *dildo* is better." The nurses laughed again as Shantel's mother stepped around them to wash her hands.

Brooke could feel Justus inside the Hibbert House when she returned that evening. The lamps in the foyer and front room had been turned off and a line of jackets hung on the wall. The only light came from the kitchen at the rear, the glow from fluorescent tubes leaking into the hallway and the edge of the living room. As her eyes adjusted she could see the black mass of his outline on the couch. The wind rattled the windowpanes. She ought to have been afraid, but she wasn't.

"Where is she?" he asked.

"Still at the hospital," Brooke said, though Shantel and her mother had left hours earlier. Brooke felt an impulse to cover for Shantel, as if by lying she could protect her. Or her baby.

"She's a liar," he said calmly. "So are you. Don't tell me she's still over there. I know she's gone. And don't tell me Cannon's not my son."

The pattern of the rug had been reduced, in the darkness, to vague geometrical shapes on the floor, like a checkerboard. Justus sat with his forearms across his thighs, his bouncing knees faintly quaking the floorboards. Brooke couldn't decide whether he was unhinged or coldly rational. "I don't know where she is," she said, "You're probably not supposed to be here."

"None of us is *supposed* to be here," he said. "But here we are."

"I meant, you could get into trouble."

"Like that means shit," he said. "Security can come bounce me if they don't want me here."

“How’s your face?” she asked.

Justus grinned and rubbed his jaw with the heel of his hand. “I’m going to sue those cocksuckers for excessive force. That whole hospital is going to pay.” Beneath his vandalized exterior he seemed to Brooke like the boys she’d gone to college with. Boys who’d grown beards to hide their baby faces and acted like punks because the only other option was to admit what they really were, which was lost. Brooke had once seen them as entitled, but now, eight feet from Justus, she wondered if entitlement was really the faith that your mistakes wouldn’t haunt you forever. All those boys in college had eventually grown into men, trading in their sweatpants for trousers and posing for family photographs with their hands atop their children’s heads. Maybe Justus had made a wrong turn somewhere; maybe he’d never had the chance to make a right one. Either way, he’d ended up here, on the sofa in the living room of the Hibbert House, so far from everything he’d wanted it felt like exactly what he deserved. She felt the same way.

The headlights of a passing car shone in the whites of his eyes. “You like it here, don’t you?”

“It’s a place to sleep.”

“You like it better than that. You think staying here makes you tough. You think it makes you better than other people. Even me, though I’m here, too.”

“I don’t think that.”

“Sure you do. But that’s okay. So many people think they’re better than me that I’ve learned to use it to my advantage. I’m most of the time misunderestimated.” He grinned again. She could tell he was testing her. “You’re pretty tough, aren’t you? A regular Katniss Everdeen, staying here all by yourself. You got these babies, but I don’t ever see your old man up in here. Never once.”

"My husband works odd hours," Brooke said.

"I'm sure he does," Justus said. "I'm sure he makes a mint working graveyard at the bank."

The dials on her watch glowed: seven minutes past ten. If she turned on the television, Harper would be in the room with them. "He has a son," she said. "My stepson. He lives with us half the time. It's hard to be in two places at once."

"Except that you like getting to say who can be here and who can't. Shantel's bitch mom is the same way. Getting me kicked out was the high point of her week. She thinks she's tough, too, and look what it got her. A strung-out daughter shacking up with a guy like me. Funny, isn't it?"

The stairway disappeared into the ceiling. She thought again of her own bed and wished she were home, buried beneath a mound of blankets while wood smoke and pine and the briny lake air drifted through the crack in the window. If Justus wasn't dangerous, he certainly wasn't safe. "I'm going to sleep now," she said. "Good night."

"Don't let the bed bugs bite." The outline of his hand rose to wave goodbye.

She turned the lock on her door, kicked off her shoes, and went to the mirror. Her breasts were heavy inside her bra and her cesarean scar, when she lifted her shirt, looked like steel wire. But Justus was right. She *was* proud she was here, that she hadn't buckled to Harper's pleas to come home or her mother's offers to help or even to Justus's attempts to scare her. Proud in a strange way of her loneliness.

The hallway light flicked on, and a shadow passed across the gap between her door and the floor. She pressed her hand to the wood. Justus was close now, she could feel him. She had another impulse, wilder than lying, to throw open the door and pull him inside simply to show him how tough she really was.

The hallway light went dark, and a pebble of fear plunged to the pit of her stomach. As if Justus could see through the wood paneling into her room. She had Denny's number in her phone, and she texted so Justus wouldn't hear. When she heard Justus yell, "That fucking bitch!" Brooke knew exactly who he meant.

11

They arrived at noon, as instructed, but still had to wait for more than an hour. Mike and Dash sat in the swivel chairs at the table in the conference room. Every other unit and corridor of the medical center had been decorated for Halloween, the windows and walls adorned with cutouts of pumpkins and witches riding brooms and ears of Indian corn tied with ribbon. Five North bore no trace of the season. Even the tray beneath the dry-erase board lacked markers or an eraser.

Dash watched body parts stream past the narrow window in the door—flashes of hair, a shoulder in a scrub top, a doctor's white coat—willing each faceless person to stop and turn the handle and come inside to tell them Landon could leave. "When the hospital says, 'lunch,' they mean any time before the end of the day," she grumbled. "They're never as fast as they hope to be. Or should be, if you ask me."

Mike nodded but said nothing. All they could do was wait.

"We do better downstairs," Dash added. "We never make parents hang out this long."

When the door finally opened it was Landon's inpatient therapist who came in. "Sorry I kept you waiting," she said. She was plump, with apple cheeks, a rounded belly, and red splotches on her arms. She wore her name badge clipped to her pants pocket and carried two folders with the HMC logo embossed on the covers. Her name was Angie Vandenhoven. She circled the table and settled in across from them.

"What's the current census?" Dash asked.

"Twenty-four," Angie said, and shook her head. "We had three admitted last night and two more this morning. We're one shy of full capacity."

"We're happy to help free up some space for you," Mike said, grinning.

"Landon's done great." Angie slid one of the folders across the table to Dash, then opened the other and began thumbing through the papers in the pocket. "He made solid progress in his one-on-ones and in group. He understands that what he did was wrong, no confusion there. We've focused on strategies for managing anger. The next time he's upset, he might try taking a walk or playing basketball in the driveway. If it's too cold to go out, he can punch a pillow."

Dash scribbled *driveway basketball and pillow punching as needed* in the margins of Landon's list of prescriptions: 400 mg of Seroquel, 10 mg of Abilify, clonidine by patch. They'd used sensory intervention techniques for most of Landon's life. When he was ten, he liked to lie on a beanbag with a Ziploc baggie of ice across his forehead. For a while Dash had buried pennies and toy cars in a bucket of rice because sifting through the grains had proven calming. She couldn't say when or why they'd stopped doing these things, only that at a certain point the rice had been emptied and the bucket not refilled. Punching a pillow seemed like a crude substitute. "What about his video games?"

"Video games are a reward," Angie said. "Not a strategy. Especially since they were the source of his trouble. Landon's agreed to play them less. Instead we've implemented a number system to describe his feelings. If he's a one, he's a little annoyed. If he gets to two, it's time to try one of the techniques we've worked with. A three means he's too upset to calm down on his own."

"What do we do then?" Mike asked. He touched the top of his bald head, raking his index finger across his freckled skin. Ms. Vandenhoven wasn't telling them anything they hadn't tried before. Dash tried to catch Mike's eye but he kept his focus on the therapist. At least she knew she wasn't crazy.

"The doctor has written a script for lorazepam," Angie said. Dash slid her finger down the list of meds until she saw it. "The pills will make him groggy, so they're a last resort. But they're there if you need them. If Landon does."

"And if he's too upset to take it?" Dash asked, recalling Landon's face that day in the kitchen, his bared teeth and faraway stare. Was she supposed to cram it down his throat in the midst of his rage?

"That's what the numbers are for. He needs to tell you he's a three before he loses control. The solution is there, but he has to anticipate." Angie said the word slowly, smiling, as if she didn't think Dash and Mike knew what it meant. "That's our word: *anticipate*. His new mantra."

"He's a Buddhist now?" If there was one thing Dash couldn't stand, it was common sense repackaged as magic.

"Just a word," Angie said. "The Seroquel and Abilify should help manage his aggressions, too. Help him sleep."

"He hasn't slept well in years," Mike said.

"His whole life," Dash said.

"He's slept pretty well here," Angie said. "The meds are working. He should try to rest up some this weekend. He'll start his day treatment program at Silver Crest on Monday, and sessions with Mr. Mogherbi start next week. Good news is that Dr. Baese says half days at Silver Crest are enough. He can go back to school after lunch."

"I don't know how we're supposed to get him back and forth," Dash said. "I'm not a stay-at-home mom. I work. I work here."

Mike touched her wrist, on top of the table. The incredulity had gone out of his face and had been replaced by his usual give-it-a-chance steadiness. "We'll find a way," he said.

"The safety measures Dr. Baese and Maggie Caras talked with you about?" Angie asked. "How are those coming along?"

At their last meeting, Maggie and Dr. Baese had discussed "shrinking the home environment" in order to facilitate Landon's "transition from inpatient to home placement." The fewer means of violence Landon had access to, the fewer opportunities he'd have to become violent. "The knife he pulled on you, for example," Maggie said. "Was it in a block on the counter?"

Maggie wore a denim jacket with a rainbow flag pinned to the pocket and big ugly glasses. In addition to the dot of silver in her nose, Dash noticed a metal stud through the center of her tongue. Of all the places to have a piercing. How in the world did she eat?

"In a drawer," Dash said, defensive. "We'd never worried about it."

"You never had any reason to," Maggie said, offering an apologetic smile. She was a pretty woman, Dash thought, with thick eyebrows and hair most women would kill for. It was too bad she tried to hide it. "We need to make sure your home is as safe as possible," Maggie said.

"Where do we put them?" Mike interrupted.

"In a locked closet or cabinet," Maggie said. Dr. Baese nodded in agreement. "The lock has to be strong," Maggie said. "Do you hunt?"

"Most years," Mike said. "Maybe not this one, though."

"Gun or bow?" Maggie asked.

"Depends, I suppose. I've done both."

"Do you have a gun safe?"

Mike pursed his lips. "In the basement. It's not very big."

"Maybe you could use it," Maggie suggested. "To store the stuff you don't need as often. Anything sharp will need to be secured, so you might want to invest in a lockbox. Your toolbox, nail files, letter openers. Dinner knives, too."

"Dinner knives?" Dash asked. "How are we going to butter our toast?"

"Some families use spatulas, others use spoons," Maggie said. She shrugged. "Some give up butter." There was something about this discussion that Maggie seemed to enjoy: rudely yanking families in crisis farther away from any semblance of comfort, tearing the veil of what had felt, up until ten days ago, like a life she knew, even loved. First social services supplanted them as parents, appointed a stranger to act as Landon's guardian. Then they made his home a *placement*. Now the county got to tell them how to cut their meat and butter their bread. There was too much government in people's lives, she thought, too much meddling, their taxes paying for services they didn't need, driving the good jobs—Mike's job—to different states. It didn't seem right. If the government really wanted to help, it ought to give her and Mike the money directly and let them decide how to put it to the best use.

Dash hoped she wasn't as cavalier with the parents in her unit. She'd sat in on plenty of family meetings with doctors and social workers. She'd argued with Lord only knows how many parents who didn't want to give up smoking even though their kid was coming home on oxygen. The Volvo-and-yoga set, they weren't any easier. They were hooked on birth plans, sour candies, and tennis ball massages, hippy-dippy doulas in maxi skirts. It all got thrown out the window the moment a problem arose. Some moms grieved the loss of their visions for birth more than they feared for the health of their children. A few times Dash had come this close to banging her fist on the table and shouting, *Childbirth is no miracle, sister. It's life, down and dirty. There's nothing supernatural about it.* Even though she didn't fully believe that herself. Before every baby becomes a person, it's first a jumble of fantasies about our best selves enlarged by their care and feeding. Those fantasies propel us into parenthood; they fortify us for the sleepless nights, the exploding barf and shit, the sieve in our bank accounts. Being forced to give up the fantasy prematurely could lead even a veteran parent to doubt her fitness for duty. That was the difference between Dash and other parents. She'd do whatever was required. She always had.

If she needed to hide the scissors and butter knives, what else had to go? How would she know which things were safe to keep out in the open? Everything they owned felt perilous. What about Mike's signed Hank Aaron baseball in its glass box on the living room shelf? Or her grandmother's pewter figurine of the Virgin Mary, its square base as heavy as a hammer? What about the meat thermometer, the brooms and mops and toilet plunger? They couldn't put their entire house under lock and key. She said, "It would be easier to lock up Landon." She meant it facetiously.

"That's what we're trying to avoid," Maggie said, no longer smiling. Dash felt a chill run through her. Maggie set her palms on the table. "The more precautions we take now, the better chance we'll have down the road."

They either needed phone lines in the bedrooms, or Kasey should have a cell phone. Door alarms and motion detectors were a good idea, too. "That's going a little far, isn't it?" Dash asked.

Maggie shook her head. "I don't think so, no. You can wait on the motion detector, but the door alarm you should get now."

"I've seen them at Lowe's," Mike said. He turned to Dash. "I can get them at a discount."

"Should we put a lock on his door?" Dash asked. "Do we need to lock him in?"

"It's not something I can recommend," Maggie said. "But some parents do it."

"Okay," Mike said. Dash could hear the fatigue in his voice. "Whatever you say."

"There's one other thing we need to talk about," Maggie said, glancing at Dr. Baese. "Landon's sex life."

"What sex life?" Dash shifted in her chair and crossed her ankles. Landon and sex in the same sentence were so incongruent the very notion made her back tight.

"Has he ever had any sexual contact?" Maggie asked, leaning farther forward, both hands on the table now as though about to push herself to standing. "Has he ever had a girlfriend? Maybe in one of his special ed classes?"

Dash tried to think. "Not that I know of." Hearing herself say it, she feared she sounded like she didn't know Landon as well as she thought. "He's never talked about it."

"Well, he bought pornography with the credit card," Mike said. "He did do that."

Dash stared hard at him. She hadn't mentioned the porn to the police or the intake social worker at the ER. Not to Dr. Baese, or Hope Wilmar, or Maggie Caras, though everyone in the room seemed to know about it. "I think he followed a link from one of his gaming sites," Dash explained. "He was curious, is all. I don't think he understands what he saw."

"Maybe not in the way we do," Dr. Baese said. "But he's got hormones. His desires are real."

"I know this isn't an easy topic," Maggie said. "The more his urges are stigmatized, the more he'll act out. He needs outlets that are safe and appropriate."

"You mean . . ." Dash said, hesitating. "You mean masturbation."

"Has he started doing it?" Maggie asked. "Have you found evidence?"

"No," Dash said. Mike, beside her, shook his head.

"Anything strange flushed down the toilet or stuffed down inside the trash can?"

"He's flushed his socks down the commode a few times," Mike said. "Clogged up the whole damn system. Had to unseat the toilet to get them. We suspected he was upset about something."

"He hides things," Dash clarified. "When he's upset. He puts the scissors under his pillow."

"He likely *was* upset," Maggie said. "He was embarrassed. If he's looking at porn, he's obviously aware enough of sex to know what to look for."

"What do we do?" Mike asked. "Teach him how to jerk his gherkin?"

Dash slapped Mike's arm.

"He's probably figured out how to do that on his own." Maggie tapped her pencil eraser on the table. "You want to encourage him to do it in private, with the door closed. I'd suggest setting a trash can beside his bed, along with a bottle of lotion and a box of tissues."

"What about the pornography?" Mike asked. He rubbed the heel on his hand along the length of his jaw. "Should we put a block on the computer?"

Again Maggie glanced at Dr. Baese. "Not everyone will agree with me. But if it were me, I'd get him a few magazines. Maybe a video, too."

Dash studied Maggie's face. "You're serious?"

"Magazines are safer than the internet," Maggie said. "Magazines don't ask for your credit card information. You can see what's in them before Landon does. Plus, they're something he can hide in his room. They might give him some sense of control over the feeling. That's really what's important. If we're lucky, they'll steer him away from the internet."

"Or toward it," Dash said.

"If he's anything like the other teenage boys I've worked with," Maggie said, "they'll keep him occupied for a while."

Mike crossed his arms and leaned back in his chair. Dash scrawled *magazines* at the bottom of her notes in lowercase, as if to hide it.

The next night, Dash drove her Chrysler Concorde two miles past the hospital to El Dorado Adult Books and Gifts, a windowless building covered in corrugated metal siding. She'd driven past it thousands of times without ever once wondering what went on inside. The door was in the back of the building and featured a neon cowboy on a bucking horse. The interior, once she worked up the nerve to shut off the engine, appeared wrapped in pastel cellophane, with candied pink lights beaming over white-paneled racks of objects she could barely decipher: crotchless panties and lace bustiers, dildos and vibrators so large she couldn't fathom them fitting inside of any body, least of all her own. She'd never once felt inclined to set foot inside a place such as this. For twenty years she and Mike had found their way to each other despite their barely overlapping work schedules, coupling in the blue-black dark after one of them came off a night shift, the sulfuric odor of the mill clinging to Mike's hands. On vacations, when they went to bed together without the looming specter of the alarm clock, they did it four times a week. If Mike had been to one of those gentlemen's clubs or watched X-rated movies on hunting weekends, she'd never heard anything about it.

A woman near her own age in a yellow fleece vest and reading glasses sat behind a glass display case. As Dash approached, the clerk closed her magazine and slid it to the side. Dash glanced at its title: *Good Housekeeping*. A picture of a young boy in a striped shirt sat next to the register. "Can I help you find anything?" the clerk asked.

"I feel awkward being here," Dash said.

"Well," she said, kindly. "You made it this far."

"I'm looking for magazines," Dash said. Inside the display case were several, all in clear plastic sleeves. "Is this all you have?"

"These are collector's items. You looking for vintage erotica?"

"I don't know what I'm looking for," Dash said, staring into the display. The soft covers showed women in fishnet stockings and babydoll nighties. Provocative but not vulgar.

"These are rare editions," the clerk said. She bent and unlocked the sliding door behind the case and reached inside. She withdrew one of the magazines and set it on the counter. The price sticker in the corner said $125.

"I'm looking for regular magazines, I guess."

The clerk pointed to a doorway in the corner, a small room beyond, where racks of magazines lined the walls. "The left side is for women. Straight and lesbo both over there."

"They're not for me," Dash said.

"Right." The clerk fanned the pages of her *Good Housekeeping*. "For a friend."

Unlike at the gas station, the magazines sat openly in the racks, ready to be browsed. Dash lifted one from the shelf and the magazine seemed to fall open to a picture of a naked woman being penetrated by three men at once. A few pages over, a young woman had been doused in oil, which made her skin look plastic, artificial, though her eyes were wide with shock. The man probing her body stood beside the table with his hand deep inside her. Dash felt queasy. She recalled her father's stack of *Playboys* when she was a girl, stored in the rafters of the garage because her mother refused to let them inside. Once, she and Dottie had taken one down and turned the pages. The models wore lace and silk pulled aside to reveal their breasts, occasionally their pubic hair. This was another kind of sex. *Animal* was the wrong word. These images bore the stain of technology, robotics. The body made into a machine. She tried to picture her son considering these pictures, growing aroused by them, and she could not. And yet Maggie had argued that magazines like *Maxim* or even *Playboy* weren't enough. Landon wanted sex, not beauty.

"Do you have anything that's not so . . . degrading?" she asked the clerk. "Maybe something with just two people together, instead of five or six. All these women appear to be in so much pain."

The clerk crinkled her lip. "You're the one who called to ask about our selection."

"I have a disabled son," she explained. "He's almost an adult and he's not always sure what to do with himself. I thought some magazines might help him avoid the internet."

"The internet is a scary place," the clerk said. "All kinds of awful stuff out there. I won't let my grandson near it without supervision."

"Does he come in here? In this store?"

"This is our business. Not our home."

The clanking release of a metal latch, and Dash and the clerk turned toward the sound. Dash watched a man step through a rear door she hadn't noticed. He was fumbling with his belt buckle, struggling to thread the leather through the clasp beneath his drooping belly. He wore large square glasses. In an instant Dash saw the telltale signs of mental delay: the jaw that required an act of will to remain closed, the unkempt neck, the lugubrious, shuffling walk. He stared into the magazine room, appraising Dash and the proprietor. It occurred to Dash that there was a viewing area of some sort in a back room, and she felt a crank turn in her chest. Here was Landon's bleak future, his forsaken destiny.

"You need anything else tonight, hon?" the clerk asked him.

He shook his head and shuffled toward the door, his heels not quite snug inside his canvas shoes. The door chime dinged.

The clerk turned back to her. Dash half expected the woman to say something about the man, but could tell by the clerk's face that she wouldn't. What was there, really, to say? That he was lonely and horny was obvious. Dash pictured him driving back to wherever he lived, likely alone.

"How old is your son?" the clerk asked.

"Seventeen. He'll be eighteen this spring."

The clerk shifted closer. "You're a good mom. I can tell."

"He's had some trouble lately," Dash said. "His social worker thinks hormones might be a part of it." She worried she wasn't being clear. "His sexual needs. I want him to stay safe."

The clerk shook her head. "Some people don't understand that. Me personally, I've seen porno do more good than harm. I was full grown before I understood the first thing about sexual pleasure. Especially about how to give it to myself."

Dash felt the heat in her face. "Yes," she said. "Well."

"It's a dangerous world," the clerk said. "At least magazines won't try to get you to meet up at a bus station. That internet, I tell you. God knows what goes on there."

"That's true enough," Dash said. Again, she considered the rack, the rows of pursed lips and hungry eyes gazing back at her. "What do you recommend?"

"Maybe try *Barely Legal,*" the clerk said. "The girls are younger and the pictures aren't quite so intense." She lifted one from the rack and turned the pages open and held it out for Dash to see. It took Dash a moment to comprehend that she was viewing the genitals of girls barely older than Landon, if they were older at all, and she could almost see a resemblance to the actors on the teen dramas that Landon liked to watch, *One Tree Hill* and *The Secret Life of the American Teenager.* She wondered if looking at magazines like this would change his shows for him. Or destroy them.

She selected two copies and another of *Penthouse,* which she at least had heard of. She asked the clerk to recommend a video, and the woman suggested one intended for couples. "Need anything else?" the clerk asked. "Maybe something for you and the mister?"

"I don't think so," Dash said. She withdrew her wallet from her purse.

"You're sure?" the clerk asked. "You're here. You should make the most of it."

"Well, what have you got?"

The clerk let her eyes drift around the store.

"Right," Dash said. "My sister says she enjoys her vibrator."

The clerk led her to a rack against the wall and began to explain the different types of equipment. The main selection looked like cacti, with arms specifically for clitoral stimulation; others were shaped like eggs, tubes of lipstick, slender wands with bulbous tips designed for hitting the G-spot. El Dorado carried vibrators that were waterproof, that glowed in the dark, that fit snugly over the tip of the finger, that could be belted around the waist, vibrating underpants controlled remotely, vibrators just for the anus. The clerk highlighted the features of each toy without embarrassment. Dash pulled from a rack a simple pink wand about the length of her hand, but when she saw that it cost $99.99 she put it back. "I think I'm okay with the magazines and videos."

"I tell you what," the clerk said. "I have a few discontinued models in the back. I'll give you one of those for half price."

"That mean fifty?"

"It cost fifty new. You can have it for twenty-five."

"Okay, then, I guess," Dash said. She was ready to finish the discussion and get out of the store. The clerk went into the back and returned with a rectangular black box, which she added to the magazines and videos on the counter. She opened the box to show Dash the vibrator, purple instead of the pink one Dash had admired, but Dash said it looked just fine. While the clerk rang up the items, Dash looked again at the picture of the boy in the frame. "That's your boy there?"

"My grandson."

It wasn't fair to ask the boy's name without telling her Landon's, so she didn't. She said, "Was he born at the medical center?"

The clerk looked up, one eyebrow cocked, her fingers still on the keyboard. "I work there," Dash said, unsure of why she'd asked the question in the first place.

"He was born in Illinois," the clerk said. "But all my kids were born at Our Lady hospital. Back then, it was the nuns who handled deliveries."

"I remember them," Dash said. "The sisters lived at the hospital until a few years ago. Some of them lived sixty years inside the building."

"They brought my babies into the world safe and sound," the clerk said. She slid the magazines into a brown paper sack. "When it comes to making babies, nuns don't know the first thing. That's where we come in."

Dash counted out her bills on the glass counter. "You're performing a service."

The clerk fit the money into the slots in the register tray. "I don't know about that. But it's not the worst thing in the world. And like most things, it only feels wrong at first."

"Everything's been locked away," Dash said to Angie Vandenhoven. "We purchased a cabinet for the garage and installed an alarm on Landon's bedroom door." She didn't mention the magazines or the videos she'd bought. If Angie asked, she wouldn't lie. But she didn't have to volunteer it.

"Then he's ready to go." Angie smiled again. The sight of her closing her folder and sliding her chair away from the table made Dash oddly nervous, the last thing she'd expected to feel. She wondered what she might be missing, and she reminded herself that when it came to Landon, no one knew him better than she did. Not a doctor or a judge, certainly not a therapist who'd worked with him for two weeks while he was adjusting to a new med regimen. Not even Mike. No one.

Landon sat on his bed, his duffel at the foot of the frame. He stared down at his sneakers. His hair had been combed to the side after his shower and he wore his navy Hanover Medical Center fleece zipped to his neck. The narrow strip of sky through the crosshatched window was hazy with cloudy afternoon light. Landon stood when Dash and Mike entered the room, his arms at his sides. "Hello," he said, and stepped toward Mike with his hand out. "Thank you for coming."

"Hey there, bud," Mike said.

Landon let go of his father's hand and approached Dash. He stepped inside her arms and laid his head against her shoulder. She gasped with both shock and joy. Her baby boy had been given back to her, returned to her arms as surely as the day Dr. Marlowe, the NICU director who'd not only cared for him but later offered Dash her job in the unit, had laid Landon in her arms and announced he was well enough to go home. Landon's hair, as it had then, smelled like no-tears shampoo, though the odor that wafted from his armpits was sour, trapped all morning in a pocket of moist skin. "I'm sorry for what I done." Dash felt his shoulders shift, the solid bulk of his frame. "I won't never do it again."

"We know," she said, and kissed his forehead.

"I won't play *Hadean Eon* neither. I'll pay back everything I owe."

"You can play your game," Dash said. "We'll work out the rest."

Mike hefted Landon's bag from the floor and slung the strap over his shoulder.

Landon climbed into the back seat headfirst, on all fours with his butt in the air, and had to awkwardly shift himself into place before reaching for the seatbelt. He looked up as the buckle clicked and Dash saw him, again, in the back of the police cruiser behind the window that had put him so far beyond her reach. She sat down beside him and pulled the door shut, her knees tight against the back of the driver's seat. Her thigh touched Landon's, but he didn't move away.

"Everything okay?" Mike asked, his eyes in the rearview.

"All good," Dash said. "I wanted to ride home next to our guy here."

Mike crossed the bridge and, coming into downtown Hanover, turned right on College rather than left, which was the faster way. Dash wondered whether he was intentionally avoiding the electronic marquees at the performing arts center and the bank, both of which had upset Landon in the past.

Their route skirted the edge of the college, students streaming across the street between the music conservatory and the main lawn, a parade of backpacks and plaid flannel and neon caps. Orange cones had been arranged in an open section of grass, and inside their invisible perimeter a small horde of bodies chased a Frisbee. Mike swung north at the light into the neighborhood, where tall paper leaf bags lined the curbs. A black limousine sat parked in front of one house while a group of teenagers stood on the walkway in tuxedoes and gowns. The boys wore colored bowties and cummerbunds, and the dresses were sequined and strapless, the girls' shoulders bare. Landon cranked his head around to peer out the rear window. He flinched when Dash touched his knee.

"You're probably looking forward to having your room back," she said. Landon stared past her, out the window.

Mike turned onto Menominee and passed Good Shepherd Lutheran. The brick front of the building had gone nearly black with soot and diesel exhaust, like a medieval cathedral, though the stained-glass window above the door swirled with color in the sunlight. A hand-lettered sign beneath the entrance read PRAY FOR PFC SCHMIDT AND HIS FAMILY. SERVICE 7 P.M. Beside the door lay a menagerie of flowers and photographs, a bouquet of small American flags in a glass jar. Landon's face remained unchanged; either he hadn't noticed or he didn't understand. That was one thing. Sending her son off to war was one thing she'd never worry about.

Landon opened the car door before Mike had turned off the engine. He circled the back of the car and stopped in the grass. He stood with his face angled in the sunlight, squinting at the top of the maple. "You all right, bud?" Mike asked, lifting the trunk. "What do you see?"

Landon didn't answer. He showed his teeth and clamped his eyes tight, then dropped to his knees and pressed his nose to the sodden leaves on the lawn. "What's wrong?" Dash asked.

"I'm home," he said. "I'm home." His shoulders and back shook.

Mike set Landon's duffel on the ground and knelt beside him, one knee on the ground and the other at ninety degrees, like a coach at a football game. He rubbed Landon's back.

She'd never loved her husband more than she did at that moment. Good old Mike. Calm in the face of crisis, steadfast and dependable even when the world was melting down. Her one and only. She felt sorry for the times she'd doubted his efforts to help Landon. He wanted the same thing she did, which was to have Landon home, to put his arm around his son and hold him close. Thank God for Mike. Dash thought of the vibrator in her dresser drawer and wondered if tonight might be a good opportunity to show it to him and suggest they try it out. She gave thanks for the clerk at the El Dorado for talking her into it, and then, flooded with relief and happiness, she gave thanks for Angie Vandenhoven and Dr. Baese, for Abdul Mogherbi, Maggie Caras with the spikes in her nose and tongue, and baby-faced Hope Wilmar, and even affable old Deputy Garb, for the medications and group sessions and Angie's corny number system, for all of it, for whatever parts they'd played, large or small, in giving her this moment. Whether Landon had been coached to fall on his knees when he got home didn't matter. At his core Landon knew what it meant to be good, even if he didn't always know how. His meltdowns and rages, the blade at Dash's throat, had been aberrations from his real self. This self. He belonged here.

Mike squeezed Landon's shoulder. "We're glad to have you back." He helped Landon to his feet and carried his bag up to his room. The sheets were fresh and tucked tightly at the corners, his shirts arranged by color in the closet. At St. Vincent de Paul, Mike had found a small television with a built-in DVD player, which now stood on a box in the corner. Landon's iPod lay on the bed beside a new pair of Beats headphones. The salesman at Target had sworn they were worth the extra money. She hadn't told Mike what they'd cost, hoping the other charges on the credit card would hide them. They'd worry about paying it off once Landon's ninety-day probation had finished, once they were back to normal. His blankie was in its bag, and she'd moved the trash can next to the bed and set out a box of tissues, the way Maggie had instructed.

Landon lifted the headphones from the bed and cradled them. "These are mine?"

"That's right," Dash said. Mike stood in the doorway, his shoulder against the frame. "We wanted to make sure you had a good pair. Dad and I want your room to be *your* space. You can feel safe here. She stepped closer and lowered her voice, "I got you some other things, too," and slid open the top drawer of the nightstand to show him the magazines. The videos were in the bottom drawer, beneath the tissues and the hand pump of lotion.

"Your sister is not allowed in here," Mike said. "We talked to her about respecting your privacy. But the things in this room"—he paused, eyes on the drawer—"The things in this room need to stay in this room."

Landon's mouth made a chewing motion.

"Can you do that for us?" Dash asked. "Keep your private things private?" She unzipped Landon's duffel bag and made a pile of clothes on the floor. She'd wash it all before it went back in his dresser. She folded the bag and stowed it in Landon's closet. "We want to do some things a little differently so we can all get along," she said. "That's our biggest concern. All of us getting along."

Landon held the headphone box in his hands. "How about you come downstairs when you're ready," Mike said. "Okay, bud?"

Dash scooped the pile of clothes into her arms and turned toward the door. Then she turned and came back and kissed the top of Landon's head, right at the whorl of his fine hair, already starting to thin. Mike was in his twenties when his started to go, and for a few years he pretended it wasn't happening by growing the sides and top long. Men were always worried about their hair, but Mike looked better now, with his sides cropped close and the top almost completely bald, as though his hair had been a husk he'd needed to shed. She hoped for the same for Landon, that along with his hair he'd shed this hard period at the end of his childhood.

Kasey came banging through the back door. Her duffel was as heavy as a body bag. "What are you hauling in that thing?" Dash said.

"My backpack's in there." Kasey dropped the bag on the kitchen floor. Her kneepads were bulky beneath her sweatpants, her face flushed from practice and the chilly air. Only five o'clock and the light was gone. The window above the sink had gone black. "Is he here?" Kasey asked.

"He's upstairs," Dash said. "Do you have homework?"

"It's Friday."

"Take a shower if you want. Dinner's not for twenty minutes."

"Maybe Landon wants to smell me before I get in," Kasey said, burying her nose in her armpit and taking a long drag. "I smell *sooo* good right now," she said. She kicked her bag. "He can sniff my sweaty volleyball clothes while he's watching his bone shows."

"Don't start," Dash said, pointing the wooden spoon. "Be nice. He's been gone two weeks. It would be helpful if you could be happy to see him."

"Whatever," Kasey said. She bent forward to peel off her long socks. She stepped out of her sweatpants and kicked off her kneepads. She casually stripped off her shorts and crossed her arms to pull her jersey over her head. She stood beneath the ceiling fan in her sports bra and underwear. The pink cotton clung damply to her skin. "What the heck?" Dash said.

"I need you to wash this stuff," she said. "We have a game tomorrow."

"I'll put them in," Dash said. "Get in the shower."

Kasey returned in clean sweats, her wet hair soaking into the shoulder of her T-shirt. Dash asked her to call the boys for dinner and Kasey stood in the doorway and cupped her hands around her mouth. "Dad! Landon! Dinner's ready!"

"I could have done that myself," Dash said. But she listened happily to the sounds of the ceiling shifting, Landon's feet on the stairs. He appeared with his headphones over his ears. He raised his eyes to Kasey and stared at her in a way Dash had never seen before, like he didn't recognize her. Dash wondered if it was a side effect of the Seroquel.

"Hey," Kasey said. She made like she was going to elbow him, but knew better than to actually do it.

"Say hello," Dash said, prompting.

"Hey," he said, his eyes on the floor, on the spot where Kasey's bag had been.

Dash had set out butter and jam for the bread, but no knives. Landon stared at his fork and spoon, unsure of what to do until Mike made a show of dipping his spoon into the jam and spreading it across the bread with the back. He winked at Landon and said, "This way I can get a big glob on there." Moments later, Landon plunged his spoon into the jam and soon they were all eating around the table.

After dinner they stacked their dishes in the sink and headed into the living room. Mike scrolled through Netflix, shaking the remote whenever it lagged. He told Landon he could pick the movie. The cursor landed on *High School Musical* and Landon said, "That one."

"You know what this show's about?" Mike asked.

"I saw it in the hospital, but only a few times."

"I like that movie," Kasey said.

"Looks like we have a winner," Mike said. He hit Play.

Kasey laid her head on the arm of the sofa and unfolded a blanket across her shoulders and legs, her bare feet poking out the bottom. Landon sat beside her, his back straight and his feet flat on the ground. He appeared as involved in the movie as his sister, moving his mouth to the songs. Four years apart, Landon and Kasey intersected in moments like these, held rapt by some ridiculous adolescent fantasy. Kasey had only recently given up cartoons and had started to download pictures of actors she liked on the computer. Dash tried to follow the movie but got lost quickly; several times she had to ask Kasey who was who before she gave up and let the story move on without her. A few of the songs she liked and was glad when the action paused so the cast could sing and dance. Across the carpet, reclined in his Lay-Z-Boy, Mike checked his watch, as bored as she was lost.

Dash looked up when she heard the siren. Fire trucks and ambulances routinely hauled down Menominee, the arterial boulevard at the bottom of their street, and on clear nights like this, the leaves down and the kitchen window cracked, Dash could track them all the way from the highway to the medical center. She usually didn't pay the sound any attention, and did so now because Landon heard it and turned stiff, leaning forward with his hands on his knees. Dash waited for it to pass, but the sound grew louder, nearer. The black windows filled with flashing light. A fire engine stopped in front of their house, followed by an ambulance.

Landon stood from the sofa, his fists clenched near his chest. "What's happening? Do I have to go back?"

"Take it easy," Mike said, dropping the footrest. "Let's see what's going on here."

"Is someone's house on fire?" Kasey asked.

Two paramedics ran up Charlie Weyenberg's walk carrying orange tackle boxes.

"I don't want to go back," Landon said.

"You're not going anywhere," Mike said.

"I'll go see," Dash said. "You guys stay here."

She crossed the lawn in her house slippers, her cardigan hugged across her chest. The temperature hovered a few degrees above freezing and the trees creaked in the wind. She approached the paramedic blocking Charlie's doorway and asked what was going on. Past the medic's shoulder she could see Charlie's massive television and smell the stale reek of his cigarettes. The paramedic told her to step back, even after she explained she was a nurse at HMC. She stepped off the stoop and slowly retreated to the lawn. Georgina Heineman's face appeared in her front window and other dark shapes started to gather on the sidewalk, in the shadow of the trucks' sirens.

The paramedic blocking her view stepped backward through the door, onto the front step, pulling a gurney. Charlie was awake and sitting up, his right arm folded across his belly and his left limp by his side. His breast pocket bulged with a pack of smokes. "Sorry about the fuss," he said when he saw Dash. "I told the 911 people not to come with guns blazing."

"What's going on?" Dash asked. "What's the matter?"

"My left side's numb. I can't move it at all. I don't know what it is, but I don't think I'm having a stroke. I don't feel like I am, anyway. It's not a huge deal."

"Big enough," Dash said. She wanted to press her fingers to his neck to feel his pulse, but thought better of it. "You should have called us. I'd have come over."

"Landon came home today," he said. "He looked pretty happy. I didn't want to interrupt."

Who else had seen them pull into the driveway? The scene beside the car? "We're glad to have him home."

"I didn't want the lights and sirens to freak him out. After the last time."

"You need to take care of yourself," Dash said. They were almost to the curb, the open doors of the ambulance waiting. She could see into her living room through the front window, the lamps on the tables glowing over the creamy walls and sofa. Landon was on his feet. Mike was, too.

"Go back to your family," Charlie said. "Don't worry about me. Tell the big guy I said to hang tough."

Back inside, Landon was pacing, stimming, hands flapping near his chin. Mike moved with him to limit his perimeter. It was a tricky business, to contain but not to cage, and though Dash hoped Charlie would be okay, it was unfair that he'd get sick now, on Landon's first night home. "Mr. Weyenberg needs to go to the hospital," she said. "Says he feels numb on one side. He seems okay. He's stable, in any case."

"Why'd a fire truck come? Is he on fire?"

"The dispatch sends them whenever someone calls for an ambulance," Mike said. He had his hands up like he intended to block Landon from crashing through the front window. "The firefighters are trained to help. They're EMTs."

"I don't like this," Landon said. He blinked rapidly. "I think I might need a pill."

"What's your number?" Mike asked. "Are you a two or a three?"

"I'm a three," he said, breathing harder. "I need one of those pills."

Dash went for her purse. The meds were still in their paper sacks from the pharmacy.

"Wait," Mike said. "Right now, you're a three? Take a breath and think hard now. What are you right this moment?"

Landon drew in a breath of air and let it out. "I'm a two. If those guys come any closer, I'll be a three. I don't want to go back."

"You're staying right here," Mike said. "The paramedics are here for Mr. Weyenberg."

Dash had the lorazepam out of the paper sack, the brown bottle between her thumb and index finger. "If he needs a pill, I have one," Dash said. Landon's eyes were darting, like he was dreaming with his eyes open. His first night home. "It's okay to take one, honey, if you need it."

"Let's give it a minute, okay, bud? We've seen fire trucks and ambulances before. They're nothing to be afraid of. If either a medic or a firefighter comes any closer, you can take one. If they go away soon, we'll hold off. That a deal?"

"Maybe you want something to drink," Kasey offered.

"That's a good idea," Mike said, grinning now. "Think you could get your brother some water, Kase?"

Dash heard the cupboard door creak open and rattle shut, the faucet turning on and off. Kasey returned with the glass, two-thirds full and without ice. She handed it to her dad.

"There you go," Mike said. He put a hand on Landon's shoulder and moved the glass closer. Dash would've given Landon the pill. "Take a sip and let's see what happens," Mike said.

The siren lights spun around atop the ambulance and fire rig. Landon watched them while he drank, and when he finished, he passed Dash the glass. She could feel his heat on the cylinder, the shape of his fingers molded into the glass. His every muscle was clenched. "Come on," she whispered to the scene at the window. "*Go. Go.*" The third time she said it, the ambulance and fire truck pulled away together. Landon's breath released in ratcheting heaves.

"What a bunch of hoopla," Dash said. "My word."

"You did great," Mike said to Landon. "Nothing to it."

Kasey came alongside her brother. She put her hand on his back and held it there. Landon looked at it, then looked at his sister and held his eyes on her for a long while. He inhaled again, more deeply this time. "I'm glad you're back," Kasey said. Landon tilted his head sweetly toward her. The window had gone dark, and in it Dash could see the four of them standing in the center of the living room, waiting for the next alarm. Mike reached for the cord and snapped the blinds shut, closing them safely inside.

12

Opal's eyes were blue, like ink from a pen. Cradled in Brooke's arms, shielded from the laboratory glow of the warming lamp, her irises turned pale and milky, like the inner lining of an oyster shell. *Opalescent,* Brooke thought. *Opal's essence.* Her eyelids, at last unfused, fluttered briefly open, long enough for her pupils to tighten to pinholes before clamping shut again. Brooke wondered what she looked like through her daughter's eyes. Whether she was a vague shadow against a blazing canopy of white or somehow different, distinctive. Maternal.

Even more amazing: Opal's mouth gripping her nipple, the milk flowing through her breast. It had finally happened. Nursing was an experiment, to see how Opal would tolerate it. She suckled for fifteen minutes at the start of each feeding, and the rest she received through the nasal gavage. Milk pooled in the corners of Opal's lips. Brooke could hear Opal's stomach gurgle.

Emery's ventilator hissed. His mouth, unlike his sister's, was slack around the endotracheal tube. Eight weeks old, he still received his calories by way of a Crisco-white concoction of fatty lipids slowly pushed into his bloodstream. The chest tube remained in place, his skin wrinkled beneath the tape, but at least his pulse ox had climbed into the eighties. The alcove beside them was empty; Cannon had been discharged or transferred to another hospital. The nurses wouldn't say either way. His Isolette had been wheeled down the hall to be cleaned and the glider stripped of its cushion. The next family to occupy the space would know nothing of the people who'd preceded them. They wouldn't even think to ask about them. In the NICU, the past meant nothing. The unit was scrubbed of every portent and calamity. Since security had thrown him out of the Hibbert House, Justus, too, had disappeared.

Brooke rubbed the tip of her nose against Opal's forehead and remembered the day—at once a lifetime ago and a single unending day joining the births to this moment—when she sat in this chair and begged for this much: a quiet morning with Opal in her arms, Emery's pulse ox on the rise. How long had it been? They'd been here, in the NICU, for fifty-six days. She felt as though she'd come down a long, unpaved road, potholed and barely passable, and had at last merged onto the asphalt, smooth and humming beneath her.

Ting left Opal in her arms while she washed out the gavage and completed her charting. She was off at eleven, and by the time Dash came on, at last returned from whatever vague personal business had kept her away, Opal had grown drowsy in Brooke's arms. "Looks like it's naptime," Dash said, coming over to her.

She could sleep right here, Brooke thought, but lifted her arms enough for Dash to scoop the baby out. She'd already received more than she expected. The nurse laid Opal on the Isolette and unsnapped her sleeper, exposing the baby's bony chest and sternum. Her preemie diaper still looked massive, but at least Dash no longer had to roll it down to make it fit. On the scale, the wet diaper ticked up to almost twenty grams. She was producing more than three cc's of urine an hour. The nurses no longer had to explain the math.

"Impressive," Dash said. "She's eating well."

"She hasn't pooped yet."

"I'm sure she will soon."

Opal's eyes fluttered again. "Does she seem pink to you?" Brooke asked, circling her finger above Opal's chest and belly. "She looks a little pink to me."

"Pink is the color we're going for."

"Is she too pink?"

Dash extracted her reading glasses from her hair and settled them on her nose. She leaned closer. "She just ate. Her body's working to digest it."

The intercom at the door crackled. "I'm wondering if Brooke is here," the voice asked.

Dash dragged her eyes from the bed to the window. Penny had taped a collage of leaf and pumpkin cutouts to the glass—the unit's only decorations. "Who's that?" Dash asked.

Brooke recognized the sweater first. "I know her."

"Anna was readmitted last night," Ingrid said at the unit door. She didn't seem frightened or even especially concerned, as though being readmitted to the hospital was no more eventful than checking into a hotel. "I figured you were probably still here. I thought maybe you'd want some coffee. I could use a pick-me-up."

Brooke glanced back, inside the unit. Dash was draping a cover over the lid of the Isolette, returning Opal to her womb-like darkness. "I'll get my purse."

She'd gone for drinks with the graphics team in her office a few times, and on plenty of client dinners, but it had been a long while since she'd done something as simple as have coffee with a friend. Largely because she didn't have very many. She'd inherited Harper's friends, the few he managed to keep in the divorce, but they, and their wives, were all at least a decade older. The movies they'd watched in high school, the music they'd danced to at prom, the places they'd been when the *Challenger* exploded or the O. J. Simpson verdict came in—they were all different. Some of the women were cordial enough to invite her to lunch, but none became friends. On her daily jaunts through the hospital Brooke had seen women walking together or huddled around a table near the Starbucks and occasionally felt a stab of envy, but it didn't last. She couldn't focus on the babies and long for something she'd never had. Today, as she and Ingrid made their way through the corridors, they passed groups of people dressed in prairie dresses adorned with bonnets, striped shirts accessorized with cat-ear headbands, colored and glittered hair. Two hay bales and a pile of pumpkins were on display near the entrance doors and the valets were dressed in cowboy hats with bandanas around their necks.

"Your daughter?" Brooke asked. "Is she really sick?"

"Anna's chloride levels are sky-high," Ingrid said. "Her forehead tastes like salted meat. I was really hoping her pediatrician wouldn't have to admit her, but here we are."

"She'll be okay?"

"All things considered. Trouble always has a way of striking on the eve of something fun. Anna's talked nonstop about trick-or-treating for weeks. Breaks my heart she'll miss it."

The parade of freaks suddenly made sense. Brooke had kept careful track of the dates, so she'd known that today was October 31, but she'd somehow failed to link the day to Halloween. Halloween was a holiday for kids on the outside: kids who could eat and breathe. Opal had only just started.

"I'd completely forgotten," Brooke said.

"Welcome to the club," Ingrid said. "I can't tell you how much gift shop shit I've brought home for birthdays. One year my husband and I gave each other bags of Skittles and

M&Ms for Valentine's Day while we waited for the doctor to answer a page." She paused, then said, "I've been thinking about you. What you've been going through."

Brooke said, "Emery got very sick. We considered withdrawing support."

The woman in front of them in line whipped her head around. She stared hard for a moment, shocked to hear such a thing said aloud, and then shuffled to the counter to place her order. Ingrid rolled her eyes but said nothing until they'd settled into their chairs. "It must have been scary, hearing your name called overhead like that. He's doing better now?"

"Steroids boosted his lungs and he's finally making urine. But he blew a pneumo and had to get a chest tube."

"If it's not one thing, it's another," Ingrid said. "Been there."

"The good news is I've been able to nurse Opal a little. This morning, she opened her eyes."

"That's terrific." Ingrid leaned over the side of the table to inspect Brooke's pants and shoes. She pursed her lips. "You haven't slept at home in a while, have you?"

"I've been staying at the Hibbert House," Brooke said.

"That place will give you scabies," Ingrid said. "You've been here sunup to sundown every day? Even weekends?" Her eyebrows were halfway up her forehead.

"Pretty much."

Ingrid took Brooke's hand across the table. "Take the advice of a grizzled veteran. You need to get the hell out of here."

The idea had occurred to her already. She'd told Harper she wasn't ready, but in the week since his visit, she'd been fantasizing about a fresh set of clothes and a real dinner. Now, as though Ingrid had given her permission, she burned with thoughts of home. Back in the unit, she opened the locker to retrieve her phone and carried it to the end of the corridor. The windows overlooked the gravel roof of the clinic building and the parking lot. The weight of the clouds appeared to sit on the roofs of the cars. Brooke asked the station receptionist to page Harper. He came to the phone huffing, his voice a roar in her ear. "Are you okay?" he asked.

"I didn't want to leave a message. I can't take my phone past the desk."

"Is there a problem?"

"Everything's fine. Opal opened her eyes."

"That's wonderful."

"I was thinking maybe I'd come home tonight."

There was a pause. Cautiously Harper asked, "Do you want to?"

"I could use a night off." She stopped short of saying she missed him. "Are you doing all three broadcasts?"

"I can probably get the ten o'clock covered. Be home by seven."

"What about Ollie?"

"Sara's night. It'll just be us."

"I'll call her," Brooke said. "Maybe we can trade. We can all be together." She hesitated, but knew she needed to say it. "As a family."

Harper was slow to respond. "Is that what you want?"

"I was thinking I could cook something," Brooke said. "Anything you're jonesing for?" They had always cooked together, she and Harper, from the very beginning. When their love was still a secret, they'd driven all the way to Milwaukee, a hundred miles in the winter blackness, not to eat but to cook. They spent three hours learning how to make stock: chicken stock and beef stock and roasted veal stock, stock made from the head of an enormous red snapper, the flattened black eye still in its socket. Harper had taken the class very seriously, jotting down notes in a small notebook he carried in his back pocket. Stocks were essential to a dish's flavor, Harper said, fundamental to a good meal, and he wanted to get his right.

"We could have fish sticks and saltines for all I care," Harper said. "So long as you're there."

She found Sara's number in her contacts and hit call, already dreading the conversation. Harper's ex was pleasant enough in public, at Oliver's baseball games and choir concerts, those unavoidable occasions when it would have been conspicuous *not* to make like they'd put the past behind them. After ten years—a period during which Sara had remarried and had another baby—Sara continued to exude an edgy, untouchable fragility for which Brooke felt responsible, no matter how many times Harper said she'd been that way for as long as he'd known her. ("She could guilt a con man into telling the truth," he liked to say.) It had taken years for Brooke to stop recalling the night Sara appeared at her dorm room to beg her to leave her husband alone. Harper had moved above the BrewHaha only a week earlier and whatever relief Sara may have felt when Harper said their marriage was over had disappeared. She stood in Brooke's doorway, dressed in gray leggings and an oversized sweatshirt. Her eyes were puffy and red from crying. Sara surveyed Brooke's room, the '60s-era cinderblock walls and the battered desk holding her computer and textbooks. Her face was pained, bewildered. Sara may have suspected Harper's unfaithfulness and may have even foreseen herself confronting his lover, but she never imagined it happening in a room like this.

Janet offered to leave but Sara told her to stay. She wanted someone to witness what she had to say, which was that she and Harper and Oliver were a family and despite their problems they needed to stay together. Sara didn't say a word about Brooke's baby and instead asked Brooke to put aside her selfish wants for the sake of others, especially Oliver. Her son, Harper's son; he was only a year old and deserved better. "I'm asking you, as a woman, to do the right thing," she said.

Sara wasn't the first one to tell her that, and Brooke had begun to wonder what doing the right thing really meant, whether such a thing—a right thing, separate and distinct from the wrong things—even existed. The right thing usually meant doing what other people wanted. Everyone, from the dean to her suitemates to her mother, spoke as though she were a fool, a Goldilocks dumb enough to believe the hot porridge and the big bed were better than the kid-sized portions. Even in her disheveled state, stripped of makeup and her hair pulled into a ponytail, Sara sounded like a condescending babysitter scolding a child. Brooke couldn't stand it, not for another second. "I'm the family he wants," she blurted out. She should not have said what she said next. She said, "He wants *me* more than he wants you. Or your son."

Behind her Janet gasped. Brooke knew she had gone too far. Sara hurried out, wiping her eyes with the back of her hand. Brooke felt a sugar rush of pride as the door fell shut. She'd finally stood up for herself. The crash came quickly enough. Janet's goodwill and loyalty disappeared; she stopped texting Brooke from class or washing her towels when she did laundry. When, a few weeks later, she miscarried in the dormitory bathroom, she felt her meanness had caused it to happen. She called Harper at the station, expecting him, now that the baby was gone, to go back to his family, just as everyone had told him to. To give up his coed and hightail it back to the real world. Instead, he said he'd have to call her back; he needed to review the A-roll before he went on the air. Twenty minutes later, there he was on television, his back straight, his jacket buttoned, his voice a velvety timbre. A woman, Brooke still remembered all these years later, had completed a 10K run after receiving a double-lung transplant. It was the kind of story Harper got excited about, people doing inspirational things. His eyes gleamed, talking to the woman. No one watching the broadcast, including Brooke, would have suspected he felt a thing.

Sara's voice on the phone now sounded distant, at the end of a tunnel. She was in the car. "I've been wondering about you," she said. "Ollie doesn't tell me anything.

"The babies are small," Brooke said. "I've been staying close to them."

"The first weeks are crazy." Sara's daughter, Naomi, was three. Brooke could hear her squawking in the background. "Not now," Sara said. "Mommy's on the phone."

"I think you're doing the right thing," Sara said. "Staying near them. Harper may grumble about it, but don't let that get to you. A mama bear has to protect her cubs, right? If I were in your place, you wouldn't be able to drag me out of there."

It was one of the dynamics that nagged at her, Sara's assumption that she knew Harper better because she'd known him first. She and Harper had been married for only five years; Brooke and Harper had celebrated ten that summer. "I'm coming home tonight," Brooke said. "I was hoping we could take Ollie."

"It's Halloween," Sara said, as if it were self-explanatory. "Ollie's promised to take Naomi trick-or-treating. This is the first year that she knows what it means." In the ongoing chess match of their shared custody, a promise was the bishop's move. If Oliver had either promised or had been promised anything, doubling back on it was nothing less than a miscarriage of justice. Tantamount to a broken vow.

Below the window, Brooke watched a dark-haired couple pushing a stroller across the parking lot. It was the kind of stroller people used when their babies were first born, with a bucket seat that could lift out and go inside the car. They stopped in front of a green minivan and slid open the side door. The woman turned and looked up at the hospital windows and Brooke saw she was the Hmong woman whose baby had been in Bed Five. She was taking her baby home. They'd never spoken to each other, and Brooke had no idea they were getting close to that point, of leaving the NICU. But it was happening. It was happening right now. The baby's father folded the stroller and stowed it inside the van's rear hatch, and Brooke felt her vision of the night taking shape. She'd cook something delicious, set out candles on the dresser and nightstand. Better than any apology she might have made.

"Please," Brooke said to Sara. "I don't know how many nights I'll get to be home."

Sara exhaled. Her turn signal clacked. "Fine. Don't let Ollie go hog wild with candy, okay?"

"What would you like his limit to be? How many pieces?" She hadn't meant it to sound sarcastic, though it likely did.

"I trust you, just not too much," Sara said. Quickly, she added, "Sugar. I meant not too much sugar."

She'd been wearing socks to bed and zipping her fleece to her chin whenever she went outside for the last several weeks, but it wasn't until Brooke stood waiting for Oliver that she registered the change of seasons. She'd gone into the hospital on Labor Day weekend; eight weeks later it was the eve of

November. She'd missed all of autumn, its panoramic flings of color, bumper crops of sweet corn for sale beside the road, apple picking and the start of football season. The maples were bare, the leaves bagged and set beside the curb, every lawn and house buttoned up and ready for the first snow. Once it fell, it would blanket the ground till spring.

The bell sounded and children flowed onto the playground, one after the other, the smallest in taffeta princess dresses, Spider-Man suits, karate gis. From their hands dangled construction-paper kites, wind chimes made from paper cups and colored yarn, plastic pumpkins half full of candy. Oliver ambled at the back with a group of older boys, their backpacks slung over one shoulder. He was in sixth grade, too old for a school that also contained a kindergarten. His hair, caked with gel, stiffly defied the wind. Oliver scanned the crowd, twice looking past Brooke before his eyes settled on her. "I thought my mom was picking me up," he said.

"I wanted to see your costume."

"Sixth graders don't wear them," he said. "That's for babies."

"Your mom said you were planning to take Naomi trick-or-treating."

"Yeah. Take her. Not do it myself. She's too little for most of the candy, so I'll end up with it anyway. Until my mom takes it away." Ollie shifted his backpack. "Am I going with you now?"

Brooke searched her stepson's face for a sign he knew about what she'd said—whether Harper had told Ollie his stepmom had disavowed him. She'd wanted to hurt Harper, and she had, but weeks later she still didn't know how deep the wound went. Ollie blinked against the wind, but his eyes were clear, unsuspecting. This wasn't the first time a different parent than the one he'd expected had met him after school. "Is it okay?" Brooke asked. "A night with Dad and me?"

"Cool," he said, and followed her toward the car.

Brooke extracted a shopping cart from the rack at Pick 'n Save and plucked several sanitizing wipes from the dispenser. She slathered the cart the way she'd seen the nurses wipe down the pumps and vents. She hit the handle, the rails, the spring-loaded seat flap (God only knew what fecal matter it held), and made a quick pass over the bottom grates. With a fresh plume of wipes, she worked around her palms and between her fingers. She tossed the wad into the trash and handed more to Oliver. "I used the bathroom at school before the bell rang," he said. "I washed my hands."

"That school is a giant petri dish." She straightened his collar and smelled the goop in his hair, the musk of the school clinging to his clothes. "Just humor me, okay?"

She needed semolina to give the tagliatelle the right chew, cured bacon and cremini mushrooms for the sauce, a good bottle of red, and a loaf of fresh bread. While she was here, she'd pick up enough to make breakfast in the morning. Once inside she found herself cruising the aisles. There was a pleasure, and a refuge, in adding items to the cart, the steady progress from the produce to the meat counter. Ollie ambled alongside her, pointing to things he was ordinarily forbidden to eat. He asked for Pop-Tarts, chocolate-dipped granola bars, yogurt pretzels. Saying yes was so easy. How satisfying to have a child ask for something in a language she could understand; how wonderful to grant his requests. She said yes to whatever Oliver asked for, including a *Walking Dead* face-painting kit. "I was thinking I might knock on a few doors," he said. Near the end he held up a box of Hostess cupcakes, the chocolate ones with the curlicues of icing across the center, something Brooke had never allowed. They were like eating Styrofoam. “Get them if you want,” she said.

Oliver pretended to read the ingredients, laboring to pronounce their pharmaceutical-sounding names. He glanced at the cart and returned the box to the shelf. “I have enough,” he said.

They pulled up to the checkout with food piled above the rim of the cart. Brooke caught Oliver looking at the checker while he transferred the food to the conveyor belt, a young girl with a rosacea of painful-looking zits on her chin, inexpertly hidden by makeup. She swiped the groceries with a practiced, unhurried rhythm, turning the boxes and cartons to their UPCs without having to look. *Beep, beep, beep.* Brooke felt the noise in her skull, behind her eyes, and without thinking she looked around for a monitor, a flashing light. Everything sailed down the slide to the bagboy, who licked his finger to open each new sack. Brooke could hear the checker in the lane behind hers working, the beeps from her scanner echoing. All at once, the noise turned stereophonic: she could hear every lane as well as the mood music over the loudspeakers behind them. The sound throbbed in her chest; it bore a hole through her gut. *Beep, beep, beep.* Her heart raced to get ahead of it only to lag ever farther behind. After all the effort she'd put into learning the sounds of the NICU, the hospital's codes and pages, the cacophony around her now didn't make any sense, sounding an alarm for which there was no intervention, no solution. She closed her eyes and saw Emery's lips and cheeks going blue. Her throat closed like a fist around a straw.

She grabbed for the orange juice and fumbled to tear off the cap. The juice burned her throat. “I'm sorry,” she said, swallowing hard. “I felt like I was going to faint.”

"You okay?" the bagger asked.

"I'm hypoglycemic," she lied. "I haven't eaten much today." She set the juice back on the belt and shook her hands. "I'm okay."

The checker hit the button for the total and the store came back into focus. Brooke's hand, though, wouldn't stop trembling. She tried several times to swipe her debit card before the checker reached for it and ran it as credit.

"You sure you're okay?" Oliver asked in the parking lot. "You sort of freaked out in there."

"Too much noise, I guess," Brooke said. She'd never had a panic attack before and wondered if it meant she'd made the wrong decision by coming home. She beat back the dread by convincing herself the opposite was true: she'd stayed away for too long. She gulped in the cold air and held it long enough to let a minivan pass in front of her.

She scrubbed down the kitchen island, though the house was cleaner than she expected. She poured the semolina on the counter and used her hand to carve a crater in the center for the eggs and water, salt and oil. She kneaded the dough until her forearms burned, glad for the workout, and then let the dough sit while she went upstairs to shower. She sat down in the tub to shave her legs and took her time moisturizing her cesarean scar with cocoa butter. She was still in her robe when she heard the garage door. It wasn't even five yet. "You're early," she said when Harper came through the door. She worried that it sounded wrong, like she wasn't glad to see him.

"I told Julie you were coming home and she told me to go," Harper said. "Brian's taking both shows." He set his keys on the counter and spread his arms. "Here I am."

"I haven't even rolled the pasta yet. I figured I had another few hours."

He bent to kiss her. "I can't believe you're cooking at all. We could have ordered."

"I wanted to," she said. "It's just pasta. It's easy."

"Dropping a box of premade noodles in boiling water is easy. This is something else."

"I'm sorry I've been gone so long."

He wrapped his arms around her waist. "The house hasn't burned down yet."

Oliver emerged from the bathroom with a mime-white face and makeup smeared on his collar. He needed help with the blood. He wanted a gash from his eyebrow to his chin on one side and a wound that would look like an animal had chewed on his face on the other. Harper mixed the reds in a paper cup, adding coloring until it turned almost black. Oliver stuck out his tongue, as red as taffy against the white of his face. He snarled. "Do I look like a zombie? Am I scary?"

"You're too cute to be scary," Brooke said. She was running the dough through the cutter, twisting the strands into clumps. "Don't worry. Cute boys get more candy."

"Who are you going with, Twist?" Harper asked.

Oliver shrugged. "No one. I wasn't planning on being here tonight."

"Can we take you?" Brooke asked. "We can eat dinner after."

"I'm eleven," he said. "I don't need a babysitter. It's not like I'm going to get nabbed by a pedo in a van."

"What about a pedo in a sportscar?" Harper asked. "Or a pedo on a bike? The Pedal Pedo."

"That's so stupid, Dad."

"If you think that's bad, stay away from the lake," Harper said, unbuttoning his dress shirt. "The Paddling Pedo hunts for kids in his canoe. If he gets you, you'll never been seen again."

"It's a dangerous world out there," Brooke said.

"Don't walk too close to me," Oliver said. "Seriously."

Brooke and Harper stayed on the sidewalk in the gathering dark while Oliver snaked between the houses, his zombie face flashing in the porch lights. Harper took her hand and she laced her fingers between his, grateful for the warmth of his palm. They admired the jack-o'-lanterns on the doorsteps, the cluster of five that looked like *The Simpsons* and the ghoulish face that appeared to be vomiting its own stringy innards. The sky was striated with orange and red; the eastern sky, over the lake, a deeper purple. As it grew darker, Brooke found herself looking through the windows of the houses, at the centerpieces on the dining room tables and the people inside. Her neighbors watching television or cooking or rushing to answer the doorbell. Each one a diorama of family life, so ubiquitous and yet also, somehow, elusive.

As a girl, her mother often worked late, assuming that Brooke and her brother didn't miss her because they were occupied with homework or music lessons, their dinners prepared by the housekeeper. On weekends, her mother read legal briefs at the dining room table while Brooke practiced her cello in the adjoining room. Occasionally, her mom would appear in the doorway to watch Brooke work through the sixteenth notes in Bach's Second Suite. She was six when her parents divorced. For the first few years, her father had flown from Hong Kong to Chicago to visit, but once he remarried and his daughters were born, the visits stopped. He talked about flying Brooke out to see him, but the trip never happened. In the pictures she saw—her father and stepmother reclined on a manicured lawn, the girls posed between their knees—the family looked so thoroughly Chinese there was no way they belonged to her. Or, more accurately, she to them. The other girls at her Chinese dance class, most of them third-generation American or the adopted daughters of white parents, told her she wasn't Chinese and should quit, which her mother finally let her do when she was twelve. The idea of seeing her father again, of showing up at his home and shaking hands with his real wife and real children, only made her feel all the more detached.

In college, before she met Harper, Brooke used to walk the neighborhoods surrounding the college, the stately homes with divided-frame windows and sun porches and chandeliers. In one house, a cat slept on a windowsill behind a sofa, sandwiched between the upholstery and glass. She could still recall the lamps on the end tables, the blanket draped over the couch's arm. It had seemed the quintessential picture of a Midwestern college town, full of simple, rich pleasures—fires on winter nights and good blankets, long books, dinners with friends. She'd hoped that by staying in Hanover, by marrying and making a family here, the place would accept her. She'd come to belong to it. Instead, her husband's ex-wife's friends glared at her across an elementary school playground. The nurses, like Ting, who encouraged her to go home had no idea. Opal and Emery *were* home. They were the key to her entire idea of what home meant.

Harper squeezed her hand. "Are you only staying tonight?"

"I'm going to start coming home more. Promise."

"Maybe we've turned a corner. It feels like we have."

"God, I hope so." She watched her shadow from the streetlamp slide across the lawn, deliberately looking away from Harper. "What I said about Oliver, a few weeks ago. I'm sorry."

"You don't have to apologize," Harper said, and breathed into the cool night. "It was a tough time. I just want to get back to normal."

She stopped and turned toward him. The amber streetlamp cast a shadow down the length of Harper's body. "Everything's different now. Opal and Emery still have a ways to go, and when they come home they'll need a lot of care. We can't just pick up where we left off."

"I know that," he said. "I'm afraid to ask and I'm afraid not to. I've tried to give you your space, even if that's meant staying away from the hospital." He looked down the block at the herd of monsters prowling between the houses. "I've wanted to be there with them. To help you. But"—he put his hand on her arm—"I haven't always known what to say."

She slid her arms inside the flaps of his jacket and circled his waist. The jacket lining smelled of his cologne and the cold. She missed being close to him. "I'm here tonight. I'm home tonight."

"I'll take it," he said.

Oliver emptied his pillowcase on the kitchen table. A dozen empty wrappers floated among the mound of loot. "How are you not sick?" Brooke asked. She wondered what Sara would think and decided she didn't care.

"I think you've had enough for tonight," Harper said. He swept the candy from the table into a bowl. Brooke fished through the pieces until she found an Almond Joy. She snarfed it down in a single bite and gathered up the empty wrappers. Oliver, when he sat down to eat, inhaled his dinner in three tremendous bites, then handed Brooke his plate and asked for another.

"I really don't want to have to clean up puke tonight," Brooke said.

"No way," Harper said. "He's got a gut like a caveman."

Oliver pounded his chest. "Me eat lots, yum, yum."

After dinner, after the dishes were washed and dried and put away, after she'd moved her clothes from the washer to the dryer, after Oliver had showered and watched *It's the Great Pumpkin, Charlie Brown* between them on the couch, after she'd kissed Oliver goodnight and whispered in his ear a quiet thank you for not telling his dad about her episode at the grocery store, after all that, Brooke and Harper shut down the kitchen and living room, killing the lights one at a time as they moved toward the stairs, the darkness pushing them forward.

Harper hung his pants on the back of the chair and walked to the bathroom in his boxers and T-shirt. Brooke set out the candles and unfolded her lace camisole and shorts from the mesh bag. When it was her turn in the bathroom she scrubbed her face with her good cleanser, chased the toothpaste with a mouthful of Scope, and ran the stopper of her perfume along her throat.

Harper had lit the candles and turned off the beside lamps. From the bathroom doorway he was a vague shape in the bed. "Ollie's still awake," she whispered.

"I locked the door."

"Very thoughtful."

"I didn't want to take any chances." How far they'd come from the illicit afternoons when they'd fucked in her dorm, sweaty and heedless, the curtains open to the snow.

The comforter settled around her as she sank into the mattress. She heard the furnace kick on as Harper rolled toward her, nuzzling his nose against her neck. Brooke raked her nails through his hair and pulled him close. His abdominal muscles fluttered against the back of her hand. Then Harper's hands multiplied and were everywhere. "Slowly," she whispered. His mouth traveled from her neck to her navel. She felt her pulse in her scar and was glad when Harper's tongue avoided it. She paused to wriggle out of her lingerie, then gripped his shoulders to move him on top. He slid inside and she let the moment take her. She disappeared inside the cocoon his body made and there was nothing beyond it—no hospital, no Opal and Emery, no Oliver, not even the line of photographs on the credenza. She couldn't feel a single part of herself that wasn't touching a part of him. When he came, she held him tight, not wanting to let any air between them, knowing that once he rolled away the world and all its trouble would rush back in to fill the space. Guiltily she wished Opal and Emery weren't waiting for her and she didn't have to go back to the hospital. Then it occurred to her that Opal and Emery weren't waiting for her at all. She was waiting for *them.*

Harper rolled off and she draped her arm across his chest. He covered it with his hand. His heartbeat was a bass drum, its cadence dragging her backward through the day, from the glowing windows she'd peered through on the street, to the supermarket, to coffee with Ingrid, moment by moment until she returned to where she began: Opal in her arms, her finely veined lids fluttering open and her lapis eyes receiving, after months of darkness, the world's blazing light.

13

All day she'd been thinking about Landon and Kasey, apart and together. Halloween was a holiday she'd grown to hate. The floating lights, the flaming pumpkins, the endless ringing of the doorbell; each one pricked Landon like a needle in his brain. Dash wished she could take him away for the night, except then he'd feel left out and that bothered her, too. That was the thing about Landon. He understood he was different but was powerless to change it. His wants were simple, yet the simple acts required to have them—knocking on doors, holding open a bag, appearing scary without actually being frightening—eluded him. Every year Dash waited for the night to pass.

To make matters worse, she was working a twelve: eleven to eleven. All the other nurses had kids except for Fran, and she was on, too. Fran had the feeder-growers against the windows, and between cares and checks she worked at the central desk so she and Dash could talk. Dash could sense her wanting to ask about Landon, about his time on Five North, his meds and day treatment program. The daily run between his morning therapy sessions at Silver Crest and his afternoon classes at the high school, when Dash gobbled her lunch in the car and power-swigged a can of Mountain Dew, was enough to make her crazy. Twice in the last two weeks she'd bawled her eyes out in the hospital parking lot. There was no way Dash could lie and say everything was fine. Fran knew her too well. It was easier to say nothing.

With Brooke out of the way, she could let her mind wander. She could check in at home without having to go on break and she could stare into Emery's bed and think about how Landon would get through the night. Mike planned to pick up Little Caesars and send Landon to the basement to play *Hadean Eon*. Headphones on, volume cranked; for once the game would serve a purpose. At five, Mike texted Dash a picture of Kasey and Izzy Huston, her best friend from volleyball, standing together in the front yard. Izzy was dressed as an ear of corn, a ruffled yellow top and a pointed green hat, and Kasey was going as a stick of butter. Mike had brought home a skinny rectangular box from Lowe's and Dash had found some yellow felt on sale at Hancock Fabrics. They did the hash marks with a Sharpie. *Girls out,* Mike wrote. *Epic battle for Earth raging in the basement. All well.* A Code Blue screeched overhead. Relax, Dash told herself, though her mind raced to the worst-case scenarios. She pilfered the Kit Kats from the candy bowl at the nurses' desk and wished she were home.

Mike texted at eight to say the girls were back and that some punk kids had started a candy fight in front of the house. They'd still be picking wrappers out of the lawn when the snow came. Landon was happy as a clam in the basement. Dash walked to the canteen for another soda and ate a bag of peanuts while standing up in the lounge, catching a few moments of CNN. There'd been a police shooting in North Carolina and people were gathering to protest. A nurse from Maternity came through the lounge and watched with her for a minute. The nurse shook her head and muttered, "Shame," though to Dash the incident felt remote, a horror in a faraway land she couldn't absorb. She didn't know anyone in North Carolina. Her brother Rick and his wife lived in South Carolina, but in Burnettown, hundreds of miles from the trouble. On the news, the trees were bushy and the lawns were green, which made it feel all the farther away. Dash balled up the cellophane from her peanuts before stopping in the bathroom to use the toilet. She scanned back into the unit, dreading the hours she had left.

She heard Opal whimpering while she was still at the scrub sink. "I'm coming, sweetie."

Opal lay with her eyes closed. The tape holding the gavage tube in place across her cheek was wrinkled and the top of her head was beaded with moisture. Dash dialed down the humidity, then unlatched and raised the giraffe neck. She slid her fingers over the baby's ears and beneath her jaw and could feel the heat through her gloves. My hands could be hot, she thought. I just washed them. She unfolded the swaddling blanket and opened the buttons on Opal's sleeper. The aroma that rose up from the cotton was sweet and floral, almost like a perfume. In the days to come, she'd recall the smell and would wonder if it had been there earlier.

She reached up and switched on the radiant overhead light. Beneath the yellow glow, mixed with urine, the gooey mass in Opal's diaper appeared dark brown. When she held the diaper closer to the bulb and stretched the batting with her fingers, she saw it wasn't brown at all. It was dark red.

"Fran!" she hissed. "Come here."

Dash held up the diaper for Fran to inspect. "Oh my God," Fran said. "Look at her belly."

Opal's abdomen was as swollen and distended as a famished infant in a war camp. Below her navel, in the corner of her gut where her large intestines lay coiled, Opal's skin was mottled and nearly black. The skin was hard when Dash pressed against it.

"When do you last change her?" Fran asked.

Dash turned her wrist to check her watch. "Three hours ago. She took forty cc's and had nineteen grams of urine." Was it possible that there'd been a hard spot at the edge of Opal's pelvis? Had it been there all day, a pebble in Opal's gut, when Brooke asked whether she looked too pink? Had she taken the baby's temperature, would she have found it elevated? Dash would wonder and wonder. Right now, she knew one thing for sure. Opal's intestines were full of blood and her temperature was rising. Her bowels were on fire.

"How much blood?" Dr. Fackelman asked. Dash heard the television in the background, dogs barking, and then both noises disappeared. "Streaks or gross?"

"Gross. And not a small amount. Belly is distended and discolored." Dash swallowed and tried to sound calm. The silence on the line grew louder. "I don't know how I didn't see it earlier."

"It might not have been there earlier," the doctor said.

A premature infant could pass a bloody stool for a dozen reasons. The feeding tube could injure the esophagus as it plumbed the throat. The temperature probe could tear the fragile skin of the anus if it wasn't properly lubricated. Breast milk fortifiers could cause allergic reactions. There were clotting factor deficiencies, vitamin K deficiencies, platelet abnormalities. A preemie's skin was so soft that even a hard stool could lacerate the skin. All those problems were treatable with stool softeners, diaper rash cream, a workup. The other possibility was infection: rotavirus, shigellosis, yersinia, necrotizing enterocolitis, or NEC, in which the tissues in the bowel suddenly began to die. NEC was the worst. Anything was better than NEC.

"Let's take one thing at a time," Dr. Fackelman said. "Put the orders in. Wait to call the parents. I'm on my way."

Dash slid the cordless receiver back into her pocket and returned to Opal. Fran helped her move Emery into the corner of Bed Eight and pulled the curtain closed around him. Bed Nine was open, cleared of the glider chair and stools, the supply cart moved around to the front. Opal lay with her arms splayed and her mouth gaping, stripped to her miniature diaper. Beneath the full power of the radiant light the streaks of interplanetary blue and green in her lower abdomen were easier to see. Dash's hands shook as she fit the syringe into the central line to draw blood for the CBC. She struggled to make the connection. Fran moved in beside her until the nurses stood with their shoulders touching. Dash fought the syringe a second time. Fran reached to take it from her. "I've got it," she said. "You've been here a long time."

"No longer than you," Dash said.

"Give it up, girl," Fran said. "Get a drink of water."

By the time Dr. Fackelman arrived, they'd started Opal on vancomycin and clindamycin, and Fran had called the float pool to ask for another nurse to come up. The technician had wheeled the X-ray machine to Opal's bedside and taken the picture without Opal having to move. The image was up on the monitor when the doctor buzzed into the unit. Dr. Fackelman pumped two generous globs of sanitizing gel into each palm and stopped to study the X-ray, lathering her arms up to her elbows. "Shit," Dash heard her say. "Shit and fuck."

"Doctor?"

"Look," Dr. Fackelman said. Dash came around the filing drawers to inspect the X-ray. There was Opal's torso and abdomen, neck to pelvis, her floating clavicle bones and small ribs, the wires and tubes squiggly white lines against the black negative of the film. Opal's intestines looked like a bag of marbles. Dr. Fackelman tapped her fingernail against the bottom of the screen. "That's free air," the doctor said, pointing to the spaces between the orbs. She touched each empty spot. "All of these are. She perforated her bowel."

"I don't know how I missed it," Dash said.

The doctor moved her eyes but not her head. "Let's not waste time worrying about that right now. Nobody knows what you saw and what you didn't." She scratched her forehead. "Who's on surgery?"

"Dr. Rubin," Dash said. "I checked to see."

Dr. Fackelman sighed as though she'd hoped for someone different. "Page him, please. In the meantime, let's do the Replogle."

Dash set out a fresh needle, syringe and catheter, iodine and sterile towels. Dr. Fackelman traced her finger along Opal's belly from her navel to her left flank, an inch below her ribcage. Dash slathered the area with iodine and draped the towels over the baby's chest and waist. She pushed a shot of lidocaine. The doctor's hands moved beneath the radiant light, her gloved fingers working swiftly to attach the syringe, puncture Opal's skin, and thread the catheter through the small opening in the needle's center. Her thumb steady on the plunger, the syringe canister filled with a dull yellow fluid that soon turned green. Then it turned black.

"Damn it," the doctor said. She did not look up. "Where's Rubin?"

"Should I page him again?"

"I'll do it," Fran said. Opal's pulse ox had slipped to eighty-eight, the number blinking red. Her temperature was up to 38.4 degrees Celsius, or above 101 Fahrenheit. Dash watched it climb to .6, then .8, as though Opal had been waiting for someone to notice. She was hot, and getting hotter.

Dr. Fackelman called across the unit for Dash to get epinephrine and atropine from the Pyxis machine. They needed pressors, too. She told Fran to call the pharmacist at home. Dash returned with the drugs and the doctor moved around to the head of the bed. She leaned over the baby's mouth, slid the laryngoscope between Opal's lips, pulled down on her chin, and threaded the endotracheal tube on her first try. She adjusted the settings on the ventilator's touch screen.

"Really?" Dash asked. Opal had never been intubated before, not even at birth.

"We're in a rescue situation now," Dr. Fackelman said, and cranked the dial on the oxygen to 100 percent. She looked at Dash. "Page Rubin until he answers. Please call the family."

Dr. Jacob Rubin wore a yellow dress shirt and a tie crisscrossed with a latticework that upon closer inspection turned out to be broomsticks. He was a meticulous man, tall with a stork-like neck and professionally manicured fingernails. He exuded confidence with patients and colleagues, but seemed attenuated and nervous elsewhere. In the cafeteria and parking lot, and the dozen or so times Dash had seen him in public, he'd avoided making eye contact. He considered the X-ray beside Dr. Fackelman, his hands perched on his hips. "Her sepsis is out of control," he said, frowning. "Why'd you wait so long?"

"We didn't," Dr. Fackelman said. Her voice was crisp and sharp. "She wasn't symptomatic."

Dr. Rubin canted his neck around the monitor to look across the aisle toward Opal lying beneath the examination lights of her bed. He didn't need to see her up close to diagnose the problem. "I've never seen NEC come on this fast," he said.

"I have," Dr. Fackelman said flatly. "I saw plenty of NEC in California."

"And?"

"*And* depends on a surgeon's willingness to intervene."

"If I take her into surgery, she'll die before I can resect the bowel." Dr. Rubin crossed his arms. "She needs a larger hospital. A pediatric specialist."

"She's not stable enough for transport."

"Not for surgery either. She'd crash the second I opened her up. I've made such a mistake before and I'm not inclined to do it again. It's better to let the family hold her alive one last time."

Dr. Fackelman nodded, yielding. She couldn't force the surgeon to operate. Dash sensed the doctor had expected this outcome from the moment she saw the X-ray, but had needed Dr. Rubin to confirm it. Surgeons *always* wanted to operate. There was a strand in their cowboy DNA that let them believe cutting and sewing was superior to almost any alternative, and certainly better than doing nothing. Dr. Rubin had cut into desiccated patients in their eighties, diabetic smokers with bad hearts, simply because he wanted to repair their reflux and their hernias, slice away their ruptured gallbladders. He'd operate even if the procedure would only extend the patient's life by a few miserable weeks. The only thing he couldn't tolerate was a patient dying on his table. Saying no now meant the situation was truly hopeless.

Dash had expected something like this to happen eventually, although, like everyone else, she'd expected it to happen to Emery. Emery was the smallest, the sickest. His organs had flirted with failure already. If any baby in the NICU was going to contract NEC, Emery was the likeliest bet. Not Opal. Opal was the miracle, the medical test pilot, the twenty-three weeker who'd avoided the vent. Babies like Opal were the reason NICUs existed, because babies like her could be saved. Dash felt her Mountain Dew and Kit Kats, her every distracted thought from the day, amassing in her throat. She told Dr. Fackelman she needed to use the restroom, where she vomited and retched and gasped and vomited some more. She'd lost babies before, most of them born far too soon and a few whose DNA had gotten scrambled in the course of writing itself out, and once, way back in the beginning, she'd almost lost Landon. But she'd never lost a baby like Opal.

She washed her face and smoothed down the hairs that had come loose from her braid. She downed a Coke, a real one, to quell the nausea. Harper and Brooke arrived, accompanied by a boy Dash assumed was Brooke's stepson. Fran pushed through the unit door to meet them in the hallway, ushering the boy to the Family Room. Brooke stepped inside the unit, her face pale and her neck splotched red. Dash felt the nausea rise again. "Don't worry about signing in," Dash said. "But you still need to wash."

Brooke moved toward the sink in a trance, either scared beyond words or already resigned. There was a relief to Harper's volume, his demands to talk to the doctor. He wore a sweatshirt, like any dad pulled from sleep to rush to the hospital. His hair stood up in the back. "The situation is very serious," Dr. Fackelman told him. She chose her words carefully, enunciating each one separately. "Opal has an infection in her intestines that's making her very sick."

"So, okay," Harper said. "What are you going to do?"

Dash saw the sweat dampening the doctor's hairline. In the two years since she'd taken over the NICU, dispensing bad news had seemed Dr. Fackelman's Achilles' heel, as though it were the lone course she'd failed in medical school.

Her predecessor, Dr. Marlowe, had been avuncular and gentle, a grandfather who could reset the world's balance with a hand on a mother's knee, an arm around a grieving shoulder. He'd understood that his patients were his neighbors, townspeople he'd see at fish fries and Rotary Club meetings, and he'd maintained professional relationships with funeral home directors, priests and clergy, cemetery sextons, knowing that at some point they would all find themselves in a room together. It was a different hospital then, in many ways a different Hanover, a city run by bespectacled men in bowties. Dr. Slovik, who came up from Madison to fill in whenever Dr. Fackelman was off, was terse and direct, the apocalypse distilled to a text message. *Your baby won't live.* Some parents appreciated it, the quick rip of the bandage. Dr. Fackelman never quite knew how to say it at all, and often tied herself into knots.

"I'm afraid we don't have too many options," the doctor said. "She's perfed her bowel."

"Perfed? What's perfed?"

"Perforated," Dash interrupted. "The pressure from the infection tore a hole in her intestine. It's leaking waste and blood into her abdominal cavity."

"So fix it," Harper said. "Close the hole."

"The surgeon can't operate until the sepsis is under control," Dr. Fackelman said. "We're doing what we can to get her stabilized. But she's very sick."

"How long?" Harper asked, baring his teeth. Brooke finished scrubbing and came to her husband's side. She stood beside him, a ball of paper towels in her hand, and didn't say a word. "How long till the medicines work?" Harper asked.

"Portions of her colon have already started to die," the doctor said. "We're doing all we can, but we're having trouble keeping her blood pressure up."

"I've heard all this before," Harper said. "You used the same words when Emery was having a hard time. You found a way then."

"It's a different situation now, I'm sorry to say."

"Then I want her transferred," Harper said. "Send us to Madison or Milwaukee. Charter a plane and send us to Chicago. We should have moved them a long time ago."

"She can't be transported until she's more stable," Dr. Fackelman said. Having an adversary seemed to calm the doctor's nerves.

"So, we're stuck?" Harper said. "We're fucking stuck?"

"We don't have a lot of options." Dr. Fackelman shook her head. "The infection came on very fast."

"Who screwed up?"

Dr. Fackelman glanced at Dash and slid one hand down inside her coat pocket. "Necrotizing enterocolitis starts in the bowel. It's hard to see until symptoms appear. It's no one's fault."

"You're her doctor!" Harper jabbed his index finger at her nose. "Don't tell me it's no one's fault. You said to trust you. You said you knew what you were doing. You were the one who said you could care for them here and we didn't need a more advanced unit. It's your fucking fault."

"Mr. Jensen," Dash said. She set her hand on Harper's back.

"Get your hands off me," he said, his face more filled with fear than contempt. Dash thought of Landon in court, his hands at his waist. She felt as helpless now as she did then.

"Do your job," Harper said. "All of you. Do your fucking jobs. Save my daughter."

The shock on Brooke's face had changed. She'd gone deep inside herself. She'd gone behind a wall, as though by holding herself apart—from Dash and Dr. Fackelman, from

Harper and even poor Opal—she could contain the implosion unleashing in her heart. Dash had seen mothers do it before, gird themselves like this, looking through time to glimpse who and how they would be after their children had gone. But steeling oneself never worked. The wreckage was always the same.

Dash remembered her own worst day as a NICU mom, the day a head ultrasound revealed Landon's intracranial hemorrhage. In her dreams she still saw the scans of Landon's brain, the hemispheres so dark with blood the folds of the brain itself were obscured. Dr. Marlowe had given her the option of letting Landon go. "It might even be considered a mercy," he'd told her. In her weaker moments, she wondered how things might have turned out had she agreed. She would have been freed from the endless years of speech and occupational therapists, the meetings with Landon's principals and teachers, the indignity of watching Robbie Heineman zoom off in a car while Landon sat alone, stimming and picking at the grass. But she hadn't agreed to let him go; she'd begged for her son's life, promising herself, and Mike, and God, that so long as Landon survived, she'd accept whatever came next. Thick eyeglasses, orthotic shoes, an oxygen canister in the bedroom. She had no way to envision the trouble that would come, but back then trouble had seemed like a sign of vitality. Spunk. She'd prayed for it.

Dash fondled her badge at the end of her lanyard, turning it over to glimpse the family picture in the plastic sleeve. She touched Landon's face through the plastic and recalled Landon on his knees in the grass, the October sun on the back of his head, the unbridled joy he took in returning to his simple, stunted life, and all her guilt and sadness passed over into rage. She wanted to grab Brooke by the hair and scream in her face: *Fight! Fight! Fight like hell until the moment she dies and not one second sooner. Tear your clothes and bargain with God and do everything you can. You're her only hope.*

"How did she get the infection in the first place?" Harper asked. He'd calmed some.

"Other than her extreme prematurity, it's honestly hard to say. She likely wasn't getting enough blood flow to her intestines. Weakened bowels can't properly process food bacteria."

Brooke looked stricken. Her eyes widened and she rubbed her throat with her thumb and forefinger. "My breast milk gave this to her?" Brooke asked. "*I* gave this to her?"

"No," Dr. Fackelman said. Dash was thankful she'd said it plainly. "Under normal circumstances, breast milk is the best thing for a preemie. I promise, it was the prematurity. Just not enough good blood moving through her intestines."

Brooke covered her face with her hands. Then she dropped them and looked hard at Dash. "I never should have left. I knew something wasn't right. I *knew* it. I let myself get talked out of it."

"There was no way you could have known," Dr. Fackelman said. "I looked in on her before I left for the day. She wasn't showing any symptoms. Temperature was normal."

"She's going to die?" Harper asked. "Like, actually die? After everything, we're going to lose her?"

"I'm afraid so," Dr. Fackelman said quietly.

"I want my son to meet her. Ollie's never met his sister."

"Why don't we find you all a private room," Dr. Fackelman offered.

Dash's shift ended at eleven, but now that she knew what would happen, she couldn't leave, not until it was over. She left Mike a message and helped Dr. Fackelman switch Opal's ventilator from the oxygen in the wall to the portable tanks. Together they pushed the Isolette on its heavy caster wheels down the hall to the room where Opal would stay until she died. The doctor called in an order of Versed while Dash arranged the stuffed fish and greeting cards from her NICU bed space on the room's nightstand and bureau, as though they'd be there for weeks rather than a few hours. Barb knocked and led the family inside, Harper and Brooke and Harper's son, rubbing his eyes and gangly in his baggy sweatpants. The boy peered into the incubator at his sister's face. Brooke dropped into the glider and stared at the window, black with night.

"You can hold her," Dash said.

Harper settled himself in the armchair. "Come sit by me, Stone. Come meet your sister."

Harper's son leaned against the arm of the chair as Dash lowered Opal into his lap. She tucked the blankets around Opal's chest to hide the lines. Harper began to weep. Dash felt the sobs leave his chest in waves of hot air. His son set his hand on his father's shoulder to comfort him. Brooke kept her eyes fixed on the window.

"If you need anything, I'll be right outside," Dash said.

It lasted all night and into the next day. Dash sat at the Maternity desk and watched Opal's monitor through the computer, the colored waves and blinking numbers, aware that the other nurses were helping to birth other babies while she waited for one to die. Once an hour she walked down the hall to check on the Jensens, bringing them ice water in plastic cups and cheese and crackers filched from the labor nurses' stash. Harper's son slept on his side on the bed, his hands sandwiched between his knees and his eyes clamped against the ceiling lights.

In the midmorning, one of the labor nurses brought to the desk several slices of birthday cake from the women's clinic. The nurse spread her arms to demonstrate the cake's size and said the staff wouldn't finish it all in a million years. She wasn't exaggerating by much. The clinic trash can overflowed with dirty plates and wadded napkins, though more than half the cake remained in the aluminum sheet pan. Dash ferried three pieces to the Jensens, aware that the small pink plates and whipped icing were too cheery, but insisting the sugar would keep their energy going. The boy ate his piece in one heaping bite while Harper picked at the edges. Brooke's sat untouched on the table.

Babies were born and wheeled into the well-baby nursery to be weighed and washed and returned to their mothers. Visitors buzzed at Maternity and sauntered down the hall. In the afternoon, Dash followed Dr. Fackelman into the Jensens' room to help remove the medications and leads and slip the endotracheal tube out of Opal's throat. She wrapped Opal in a receiving blanket and then in one of the sister's hand-knit afghans and laid her in Brooke's arms. She returned to the desk while the doctor stayed with the family. Dash watched the door and waited.

The windows had begun to darken when the door opened. The day had passed and night was falling. Harper had his hand on his son's shoulder. Dr. Fackelman followed them out, leaving Brooke inside. Dash went down the hallway and stood against the wall beside Jenny Ramirez, who held a manila folder containing the necessary paperwork. No one said a word. Brooke came out of the room with her jacket already zipped up, her purse over her shoulder. She didn't look at Dash or Dr. Fackelman or Jenny, didn't seem to register any of them. Harper let out a long breath and led his son toward the elevator. Brooke followed them around the corner and was gone.

Part Three

14

The woman at the door said her name was Camille, which sounded pleasant enough. Like a cup of herbal tea. She stood at least six feet tall, if not more. In her khaki trench coat and hedge of scrunchy blond hair, she looked a little like Big Bird. She had a wide smile and probably, Dash suspected, oodles of friends who admired her selflessness and altruistic spirit and told her a thousand times that they didn't know how on God's green earth she did her job with all the hard-luck and tragic cases she must see. Yet when Camille Martin handed over her card with the county seal in the corner and the title Juvenile Delinquency Social Worker beneath her name, Dash was inclined to hate her. Camille said she'd been referred by the police.

"We've been working with Maggie Caras," Dash said, the card pinched between her thumb and index finger. "She's our social worker."

"Maggie works in child protection. I'm in a different division. Is this an okay time?"

The streetlamps cast spotted halos of jaundiced light over the road. The unlit houses across the street were nothing more than blank spots in the line, as though they'd been hauled off their foundations. Fine grains of icy snow swirled like insects beneath the porch light. There was something predatory about the county sending out one of its agents like this, unannounced and so close to dinner, as though hoping to catch her off guard.

"I had an appointment in the area, so I thought I'd stop by to see how things are going," Camille said, sliding her coat off her shoulders. Dash reached to take it and was surprised by its weight. It was the kind of coat hookers wore to hotels to hide their fishnets and teddies, or hitmen to hide their shotguns. At least in the movies. Dash almost said something about the coat when she noticed Camille removing her shoes and placing them neatly on the mat. Her toenails, visible through her pantyhose, were painted red. This visit wouldn't be brief.

Dash led Camille through the living room toward the kitchen, willing herself not to call attention to the basket of unfolded laundry beside the sofa or the plate of crumbs on the coffee table. Camille pulled one of the chairs away from the kitchen table and turned it to face the stove. Dash noticed the woman's earrings were little silver birds and wanted to ask whether they were turtle doves for Christmas or a sign that her first impression of Camille hadn't been accidental.

Camille pulled a yellow legal pad from her bag. "I want you to know," she said, clicking her pen, "this isn't an investigation. Landon's case has been adjudicated. I'm here to make sure he's getting the services he needs. I also want to make sure you feel supported."

"Me?" Dash pointed at her own chest. "I have my family. We have all we need." Her choice of pronouns was deliberate. "More than anything, we need this mess to be over."

"Does Landon's father live here?" Camille asked, looking down at her pad. "Does he live in this house?"

"Of course he does," Dash said. "Didn't I just say that?"

"It's not always the case. I'm trying to get an accurate picture of his home environment."

"This is the only home Landon's ever known."

"Good," Camille said, scribbling. "Stability is good. Problems sometimes result from disruptions to a routine." Camille dragged her eyes up from the table. "Anything like that going on?"

Dash lifted the wooden spoon from the cruet and stirred the sauce, though she'd turned off the burner to answer the door. As with every inquiry and interrogation she'd faced in the last two months, she had no choice but to endure it. She needed to get through the next fifty days, when Landon's probationary period would end. "My husband was a supervisor at the Northern Waters Mill before it shut down. Worked there twenty-two years. My sister's husband worked there, too, but they relocated to Georgia to stay with the company."

Camille leaned back in the chair and crossed her ankles. "Has that been stressful? Your husband out of work?"

"He *is* working," Dash said, defensive. "He does loading and assembly at Lowe's and is taking accounting classes at the tech. He got on at UPS for the holidays. He doesn't pull down what he used to, but we're scraping by."

"What I meant was whether the changes have been stressful for Landon. If the tighter budget is something he's felt. Things you've had to cut, stuff like that. Kids have an uncanny ability to absorb their parents' worries, even when their folks try to keep it from them."

It was possible the knife at her neck was Landon's way of trying to protect something, though what that thing was she couldn't say. It was her instinct to protect, too, and to admit that Landon's troubles had something to do with Mike losing his job would wound her husband, were he to learn of it. "Landon's in his own world most of the time." She looked up at the ceiling. "He likes movies and video games."

"How do you think he sees himself?" Camille asked. "As a boy or as a man?"

How Landon thought about himself was a question she'd never been quite sure how to answer. Buying his smutty magazines, she'd felt as though she were contributing to the delinquency of a minor. Dash noticed the splatter of sauce on the back splash, the grease on the vent hood. The kitchen could use a good scrubbing. "A little of both, I'd guess. He's seventeen."

"It's an important thing to think about. He might feel confused by the changes going on around him, but it's also possible he's jealous of the things other people get to do."

"Could be," she said, remembering Robbie Heineman driving off to meet his friends while Landon sat on the lawn.

Camille asked her to recount the day Landon attacked her and Dash told her about the credit card bill and the charges Landon had racked up. She said she'd been the one to blow it by reacting so emotionally. "Things had been crazy at work, and I was tired," she said. "It was my fault more than his. Landon can't always control his feelings, but I can certainly control mine."

"Where do you work? What was going on?"

"At Hanover Medical Center," Dash said. "I'm a nurse in the NICU."

"That stand for neurological ICU?"

"Neonatal. Premature infants. We had a complicated case and I'd been working extra shifts." Dash lowered her voice and rocked her weight onto her heels, let her toes rise up from the floor. "We had a high-risk multiple birth and not all of the babies survived. The two that did were sick as stink, and then one of *them* died two weeks ago. She contracted an infection in her intestines and was gone in a matter of hours."

Camille's eyes grew wide. "Does that happen often? Infections like that?"

"Not often. But they happen. Preemies are incredibly fragile. Things can turn on a dime."

"Wow," Camille said.

Dash felt calmer, back in control. Not so smart now, she thought. She turned to the stove and let her mind flit, briefly, to Opal. After the Jensens had gone, she'd returned to the room where Opal lay on the open bed of the Isolette, wrapped in a hospital blanket inside a handmade afghan donated by the sisters. Long moved to a retirement village, the nuns continued to make afghans for the dying and the dead. It was not for them, or Dash, to understand the mysteries of life and death, but to attend to them and to be amazed. Seventeen years in the NICU and holding a preemie could still fill her with a private awe. That Opal had lived at all was miraculous, though it was precisely that, the miracle, that made her death so much harder to take. Miracles were supposed to alter the universe, not run aground after eight weeks. She'd seen her share of catastrophes over the years. Full termers that died in utero a week before their due dates; babies born with undiagnosed congenital defects; babies born too early, too small, too sick to save. Regardless of the cause, a preemie's demise seemed to pose a kind of riddle: How long did a life have to last for it to count as having been? An hour? A second? If a baby had only ever lived in a Plexiglas box in a locked room inside the hospital, had she ever really lived at all? And yet when she'd stepped inside Opal's room, Dash had registered the change, the palpable absence of a force that remained undetected up until the moment it went missing. She'd felt the same void when her father died at eighty-one, surrounded by his adult children—this sudden disappearance of animus. Every time she moved toward a room in the hospital where a death had occurred, she doubted whether she'd feel it again. Then, closing the door behind her, there it was: the moth hole in the fabric of space and time.

She'd laid Opal atop a fresh blanket spread across the warming bed and opened the swaddling clothes. She spent the next several minutes snapping pictures with the unit's old Canon. The pictures came out a little grainy, but they were better than nothing. Dash set the camera on the counter and went to the supply room for the molding plaster and four Styrofoam cups. She sprinkled gel powder into each cup, ran the cups under the tap, and stirred until the yellow clay tuned viscous enough to resist the pressure of her finger. She pressed Opal's hands one at a time into two of the cups, then her feet into the other two, holding each one in the clay long enough for it to record the wrinkles in her palms and soles, the spindles of her fingers. After the gel hardened, Dash mixed the plaster in a bowl and poured the milky batter into the impressions, then locked the cups in the cabinet to dry. In three days, she'd use a scalpel to cut away the Styrofoam and mold to reveal the statues of Opal's hands and feet. Months might pass before Brooke or Harper were ready for them, but one day, hopefully, they'd be glad to have them. And anyway, Opal deserved a monument, a record to prove she'd once occupied a place in the world, even if a small one.

She'd reswaddled Opal, covered her head with a cap, and gathered her into her arms. Jenny Ramirez had arranged for the funeral home to collect Opal's body. They'd cremate her for free, as they had the other two Jensen babies, as they did for every baby who didn't make it. She rode the elevator with an elderly, blue-vested volunteer who tried to peek inside the bundle, but Dash turned her shoulder so the woman couldn't see. The woman got off the elevator on the ground floor but Dash stayed on, and in the basement followed the steam pipes and colored internet cables through the cool, silent maze, past Maintenance and Environmental Services, past the blood bank, to the morgue, its steel doors at the end of the corridor—a scene from every cop show and horror movie. The pathology tech had set out a cart draped in a clean sheet, but Dash couldn't leave Opal there. She waited by the loading-bay window, grayed by years of vans and ambulances backing down the ramp. She sang "A-Tisket, A-Tasket," "This Little Light of Mine," and "John Jacob Jingleheimer Schmidt," the songs her father used to whistle while he cleaned fish or tinkered with old radios. He'd been a mechanic at the Sylvan Mill and had been proud of Hanover's status as the country's paper capital, proud that it was his responsibility to keep the machines running, as if the entire industry, the entire city, depended on him. In the same way, Dash had taken pride in the NICU, the fact that little old Hanover had the resources and know-how to care for the most vulnerable humans on the planet. She felt nauseous thinking that she'd failed Opal, had somehow missed the sign that might have saved her. Dash sang to quell her sickness, hoping that by tending to Opal now, by going the distance with her, Opal or God or whoever was watching might forgive her.

Now with Camille Martin in her kitchen, scratching at her legal pad, Dash saw she had farther to go.

"Landon was a preemie, too," she said. "He had a grade IV bilateral intracranial hemorrhage and spent sixteen weeks in the NICU."

"You worked there then?"

"Not when Landon was born. I moved to that unit after he was discharged."

"Interesting," Camille said.

"Like I said, I've always taken care of him."

The back door swung open and Kasey stepped into the kitchen, pushed inside by a gust of cold wind. With both hands, Kasey pressed the door closed, using her weight to shove it inside the cold-shrunken frame. She wriggled out of her parka and shoes. Her wet hair hung in strings from her knit cap. Volleyball season was over; she was playing basketball now. "Dad home?" she asked.

"He's at class tonight and then he's going to work," Dash said. "Please say hello to our guest. This is Camille Martin."

Camille unfolded her long legs and stood to greet Kasey. Her height seemed, once again, an imposing presence. Flyaway strands of her hair shone beneath the ceiling fan. "Nice to meet you," Camille said.

"Okay," Kasey replied. Dash frowned. Kasey was raised to have better manners. In the weeks since Landon had come home, Kasey had become a real handful. She was more snappy than sassy, oftentimes downright rude. She refused to unload the dishwasher or run the vacuum and lately had started squirreling food up in her room, leaving apple cores and spoiled yogurt containers under her bed. Her whole room smelled like vomit, but Kasey seemed not to notice it. She'd hole up there for hours, but then barge into Dash and Mike's room while they were getting ready for bed, crawling under the covers and telling Dash to go sleep downstairs. "This is *my* bed," Dash said. "And a thirteen-year-old girl shouldn't sleep with her dad." Kasey told her to take a long walk off a short pier, to go suck an egg. Once, she even said, "Bite me," which Mike said would earn her a sore butt if she ever said it again, he didn't care how old she was. Kasey burst into tears and wouldn't stop crying, but then wouldn't say why she was carrying on. It was driving Dash nuts. Mike said it was either hormones or that Kasey didn't know how to deal with the stress they'd been experiencing. Whether

Kasey was embarrassed by Landon or jealous of the extra attention he'd been getting, she needed to get with the program. Landon's future was on the line.

"Ms. Martin works for the county," Dash said. "She's a social worker."

Kasey retreated from Camille's hand. "You're here to talk about Landon."

"I'm only checking on him," Camille said, smiling. "On all of you, really." Watching them stand together, Dash had a vision of Ms. Martin leading not only Landon from the house but Kasey, too, the sum total of her life's labor and love. She coughed into her fist. "Do you need to talk to Kasey as well?"

"We can talk next time," Camille said. "I'm glad we got the chance to meet."

Next time, Dash thought. God. "Go on and watch TV," she said. "Dinner will be a bit yet."

Kasey slid around the corner and a moment later, Dash heard a laugh track going, an awful chortling like a burst of gunfire.

Dash showed Camille Landon's backpack, the workbooks of exercises for "Cool-Down Tools" and "Reading Social Cues" he'd learned at Silver Crest. The pages were inked with Landon's wobbly handwriting and his stick-figure renderings of people, as well as more abstract—and more beautiful—pastels of colored stripes. Art therapy, she said, was Landon's favorite because he liked to use his hands. The commute from the day treatment center in the mornings to school in the afternoons wasn't easy, but they were making it work. Landon had also resumed his applied behavior analysis sessions with Abdul Mogherbi. He'd had to quit managing the basketball team, but he still put furniture together on occasion. With Christmas coming, more people were calling.

"CPS talked with you about safety precautions around the home?"

"We took all the knives out of the kitchen, and my husband locked his tools in the garage. We installed an alarm on Landon's door upstairs, for when he goes to bed."

"Can I see?" Camille asked, standing up again.

"You want to see his room?"

"If you don't mind."

She didn't want Camille Martin to peer inside their bedrooms and catch the scent of her children. Or to look upon her own bed, still unmade since she left Mike sleeping in it when she rose to shower for work at 1:30 A.M. Climbing the stairs, Dash wondered if Camille noticed the frayed carpet fibers, the spiraling bare spots on the risers and the landing, or the hieroglyphic nicks in the baseboards, etched into the wood with a paperclip. "I'm sorry it's not neater," she said. "I haven't had time to clean. It's on the docket for tomorrow."

Behind her, Camille said, "Compared to most homes I visit, yours is a five-star hotel."

From her open doorway, Dash could see that Kasey's duvet had been pulled up and the blinds dialed open. Dash showed Camille the shiny brass door handle with the lock in the center of the mechanism. Mike had installed a lock on Landon's door, too, only the other direction, facing the hallway, as well as an alarm attached to the frame. Camille examined the ceiling. "No motion detectors? Do you have a camera in his room?"

"Motion sensors are expensive. Maggie Caras told us the alarm was enough to start with. And Landon deserves his privacy, like the rest of us."

Camille nodded. "I'd like to say hi."

Dash knocked and swung open the door. Landon lay on his bed with his headphones around his ears, the wire snaking along the length of his mattress to the television on his dresser. He had his hand down the front of his sweatpants. She nudged his elbow. He looked up at her but didn't remove his hand. Dash widened her eyes and waved. "Can you sit up, please?" she said. "Someone is here to talk to you."

"What?" He used his free hand to remove the headphones.

"Someone's here to talk to you."

Landon looked around her arm, toward the television. Dash had not yet managed to command his attention and she turned to see what he was watching. Camille had followed her inside the room and stood a few feet behind her, also facing the screen. A naked woman lay partially reclined on a kitchen counter, her weight on her elbows, one bare leg over the shoulder of a naked man who stood facing her. The man thrust into the woman with his bottom lip clenched in his teeth. The woman's fingertips were clamped around her nipples. Dash could hear their rhythmic grunts and moans rising from Landon's headphones lying on the mattress.

"Whoa," Camille said. "Holy cow."

Dash's hand flew to the television and switched it off. Her tongue was so thick she found it hard to speak. "I bought the video for him," she tried to explain. "Maggie Caras suggested it. She said a few magazines and videos would help keep him away from the internet." She glanced at the trash can. A few wadded tissues lined the bottom, but, thankfully, it wasn't overflowing.

"I see," Camille said.

"It was CPS's idea."

"It makes sense," Camille said.

"Landon, say hello," Dash said. "This is Camille Martin. She's a social worker."

He swung his legs over the side of the bed. There was something about sweatpants that made the body look incapacitated, suited only for repose, not for industry.

Camille touched the earring looped through her lobe. She scratched the bridge of her nose. "Hi, Landon," she said. "You like watching videos?"

What kind of question was that?

Camille turned to Dash. "Do you mind if we talk for a few minutes? Alone?"

"Landon, why don't we go downstairs?"

"No, that's okay," Camille said. "He's comfortable here. We don't have to go anywhere."

"When's dinner, Mom?" Landon asked. His eyes fixed behind her, on the darkened TV.

"Soon," Dash said. "Once you're finished with Ms. Martin."

"It's almost six," he said. "We eat at six so I can shower by seven."

"We have plenty of time," Dash said.

"I have to shower by seven."

"It's almost ready."

"We won't talk for long," Camille said. "Your schedule is important to you, huh?"

"We eat at six," Landon said. "We need to eat by six."

"Get talking and I'll have it ready for you," Dash said. She left the door ajar enough to hear Landon's mattress creak. The springs creaked again, the pressure lifting, and Dash felt the air on the other side of the door collapsing, and she backed away. She paused on the landing, but once she heard the latch click solidly into place, she went the rest of the way down.

She turned the stove back on and busied herself setting the table. She expected to wait a long while, but heard the stairs creak before the water had begun to boil. "Sweet kid," Camille said.

"He is, isn't he?" Dash said. It wasn't that she ever forgot about Landon's sweetness, just that she too often let all her other worries gum up her thoughts. Right up until the cold snap, and even a few times since, Landon and Mike had spent an hour each evening throwing the football in the front yard. Through the living room window, Dash had watched Landon take care to place the first knuckle of his ring finger over the ball's second lace, his index finger on the stitch line, the way his dad had shown him. He'd taken great care to do this, as though learning to play a musical instrument. Laying his hand on the ball had taken more time than the throw. And when the ball finally rolled off his fingers and spiraled through the air, Landon ran across the yard to hug his dad. An actual hug. Had Dash not seen it with her own eyes, she never would have believed it.

"Listen, about the video."

Camille held up her hands. "I see where Maggie's coming from. I can't say I completely agree, but I understand her reasoning."

"He also has a few magazines," Dash said. Better to get everything out in the open now. "Did he show you those?"

"I didn't dwell on any of that. We talked about how he's been feeling since he came home. He must have told me he was sorry a hundred times."

"I honestly think this whole thing has been blown a little out of proportion."

"Maybe," Camille said. "If that's the case, you won't see me after his ninety-day period concludes." She set her hand on the counter and balanced her weight against it, one bony shoulder rising. The bridge of her nose crinkled. "It's clear you love him and this is a stable home. But there are still some services he could be using."

"We've had services for years. I know the system pretty well by now."

"He's eligible for Social Security," Camille said. "Did you know that? There are family groups, supplemental programs.

There's a waiver for added safety measures that could pay for the motion detectors. Respite care centers, for when you and your husband need a break."

Social Security, she'd assumed, was for when he turned eighteen. The waivers she'd never heard of. She'd tried a family support group once but had found the other parents whiny and eager to hear themselves talk. Respite care was as good as admitting Landon was too much for them. "We're fine," Dash said. "We're managing. We always have."

"That's my point," she said. "You try to do too much on your own."

"I appreciate your recommendations."

Camille looked at her watch. The water was bubbling, clouding the vent hood and the light in the center of the ceiling. Dash reached across the sink to crack the window. She felt the kitchen's heat rush through the opening, and when she turned around she saw the steam from the pot pour down the front of the stove, flow across the linoleum floor, and climb the cabinet to the open sash. Dash and Camille watched its path together without speaking, in awe. Dash wanted to touch the steam but afraid that doing so would cause it to disappear. Camille said, "I'll let you get dinner on the table. I'm sorry if I came at an inconvenient time."

Dash lifted Camille's coat from the back of the chair. The satin lining was yellowed and smelled of winter, of cold metal and old smoke. Camille fed her arms down the sleeves, hefted the coat over her shoulders and closed the flaps. Dash pulled open the door and the glass storm door went instantly opaque with frost. Camille pulled her coat tight across her neck. "Weather report says tonight's the night. At least three inches, possibly as much as six. I'm not ready."

"It's November," Dash said. "We made it this far. We should count ourselves lucky."

Camille stepped onto the stoop. She turned back to Dash. "Things happen," she said, her breath puffing beneath the porch light. "Sometimes without warning. You think you have it all handled and then you don't." She put her hands in her pockets. "If something *does* happen, call me. I can help you. You might not think so, but I can."

"Will do," Dash said. She let the storm door swing shut. The springed hinge bounced until the latch caught. Camille receded behind the frosted glass, into the darkness, and Dash leaned her shoulder against the door to make sure it sealed tightly and held in the heat.

That night she dreamed of falling leaves, the wind chimes tinkling from the overhang, bare tree branches scraping and knocking against the window. When she opened her eyes, she could still hear the knocking. Soft but steady, almost rhythmic. She lay blinking in the dark, listening to it, *tap, tap, tap,* like a faucet dripping over a cutting board, transported in the night's time warp to the years when Landon was three, before Kasey was born, those interminable stretches when it seemed he never slept. All the nights he lay in bed kicking the wall until, desperate and exhausted, Dash forced herself to sleep through it. The red numbers on her alarm clock came into focus: 2:17 A.M. She woke enough to separate now from then. Mike was asleep beside her though she had no memory of him coming home. The knocking hadn't stopped.

She folded back the blankets. The tapping stopped when she paused before Landon's door. She flipped the switch on the door alarm. "Landon?" she asked, turning the knob. "You okay?"

The smell was overwhelming. Landon stood in the center of the room, looming in the dark. His beard made shadows on his face, and his teeth were white in the moonlight. She flicked on the light and saw the stain on his sweatpants. It wasn't like entering a baby's room, the sweet and downy aroma of their sleeping, soaked diapers perfumed by baby powder. This smelled more like a hospice ward, the adult body functioning despite itself. "What happened?"

"I had to go," he said.

"Why didn't you come out?"

"I didn't want the door to make the noise."

Dash balled up his sheets and blankets. "Let's hop in the shower."

"I showered before bed. I always shower before bed."

"Well, this is a special case," she said. "It'll make you feel better."

"I shower before bed."

"You can shower tonight, too. This is extra."

"We ate dinner too late," he said. "It was after six."

"We'll get back on schedule tonight. I promise it won't happen again."

She set the sheets on the floor outside the bathroom and turned on the light. Landon blinked, surprised and afraid, and turned his head from the mirror. He held his clenched fists to his chin, paralyzed. Dash touched his elbow to move him toward the tub. He stepped over the rail and stood inside the basin, his eyes still closed and fists still clenched. "Give me your clothes," she said. When Landon didn't move, she said it again. "Landon, honey, give me your clothes."

She lifted his T-shirt from his waist, and once the hem was above his diaphragm, he helped her by sliding it over his head. She tugged on the waist of his sweatpants, but now he stood still, letting her do the work, and she had no choice but to pull them all the way down into a syrupy puddle and wait while he removed his feet. She hadn't seen him naked in a long time, and though she told herself to turn away she considered for a moment the dark thatches of hair at the base of his stomach and around the knob of his genitals. She thought again of Camille's question, whether Landon saw himself as a boy confused by his body or as a man confined to the life of a child. She slid the plastic curtain shut and reached around the front flap to turn on the water. She let it run warm over her hand before pulling the lever for the shower. "Start with the shampoo and then use the soap," she said through the vinyl. "Wash your hair and then wash your body. Rinse when you're all finished. I'll go put your sheets and clothes in the wash and come back and check on you. Okay?"

"I'm supposed to shower before bed."

"After this you're going back to bed. It still counts, right?"

In the basement she discovered Landon's other set of sheets in the laundry basket, along with the heaps of dirty clothes she'd let sit the last few days. She'd tackle the backlog tomorrow. She rifled through the linen closet for a spare set of sheets, and at the back she saw found an old set of Landon's from when he was a toddler, decorated with trains. They were slightly musty, and smelled like cedar and hairspray, but they were clean and dry. She snapped the fitted corners around Landon's mattress, flicked open the top sheet and let it fall across the bed. She remembered the nights she lay beside him on these very sheets, her palm pressing on his chest to quiet him, and felt a surge of joy that she was here again, making his bed with his train sheets. In this gap between night and morning, she was once again, if for only a short while, the mother of a little boy.

"Are you finished?" she asked through the shower curtain.

"Yes."

"Did you shampoo and use soap?"

"Yes."

"Did you rinse?"

His hand and arm appeared above the curtain railing. She heard the water against his armpit.

"Okay, go ahead and turn off the water." She reached through the curtain to hand him a towel. "I set some clean pajamas on the toilet."

She closed the bathroom door and stood in the hall. He emerged with his hair standing in a wet spike. She patted his back and reached around to shut off the light. "Let's go back to bed."

At the end of the hall she could see Mike asleep on his side. Neither he nor Kasey had stirred. She'd return Landon's regular linens to his bed in the morning and her husband and daughter would never know what had happened. Landon might himself forget, recalling the shower and change of clothes only in fragments, like a portion of a dream. She could contain it all.

Landon gazed down at the railroad sheets, as if remembering them, and then nestled his head into the pillow. Dash lifted the blankets so he could get his feet in, then pulled them to his chin. His eyelids drooped and his head rocked to the side. She bent toward him, her heart surging, the answer to Camille's question so clear it no longer seemed worth asking. She kissed his wet hair at his temple. "Sleep well, my sweet boy," she whispered.

15

Linda Stark, Brooke's next-door neighbor, apologized for not coming sooner. "Of all the times for us to be out of town. We were sunning ourselves like a couple of idiots while you and Harper were going through hell." Linda sat on the edge of Brooke's sofa with her weight on her toes, ready to spring into action. Brooke could hear her mother, Pamela, in the kitchen, opening drawers and cupboards, boiling water and pulling out plates and spoons and cups.

"It's all right," Brooke said, surprised by Linda's concern. "There was no way you could have known." Or would have. In the ten years they'd lived next door, friendship with the Starks had never progressed much beyond the "How 'bout this weather?" or "Go Packers" stage. A few times Jerry, now sitting with his arm extended across the cushion behind his wife, had suggested getting together for dinner, but it had sounded more like a genial way to end a conversation than an actual invitation. Brooke didn't know how the news about Opal got out, whether Harper sent out a tweet or Ollie said something at school, but food had once again been showing up. Trays and Tupperware left on her doorstep, casseroles swaddled in dish towels. The Starks had appeared that morning bearing a crusted salmon on a bed of glazed radicchio, and an iced lemon cake. Their card said, *We can't control the direction of the winds, but we can always adjust our sails.* Jerry was gaga for boats.

Their noses were shiny, their cheeks slicked with aloe. Linda wore her blouse open to the third button, exposing a neck so red that heat appeared to radiate from it. The Starks went on a cruise each November, which Linda claimed was the absolute best time: the tail end of hurricane season, but after the big storms had passed. Prices were rock-bottom and crowds practically nonexistent, the weather rarely a problem. Linda and Jerry had visited every country in the Caribbean and every port of call in the Yucatán. In recent years they'd begun to go farther, sailing into waters where hurricanes weren't an issue. Thailand, French Polynesia, along the Danube. This year they'd island-hopped in southern Greece.

Pamela rounded the corner carrying a tray with a pot of coffee and four small squares of the Starks' lemon cake. She'd arrived a week ago, her court docket cleared, vowing to stay for as long as Brooke and Harper needed her help. Brooke didn't know what help she needed, but Harper had called her and she'd responded. She'd tied an apron over her cashmere sweater and black trousers. On her it looked like a costume, a woman pretending to be a grandmother. Brooke couldn't recall a single instance of her mother baking anything. As a girl, birthday cakes and cookies for school bake sales all came from Laury's or Vesecky's.

Her mother poured coffee before sitting on the loveseat next to Brooke. "You had a pleasant trip?" she asked.

"*Fantastikós*," Linda said. She tugged at her shirt buttons to fan herself. "Perfect weather. Rhodes and the Asklepieion were on my bucket list."

"We drank a bottle of wine with every meal," Jerry said. "Breakfast, lunch, and dinner."

"Not breakfast," Linda said, slapping her husband's thigh. "Well, not every breakfast."

"Did you see any refugees?" Pamela asked. "Or were they all hidden away when the cruise ships came into port?"

"The islands did a nice job of cleaning up," Jerry said blithely, not catching Pamela's tone. "We saw a few panhandlers and some absolutely filthy gypsies, but not so many that they ruined our experience."

"You must have been relieved," Pamela said. Brooke tensed, fearing her mom would unleash a diatribe against her neighbors. Pamela glanced sideways, then lifted one of the cake plates and passed it across the coffee table.

"*Efharisto*," Jerry said, grinning. "I picked that up on the ship. It means 'thanks.' I also had to learn *poy ine e toualeta* pretty darn fast."

"All that breakfast wine," Brooke said.

Linda leaned forward again and wrung her hands. "I'm sure everyone and their brother has been reaching out," she said. "But I think we can relate to what you're going through."

"I appreciate that," Brooke said. The Starks' youngest son had died sixteen years ago from a heroin overdose, long before Brooke knew them. Their cruise dates coincided with the anniversary. Brooke understood that her neighbors had come not only to save her the hassle of cooking, but to offer themselves as example of life after grief. The secret pleasures, the freedom, even the adventure, that surviving could bring.

"I know the circumstances are different, but loss is loss," Linda said. "Especially when it's your child. Nothing's worse than that." She balled her hands into fists, then let them relax. "You probably don't know this, but Hunter went to rehab eleven times. Eleven! We tried everything. Different counselors, different programs, one time a ranch in Nevada."

"We were stupid enough to think that sticking his hand up a cow's ass might do the trick," Jerry interjected, his mouth full of cake. "He could've shoveled shit around here for a lot less."

"We were desperate," Linda said. "We knew something would happen eventually, but it was still a shock when it did."

"He wasn't the boy we raised," Jerry said. He returned the fork to his plate and wiped his mouth with a napkin. "That garbage made him into a different person. I look at old pictures and can't believe how things turned out. He'd be forty-one now. I like to think he'd eventually have grown out of it."

Maybe Opal would have grown into a horrible person. A drug addict, like the Starks' son, or just shallow and narcissistic, her Instagram account nothing but selfies. Pouty faces in front of the bathroom mirror, peace signs from the front seat of a car, sticking out her tongue with her hand on her hip. Maybe she'd have robbed banks, clad in black leather and a balaclava. It amused Brooke to think of Opal as a badass biker chick wielding a shotgun, the barrel between the shoulder blades of a pudgy branch manager while he stuffed cash into a sack. Maybe she'd have ended up a stripper, a compulsive gambler, a gold digger, a pot farmer, a libertarian, a whiny, codependent bitch who blamed the world for her problems. No matter what she came up with, she couldn't give thanks for having avoided it.

Jerry dabbed at his eyes with his napkin. "No one remembers Hunter as a person. He's just a statistic now. Another domino in the chain. Meanwhile this junk keeps tearing through the community and no one's doing squat about it."

"There's a class-action suit against the company that sells OxyContin," Pamela said. "Are you a party to it?"

Jerry shook his head. "Hunter only took pills after his knee surgery. That was long before things got out of hand. It wasn't the pills that got him."

Brooke sensed the conversation had gone from empathic to invasive and Jerry's walls were going up. She imagined it like that: Jerry stacking cinder blocks in front of his feet, one atop the other, until he disappeared behind them. She wanted the same for herself: a small, enclosed space where she could hunker down. A compartment, a cubby. A cell. Alone in the shower or the car, she replayed the tape of Halloween, minute by minute, right up until her phone started buzzing. It was like watching a scary movie she'd seen a dozen times. Knowing the end allowed her to relish each scene and hunt for the clues she'd missed the first time through. Savor each one.

"We're heading to the hospital soon," Pamela said. "What do you two have planned for the rest of your day?"

Jerry laced his fingers behind his head, leaned back against the sofa cushion, out of hiding. "We're retired," he said. "We'll follow wherever the wind blows."

"Don't forget to adjust your sails," Brooke said, and quickly regretted it. They'd meant the card to be kind. What could any card say that *didn't* sound totally lame?

Linda forced a smile. "Just bake the salmon for twelve minutes at four hundred degrees. There's no rush on the dishes. Bring them back whenever it's convenient."

"Or chuck them over the fence," Jerry said. "Who cares?"

They took Lake Drive toward the city. The water's boatless surface rippled with wind, and heavy gray-brown waves crashed against the granite slabs lining the shoulder of the road, the beach and sedge grass drowned beneath the water. The hospital's mirrored windows gleamed in the noonday sun on the eastern shore, beyond Hanover's small skyline. The road curved away from the shore as it came into downtown. Brooke stopped at the first light, at the edge of the college. Her college. Students in fleece jackets and wool caps ambled along the sidewalk with their hands in their pockets and their eyes on the ground. Across the avenue, a trio of trombonists played on the steps of the concert hall, brass slides gleaming and the dark velvet of their open cases absorbing the sun. "They should take their instruments inside," Pamela said. "The cold air can't be good for them. Their parents probably paid a fortune for them."

"It's warm in the sun," Brooke said. "The practice rooms get so stuffy when the heat's on."

"Do you ever play? To see what it feels like?"

"Not in a long time," Brooke said. Her cello was in the basement, somewhere.

Pamela frowned. "That's too bad. Such a beautiful instrument."

Brooke had arrived at college her freshman year with her cello in the back seat of her mother's Lexus, and her clothes, towels, bedding, and boxes of sheet music all crammed into the hatchback. Her studio teacher, Ms. Gui, had called her personally to convince her to come there, over Oberlin and Northwestern, noting her connections at Julliard and Curtis and Eastman for when Brooke was ready to audition for graduate school. Brooke cut the fingertips off a pair of gloves so she could practice during the winter, the way David Helfgott did in *Shine*, picturing Hanover snowed under and trapped in perpetual night, like some arctic outpost, though it was only four hours from Chicago and had its own airport, a mall next to the freeway, a Starbucks two blocks from campus. She'd rehearsed the fingerings for Tchaikovsky's Variations on a Rococo Theme all summer, eager to play it at her first lesson. By the end of her first year, she understood she wasn't cut out for a professional career. Changying Xu, the orchestra's first cello, could coax sounds from her inexpensive Cecilio that Brooke couldn't replicate on her Edler. Brooke was good, but she wasn't *that good,* not the way her brother was good at math or her mother at the law. Spending the next three years holed up in a soundproofed room in order to become a junior high music teacher felt like a waste of time. It was better to find something else to do, someone else to become.

The light changed and they moved past campus, into downtown proper, the awnings over the shops weighted with icicles dripping onto the sidewalk. City workers in orange vests were busy wrapping lights around the trees. "I don't think I'm up for the hospital today," Brooke said.

She'd gone back right after Opal died, but with the second Isolette moved out, the bed space seemed massive and vacuous. All the nurses, even Dash, tiptoed around her, slipping off to whisper in the corner by the laundry, as if Brooke had been the one to do something wrong. Lately she'd begun to wonder if it wasn't her absence that had cost Opal, but her presence.

Her mother didn't argue with her or ask her to explain. "Well, we can't keep sitting around the house all day," Pamela said. "Now that we're out, let's go somewhere."

Brooke wanted to lie on her narrow bed in her tiny room in the Hibbert House. But the room was no longer hers. She'd collected her clothes and returned the keys the night Opal died. "Any ideas?" she asked.

Pamela put her finger to the passenger window, clearing a hole in the damp fog. "The paper's been advertising all sorts of early Black Friday sales. Want to go shopping?"

The suggestion was so unexpected and uncharacteristic that it intrigued her. Her mother hated malls and blamed them for every social illness from runaway consumer debt to suppressed middle-class wages to environmental exploitation. Mall construction in Texas had displaced North America's largest migration of snow geese; in North Dakota, the Sheyenne River had been poisoned with sludge. On some level, Brooke had sought a career in advertising as a way of sticking it to the old lady, a challenge to Her Honor to choose her politics over her own daughter. Brooke's small firm in Hanover was a far cry from Ogilvy. Nearly all her clients were locally owned businesses with limited marketing budgets. Brooke had helped the Barkery develop a website so it could ship its scratch-made, non-GMO pet treats all over the country, and she'd persuaded Nixon's Jewelers to offer free professional engagement photos for every couple who bought a ring in the store. They hung the pictures in their front windows, captioned by phrases like "He put a ring on it!" and "Thank God he didn't go to Jared!" In warmer months, the shop set out baskets of dry-erase markers so people walking by could scrawl congratulatory messages across the glass. The markers had been Brooke's idea, and they'd worked like a charm.

Brooke expected Pamela to change her mind as she crossed beneath the interstate and turned into the mall. Instead, she read aloud the names of the chain restaurants flanking the parking lot, trying to decide where to eat. Brooke wondered if Pamela suggested coming here because she assumed the mall was a place Brooke loved, the way she loved it as a teenager, and likewise, whether her mom still saw her as a foolish girl ill-equipped to make adult decisions.

The noisy food court worked like an analgesic. There was no way to think straight among the overwhelming clamor and mash-up of smells. It was easier not to think at all. In the center of the expansive glass room, a bearded Santa filled a velvet chair surrounded by cottony artificial snow. A miniature train carried toddlers around the circumference of the makeshift village. Thanksgiving was a week away, but here it was Christmas. It was the one thing Brooke loved about malls, the way they hopped from holiday to holiday, skipping over the drudgery in between.

"You don't get enough snow in Wisconsin?" Pamela asked. "Had to import fake stuff?"

"It's the most wonderful time of the year," Brooke said. "You're sure you're game for this?"

"It's a holly jolly Christmas," her mother said. "Lead the way."

Brooke moved aggressively from one store to the next, striding the concourses with purpose. As in the hospital, so long as you knew where you were going, no one questioned your right to be there; two women shopping together could go into any section of any store, from lingerie to boys' shoes, and no one would find their presence strange. Brooke had forgotten the pleasure of moving with freedom and anonymity. There were so many things about her that people didn't know and never would.

She bought two shirts with coordinating ties at Jos. A. Bank and a bottle of cologne for Harper. Her mom held the paper-wrapped soaps to her nose in L'Occitane and told Brooke the Shea Milk Verbena smelled more like Chloe, Ian's wife, while Hannah, their daughter, would probably prefer the Cherry Blossom. In Talbots, Pamela dutifully tried on cardigans and twin sets and agreed the mocha and the turquoise were the prettiest. The sweaters were buy-one-get-one, and Pamela encouraged Brooke to pick one for her and to give the other to Harper's mother. "That way I'll still be surprised." Together they glided in and out of Williams-Sonoma, Godiva, the Packers' Fan Shop, collecting tins of peppermint bark, martini glasses, hand-dipped chocolates, scarves, and mugs.

She considered springing for Ollie's cell phone, to preempt the fight between Harper and Sara about when he'd be ready and which parent would get the privilege of buying it for him. If history was any predictor, Sara would try to get it before Harper could say no. So many little ways we find to hurt one another. Brooke envisioned sliding the box across the table, Oliver using it to call his mom to break the news. But at $700, it would be an expensive fuck you. It was better to play nice. She settled on a haul of Nike, the only brand Ollie wanted to wear.

Leaving Macy's, Pamela looped her arm through Brooke's elbow, one more in a string of foreign gestures and solicitous acts Brooke didn't know how to interpret, other than the obvious. As they walked, their faces now only inches apart, Brooke noticed her mother's breath growing heavy. She hadn't been this close to her body in a long time. She'd never thought of her mom as old. She'd only ever thought of her as unchanging and steadfast—though she could remember swimming with her as a little girl at the West Cook YMCA, her mom floating on a foam noodle, the skirt of her bathing suit billowing around her like a jellyfish, liquid and untouchable. Her mother's naked warm body in the locker room shower, kneading shampoo into her hair. When Brooke was a teenager, her mom had become repugnant to her, the way most parents did, and she had recoiled from her touch. She expected to come back, to one day reclaim her place as a loving, loyal daughter, to acknowledge Pamela's outsized role in her development. She'd married Harper instead.

If I can have Harper, I'll never need another person ever again.

"Do you need a break?" Brooke asked.

"I could use a restroom. And I'm a little hungry."

"Give me the bags," Brooke said. "I'll meet you at the tables over there."

Her mother turned down the hallway toward the bathrooms and Brooke ducked into Carter's. She'd been avoiding it all day but figured she was safer on her own. It wasn't much different from any of the other stores: full of clothes and accessories, things to buy, only smaller. The fleece sleepers at the front were on sale, and she took her time weighing which ones she liked best before remembering that Emery couldn't wear pullovers because of the vent.

"Need any help?" the salesgirl asked. She was young, not even twenty years old, with dots of acne on her chin and cheeks. Brooke wondered if the clerk worked here because she had children or hoped to one day, or if this was just a job, something she did for money.

"I'm looking for sleepers with front snaps," Brooke said. "Do you have any of those?"

"Not a lot," the salesgirl said. "What size do you need?"

Preemie was correct, though to ask for them by name would prompt questions she didn't want to answer. "Newborn," she said, hoping the preemies would be nearby. The girl looked her up and down, as though pondering the same question Brooke had about her. If she had a newborn, where was it? Since Opal had died, Brooke had stopped pumping (Emery was on total parenteral nutrition and showed no signs of coming off), but she still wore nursing pads inside her bra. Maybe the salesgirl could tell. The snap-fronts were at the back of the store. None were as cute as the sleepers up front and none were on sale.

"Are you looking for a boy or a girl?"

"It doesn't matter," Brooke said. The trappings of gender often seemed irrelevant, a later concern, like worrying whether they'd be good at chemistry or make the soccer team. The salesgirl looked at her quizzically. Brooke added, "A boy, please. I'm looking for a boy."

She picked the first two she found, one with baseballs and the other camouflage, which the salesgirl said she was lucky to find because the camo print was their best seller and they could never keep them in stock. To make up for only buying two, Brooke added sets of matching hats and socks. The salesgirl returned her credit card and passed the sack across the counter. “Happy holidays.”

She reminded herself to smile. Looking happy, like knowing where you were going, was key. “You, too,” she said.

Pamela waved to her from a small table in the main corridor, outside the Gloria Jean’s. She’d bought two soft pretzels and had set them atop their paper sleeves. Pamela eyed the Carter’s shopping bag among the bundle in Brooke’s hand. She tore a piece from a pretzel dusted with cinnamon sugar and held it out to her. “This is surprisingly tasty.”

“Carbs make everything better,” Brooke said.

“My doctor told me I need to gain weight. I’m a little anemic and my blood pressure is on the low side. I’ve been eating ice cream after dinner almost every night. It’s wonderful. The market carries a flavor called ‘salted caramel truffle.’ I can’t get enough of it.”

“I can’t imagine being able to eat whatever I want.”

“I spent so much time and energy fretting about my weight when I was your age. I worried my robe made me look heavy. Now I worry more about falling. Gina Halley fell off a ladder while cleaning out her rain gutters and broke her femur. She spent months in a wheelchair. I’d be up a creek if that happened to me.” She took another bite. “I’d rather get fat. Who cares what people think.”

The stairs in Brooke’s childhood home, the house where her mother still lived, were steep, narrow, and wooden.

When she was eight, Brooke had tried to slide down them in a sleeping bag and had broken her collar bone. She lay at the bottom of the stairs, paralyzed by fear and pain, for what felt like a long time, until Ian came home and called their mother's chambers. A clerk came to take her to the emergency room and Pamela met her there after court. Brooke pictured her mother lying at the bottom of the stairs after a fall, studying the fractured colors in the stained-glass window, the way Brooke herself had, waiting for someone to find her.

A teenage couple walked by their table, a boy and a girl with long chains joining their jackets to their jeans' pockets and rings stretching the holes in their earlobes. They were chased by a toddler in overalls, a little boy with blond curls and candy-red Nikes, a miniature version of the shoes she'd bought for Ollie. The teenagers stopped to look at the toddler and the girl stuck out her index finger, one long black nail. A woman in jeans and a green sweater ran up and scooped the boy off the ground. "You little speed demon," she said, hoisting him. The boy draped an arm over his mother's shoulder. "Sorry," she said. "I think he wanted your chains."

The teenagers shrugged and the mom carried her son directly toward Brooke. For a moment, she feared the woman would pass her son to her and ask her to watch him. A jolt of panic buzzed through her. Yet the woman glided past, to the next table, where a group of women had pushed two bistro tables into a figure eight and had parked their strollers between the chairs. The women wore earrings shaped like snowflakes or silver hoops or small diamond studs. The children seated on their laps pinched Cheerios one at a time and placed them inside their mouths.

"I'm so sorry," Pamela said. "I didn't even notice them. Do you want to find another table?"

"It's fine," Brooke said. "It's not like I haven't been around babies before."

"Yes, but now—"

"Really," Brooke said. "I'm okay. We don't need to move."

Pamela studied the women. She took in their black leggings and fleece vests, their boots and paper coffee cups. Brooke could only catch pieces of their conversation over the Christmas music blaring down from the ceiling and the whir of the blender at Gloria Jean's, but she heard one of the women say that the Honest Company offered free shipping if you spent more than a hundred dollars. "We go through that much in a week," said the woman wearing the silver hoops.

"God, every three or four days," said the diamond studs. She caught Brooke watching, smiled, and turned back to her friends.

"There's a word for women like them," her mother whispered, leaning in. "One of my clerks used it. Standard? Base model? I can't remember."

"I think you mean basic," Brooke said. "I haven't heard that in a while."

"That's right. Basic. I liked it when I heard it. A uniform of sameness, and of disregard. So many women spent decades fighting for equal pay and sexual harassment protections, so many things big and small, and these ladies"—she nodded in the group's direction—"they turn their backs on all of it. Live the life of vicarious consumers for their husbands. Veblen saw it more than a hundred years ago. Wives as prized cattle. Women as trophies. I'll bet every one of them went to college." She clicked her tongue. "What a waste of brain power."

"Childcare is expensive," Brooke said.

"It certainly is expensive," Pamela said. "Way too expensive. But that's not the problem here, with them. They had choices." She looked around the concourse and tore off another piece of her pretzel. "When you were in school, women like that envied you."

"No one envied me in high school," Brooke said. "Especially not the popular girls. I was in the orchestra."

"Oh yes they did." Her mom smiled, brightly. "Who was that one girl in the CYSO who wouldn't leave you alone? The one who wore all the turtlenecks? Wendy something."

"Wendy Whitehall."

"That's right, Wendy Whitehall. Every time I saw her, she was in a white turtleneck. Drove a white Jeep Wrangler with her name on the license plate. Wasn't her hair white, too?"

"It was blond." Brooke remembered that Wendy didn't shave her legs above her knees, but that the hair was so fine and light it was invisible. She noticed it when their bare thighs would rub against each other during summer rehearsals. She recalled the funk of the orchestra room, the rosin and slide oil and cork grease, the pools of saliva on the carpet beneath the trumpets and trombones.

"She was a towhead." Pamela grinned again. "Some people are whiter than others. Wendy Whitehall may have been the whitest person I've ever met."

"Like I'm not?" Brooke asked.

"Your father is half Chinese. My grandmother was Jewish. She was disowned by her parents when she married Papa. My point is that Wendy used to burn with envy. I'd see her glancing at you while you played. She was never as musical as you. Proficient, but not musical."

"That's how I felt when I went to college," Brooke said. "Why I dropped out of the conservatory. I wasn't as good."

"You were very good. But you were also very hard on yourself. Everyone envies someone for something. Life is a circular firing squad, especially for women. No one's harder on women than other women." She glanced at the table of moms. "I guess that makes me a hypocrite, but it's true."

"What about Dad?" Brooke asked. "Did you envy him?"

"Good heavens, no. Why would I?"

"When he moved. When he remarried. For leaving you all alone."

Her mom leaned closer. "I'll tell you something, if you promise not to hold it against me. If you do hold it against me, I guess it's your right to. I was relieved when he moved back overseas. He never intended to stay in the States for good, but then we got married and I had your brother. By the time you were little, Hong Kong was gearing up to return to China, and there were opportunities for him there. I knew he wasn't happy in Chicago, and I knew if he stayed, you and Ian would have grown up with a miserable father, like I did. My dad was an alcoholic, and my mother spent her whole life trying to mollify him. It made me sick to watch it. I knew that if your father stayed, the same thing would have happened to me. When you told me you'd be staying here, I worried it would happen to you. Our family has a long history of women sacrificing their lives for men. I feared you'd wake up one day and realize you'd made a huge mistake."

Brooke thought of her mother wiping her eyes at the window of Harper's apartment, all those years ago. The way her voice cracked when she said, *I guess you're here now.*

"Weren't you lonely?" Brooke asked. If the sum of her life's decisions pointed in a direction, it was that: solving the problem of loneliness. Brooke leaned closer. "Haven't you been lonely, by yourself all these years?"

"No," Pamela said. She ran her finger through the sugar clinging to the wax paper, and licked it off. "I was concerned about you and your brother, but I wasn't lonely. I was too busy. As the years went by, I grew to value my autonomy, and my privacy."

It was strange to imagine solitude as a state one could prefer, but her mother seemed to prefer it. "What about me?" Brooke asked. "Do you think I've made a mistake with my life?"

Pamela looked at her without speaking. Her eyes softened, and Brooke felt her body warm, as if an inner dam had given way. After a time, her mother said, "You were a very determined young woman. *Very* determined. Your brother was gifted, math came easy to Ian. He didn't have to try very hard. You were the opposite. You worked so hard, Brooke, at everything. You used to saw away at your cello like you were trying to start a fire. I only wanted your work to pay off. I wanted you to get what you wanted."

Brooke recalled the small upstairs lamp her mother would turn on before going to bed. Nights when Brooke came home late, the faint glow would spill down the staircase, just enough to guide her up the stairs. Her bedroom had been beneath the eaves of the roof, her twin bed in the corner, her music stand and chair and poster of Rostropovich tacked to the wall. So many of the rooms she had known in her life had been like that, sequestered from the world and the people in it. She'd been so lonely, so unbearably alone. Even Wendy Whitehall, in her white turtleneck and white car, with her almost-white hair, had gobs of friends. The violinists were Wendy's friends; so were the violists, the oboists, the flautists, the clarinetists. They crowded together into the corner booth beneath the stairwell at the Artist's Café. If Wendy envied her, she likely did so because she believed Brooke didn't deserve to occupy the chair ahead of hers. Brooke's favorite part about the Chicago Youth Symphony Orchestra had been taking the Green Line into the city for rehearsal, the cars steadily adding people until the train stopped at Adams and Wabash and everyone spilled out toward Michigan Avenue. On so many Sundays she had been tempted to walk past the Fine Arts Building simply to stay inside the crowd, the crush of bodies, hoping it would absorb her and her loneliness would end.

All she had ever wanted was to belong. Cut away all the husk and casing, the Christmas carols and bad hair and unused college degrees, and Brooke had longed for the very thing her mother despised. A spot in the corner booth, an invitation to join the group of moms at the next table. There was nothing ridiculous about their conversation, certainly nothing evil or tragic. The women were only discussing how their children grew, the things that went into and came out of their bodies. Not so different from the vocabulary of neonatal medicine—pulse ox and blood gases and creatinine and total parenteral nutrition. For the last three months, Brooke had clung to the hope that if she could wait out the wires and pumps and breathing machine, she'd one day receive the things these women took for granted. Babies in strollers, babies tweezing Cheerios between their fingers, babies motoring after strangers. Now she understood she'd never talk the way other women did. Motherhood was one more sorority she couldn't join. The universe had been teaching her that for a decade, the hungry ghosts of her own vanished children had whispered it in her ear, and yet she'd stubbornly, stupidly, refused to learn it.

"No matter how old you get, your heart never stops breaking for your kids," Pamela said, crumpling her pretzel wrapper and napkins. Brooke gathered her shopping bags and pushed in her chair, while Pamela wiped the crumbs from the table and carried their trash to the bin. The mall was at its most crowded, though it was a weekday, a Thursday, a week before Thanksgiving. Brooke offered her mother her elbow again, but Pamela said she was fine. The pretzel had helped. She took two of the shopping bags, one for each hand. Brooke kept her back to the moms seated around the tables. She knew that looking back was a waste of time. None of the women had noticed her enough to notice her going away.

16

Fran returned from lunch on Christmas Eve with news. "Huge," she said, holding her arms above her head. She'd seen Julius Robinette in the lobby, taking pictures in front of the water wall with the senior administrators. Leif Gunnarson, several vice presidents, the chief of medicine, all wearing Packers jerseys over their shirts and ties. "They wore *his* number," Fran said, breathless. "Someone bought them special for today." Julius wore his jersey, too, only his was white while the administrators wore green.

There was more. Greg Venneck, the VP of communications, had pulled her aside to whisper that Julius would be coming up to the third floor. Their floor. He'd asked to see the kids.

"What kids?" Dash asked. "How many do we even have on Peds?" Since Opal's death, any child requiring surgery, any child who even *might* require it, had been transferred out. The last time Dash wandered past the Peds unit, the corridor had been dark, the nurses all sent home.

"There's one down there," Joanne said. She adjusted her glasses and looked at the admissions board on the computer. "Eighteen-month-old with RSV."

"He won't be able to see him," Dash said.

"He can help deliver babies," Fran said. The pens in her breast pocket rattled. "I mean, he has good hands, right? He knows how to catch."

"He's a linebacker," Joanne said. "Not a receiver."

"He can line my back all he wants," Fran said. "He can blitz my line of scrimmage."

"Guys," Dr. Fackelman said. "Please."

The holidays were a magnet for would-be and had-been celebrities. The Niminose Casino, northwest of town, booked a steady stream of one-hit wonders from the '80s, acts like the Fabulous Thunderbirds and Cutting Crew, and members of the bands sometimes stopped by the hospital. At least once a year, they got players from the Green Bay indoor football team, though nobody cared about them, and one Christmas, the entire touring cast of *The Lion King* showed up in full costume, leotards and wigs and layers of thick stage makeup, expecting to bring Yuletide cheer to a wing full of chipper bald kids coloring pictures while they waited for their hair to grow back. They'd found a ten-year-old with pneumonia, so heavily sedated the nurses couldn't wake her, an eleven-month old who'd had an anaphylactic reaction to cranberries, and a four-year-old tonsils-and-adenoids kid who'd screamed bloody murder when a rainbow-faced Rafiki bounded through his door. A starting player for the Packers was the closest they ever came to an actual famous person.

Streamers draped the hallways, though in the NICU only a few paper snowflakes dangled from the ceiling, turning in the breezes from the ducts. Fran had found preemie-sized hats outfitted with reindeer antlers; every baby got one, along with a dot of rouge on the end of his or her nose. Penny's radio played a god-awful Mannheim Steamroller CD, all synthesized and too fast, not the slightest bit Christmassy. Emery's ventilator drowned out most of the noise if Dash sat close, but whenever she left the bedside to snatch another fudge square or chocolate-dipped pretzel from the smorgasbord at the nurses' desk, the music was all she heard.

Peds was empty but Maternity was nearly full. Christmas Eve was one of the busiest birthing days of the year because every new mom wanted to be home by Christmas. "Squeeze 'em out and send 'em home," Fran joked, and throughout her shift Dash had noticed the steady stream of visitors in Christmas sweaters moving past the NICU windows on their way to the birthing and postpartum suites. Both of the costumed Santas, several hours apart, rang the unit's intercom and had to be pointed in the right direction. The activity made the shift go faster, though when Dash retreated back to Emery's corner, she thought ruefully about the next day when the corridors would be deserted, and anyone stuck in this place would spend Christmas alone. Brooke had been calling every other day to check in, but it had been close to two weeks since she or Harper had visited. Jenny Ramirez said parents had to go seven days without any contact before she could get Child Protective Services involved. A phone call was a poor substitute for actually showing up, but it still counted. Emery still had a ways to go before discharge or transfer were even possibilities, so there wasn't much they could do about it now. If he crashed or required emergency surgery, that could change things, Jenny said, but no one was rooting for that. Dash held out hope Brooke and Harper would make it in tomorrow, simply because tomorrow was Christmas and Emery was their son, though she knew there was a possibility they would not. Brooke wouldn't be the first mother to disappear from the NICU, nor would she be the last. Like every other unit in the hospital, the NICU kept going regardless of who visited. Or who didn't.

A little after two o'clock, she noticed the nurses and techs from Maternity and staff from the OB clinic beginning to amass in the foyer outside the NICU, their backs against the window. Penny knocked against the glass and waved for people to get out of the way, but as soon as a space opened someone new stepped in to fill it. It didn't matter. Julius was easy to see above the horde of bodies, the glowing white polyester of his jersey, the beaded ropes of his tight braids hanging below his shoulders. He stopped at the NICU window and lowered his face to the glass, scanning the room before settling on Dash at the mixing table in the center. He smiled before leaning up, out of view. The doors to Maternity swung open and closed behind him.

"Ta-ta," Dash said. Despite Brooke's disappearance, Dash was in a good mood. It was Christmas Eve, she was off tomorrow, and in only in two and a half weeks, Landon's probation would end. County services would be out of their hair for good. They were in the home stretch now.

Fifteen minutes later, Julius was back, this time without the crowd. He stood alone with Greg Venneck, the hospital's vice president only as tall as the football player's shoulder, even with the Santa hat. Penny buzzed them in, and once inside Greg Venneck said that Mr. Robinette had been visiting units at the hospital and had specifically asked to stop in at the NICU. "Welcome, Mr. Robinette," Penny said. "Thanks for dropping by to see us."

"Merry Christmas," Julius said, flashing a bright smile, his telltale diastema. Dash had seen him smile on television dozens of times—his face behind the grid of his face mask, his breath a fog inside his helmet. It was surreal to see in person, in the unit.

Fran leaned in close to Dash. "Look out, girl. Penny's in the red zone."

"Call me Julius," he said. He carried a small velveteen sack, the size of a pillowcase and weighted at the bottom. He set his free hand on Greg Venneck's shoulder. "How about I meet you down in the lobby in a few? I want to talk to the nurses."

"Really?" Greg Venneck appeared shocked by the request. "You want me to go?"

"These nurses will look out for me," he said. "These are my people here."

"You think you can find the lobby on your own?" Greg asked.

"I'll go the elevator and push L," he said. "That should get me there."

"Okay then," Greg said. The door latched behind him and he turned to look through the window. He looked not only awkward but even slightly sad in his jersey and tie and Santa hat.

Penny led Julius to the sink, showed him the timer, the foot pedal, the paper towels. He soaped his forearms to his elbows and between the webbing of his fingers without being told to. Dash had seen her share of large people—gestational diabetes was a good way to land a baby in the NICU—and she could recall a few moms and dads who'd weighed close to four hundred pounds; their weight hadn't seemed gained so much as accumulated without intention. Julius's size had been sculpted with great deliberateness, designed to stop a grown man running at full speed. Dash instinctively positioned herself in front of Emery's Isolette, as if to guard it.

"I'm glad to see ya'll," he said, shaking Dr. Fackelman's hand. "My baby girl was in the NICU for sixty-seven days, and I can remember every last one of them. Those were hard days."

"Your daughter was here?" the doctor asked. "In this unit?"

"Not here. In N'awlins." He glanced around and said the word again, more slowly, his mouth cocked to the side, "New Or-*leans*. She came at twenty-seven weeks. Three pounds, three ounces, smallest thing I've ever seen." Julius blinked twice. His eyelashes were longer than Dash expected, his palms pink and soft. "So many days I didn't know if we'd get to keep her."

"How is she doing now?" Dr. Fackelman asked.

"She's six. Has some sensory processing disorder and goes to therapy four days a week. A little trouble with balance, but she can pedal a bike with training wheels."

"That's wonderful."

"I prayed to Jesus that if my baby got better, I'd never forget it," Julius said, reaching inside the sack. "I promised I'd give back." He pulled out a box, a Nikon DSLR camera, and handed it to Dr. Fackelman. "I figure even if ya'll got one of these already you could use another. There ain't ever enough pictures of the babies in here. Like people are afraid to remember."

"It's true," Dr. Fackelman said. "Most parents wish they had more photographs later."

"The camera we're using sucks," Fran said. "The DMV has a better lens."

"The NICU is probably the most invisible place in the hospital," Julius said. "It's like that door shuts and everyone outside forgets about you. More people know about the morgue than know about the NICU. I vowed to never forget."

"We appreciate it," Dr. Fackelman said. "It's nice of you to say."

"Nah," Julius said. He reached inside the sack again and withdrew a pile of gold foil-embossed envelopes. "I also brought some things for ya'll personally, for Christmas and all. My wife suggested I get ya'll pedicures since you're on your feet all day, but I wondered if maybe you didn't want that. This way you can pick you something for yourselves."

"It's not necessary," Dr. Fackelman said.

"Yes, it is," Julius said. He set the envelopes on the counter. "I promised God."

"Do you want a treat?" Fran asked him. She pointed to the spread on the counter. "All homemade."

"Better not," Julius said, a hand to his stomach. "We play on Sunday."

"Maybe you want to say hi to the babies?" Fran offered. NICU parents weren't supposed to visit other babies in their bed spaces. But Julius Robinette wasn't a NICU parent, at least not at the moment. He'd been in commercials for Campbell's Soup and Icy Hot, and he'd sacked Eli Manning to end the game that sent the Pack to the playoffs. He'd lifted the NFC trophy above his head at Lambeau. He nodded solemnly and Fran led him to Bed One, near the window.

He came to Emery's bed last. His cologne was sweet and orangey, and as he stepped past the supply cart and into the bed space, an image entered Dash's mind, unbidden, of Mike wrestling in high school. How she used to imagine herself beneath him on the mat, his chin to her shoulder and his flexed quads gripping her waist. This was before she'd had sex and wondered what it would be like, the exertions it would require. Now she thought of Julius in his uniform and pads, pressing her body into the earth, the grass and dirt beneath her cratering around her shoulders and back, giving way, her tissues and bones compressing until she shrank to the size of an acorn, a mustard seed. For years she'd watched him break through an offensive line and bring down a quarterback, and she wondered if the quarterbacks, knowing what was coming, had at some point given over to it, let Julius take them down like a wave crashing over their heads. If a part of them even came to crave it.

Julius squinted at Emery inside the Isolette. He studied the digital readouts on the ventilator, the pump, the scroll of the monitor. Emery had taken sixty cubic centimeters of fortified formula by nasal gavage, which was real progress, but his patent ductus arteriosus was still an issue and he was probably headed for surgery. Whenever Dash blew against his face, his eyes swam around, unable to hold focus, and his tongue worked against the ET tube, searching for an opening through which to protrude. Not good signs.

Julius's eyes narrowed further. His head dropped closer to the lid of the Isolette. He seemed to study Emery with the entirety of his focus. He blinked three times and said, "This baby's sicker than the others."

"He's had a rough time," Dash said. She looked around the unit to see who was watching. Dr. Fackelman was, but the other nurses had turned back to their patients and computers. If someone from the Joint Commission walked in right now and caught her giving information to a non-family member, she'd be screwed.

"Can I touch him?" Julius asked. "I want to pray for him."

Dr. Fackelman shrugged and nodded, faintly. They were co-conspirators now. If any of the nurses were to report that she'd allowed a visitor to touch a patient without the parents' consent, Dash could lose her job, even her nursing license. Dr. Fackelman nodded a second time, and Dash sighed and released the latch and opened the porthole door. Her breath caught watching him extend his hand inside. His palm was larger than all of Emery; the baby disappeared entirely beneath it. Julius lowered his palm to Emery's chest. His fingers curled over the blankets, his thumb and finger parting to make room for the ventilator tubing. "I remember that smell," he said.

"What smell?" Dash leaned closer, to catch the scent.

"The inside of the boxes," he said. "The medicines and plastic, the babies' little bodies. I smelled it every day for sixty-seven days. The better my daughter got, the more I smelled it. It's a good smell." He gazed down at Emery through the lid of the Isolette, his hand still in place. He closed his eyes and said, "Lord, whatever you do for the least of these, you do for me. This baby is the smallest, sickest life inside this whole hospital. Send your power to make him better." Dash let her eyes fall closed while Julius spoke. His voice washed through her. His cologne, now mixed with the interior of the Isolette, smelled like incense. Her head was almost touching his. Emery made a small noise, a baby noise, and Dash hoped he knew somehow that Julius was there, praying over him. She hoped that God, too, heard Julius, and would answer.

Julius opened his eyes and said to Emery, "You get better now. You do what these nurses here tell you, and you get better. Then you come see me play, okay?"

He shut the porthole door. "You're the angel of the Lord," he said to Dash. "All ya'll. These babies are like Jesus in his manger and ya'll are the angels keeping watch."

"More like the donkeys," Fran said.

Julius pretended not to hear. He spread his arms and Dash opened hers to receive him. She felt him close around her. She felt the taut muscles in his back, again imagined the ground opening. His cheek was smooth and soft. The diamond in his ear dragged across her jaw. "God bless you," he said. "May God bless you and keep you."

They waited until he'd gone to open the envelopes. Each one contained an American Express prepaid gift card, the words *A Gift for You* embossed along the bottom where their names would have been. The number in the corner said $500.

"Score," Fran said. She did a little chicken dance and made like she was spiking a ball.

After all the expenses associated with Landon's case and treatment—their co-pay and court fees, the changes they'd made around the house and the portions of Silver Crest their insurance didn't cover, to say nothing of the charges Landon racked up in the first place—Dash already carried an astronomical balance on her MasterCard. She'd bought Mike and Landon shirts and Kasey a jacket, all from Kohl's, telling herself that Mike never wanted anything and Landon's headphones ought to figure into the tally. Besides those things, she didn't have much else for them to open. She could go straight from the hospital to the mall. Or cash in this card for two smaller ones so Kasey and Landon could shop for themselves, and use whatever was left over to buy something for Mike, maybe a bottle of VO to sip after the kids went to bed. The image of Julius's hand on Emery made her nervous all over again, the consequences she'd face if anyone found out. Eighteen days, she thought. Landon had eighteen days to go.

"We're not supposed to accept gifts," she said. "We should give these to the hospital."

Fran clutched hers to her chest. "He gave them to us."

"It's hospital policy."

Fran came closer, past the supply cart, close enough for Dash to smell the chocolate on her breath. "Don't ruin this, Dash," she whispered. "Didn't you see how sweet he was? Most people who come to the hospital don't even know we're here. He came to see us."

"We'll get in trouble," Dash said.

"Only if someone finds out. And you're not going to say anything, are you?" Fran stared at her, her voice lower still. "I know you could use it. We didn't get shit for bonuses this year."

"Go on and keep it," Dr. Fackelman said. "I'll take the heat if anything comes of it. You think the administration wants a story going around that they confiscated gifts given by one of the stars of the Packers?"

"Hell, no," Fran said. "Greg Venneck would brown his shorts."

"Spend it on yourself," Fran said, touching Dash's arm. "If it disappears, no one'll ever know you had it."

"I can't keep it," Dash said.

"God, you are so frustrating sometimes," Fran said. Her lip curled. "Lighten up, for once."

Dash set her envelope on the mixing counter. "I won't say anything, but I can't keep it. And if someone asks me about this, I'm not going to lie."

"No one'll ask," Fran said. "Don't you go looking for someone who might."

"I already said I won't."

Fran slid Dash's envelope from the countertop. She withdrew the card, separated it from the paper backing, and slid it down her breast pocket, behind her pens. "Go, Pack, go."

The news was forecasting a winter storm, starting on Christmas night. Travelers in the Midwest could have a hard time of it. Another, even larger system was already shutting down airports in Oregon, Washington, and parts of Canada. The terminal lines snaked out the door. She'd overheard one of the obstetricians talking about his skiing trip out that way and Dash wondered if he might be among the huddled masses trying to sleep on the floor. She was glad to be home in Wisconsin, even if Wisconsin was the only place she'd ever really been.

As a young girl, her family spent Christmas driving between relatives, the nine of them piled into her father's Ford van as they crossed between her grandparents and aunts and uncles in Scandinavia and Ogdensburg and Manawa. The youngest of the seven, Dash rode on the front bench between Vanessa and Andrea while Dottie sat in the back with the boys. The year Uncle Verlyn lived with them, all the girls had to squeeze into the first row, though even then Dash got the middle, a clear view of the road between her parents' shoulders, strips of sand down the center of the silted asphalt, the snowbound fields and trees. The van tended to fishtail, and whenever it did, Vanessa would clamp down on Dash's arm. The worst thing that ever happened was a flat tire, which required them to empty the van onto the side of the road so their father could get to the jack and iron. They were all still shivering when they arrived at their aunt's house and Dash curled in front of the fire until she fell asleep. She woke when her brother Marty picked her up to carry her back to the van, and in the morning she found a ten-dollar bill in her pocket, slipped there by her uncle or aunt.

The sum total of their family left in Wisconsin now consisted of Aunt Helen and Uncle Rolph, in Omro, and Mike's brother in Helmond. They took dinner to Helen and Rolph, who had four cataracts and one good ear between them, and went on to Dan and Carol's for dessert and the football game. Helen and Rolph gave the kids cash in envelopes, twenty dollars each, and at Dan and Carol's Kasey and Landon both unwrapped remote-controlled drones, little whizzing helicopter-like machines. Landon clapped at the sight of his and tore the box in half trying to get it open. Kasey smiled and said thank you in a voice so quiet that Dan said, "I'm sure you're too big for toys nowadays. This one's just for messing around." Dash felt bad there hadn't been more to open. She thought of Julius Robinette's gift card and tried to reassure herself she'd done the right thing. Flying the drones in the backyard, Kasey wore her new jacket and Landon wore his navy Hanover Medical Center fleece, the only jacket he wanted to wear, no matter how cold it got. They stood several feet apart, their feet spread and their necks craned at the sky. Whenever Landon moved toward his sister, Kasey shuffled sideways, maintaining the gap between them. Dash figured their drones, like kites, would crash together if they got too close.

The snow began right as they were turning down their street. Had they left Helmond an hour later, they'd have been on the highway during the most dangerous time, when the road started to freeze and snow fell over the ice. Dash felt lucky they'd made it home when they did. The kids carried their presents upstairs and she called to Landon to take his shower. Mike locked the front door and said he was heading up, too. The day after Christmas was a major shopping day at Lowe's and he had to work in the morning. Dash had volunteered for Christmas Eve and New Year's Eve in exchange for the days after off, and was glad to have another morning to sleep in. She turned off the lights in the front room except for the tree in the corner, the bulbs shining in the ornaments and coloring the wall behind it. Needles lay on the carpet and the living room smelled softly of pine. She moved toward the kitchen, the morning's dishes waiting for her in the sink. She turned on the water and lifted the first dish, but then set the plate down and cut the water and the lights so she could watch the snow fall in the moonlight. The street and house lights on the next block were diffused behind the granulated curtain of snow, causing the sky to throb orange, and in the windless night the flakes covered the lawn as though over a pastry, in thin sugared layers. Each branch on the maple was distinct from every other and the tree appeared three-dimensionally thrust forward. The snow that landed against the glass melted and ran toward the casement. December often felt to her like caring for a patient in end-stage renal failure, edematous and jaundiced but somehow managing to hang on from one day to the next. That a real storm had finally come felt like a relief, even a cause for joy: 2012 was going under. In a few days, they'd begin a new year.

The snow was still coming the next morning, eight fresh inches overnight. Dash watched it from the sofa with her coffee. Christmas lights still glowed beneath the blankets of snow covering the front hedges. Mike had shoveled the driveway before leaving for work and the inch that had fallen in the last hour looked, in the flattened gray light, like a sheet of velum laid across the pavement. Occasionally a car drove past the house, slush spinning up into its wheel wells, but once it passed the street fell silent. She'd been watching for an hour when Charlie Weyenberg emerged from his garage in his orange hunting parka, carrying a shovel in one hand and trying to push his oxygen canister through the snow with the other. She summoned Landon from the basement.

"Would you go help Mr. Weyenberg?" she asked him. "He hasn't been well and the slush is heavy. I don't want him to have a heart attack."

"I'm on the computer."

Silver Crest and school were closed until after New Year's. She worried about the disruption to his routine and knew he couldn't just play his game the entire time. She opened her purse and withdrew a ten-dollar bill from her wallet. "You can have this if you go now," she said.

Landon folded the money in half and slid it into his pants pocket.

"You have to go now," Dash said. "You can't wait till later."

"I know," he said. "I'm going."

Landon went out in his snow boots and fleece, his headphones over his ears. Charlie extended his hand, but Landon didn't shake it. He stuck his shovel in the snow and got to work.

He worked for two hours without stopping, until Dash called him in for lunch, a big grilled ham-and-cheese sandwich and a bowl of tomato soup. Landon ate greedily, bent over the bowl with the spoon in his fist, snowmelt puddling around his boots. His hair was frosted and his ears were pink, but he said that if she made him wear a hat he wouldn't go back out. Ray Krueger and Lisa Hogan came out to talk with Charlie while Landon shoveled the walks, and when Charlie's house was finished Landon moved on to their places. He made seventy dollars that day, including the sawbuck from Dash. The money excited him, as did the forecast for more snow.

Freed from school, Kasey bounced between friends' houses, watching movies, sleeping over. She spent two nights at Izzy Huston's and the next day, when Dash came home from work, the girls were in her living room, slumped low on the sofa. Their silence felt like an echo, and Dash got the impression they'd stopped talking abruptly when they heard Dash coming inside. Izzy widened her eyes at Kasey and nudged Kasey's shoulder.

"Something you'd like to ask?" Dash said.

The girls' silence grew heavier. It was Izzy, not Kasey, who asked the question. "You see, the thing is, Mrs. Coenen, my parents are going out tonight, for New Year's. I'm supposed to go to my aunt's house, but my cousins are babies and everyone goes to bed super early. So, I was wondering."

Dash held up her hand. "Izzy, we'd be delighted to have you stay with us."

"Is Landon going to be home?" Kasey asked.

"Where else would he be?"

"It's more fun at Izzy's house. I wish we could go there again."

"Not by yourselves. Not without parents there."

"I don't know if I want to," Kasey said. "We stayed up late last night."

"I haven't stayed here in forever," Izzy said. She draped her arms around Kasey's shoulders and laid her head against Kasey's back. The sides of Izzy's hair had been braided into tight rows that flowed over her ear. Her ears glimmered with small gold studs. "Don't be a baby,"

"Don't be a lesbo," Kasey said, shaking her off.

"Lil' baby needs her sleepy," Izzy said.

"You're such a skank."

"Language," Dash said. "We talked about this."

"It's boring over here," Kasey said.

"Let's talk in the kitchen for a minute, okay?" Dash said.

Around the corner, Dash backed her daughter against the refrigerator. Her teenage angsty nonsense, her weird avoidance, the way she sat curled against the window in the back of the car—it had gone on long enough. There was no excuse for nastiness. "What's the matter with you?"

"Nothing."

"Then cool it, okay? Izzy's family let you stay there for two nights in a row. She can spend one night here."

"I don't want to."

"Because of your brother?"

Kasey shrugged. "Maybe."

She swallowed hard in an effort to keep her voice down. "Half our neighbors think he's some kind of monster. The county would just as soon take him away."

"Maybe they should," Kasey said. "Maybe somebody should lock him up."

A small wad of white gum rolled around the back of her teeth. The sight of it made Dash even more furious. "You don't mean that," Dash said.

"I don't know," Kasey said, rolling her eyes. "Maybe I do."

She squeezed Kasey's bicep hard enough to make her wince. "You have no idea what you're saying," she hissed. "None."

Kasey jerked her arm away. "Fine. Sorry."

"You think he doesn't sense how weird you've been with him? That he doesn't know? It wouldn't hurt for you to try to be nice every once in a while. You're still his sister."

Kasey looked past her. "Whatever."

They ordered pizza for dinner. Dash ate three slices and vowed to start eating better tomorrow. No more treats at the nurses' station, and she'd make time to use the staff gym at the hospital. Kasey and Izzy sat cross-legged on the carpet and argued over which movie to watch, *Sleepover* or *10 Things I Hate About You.* When they asked Dash to break the tie she picked *Sleepover* because it sounded nicer. Mike played *Hadean Eon* with Landon for an hour, then came upstairs and caught the end of the movie. He settled into the sofa and Dash slid her socked feet beneath his thigh. She could hear Landon through the furnace vents, his high-pitched squeal, "Pow! Pow! Pow!"

Izzy laughed. "Your brother is so loud." She said it like an insult. Dash studied the makeup on her cheeks—too much of it, she thought, and too soon. The outlines of both girls' bra straps were visible through their shirts, but Izzy deliberately pulled her collar to the side to expose one shoulder, the satin red stripe across her skin. She sat with her shoulder cocked, posing.

"He gets caught up in his games," Dash said. Izzy turned her ear toward Dash, her face in profile enough to see Izzy's right eye appraising her. Without a word, she turned back to the set.

She went to the kitchen and called down the basement stairs, "Landon, keep it down, okay? The girls are watching a movie."

At the end of the night, Dash collected the empty popcorn bowl and the glasses and carried them back to the kitchen. Mike slept sitting up in his chair, his mouth open. The girls lay on the carpet, Izzy's head on Kasey's stomach. "Okay, ladies," Dash said. "I think it's time to turn in."

"It's New Year's," Izzy said.

"Can we stay up to watch the ball drop?" Kasey asked.

It was only ten o'clock. "I don't think I can make it that long," Dash said.

"We'll go to the basement," Izzy said. Landon had already gone upstairs to bed.

Dash raised her index finger. "You'll turn off the light right after midnight. Got it?"

"Got it," the girls said in unison.

She unfolded the sleeper sofa in the basement and carried down a fresh set of sheets, extra blankets. She left the girls lying on their bellies, hugging pillows with their feet in the air. She kissed them both, Kasey's cheek and Izzy on the top of her hair. She felt sorry for scolding Kasey earlier that day and for not scolding her sooner. They'd needed to have it out for weeks, and it was too bad that the first shots had been fired while they had company. After Izzy went home, she'd sit Kasey down and clear the air. Start the new year off fresh. She left on the stove light so the girls could find their way to the bathroom, then eased open Landon's door to check on him before going to bed.

He slept on his side, his head close to the wall, his hair swirled around his ear. Dash could see the veins crosshatching his eyelids, the creases in his pursed lips. She backed out of the room. The last thing she did was flip on the door alarm. Everyone, even Landon, had been sleeping so much more soundly since he'd started on the Seroquel. Since he'd come home, they'd never heard the alarm go off. Not once.

Dash was still on her first cup of coffee when Izzy emerged from the basement and said she wanted to leave. She didn't want to wait for breakfast. She wanted to go now. Dash offered to drive her, but Izzy said she'd rather walk. She wore her jeans beneath her nightgown, the long hem of her nightshirt hanging past her knees. Her ratted hair hung in front of their eyes. The girls hadn't slept much. "Did you two fight?" she asked Kasey.

"Too much time together," Mike said. "Like candy at Halloween. You think you want it until you overdo it. Then it makes you sick."

"We didn't fight," Kasey said. "I don't feel well."

"Okay," Dash said. "Last day of Christmas break. You can rest if you want."

Mike and Landon watched bowl games. Dash stripped the foldout of its sheets, switched out the laundry, and got started on disassembling the Christmas tree. Starting tomorrow she had five twelves in a row, Wednesday through Sunday, and the kids would be back in school. By three that afternoon the tree stood bare in its stand, a wreath of dry needles skirting the base. Mike promised to take it to the curb after the game.

Dash stared up at the ceiling. "How long is she going to sleep?"

Mike shrugged. "She might as well."

The player on the field dropped the football. It bounced across the screen in slow motion. Landon peacocked his fingers and shouted, "Fumble! Fumble! Fumbalya!"

"That's enough now, bud," Mike said. "Your sister's sleeping."

"She should get up anyway," Dash said.

The phone rang that afternoon when the last band of golden light was streaking across the trees. "It took us all day to get it out of her," Ben Huston said. "We still don't have a clear picture."

"Izzy seemed upset when she left," Dash said, relieved to hear from him. "Kasey said they didn't argue, but she hasn't said anything more."

"Not between the girls," Ben said. "With Landon. Something happened with Landon."

"He was in his room all night," Dash said.

"It's what she's telling us," Ben said. "He scared Izzy pretty badly."

"We were both home," Dash said. "Mike and I slept in the next room."

"She's never lied to us before," Ben said.

What parent doesn't believe that? What teenager *doesn't* lie? Dash could easily imagine Izzy blaming Landon for some phantom offense.

"Karen wants to call the police. I thought I'd give you the heads-up."

Dash swallowed hard. "Have you called them? Have you called the cops?"

"She's calling now," Ben said.

Dash and Mike left Landon sitting on the couch and went upstairs. Dash knocked on her door and tried the handle, but Kasey had locked it. "Kasey, honey, can you open up, please?" she said. "Dad and I need to talk to you."

They heard movement, the muted thud of Kasey's feet hitting the floor, and when the door opened the room was nearly pitch-dark. The blinds were drawn and Kasey still wore last night's pajamas. The top had a picture of a donut with antlers and glittered lettering that said I DEER-LY LOVE DONUTS! The room smelled of old clothes. Dash flipped on the lights and Kasey crawled back beneath the blankets. "What happened last night?" Dash asked. She sat on the foot of the mattress. "Why did Izzy run off so fast this morning?"

Kasey shrugged. "Tired, I guess."

"Kase," Mike grumbled. "Mr. Huston called us. Izzy's mom wants to call the police."

Kasey's eyes drifted toward the wall and grew wide. "She's so hysterical," she said. "Nothing even happened to her."

"What did happen?" Dash asked, setting her hand on the mound of Kasey's feet.

Kasey moved her feet under the blankets, away from Dash's hand. "Landon's so gross."

"What'd he do?"

"We went upstairs to use the bathroom. He was in there, playing handy shandy."

"What?" Dash almost laughed at the rhyme.

"He was spanking the monkey, Mom. God."

"You and Izzy saw him doing that?" Mike asked.

"Pretty hard not to. He didn't have any pants on."

Dash turned to Mike. "How did he get out of his room?"

"He knows how to turn off the alarm," Kasey said. "You turn the battery around and it doesn't work. The lock, too. There's a little catch inside the hole that you can get with a paper clip. It's not even hard."

"Well, honey," Dash said. "He *was* in the bathroom. Maybe you should have knocked first."

"Jesus, Mom!" Kasey's hands shot into the air. "I can't believe you're defending him! He didn't have the door shut. We just came upstairs and there he was, burping the worm.

Then he got all embarrassed and chased us back down to the basement. He said he'd kill us if we told."

"He said that to you?" Mike asked. Deep lines appeared on his forehead.

"He didn't mean it," Dash said.

"How do I know what he meant?" Kasey said. "He looked like he meant it. He said it, like, a thousand times until I promised I wouldn't say anything. So now I've screwed up twice."

"You haven't screwed up, Kase," Mike said. "This isn't your fault."

"Izzy wanted to go home, but I begged her to stay. If she left, then Lan-dork would come back downstairs again. Or he'd come in my room."

"You have a lock on your door," Dash said.

Kasey threw back her comforter and leapt up. "God, Mom, wake up! The lock doesn't work. Nothing works. He can open it whenever he wants. He's just his big crazy gross self all the time. I told you I didn't want Izzy to spend the night. *I told you.*" She moved to the center of the room, beneath the stilled ceiling fan, the blades rimmed in powdery dust. "I hate him," she said.

"Don't say stuff like that," Dash said. "You don't mean it."

"I do mean it. I hate him. He freaks me out. I'm scared around him all the time."

Mike's eyes were wide. "He scares you, Kase?"

"He whacked Mom in the face and then tried to stab her in the neck." Kasey wiped her nose and looked hard at Dash. "He said he was going to kill you. If you took his money, he said he was going to kill you."

Mike whipped his head toward Dash. "He said that to you?"

"I heard him," Kasey said. "I was standing right there."

"Dash?"

"Yes," Dash said, weakly, almost mumbling.

Mike was pacing some now, a few steps to the left, then back to the right. "You never told me that. Why wouldn't you tell me something like that?"

"He was upset. He wasn't in his right mind."

"All our meetings with the doctor and therapists. His public defender, for Christ's sake. Never once did you mention him threatening to kill anyone."

"Take a breath," Dash said. "We need to stay calm."

"I've stayed calm for a long time," he said, his voice rising. He hooked his thumbs through his belt loops and twisted them around. "I've stayed pretty damn calm for the last months, haven't I? We've made a lot of excuses for him. But he knows better. By God, he *knows* better."

"He can't help it," Dash said.

"Sure he can!" Mike yelled. "We've never asked him to learn calculus or memorize the dictionary. We've only ever asked him not to hit, not to hurt. And what does he do? He punches you in the face and holds a knife to your throat. Now you tell me he said he was going to kill you?" He began to cry, then abruptly bit down on his lip. "And kill his sister?"

Mike stopped pacing and knelt down beside Kasey's bed. He propped his elbows on the mattress as if to say his prayers. His shoulders moved up and down. Her husband's anguish was harder to watch than her daughter's. "I'm sorry, Kasey," he said. "I'm sorry I let it go on this long."

"What choice did we have?" Dash asked, indignant. "We can't just send him away."

"Yes, we can," Mike said. He was still looking at the wall. "That's exactly what we should have done months ago, and what we ought to do now. Or Kasey and I can leave. We're not staying here another night, the way things are." His voice cracked and he turned to look at Dash, so there'd be no misunderstanding. "Either he goes or we do."

Kasey crossed the floor to stand beside her father, her hip tucking behind his shoulder. She laid her hand there. The carpet between Dash and her husband and daughter seemed as wide as an ocean. She'd dreaded this moment for years, for all of Landon's life, perhaps, knowing it would one day come—when she'd have to choose between her son and daughter, between Landon and everyone else she loved. She'd foreseen it, dismissed it, shut it down, fought like hell against it. She'd done everything she could to keep it from happening. It had come anyway. The moment had finally come.

"Don't go," she said, and put her face in her hands. "I'll call Camille."

17

The ambulance was waiting beneath the emergency room overhang when Brooke arrived. Her taxi pulled up close behind it and the cab's headlights beamed on the ambulance company's name, Gold Cross, in glittering metallic lettering across the back doors. Brooke could see the ambulance's glowing interior through its rear windows, the instrument panels and colored drawers along the walls. The engine was running and exhaust clouds curled up from its tailpipe.

The taxi driver wheezed while he waited for Brooke's credit card to go through. During the drive, he'd suffered a coughing fit so intense he'd had to take his foot off the accelerator, and the car had slowed to twenty miles per hour. His hair was combed in greasy rows down the back of his neck. He turned to pass Brooke her credit card and she saw the thickness of his glasses.

"Need a copy?" he asked. They were the first words he'd spoken to her.

"No, thank you." Brooke slung her duffel bag over her shoulder and shut the car door behind her. The wind smelled like lake brine and paper pulp; the temperature had climbed into the twenties ahead of a storm, the third since New Year's. The emergency department waiting room, visible to her through two walls of windows, was empty except for a hunched man in a barn jacket and a red stocking cap. He sat with his back to the windows. The sensors above the hospital entrance were too cold to detect her. Brooke had to wave her hands to prompt the doors to open.

Avoiding the hospital in the last weeks had become a project. Every morning she called the NICU to say she'd be in later. Once in the car, however, she discovered a new reason not to go. The Starlite Theater was showing all three *Lord of the Rings* movies, one after the other, and Brooke spent nearly nine hours in the same seat. The next day she returned and watched them again, in the same order. Another day she lost five hours reading *National Geographic* articles about Mars and Madagascar in a corner of the public library. A day or two later, she was in Sears when she saw Ingrid pushing Anna in a shopping cart. Brooke had only ever seen Ingrid's daughter in the hospital, but here she was sitting up, her hair in pigtails, eating raisins from a plastic baggie. Brooke fled down the aisle of socket wrenches and moved along the back wall until she reached the escalator. After that, she avoided most stores and instead began to drive: into the country to the west of Hanover, the fields white with snow, yellowed stalks poking up through the crust. The ice formed gelatinous skims on the kettle ponds before freezing solid and going under the snow. The days the clouds opened the sunlight was as hard as metal.

She liked the fabric enclosure of the car, the steady hot wind through the vents, the heat thickening around the tip of her nose. She brought food along, cans of tuna and hard-boiled eggs, which she cracked against the steering wheel and peeled with one hand. Harper had promised his news director he'd be as dependable as a Swiss train in the new year, Ollie was either in school or at his mom's, and Brooke had nothing to do but drive. As long as she called the NICU to check in and Harper came home to a plate of food in the microwave, no one questioned where she'd been.

She wondered how far she'd have to go before she went too far. Some days she made it as far as the Mississippi River before she turned around. She paid to have her oil changed and tires rotated at the How-Dea truck stop in Belgium, then spent the afternoon sitting in the car at Harrington Beach, watching Lake Michigan slam and burst against the ice, earlier waves frozen in their upwelling, ice dripping like candle wax over the tops of the crests. She sometimes thought of Emery, of Dash and Fran hovering over him, but if she let herself linger too long her thoughts slipped and she saw Dr. Fackelman easing the oxygen cannula from Opal's nostrils, peeling the Tegaderm from her skin. It was best to keep moving.

The third week of January, Jenny Ramirez called from the hospital. "The holidays," Brooke said by way of an explanation.

She waited for the lecture, for Jenny to tell her she'd failed as a mother and was no better than any of the trailer-trash moms who fled the unit every fifteen minutes to smoke. But Jenny said, "They're ready to schedule Emery's surgery."

"What surgery?"

"The PDA ligation. He'll need to go to Madison. The surgeon there gets very good results."

The very idea of a good result didn't make sense. Good results were no longer available. Brooke wondered what Jenny meant, but she didn't want to ask. She didn't want the answer, whatever it was. She said, "That's good."

"Dr. Kadlec is very capable," Jenny said. "He'll also evaluate Emery for a tracheostomy and a G-tube. There's a possibility all three procedures can happen while he's down there." Jenny paused and Brooke heard papers rustling. "We need your consent. You or your husband's."

"It's fine," Brooke said. "You have my consent."

"We can't do this over the phone, Brooke," Jenny said. At last, she betrayed a hint of annoyance, though only a hint. "You need to come in. There are papers to sign."

The transfer was scheduled for Tuesday evening. The surgery would happen on Thursday. Jenny had arranged a room in Madison in the Ronald McDonald House, the real one, and had talked the transport team into allowing Brooke to ride in the ambulance. All Brooke had to do, Jenny said, was show up on Tuesday night with a bag of spare clothes.

"Okay," Brooke said.

"You'll be there?" Jenny asked. "I can tell the team they'll see you on Tuesday night?"

"In the flesh," Brooke said, and hung up.

She'd been lying to her husband, but now Brooke told Harper the truth about the transfer to Madison, the surgeries, the arrangements Jenny had made on her behalf. Harper nodded without questioning the plan, and Brooke saw that her lying had only ever been a charade. He'd known all along that she hadn't been going to the hospital. They were both waiting for the inevitable end, the meteor's final impact. The fireball was already streaking across the sky. It was only a matter of time.

Harper offered to go with her.

"Surgery's not till Thursday," Brooke said. "Why miss two days of work to just sit around?"

"I can call out for Tuesday, at least. Take you to the hospital and see him off."

Brooke saw in his eyes that he did not want to do this. He had no desire to return to the place where they'd last held Opal, even if Emery was all they had left.

"Don't lose a night on the air," she said. "I can get there."

Harper nodded, as though all of this—broadcasting the news while an ambulance carried his son a hundred miles away so a stranger could sew closed a hole in his heart and open new holes in his throat and gut—were reasonable propositions. In a dimly lit corner of her subconscious, she understood he was as saddened as she was by what had befallen them. Her thoughts flashed on their first night above the BrewHaHa, Harper's stubbled chin against the belly of her T-shirt. *I get to keep you,* he'd told her. So blissfully unaware of the sacrifices that keeping would require: his career oxbowing in Hanover, the sins his ex-wife would forever hold over him, the family he and Brooke would try and try and try and fail to create. He was the only other person on the planet who'd lost what she'd lost, yet the shared nature of their losses made loss itself feel trivial—she felt she had no right to her sorrow and neither did he. Harper seemed to sense this, too. Emery was now a problem to solve. "We need to start making plans for how we're going to care for him in the long run," Harper said, softly. He pushed himself deeper into the sofa corner. "He's going to need to a lot, Brooke, and I'm not sure—" He paused to summon the courage. "Maybe he'd be better off in a place with a staff who can look after him. You shouldn't have to bear the burden on your own."

"On my own?"

"We," he said. "Us. You know what I mean. He's going to need a lot of help. I'm not sure we're up for it."

It was the truth. They weren't up for it. She wasn't up for it. She'd as much as proven it.

She let the hot water run over her hands at the NICU sink until the last grain of sand tumbled through the hourglass. More books had been added to the shelf, *Knuffle Bunny* and *Don't Let the Pigeon Drive the Bus!* Brooke recalled the frumpled dad in his flannel pj's who read to his baby every morning. Where was that baby now? The dad? Most likely home together on a winter night, the NICU already a fading memory. She balled up the paper towels and tossed them in the trash.

The transport team stood with their backs to her, two men and a woman in blue astronaut jumpsuits with reflective stripes down the arms and legs. The woman, the nurse, was older than the men. She wore her hair parted down the middle and looked a little like Sally Ride. Strangely enough, the patch on her breast said her name was Sally. She looked over Dash's shoulder at the computer, tapping the screen with her pen and writing on a clipboard. The younger of the two men had a blond crew cut and mustache. He fiddled with the settings on the Isolette until the monitor toned and the red light began to flash. Brooke couldn't see Emery, but she could hear the hiss of the ventilator. He was somewhere among them, alive.

"Oh good, you're here," Dr. Fackelman said. Brooke strained to detect in the doctor's face, as she had in Jenny's voice on the phone, some hint of reproach, of judgment or scorn, but she could not. Which only made it worse. The doctor touched the elbow of the man she'd been talking to. "The baby's mother is here."

The man introduced himself as Dr. Kothari. He explained that he was a fellow in pediatric surgery. He'd be overseeing the transport to Madison, where Dr. Arjun Kadec would perform the procedures. Behind him stood the transport incubator, a box attached to a yellow accordion base, the monitors strapped on top and the oxygen canisters slotted horizontally beneath the stretcher board. The doctor shuffled sideways and there was Emery, stripped to his diaper and lying in a nest of wires, the artery of the ventilator tube snaking through the porthole window. He'd lived his whole life in a box and now he was in another. He gripped the respirator valve in his small hand.

"We're letting him settle in for a few minutes," Dr. Kothari said.

The doctor moved farther aside so Brooke could get closer. It would be wrong to stay back, so she leaned in for a better look. Emery's eyes were open and calm, though given the damage to his retinas caused by the steroids and prolonged oxygen use, it was unclear how much he could see. Even less certain was whether he recognized her. Brooke tried to register what she felt, to note and file in her memory her emotions not only of what she saw but of what she thought, the places her mind went. She set her hand atop the Isolette and leaned down until her face was close enough to fog the Plexiglas. She opened the porthole door in the side, and Emery's smell wafted out: a new diaper, semi-liquefied plastic, his little body—as individual as a fingerprint and knowable only to those who lived close to it. His atmosphere misted over her. She breathed his humidified air. She whispered Emery's name as she extended her hand to touch his downy fine hair. She wished she could make herself cry, but she found her heart was empty, the organ in her chest only a container from which all feeling had leeched away. The acknowledgement of it, that what she'd suspected of herself in November was still true in January, fell through her like a stone. To her relief, it made her well up. At least she didn't look as cold as she felt. The tears, though, were phantom pains, the echo of a lost capacity, and they didn't last.

"We'll take good care of him," Dr. Kothari said, his hand on her shoulder. "I understand you'll be riding along with us."

"If that's okay," Brooke said, and caught Dash's eye. The nurse frowned and stared hard at her. At least Dash had the decency to disapprove. Brooke waited for the nurse to tell her she had no right to accompany Emery anywhere and was disappointed when Dash turned back to the computer and clicked through the screens. After several minutes had passed, Dash whispered something, and Sally whipped her head around to look at Brooke, her expression haunted.

"We're glad to have you along," Dr. Kothari said. He turned to Nurse Sally. "Let's bump O_2 to sixty and give him a touch of Versed to make sure he's comfortable."

Sally drew a syringe and fed it into Emery's central line. Emery's eyelids drooped, blinked open, and settled heavily. Sally handed Brooke a folder with the forms she needed to sign: consents for admission and the surgeries, for emergency procedures en route, a do-not-resuscitate order if she wanted. Brooke's pen hovered over the pages. Wasn't his entire existence a resuscitation? Wasn't Emery kept alive, every second, by the air being forced into his lungs? She signed the consent forms, shuffling the DNR to the back of the pile.

The shelf behind Emery's bed had been cleared of the stuffed animals and Polaroids. Once Emery was wheeled through the doors, his bed would be taken away, and all evidence of him—like Opal, like Ruby and Pearl, like Brooke herself—would be gone. Emery had only ever lived here, in this one room, and even here incompletely.

Sally looked at her watch and moved to the nurses' station to use the phone. She stood while she talked, pacing back and forth and reading numbers from the sheet in her hand. "ETA is two hours," she said. "We'll call at ten minutes out. Yes. Yes. Very good. Have a nice evening." She set the receiver back in the cradle. "We're good to go."

"Well then," Dr. Kothari said.

The crew cut kicked the brakes free, and Sally stepped around the other side to help push the incubator while the doctor followed behind. “Bye-bye, Emery,” Ting said, coming to the front of the unit to stand with Dash and Dr. Fackelman. “Bye-bye, sweet thing.”

Dash kissed her fingertips and pressed them to the side of the box. “Don’t give them any trouble,” she said. “You gave us plenty, so just be good now, okay?” She looked up at Brooke. “Wait,” she said, and jogged back to the bed space. She came back with the plastic laundry sack filled with Emery’s things. “Don’t forget this stuff.”

Dash again looked hard at her, her bottom lip between her teeth. Her face shifted from stern to pity, and she opened her arms. “Take care of yourself, Brooke,” Dash said. Her grip was tighter than Brooke expected. Her nose touched Dash’s hair. “Take good care.”

The snow had turned heavier and was falling faster. It stung her cheeks and nose when Brooke stepped into the night. The ambulance chugged in the dark. Sally swung open the bay door, climbed up, and turned to receive the incubator. The medic pushed the incubator forward until its base collapsed and the entire thing slid inside the ambulance like a drawer. The medic secured the safety harnesses while the nurse plugged the incubator into the outlet on the panel.

Brooke recalled the only other time she’d ridden inside an ambulance, that January afternoon when she’d waited in the winter sunlight with her stillborn daughter wrapped inside a blanket. It felt like another life, though it had only been a year. The ambulance then, as now, had had the same colored supply drawers, the wall of electrical outlets. She remembered the paramedic she gave her daughter to, the rubber bracelets on his wrist, the firm ball of his belly like a small pregnancy. He was Chinese, and Brooke had wondered briefly if he could see her father's face in hers, the faint shadow of a phenotype she'd never felt she could claim as her own. The medic rode with the baby in his arms while a second EMT took Brooke's blood pressure and gave her an electrolyte drink. At one point, the first medic lifted the bundle containing her daughter and offered it to her to hold, but Brooke didn't move. She kept her hands folded in her lap. He sat back against the vinyl seat and stared at her in a way that told Brooke he saw her for what she was. He knew every horrible thing she'd ever done.

Her zipper froze to her bare fingers. She scrambled her hands down inside her gloves. The nurse and medic sat down on opposite sides of the incubator and slid their arms inside the shoulder harnesses. Dr. Kothari hoisted himself up and turned to offer Brooke his hand.

"Actually, I just talked to my husband," Brooke said, taking a small step back. "He wants to drive down with me. I'll wait for him, if that's okay."

"Of course," the doctor said. His relief was plain; the ride would be easier without her. He reached out to grip the door handle. "It'll take us a little while to get him settled, so there's no need to rush. Arriving in the morning is as good as coming tonight. Your son's in good hands."

"Maybe tomorrow will be better," Brooke said.

Dr. Kothari pulled the doors closed. Brooke watched his head through the glowing rear window as he wrestled his arms into the harness and buckled it across his chest. The ambulance rolled forward, the exhaust from the tailpipe dissipating in the cold air. It braked at the stoplight, its signal blinking, before rounding the corner.

Brooke watched the traffic light change from green to yellow to red. The door to Seoul Food, across the street, swung open and a white rectangle flashed in the center of the unlit wall. Two people emerged, silhouetted in the bright doorway, and when the door fell closed behind them, snuffing out the light, the world froze in place and was still. The stoplight held at red. No cars moved along the street. The snow stopped falling. The cars in the parking lot were crusted with pixelated ice and salt that sparkled beneath the lamps. The old man in the red stocking cap hadn't moved inside the ER; he sat in the same chair, as still as a mannequin. In the blackness beyond the overhang, she saw a tiny orange glow and could smell tobacco burning. She moved toward the small fire. The outline of his body was only just visible in the ambient glow from the building. Brooke recognized his shape before she saw his face.

"Hey," Justus said.

"Can I have one of those?"

He shook a cigarette from the pack and kissed the tip to the burning end of the one he was smoking. She took it and inhaled, holding it in, resisting the urge to cough. She'd never smoked more than the occasional cigarette at parties in college, after she'd had too much to drink and wanted to show her friends she wasn't the goody-two-shoes everyone thought she was. To break a rule no one cared about in the first place.

"That was your kid?" Justus asked.

"He's going to Madison to have his PDA ligated."

"The hole in his heart."

"That's right."

"The indomethacin didn't close it up?"

"His kidneys were too weak for it." She let the smoke stream from her mouth and again fought the urge to cough. "How do you know about that?"

"I know things," he said. "I'm not stupid."

"I didn't think you were." His cigarette brightened as he drew on it. The snow creaked under his feet. "What are you doing here?"

"Cannon was readmitted. Failure to thrive or some shit. This is as close as they'll let me get."

"Oh."

"Funny, isn't it, how I'm the one to get bounced from this place? Shantel takes the baby home to Mommy and Daddy and ends up back here. She doesn't know what the fuck she's doing. Or she's too wasted to care. I hope the social worker takes him away, just to prove the point." He sounded neither angry nor sad. He flicked his cigarette butt onto the ground, where it burned a hole in the snow. "When's Daddy Warbucks getting here?"

"I made that up. I didn't want to go in the ambulance."

He laughed, and his breath clouded his face. "You need a ride somewhere?"

"Are you offering?"

"Depends on where we're going."

"Anywhere that's not here." The thought of following the ambulance made her nauseous, as did arriving at another hospital, another place where people knew of her failures. How she'd fought for Emery's life when the compassionate thing would have been to let him go, and how, once he was all she had left, she'd abandoned him. She didn't need Dash to tell her she had no right to accompany Emery; she knew it well enough on her own. All that remained was the final disappearance. She wanted to close her eyes and open them somewhere else.

"Then yeah, sure," Justus said. "I'm offering."

Part Four

18

Dash sought comfort wherever she could find it. In her morning coffee, in the hushed rhythm of the unit, in Camille Martin's voice on the phone each afternoon. Landon had been placed in a treatment foster home on the north side of the lake, close to Papasay, with a family trained in caring for kids with special behavioral needs. In their one-car garage, fragrant of rubber and gasoline, Dash watched Mike lean beneath the propped hood of her old Chrysler Concorde. His belly rested against the car's quarter panel, the outline of his wallet a faded rectangle in his back pocket. Her windshield wipers had crapped out and Mike was checking the fuses. He'd kept the car running long past the point it should have gone to the scrapyard, replacing the brakes and rotors, the timing chain, the gasket head, flushing the coolant. Repairs that would have cost them thousands in the shop. It had been a long time since she'd seen him work on the car and the sight of it soothed her. At least one thing was where it ought to have been.

Mike held a pronged fuse in the beam of his flashlight. He turned it, blew into it, and slid it into place. "Try it now."

Kasey twisted the wand on the steering column. "Not yet."

Mike wiggled the fuse in its housing. "One more time, please."

The wiper blades swept across the windshield, squeaking against the glass. "It worked, Dad!"

"Eureka," Mike said. He lowered the hood, holding it in his fingertips before letting it fall the last inch. He wiped his hands on a rag. "We're off."

"Like a prom dress," Kasey said. She dropped into the passenger seat. Mike sat down behind the wheel and Dash climbed in back. Dash and Mike's family therapist had encouraged them to change up the family dynamic, to break down whenever possible the adults-versus-kids binary so that Kasey might feel more comfortable opening up. Dash was perfectly happy to let Mike drive her car and to let Kasey ride up front. She didn't mind the back seat. She could stretch out her legs and close her eyes.

To distract them from their problems, Mike had scored a last-minute deal to the Amazon Rain Forest Resort in Wisconsin Dells, an hour and a half southwest of Hanover. Money was tighter than ever—Kasey was seeing a counselor now, and they had to pay child support for Landon's foster care—but Mike said they could do for a break. Missing a few days of school wouldn't hurt. Their $99 midweek rate included a night in the hotel, a pizza and a pitcher at Antonio's, and two days' admission to the indoor water park.

Mike bypassed the interstate, opting instead for Highway 23 through Princeton and Montello, then the two-lane roads across the farmlands where red barns and navy silos rose, island-like, out of the wide plains of untrampled snow. The sky was low, white on white with a streak of blue against the horizon, like a long crack in the sky. Dash was glad to be away from the larger highway and its chains of billboards for adult novelty shops and gentlemen's clubs, signs she now took personally.

The power lines disappeared and the Amish farms they passed looked all the more remote among the drifts and bare trees. Driveways sat unplowed, chimneys puffed thick clouds of smoke, utterly absent of electricity, of computers or video players or door alarms. Dash felt like she was playing hooky, shirking her responsibilities. She hadn't told Camille they were going out of town and she nervously palmed her cell. They overtook a buggy pulled by a single horse, a triangular orange reflector affixed to the back, half covered with muddy snow. Dash tried to see the people inside, but the buggy was enclosed and the windows frosted.

"Freakazoids," Kasey said. She rode with her pink socks on the dashboard.

"Just different is all," Mike said.

"What is there to do without electricity?" Kasey said. "I'd be bored out of my skull. I'd literally cry all day. *Literally.* I'd wake up in the morning and be like, 'Oh great, I'm still Amish. Guess I'll churn some butter. Waah waah.' "

"Those folks build some awfully sturdy furniture," Mike said. "Quality stuff."

"When they're not humping their cousins."

Dash winced but kept her mouth shut. The therapist had told her not to correct Kasey, not to give her any reason to clam up. There was a chance that Kasey had been trying to get Dash and Mike's attention for some time but hadn't known how. The therapist also said not to freak out if Kasey dyed her hair or started going heavy on the makeup. If she asked to pierce her belly button, maybe they should consider it. Trying to shock them wasn't the worst thing. If she started losing weight, that's when they needed to worry. Dash leaned forward, between the two headrests. "How's it going with Deborah?" she asked. "That's how you say her name, right? Deborah?"

"She pronounces it De-*bor*-ah," Kasey said. "'Cause she's de-*boring*. She sits and stares at me for, like, ever. Or she tries to get me to play cards."

"Do you play?" Dash asked.

"She lets me win. It's so lame. I could beat her anyway."

"Maybe she's not letting you win. Maybe you're really winning."

"Does it help, talking to her?" Mike asked. He leaned his elbow on the rest and steered with his wrist hinged over wheel.

Kasey shrugged. "Not really. She keeps trying to tell me it's not my fault that Landon ruined my life. Like now I'll never date a nice guy and I'll have huge daddy issues, except in my case they're brother issues, and one day I'll probably turn into a crackhead. I mean, come on, sister. It's not like I've never seen someone wax the dolphin before."

"You have?" Dash asked, alarmed. Mike looked over at Kasey, too.

"Well, no," Kasey said. She leaned her back against the door handle. "But we talked about it in health class. Ms. Zeman said, like, 80 percent of all boys do it."

"Not in front of their sisters," Mike said. His teeth clenched.

"What about Izzy?" Dash asked. "Has she said anything?"

"She's, you know, not supposed to talk to me, but she does sometimes. Just not about *that*. Maybe she'll end up a crackhead."

"That was me when I was a kid," Mike said. "A crackhead."

"You smoked crack, Dad?" Kasey said. She pulled her feet from the dashboard and crossed them beneath her. "Really?"

"Oh, you did not," Dash said.

"Who said anything about smoking?" Mike said. "I took a nasty spill on my ten-speed and hit my head on a parking block. Cracked my noggin wide open." He set his Cabela's cap on the dashboard and reached across the seat for Kasey's hand. He guided it to the side of his head, above his right ear. "Here. Feel it?"

“Freaky,” Kasey said, feeling the scar. “Did your brains spill out? Were you like, ‘Oh perfect, there goes four years of Spanish class’?”

“I coulda been a contenda!” Mike said.

Dash knew that scar. She’d felt it in the dark for more than twenty years. She knew it as well as she knew the mole between his shoulders, the birthmark on the back of his left knee. Kasey’s finger on the scar was a reminder that Dash’s daughter had always been Mike’s child. That had always been their unspoken deal. She took care of Landon and Mike looked after Kasey. No one got left behind that way, every need was met. Now Landon was gone and she was alone in the back seat.

They came out of the flatlands and into the valley of the Wisconsin River, pine trees on both sides of the road and honey-colored sandstone towers along the river. Dash hadn’t been here in years and the place didn’t look much changed. Coming into town they passed signs for Dells Boat Tours and Original Wisconsin Ducks, then the Chalet shopping center that sold T-shirts and saltwater taffy. On summer evenings, the Dells were as gaudy and luminous as Las Vegas. In winter, the streets were empty. The wooden roller coaster at Mount Olympus looked like a heap of sticks. Antonio’s, their dinner destination, sat beneath a tattered awning sagging with ice. Dash hoped the food was better than the ambience.

Twin bronze jaguars, each with a paw raised, marked the front entrance of the Amazon Rain Forest Resort, a sprawling complex of buildings with faux-thatch roofs that were supposed to look like jungle huts. Mike circled a plowed mound of snow large enough to ski down and parked near the front. Dash wondered how Mike would react if she spent the afternoon in the room while he and Kasey went to the water park. She'd been picking up double shifts the last several weeks to help get Emery ready for transport to Madison, and to fend off missing her boy. Alone with Emery after midnight, the unit empty of parents and the other Isolettes covered with blankets, it often felt that they were the only two people awake in the hospital. They had only each other. Now that Emery was gone she wanted to watch TV in bed, call Camille, and soak in her brooding thoughts.

The hotel was only half full, so the desk attendant upgraded them to a two-bedroom condo with a full kitchen, a Jacuzzi, and fireplaces in both the sitting room and master bedroom. The king bed looked like a floating dock. Mike flopped back on it while Dash unpacked their bathing suits. "Talk about room to spread out," Mike said. He made a snow angel on the comforter.

"You won't even know I'm here," Dash said. She draped her jeans over the arm of the chair

"Maybe you will," Mike said. "Maybe I'll sneak on over."

"Oh yeah?" She stepped closer to him, in her sweatshirt and underwear. She ran her hand through his hair until her finger found his crackhead scar. It was still hers, despite everything. Mike reached around her waist and patted her rear end. "A fire later could be nice."

"Hey, Mom?" Kasey said, behind her. "Oh, geez. Gross."

She stood in the doorway in her bathing suit, a towel wrapped around her waist and her phone in her hand. Dash pulled her jeans from the chair and draped them in front of her legs.

"Could you guys at least wait until I'm, you know, like asleep?"

"What's up, Kase?" Mike asked.

"Did you hear about the kidnapping at my school?"

"What?" Dash said. Her stomach dropped. She stared at the phone in her daughter's hand. There was no safe place left in the world. Not one place. "When did this happen?"

Kasey's mouth curled. "Don't worry, he woke up."

Mike slapped the mattress. "Nice one."

Dash didn't get it until she repeated the joke out loud. "So that didn't really happen?"

"Too soon?" Kasey asked.

"Seriously," Dash said. Her stomach still hadn't calmed down. "Did you need something?"

"Yeah," she said. "Hurry up. I'm ready to go."

The carpeted hallways led through a tunnel that crossed beneath the parking lot. Dash could smell the chlorine and hear the rush of the water, as though they were moving toward something dangerous. It was late January and they were in bathing suits; it didn't feel right. She expected to find the water park deserted, but when they followed the ramp back up to ground level she saw a line of yellow school buses parked out back. The sign at the reception desk said WELCOME TO THE RAIN FOREST, and a wall of floor-to-ceiling windows looked into a room the size of an airplane hangar: towering slides painted to look like trees, plastic vines suspended from the ceiling, snaking lines of kids and teens, their hairless shoulders and backs shiny and wet.

Through the locker room they stepped into the warm damp air, the thin winter sun concentrated by the glass panels in the ceiling. Birds and monkeys squawked from the speakers. Dash began to sweat in her terry coverup. Kasey yanked her T-shirt over her head and kicked her shorts onto a plastic chaise lounge. "Let's go, Dad," she said, waving. Kasey bounced on her toes as Mike peeled off his shirt and seemed indifferent about whether Dash would come along.

Her earlier idea about staying back hadn't been far off. She wouldn't have been missed.

She followed her daughter and husband to the Piranha Plunge, Kasey charging up each flight of wet stairs and then waiting impatiently for her and Mike to catch up. At the top, they had their choice of three tunnels and Kasey made them each stand in separate lines so they could race. When it was her turn, Dash sat in the water and waited for the lifeguard to wave her on. She crossed her arms across her chest, the way the diagram instructed, but still felt the water driving her swimsuit up her rear and water spraying her face. She slid up one wall of the slide, then the other, water shooting up her nose and into her mouth until at last the bottom disappeared and she dropped, blind, into a tank of churning water. Her feet went above her head and her arms twisted before her face. She couldn't find the surface or the bottom. She fought the urge to gasp. Someone took hold of her arm and pulled her up. Her feet hit the bottom and she pushed the hair away from her eyes.

"Exit to the left, please," the lifeguard said. She was hardly older than Kasey, a red float under her arm. The water was only up to her thighs.

"Took a little spin in the Maytag there," Mike said. He stood with his hands on his hips, his trunks high on his waist, like a boxer.

"I think I'm better off in the lazy river," Dash said, wiping her face again.

"It's not that bad," Mike said.

"Stay with Kasey," she said. "I'll go again in a minute."

"Take a load off," Mike said. "Relax a while. We're supposed to be having fun."

Mike headed back up the stairs and Dash followed the footpath toward the wave pool. An artificial beach sloped into the water, the textured concrete the color of sand. A pair of young women in sunglasses sat at the edge of the water with their ankles crossed and their weight on their wrists. Between them, a toddler in a sunhat splashed in the rippling waves that crashed against her legs. Beyond the windows she could see the snow-covered pines at the back of the parking lot, the line of school buses dulled by salt and silt. Temperatures were in the single digits. Yet close one eye and the women and the baby could have been on a real beach. She'd only been to an indoor water park one other time, nearly ten years ago. Landon hadn't liked the noise of the room, the music clanging over the rushing water, and when Dash had tried to hold him in her lap down one of the slides, he'd screamed so furiously she'd had to take him out. She'd spent the rest of the day sitting in the lobby while Landon played video games in the arcade and Mike stayed with Kasey.

Dash stepped down the beach until the water crested her ankles. She wiggled her toes in the water. She couldn't remember feeling so warm, and the unexpectedness of the pleasure only intensified it. She backed away when a horn sounded and the waves began to roll. The women with the baby didn't move.

She noticed people drinking beer and frozen drinks that looked like margaritas. On the other side of the wave pool, she found the bar, a four-sided thatched hut decorated with paper lanterns where a line of shirtless men stared blankly at the basketball game on the flat screen. She pictured Landon watching *The Golden Lance* on the living room carpet and tried not to feel sad. She gave the bartender her room number and asked for a Bloody Mary. It came with a bottle of High Life on the side—not a pony bottle like in most taverns, but a full twelve-ouncer. She carried the drinks to the hot tub, built into a rock grotto with warm water cascading down the face. A tattooed couple sat beneath the waterfall with their tongues in each other's mouths, a scene out of some trailer-park version of *Fantasy Island*. Dash eased her way into the water and turned her back to the couple. The ice melted and beaded on the side of her cup. She sucked on the olive and watched the river flow past, growing drowsy in the somnambulant heat. She rested her head against the coping and let her thoughts drift back to Landon. He was four, the day he spoke for the first time; Dash was pregnant with Kasey, and for months she'd been trying to coax him to say one word. A single word would have vaulted him over the wall between silence and speech; a single word would have proven that language dwelled somewhere inside him.

When the word came, they were in the car. It was late summer, the lawns gone brown from lack of rain. Flowers wilted in their pots. She turned a corner and heard him in the back seat. "Wata."

She pulled over and rammed the car into park. She turned to face him in the back seat. Landon pressed his finger to the window. "Wata." Everything was dry, the gutters along the curb caked with cracked mud. Landon pulled his finger from the window, leaving behind a cataract smear on the glass. Through the smudge, a block away, she saw it: a man holding a garden hose over a bed of flowers. The water flowing from the hose arced, suspended, between the nozzle and the ground and the afternoon sun shone through it. She said it the way Landon had: *wata, wata*. It sounded like a conjuring spell. Naming the water had caused it to appear.

Other words followed in time, each with the same singular obsessiveness. *Milk. Robot. Pop.* Landon repeated each one for weeks, that one word and no other, until it began to sound prophetic, a word a monk might utter after years of contemplation. Dash sometimes imagined him that way, draped in a brown robe, diving in an unfathomable well of mystery. She wondered what he was doing right now. She and Mike were going to visit him on Sunday. She didn't know how she'd wait.

"Mom!" Kasey called. "Mom!"

She opened her eyes. Mike and Kasey were floating toward her on the lazy river on blue plastic inner tubes. Dash sat up and waved.

Mike grabbed the ladder rail and hauled himself and Kasey to the side. "We wondered where you'd got off to," he said.

"This place is amazing." She was feeling better than she expected.

"They did a nice job with it," Mike said, climbing out of the river.

"Mom," Kasey said. "That big slide right behind us, do you see it? It's called the Anaconda. You go in a double tube with a partner. The first part drops into this big swirly bowl. You go around and around a few times and then the tunnel at the bottom dumps you right out at the bottom. Like, who cares, right? But if you can steer your tube up the bowl there's another tunnel. It's that big green pipe that goes outside the building. Like through the snow and everything. Dad and I tried like a hundred times to get it."

"I'm too fat," Mike said. He cradled his wet belly in his hands.

"You are not," Dash said. She lifted her hand from the water. "You want my beer? The Bloody Mary is enough for me."

"Beautiful," he said. He sat down and submerged his feet and calves in the hot tub. Tilted the bottle back. "Beautiful."

A school group floated past them, maybe twenty boys and girls close to Kasey's age, linked by ankle and elbow into an amoebic mass. Several of the girls wore bikinis, their breasts hidden by either bands or triangles of Lycra; they kept leaning backward over the tubes to dip their hair in the water, their bellies pointed at the ceiling. One boy, his thin chest spritzed with acne, rode his tube on his hands and knees. He looked at Kasey and sprang to his feet, his arches curved around the top of the tube. For a moment he managed to hold his balance, his arms thrust out like a surfer, before another boy kicked the underside of his float and he tumbled sideways into the water.

"I'm going again," Kasey said. She shoved away from the wall and floated downstream, seconds behind the group, her arms and legs draped over the sides.

"Is she having fun?" Dash asked.

"She's distracted," Mike said.

"Is that the same thing?"

"It'll do for now." He sipped again from his beer.

"That joke she told upstairs. I about threw up."

"She wasn't trying to be hurtful," Mike said. "Things have been pretty tense lately, especially between the two of you. She won't say so directly, but I think she's feeling guilty."

"I don't blame her," Dash said. "For Landon going away."

"I'm not sure she knows that."

"I can't stop thinking about him," Dash said. "What it's like where he is."

"We'll know soon," Mike said, frowning, disappointed she'd changed the subject.

"You'll be okay? Seeing him?"

"I'll be fine," Mike said. "I miss him, too."

"Do you regret making him go?"

"I don't know yet. Only been a few weeks. I don't mind not having to lock my bedroom door when I go to bed, though. Or hide all my tools in the gun safe. Everyone feeling scared to death all the time."

"I didn't feel scared till last year," Dash said. It was another truth she'd only recently been able to admit: she'd been scared of her own son. A bolt in her spine had torqued whenever he came into the room.

"A year is long enough," Mike said. "Something had to give."

"Would you have really left on New Year's? Would you have really done it?"

Mike set his bottle on the side of the hot tub. He eased himself down into the water, his chest and shoulders going under until his face was next to hers. "Yes, Dash. I would have. I didn't want to, but I'd have gone. You and I feeling scared is one thing, all the trouble we've faced. But Kasey—" He splashed his face and ran his hands backward across his head. "She deserves better."

They heard the school group coming around again. They emerged beneath the bridge spanning the lazy river and Dash saw that Kasey had joined the flotilla. She had her feet hooked under the tube of the boy who'd tried to stand up on his float. The kids up front paddled toward the exit, letting their tubes continue on without them as they climbed out of the water and headed toward the Anaconda. Dash watched Kasey move along the footpath and up the stairs, inside the crowd like a herring inside a shoal. The boy following behind her kept pulling at his shorts. Dash's eyes watered in the chlorinated air. Despite the thousand ways Dash told herself, and Mike, that Landon's troubles weren't Kasey's fault, in the secret, shadowy corner of her heart where she hid her worst truths, she knew she blamed her daughter—not for her sassy teenage mouth or her sassy teenage friends or even for catching Landon in the act of touching himself. But much, much worse: simply for being. She swallowed the dregs of her Bloody Mary, the swirl of pepper and hot sauce. It burned her throat all the way down.

Kasey and the boy disappeared at the top of the stairwell. Mike pointed to the pool where the Anaconda finished and told her that the purple tunnel in the center was the easy one; the green tunnel to the right was the hard one. Every thirty seconds a pair of kids shot out of one tunnel or the other, their tandem inner tube skimming across the water.

Dash heard a high-pitched shriek echo through the tunnels. She knew it was Kasey. A mother knows her child's scream. She'd heard Kasey wailing from down the hall the day she was born, amazed and relieved that it was her baby—full-term and healthy, a perfect ten on the Apgar—crying in the well-baby nursey. She watched the water tumbling from the ends of the colored tunnels and tried to guess which one Kasey was in. The water in the green tunnel slowed to a trickle and then, with a sudden gush, they came rocketing out. Kasey up front and the boy behind her, his feet under her armpits. Kasey's hair was plastered to her face and her mouth was open. She was kicking her feet and squealing happily, like a girl. Which was exactly what she was.

19

Brooke came to in the flattened half-light aware that she wasn't alone. The horseshoed coils of a space heater glowed in the corner and the wind whistled through a window seam. The room quaked as though the house were set atop an enormous underground turbine. A shadow fell across her and the darkness grew thicker, closer. She tried to will it away by pulling the quilt over her ear and burrowing deeper into the couch. The quilt was stale with cigarette smoke and the end of her nose grew moist from her breath. The silence in the room was a weight on her shoulder. Brooke lifted her head and saw a girl at the end of the couch. She floated, legless, above the black void of the carpet. Brooke recognized her in an instant. Her own daughter. Not Opal or Pearl or any one of the children she'd carried and lost, but all of them at once, a decade's worth of heartbeats and brainwaves condensing into a human figure.

She lay still, not wanting to scare her off.

"What are you doing here?" the girl asked. Her voice was small and high, a sound from far away. The dark muffled and absorbed it.

"I left your brother," Brooke said.

"You know my brother?"

"I stayed with him for a long time," Brooke said. "I stayed with him until I lost you. I tried my best." Her daughter moved closer. Brooke could see the outlined pout of her lips, the slope of her ears, the tinseled glow in the flyaway strands around the crown of her head. This girl, this daughter brought forth from the netherworld, seemed more real to her than Emery. It did not seem that Emery existed, that he'd ever existed, that he'd ever been anything more than a dream. All of her life—her life with Harper and Oliver, her house and job—it all felt unreal, a long unspooling vision from which she was groggily starting to emerge. Where was Emery now? Where were Harper and Ollie? They were nowhere. So was she.

"Who are you?" the girl asked. "What's your name?"

"Mom," Brooke said. She reached out her hand. She wanted to smell her daughter's scalp. "I'm your mom."

"You're not my mom," the girl said. "You're no one I've seen before."

The girl retreated across the floor and faded into the darkness beyond the couch, away from the whistling wind. "Wait," Brooke whispered, but she was already gone.

When she woke again dawn had broken and she could see the room where she'd slept. A water stain spread across the ceiling and the carpet beside the sofa was pocked with burns. A tangle of wires spilled from the television perched on plastic milk crates beside a DVD player and an Xbox. Justus sat at a table in the corner, tapping his ashes into a longneck bottle. He wore a gray hooded sweatshirt several sizes too large. The extra material around his neck and slim shoulders made his head appear smaller, his face more boyish, despite the scruff on his cheeks and jaw. He watched her with a strange expression, trying to gauge something in her, what she remembered or what he might expect from her. She tried to remember the previous night, her journey to this place. She could recall finishing her cigarette before following Justus across the hospital parking lot, but not much else. She lifted the blanket and looked down and was relieved to find she was still wearing her jeans.

A white coffee maker and black microwave oven sat atop the table beside a desktop printer. Two large sheets of plywood, covered in plastic, had been nailed tight to the wall behind him, wide enough to cover the doorway to whatever room lay beyond it.

Justus raised his coffee mug. "Want some? I have some sugar, but I'm fresh out of cream."

"Black is fine," Brooke said.

Justus tipped the carafe into the mug and carried it to her. "It's not that French press stuff, but it's hot."

Brooke sat up to accept it. She could smell the musk of the couch on her clothes and hair. "I didn't plan on doing this," she said.

"That's the way most things happen." He smiled and Brooke saw that one of his canines was missing, something she'd never noticed before. It struck her that these subtle changes, our teeth and hair and what we did with them, could make a good person look like a bad one, and the other way around. And yet she felt she'd known Justus for years, as though they'd been children at the same time and had been reunited after a long separation.

Justus circled the table and tugged at the plastic covering the plywood. The wood had been secured by a line of nails around the perimeter, the flattened heads white against the yellow wood.

"What happened there?" Brooke asked.

"Little science experiment," he said, grinning again. "Stove caught fire. Nothing to be done about it till the snow melts some."

The coffee was too strong and bitter; it clung to the roof of her mouth. She needed to pee. She asked Justus if she could use the bathroom and he led her down the hallway, past the closed doors to the rooms she'd hadn't yet seen. Justus pushed open the door at the end of the hallway and reached across her to flick on the light. Brooke caught a whiff of his hair and the ripeness of his T-shirt and felt in her spine the sounds he and Shantel had made in the Hibbert House, his fists against the NICU windows. She braced, half expecting him to shove her inside the bathroom and shut the door. The light, when it came on, revealed only an ordinary bathroom: a toilet, a sink atop a wooden cabinet, a bathtub rim crowded with bottles of Suave and baby shampoo, grimy circles in the sink basin. The faucet was running, a slow but deliberate stream. "Don't shut that off," Justus said. "Pipes'll freeze."

She locked the door before she unbuttoned her jeans. The toilet seat was freezing, and the chill traveled up her thighs. When she turned to flush, her lower back touched the toilet lid and the cold made her gasp. She opened the tap until the water warmed and then washed her hands and face, ran her wet hands through her hair, washed her hands again. She cupped her hands and scooped water into her mouth, swished and spat, then submerged her face. In the mirror she told herself she was a fool. She didn't need to be afraid. Justus didn't need to trap her anywhere. She'd come willingly, on her own.

In the living room, a quartet of colored animals bounced across the TV screen. Brooke recognized the show first, *The Backyardigans,* one of Oliver's favorites when he was little. Then she saw the little girl sitting cross-legged on the floor, staring at the TV with her mouth open. My daughter, Brooke thought. But quickly she understood the girl wasn't hers. She was nobody's mother. The girl turned and stared hard at her. She wore a pink Minnie Mouse nightgown with gray sweatpants underneath. Her hair was in knots.

Brooke said, "I like this show."

"You're not my mom," the girl said.

"I know. I'm Brooke."

"You said you were my mom, but you're not."

"I thought you were someone else," Brooke said. "Is Shantel your mom?"

"She's not my mom either."

"What's your name?"

"Atlantis," the girl said.

"Alanis? Like the singer?"

"Atlantis," Justus said from the table. "Like the lost city. A friend was supposed to come get her when I went to the hospital, but she didn't show. She was here alone for a while."

Justus had abandoned his own son as surely as Brooke had abandoned hers. Did that make them accomplices in each other's crimes? "How long will Cannon stay?"

Dual exhausts of smoke streamed through his nostrils. "Beats me."

"Is she your girlfriend?" Atlantis asked.

"Not yet." Justus laughed and tapped his ashes. "She's only a nice lady who needed some company." Atlantis turned back to the TV. Justus said to Brooke, "You want I could take you somewhere."

You already have, she thought. Here. At last fully awake, she could now recall the techno-blue glow of Justus's dashboard, the city lights thinning as they headed north before disappearing altogether. Through the silhouettes of the trees, she'd caught glimpses of the moonlight shining on the frozen lake.

Justus dropped his butt down the neck of the bottle. "You don't have to rush off. In fact, I have a proposition for you. There's a doctor in town that prescribes certain medications. I'll pay for the visit and the pills."

“I don’t want any pills,” Brooke said. Had she taken one the night before? It would explain the gaps in her memory, her missing hours, but she couldn’t say for sure.

“They’re not for you,” he said. “They’re not for me either. They’re for a friend who can’t get them. The doctor, the drug store, it’s all legal.”

“Doesn’t sound legal.”

“It’s legal enough that one time won’t raise any concerns. What I’m saying is that if you get the meds and stay with Atlantis for a few days while I do some business, I’ll take you anywhere you want to go. I’ll buy you a plane ticket, if that’s what you want.”

What she most wanted was to look out a window while lying in bed, the way she had in the hours after the births, before she’d ever seen the inside of the NICU. To return to that gap in time before Ruby and Pearl were gone and Opal and Emery were real. “How long?”

“Not long. Two days, maybe three.”

Brooke looked at the plastic shelf behind the table. “Do you have anything to eat?”

“Cereal,” he said. “We’ll pick up some things when we’re out.”

She wanted to lie down again, hide beneath the quit. Brooke hoped that if she agreed to what Justus asked, they could leave soon and return quickly.

Backing down the driveway, Brooke saw the extent of the kitchen fire. Justus’s science experiment. The exterior siding was charred, the clapboards broken away in sections to reveal the weather wrapping and insulation beneath. The visible lathes were blackened and scaled and the window glass was opaque with soot. A stranger driving by the house would think the place had been abandoned. “How do you have power?” Brooke asked.

"I rerouted some of the circuits in the box," Justus said. "Nothing to it."

"Are you an electrician?"

He shifted into drive. "I'm a little bit of everything."

The road wasn't plowed, but Justus's truck moved easily through it. There was only one set of tracks in the snow from their arrival the night before. The other small houses on the road, all wood-sided and weathered, sat isolated among the stands of trees, too far apart to see through any of the windows. None had cars in the driveways or lights on and Brooke guessed they'd been winterized and shut up for the season. The road ended at the lake, an infinite white plain that devoured the horizon, the crystallized sky fuzzy at the edge, like a mirage. If Justus were to drive onto the ice, it would devour them, too. Justus turned south, toward town.

Atlantis had changed out of her nightgown but not her sweatpants. Even from the back seat she smelled a little like urine, though Brooke couldn't tell if she was smelling the girl's body or the house where she lived. For once, she was glad for Justus's cigarette. Other than the smell, the interior of his truck was immaculate. The seats and dash were wrapped in leather and a large touch screen, the size of a small television, filled the center of the dashboard. "This is a nice ride," she said.

"My baby."

"You take care of it."

"After what I went through to get it, I ought to." Brooke thought he meant drugs, but Justus said to the windshield, "I was going through some things a while back. I ended up—" He glanced in the rearview at Atlantis. "I ended up in a mental health facility for a while. One of the therapists took a little too much interest in my well-being. She wasn't bad looking, so it wasn't like anyone put a gun to my head. But I had a good lawyer. He got me out and got me this truck." He glanced at Atlantis again. "Got me my girl back, too."

Brooke recalled Jenny Ramirez talking to Fran about Justus, the day Cannon came into the NICU. His pending charges for false imprisonment. "You held your girlfriend hostage."

Justus looked at her across the center console. "Where'd you hear that?"

"I wasn't supposed to," she said, quickly. "The social worker and one of the nurses were talking. I wasn't supposed to hear."

"Oh, that's good," he said, nodding. "That's a big fat violation right there. I can't wait to tell my guy about that. The NICU reminded me so much of the other place. Nurses and that bitch social worker thought they knew everything. The doctor was the worst. I knew the moment I met her she had something to hide."

"Dr. Fackelman."

"Yeah, her. Dr. Fuck You Man." He laughed and pulled his cell phone from his pocket. "I've got hours of her on tape. Not tape-tape, but recordings I made on this baby. My lawyer's going through them. That bitch is toast."

"I thought Cannon was okay," Brooke said. "I thought everything worked out fine."

"What I want to know is, why was he there at all? They stuck a tube down his throat that made him bleed so much it almost killed him. They won't cop to it, but someone fucked up."

"Why not be grateful that he was okay? Why sue?"

"Why *not* sue?" he said. "There's so much cash floating around that hospital it's not even funny. All those doctors in their Porsches and Bimmers raking it in hand over fist. This one time I saw a freaking Tesla with an extension cord running to the hospital. Those cars cost more than my house, and the jagoff's mooching electricity. Why shouldn't we get ours?"

"Fair enough, I guess."

"Not even close to fair," Justus said. He leaned against the window and exhaled out the side of his mouth. "I bet something happened to you, too. You wouldn't be here if everything had gone right. My lawyer would *love* to get his hands on you."

Hadn't Harper said the same thing? Had Brooke delivered in Madison, or had they transferred the babies there, they might have fared better. Emery wouldn't still be on the ventilator and Opal, and maybe even Pearl and Ruby, too, would still be alive. But why stop there? Had she and Harper moved away from Hanover, like they'd once talked about; had she not organized the team for the charity spelling bee her senior year of college. Change any one of the factors and the product would have come out differently.

She wondered whether Harper already knew she wasn't in Madison, and whether he'd try to find her. Either way, it didn't much matter. He'd never find her here.

"So, did you do it?" she asked Justus.

"Do what?"

"Hold Shantel hostage?"

He shook his head and glanced once in the rearview mirror. "Her dickwad dad didn't like his angel shacking up with the likes of me. Showed up at my house with the cops, and I told them all to fuck off. Slammed the door right in their entitled faces. They acted like I was a fucking terrorist. In the end, nothing much came of it. I tell you, my guy's a genius."

They passed bait shops and small motels, Fishermen's Paradise and Musky Mecca and the Out O' Town, all closed for the season, their parking lots thick with snow. Papasay's main street was three blocks long, with stop signs at each intersection and a line of squat storefronts with signs for Red Wing shoes and Amana appliances. Most buildings were clad with the same weathered brown siding as on Justus's house, as though the entire town had been built at once. The pale blue orb of a water tower rose above the trees. The credit union marquee said the temperature was nine degrees.

Justus turned at the Piggly Wiggly and pulled up to a small house adjacent to the supermarket's back lot. The lettering on the window said PAUL KLEINSCHMIDT, M.D., PAIN CLINIC. Justus shoved his hand inside his jacket pocket and produced a roll of cash held closed with a rubber band. He separated four one-hundred-dollar bills from the curled stack and handed them to Brooke. Three hundred, he said, she should give to the receptionist at the front. The fourth she should give right to the doctor. He handed her a manila envelope and said the doctor might want to have a look at what was inside. Brooke bent the brads and lifted the flap and slid out a black-and-white MRI image of a spinal column, clusters of numbers in the upper and lower left corners. Most surprisingly, Brooke's name appeared on the label affixed to the lower right. "This is mine?"

"Sort of," he said. "It's backup."

"How'd you know my last name?"

"Your driver's license," he said. She pictured his hands in her purse, in her duffel bag, pawing through her underwear. She'd yet to say no to anything.

"Take Atlantis with you. A woman with a kid looks more real. I'll pick you up after."

The wind roared. Brooke had to use both hands to pull open the clinic door enough for Atlantis to scurry through, and then brace it with her back to keep it from slamming shut behind her. The front waiting room had a line of metal folding chairs arranged along the window and side walls, here and there occupied by patients waiting to be seen. There was an overweight woman with bright orange hair and a gemstone stud in her upper lip; a skinny young man in a neon vest; an older man with a poverty-ravaged face, cratered and unshaven, who held the fingers of his left hand inside the fist of his right. The episode of *SpongeBob* on the TV immediately drew Atlantis's attention.

The receptionist sat behind a desk in the corner, near the hallway, the gatekeeper to the rest of the house. In her brown turtleneck and reading glasses, she looked more like a librarian than an accomplice in an enterprise not quite on the up-and-up. She asked Brooke if she had an appointment, and when Brooke said she didn't think so, the receptionist said that drop-ins were cash only. Brooke put the money on the desk and the woman gave her a clipboard of forms to fill out.

While Brooke checked the boxes on the medical history, Atlantis watched the show with her thumb in her mouth, her knuckle wedged into her nostril. She sat with her knees tucked up to her chin. "Have you ever been here before?" Brooke asked her.

Atlantis shook her head.

"You ever been to a doctor?" The receptionist looked up from her desk, then back down at her papers.

Atlantis nodded. "I had to get shots before I went to school."

"Why aren't you in school now? Aren't you old enough?"

Atlantis shrugged.

"How old are you?"

"Six."

The receptionist called her name. Brooke asked Atlantis if she wanted to stay out here. "I like this show," she said. Through the gaps in the blinds in the front window, Brooke could see Justus's truck parked across the street.

The exam room had elephant wallpaper, a closet door, wood molding on the baseboards. The window was covered by a vinyl shade. A family had once lived here; a child had once slept in this bedroom. A padded table covered with white antiseptic paper stood in the center and a poster of the muscular system hung on the wall near the door, a skinless human with bulging eyes and crenellated muscle fibers. There was no computer, no jar of cotton balls or wooden tongue depressors, no blood pressure cuff. Brooke sat on the table, crinkling the paper beneath her.

The doctor had a high forehead and wire-rimmed glasses, his thinning gray hair combed to the side. The splotchy lines in his creased neck were amplified by his collar and tie. Dr. Kleinschmidt was embroidered on the pocket of his white coat. If he was a fake doctor, he was a good one. "How are we this morning?" he asked.

She remembered she was supposed to be in pain. "Okay. All things considered."

He asked where she was hurting and she said her lower back. On impulse, she said her pelvis hurt, too. "I had surgery a few months ago," she said.

"Let's have a look," he said. "Open your pants button, if you don't mind." She did as she was told, lying back on the paper while Dr. Kleinschmidt squeezed hand sanitizer into his palm and rubbed his hands together, the way Brooke had seen the doctors in the hospital do a thousand times: palms first, then backs of the hands, between the fingers and around the wrists. His hands were warm and the hairs on his hands were netted with Purell. He pressed the skin above her navel and below it, palpating the contours of her organs and bones. His fingers crossed her scar and Brooke winced. The doctor moved his hands away. "You've had a cesarean," he said.

"In September."

"Are you nursing? These medications aren't good for breast milk."

"Not anymore," she said. She looked at him for a while, hesitating, before she said, "My babies didn't live."

"Babies?" he asked, eyebrows raised. "With an s?"

"Quadruplets," she said. "Two died during the delivery, and the other two in the NICU."

"Good God." He stepped back and crossed his arms. "They were premature? How early?"

"Twenty-three and three."

"You've been through hell." He held out a hand to help her sit up. "You're in hell now."

"Does that make you the devil?"

He smiled and set a hand on her knee. "I've been called worse."

She held out the MRI envelope and asked if he needed to see it. "That's not necessary," he said. She plucked the hundred from her purse, which he folded and slid inside his coat pocket. He wrote on his prescription pad, tore off a sheet, and handed it to her. "I wouldn't try to get this filled at the Piggly Wiggly," he said. "You'll have problems there."

"What kind of doctor are you?"

Dr. Kleinschmidt stepped farther back and put up his hands. "I'm only providing a service."

"I meant what were you trained in. Your specialty."

"Orthopedics," he said. "I used to do surgery. Mostly knees and hips."

"How did you end up here?"

He slid his pen inside the pocket with the money. "It's a sad story," he said. "But nowhere near as sad as yours."

East of town, Justus pushed the accelerator down. Brooke felt her weight against the seat, the belt tight across her chest and lap. The readout on the navigation system said they were going seventy-five, then eighty, then above ninety. The brown stalks rising out of the snow began to blur. Justus drove with both hands on the wheel and his elbows locked.

After twenty minutes they came into the little town of Runyan, smaller than Papasay, but with a Hometown pharmacy across from the Kwik Trip. She had never been to any of these places, to this side of the lake. Justus counted out more bills and told her to take her purse. She'd need to show her ID to get the prescription filled.

Justus and Atlantis roamed the aisles with a cart while she waited at the counter. The cashier studied her face when she saw what the prescription was for—the reason, Brooke understood, that Justus had asked her to go to the appointment in the first place. The challenge wasn't getting the script, but getting it filled. Brooke offered her license, the cashier punched in the information, and a screen appeared on the debit reader for her to sign her name. The pharmacist carried the bottle to the counter and warned her that oxycodone was very strong, and habit-forming. She shouldn't take more than one pill in a twenty-four-hour period, or while driving or drinking alcohol. She shouldn't break them apart because the pills were timed to release a set amount of medicine over a given period. She should stop taking the pills when the pain went away, and she should keep them far from any place a child might access them. Brooke nodded and the pharmacist stapled the bottle inside a white paper sack. She carried it to the front of the store where she twirled the makeup displays while Justus unloaded his cart onto the counter. He bought loaves of white bread, cans of tuna and beans, crackers and Doritos, Crunch 'n Munch and Froot Loops and Frosted Flakes, Oreos and Chips Ahoy, microwavable rice bowls, mac and cheese, soups, half a dozen twelve packs of soda.

Brooke climbed up inside the cab of the truck while Justus was still loading in the groceries. "You get what you need?" he asked after he pulled the driver's door shut.

She passed him the paper sack. Justus pulled out the brown plastic container and held it to the light beneath the rearview mirror, the egg-shaped capsules nested against the bottom. He uncapped the bottle, pinched out one of the pills, and held it against the black disk of the steering wheel like a jeweler inspecting a diamond against a felt pad. "You're a gold mine," he said. He held the pill close to his lips and kissed it before dropping it back inside the bottle. She didn't care who the pills were for or whether they made someone well or sick or first one and then the other. Or made Justus rich. She only wanted to get to a place where she could close her eyes. She wanted to lie in the still, cold darkness until her daughter appeared again. Even with Atlantis in the back seat, last night's visitation still felt real—more real than anything that had come after it.

Justus shifted into reverse, his arm across the seat so he could look out the back window. He caught her eye and winked. "Watch out," he said, grinning, his missing tooth gaping. "I might never let you go."

20

The Packers game on the radio saved them from having to talk. Mike turned onto County Road QQ, and Dash switched off the game so she could concentrate on the directions Landon's foster mother had given them. Mike didn't argue; it was past two in the afternoon, close to halftime, and Green Bay was up by ten. He slowed at every mailbox to read the numbers until they saw the sign for Heron Lane. A novelty road sign, the letters too large to be authentic. The house at the end of the long, compacted gravel driveway looked tiny. Cyclones of granulated ice spun up from the snowbound fields, and the sharp winter sun caused Dash to lift a hand to her eyes and Mike to pull on the brim of his cap.

"Do you think they own all this land?" Dash asked.

"I don't know how they'd work it if they did."

"Taking in boys would be one way. Slave labor funded by Uncle Sam."

He squeezed her knee. "Let's not worry about that right now."

The house was yellow with a sharply pitched roof and foil Tyvek wrap glinting through the gaps in the siding. The snow on the driveway had been graded and packed hard and sand had been thrown across it. Opposite the house was a garage with space enough for four or five cars plus a tractor, and sided with white vinyl instead of yellow. Mike reached behind the seat to collect the bag of clothes. Dash carried the paper sack of groceries against her chest, the way you held a toddler.

The storm door led into a makeshift vestibule, with bare plywood walls and a dirt floor. The small enclosure blocked the wind but trapped the cold, and Dash felt the temperature on her cheeks. She hugged the groceries tight. Mike rang the bell.

Landon's foster mother, Valerie Heron, was maybe thirty, maybe not quite that old. Dash had talked to her on the phone but hadn't seen so much as a picture of her, and the woman's youth surprised her. Her hair was frizzy, aggressively sprayed and dyed, her chin and jawline textured with blemishes. Her pinched nose made her look either wildly distracted or hyper-focused. Had Dash encountered her in the hospital, she'd have pegged her for a meth head.

"Dolores and Michael?" Valerie Heron asked. A golden retriever nosed at her leg.

"Dash and Mike," Mike said.

It bothered her that Valerie didn't call them Mr. and Mrs. Coenen.

"Come in," Valerie stepped backward, pulling the dog by its collar. "Come on in."

In the kitchen Dash discovered the source of Valerie's expression. Portraits of Jesus, some hand drawn and others purchased, were tacked to the paneled wall and trapped beneath magnets on the refrigerator. It was worse than the Heinemans' house. Among the paraphernalia, Valerie Heron reminded Dash of Georgina. Self-righteous. Holier than thou. Certain they know how to solve a problem like Landon because they'd heard some quack on the radio. A plaster Jesus, arms spread from the folds of a white robe, stood on the sill above the sink, which, Dash couldn't help but notice, was crowded with plates and mugs and silverware.

The kitchen smelled like maple syrup, cheap and too sweet, almost like wine.

The dog sniffed at the shopping bag in Dash's arms and Valerie shooed it away. It loped around the corner, into the next room. "Did you find us okay?" Valerie asked.

"Took some doing, but we made it," Mike said. "You're out here."

"We like it," Valerie said. "It's so much more open. And lower taxes."

"Taxes," Dash echoed, as if taxes were the problem. Never mind that taxes, along with the child support deducted from Dash's paycheck every other week, paid for Landon to be here.

"How far are you from the lake?" Mike asked.

"Maybe two miles, as the crow flies," Valerie said. "Papasay's on the other side of those trees. The road, though, goes all the way around. Closer to ten from here."

The living room was too small for the furniture that filled it. A man sat in an overstuffed chair against the near wall, his back to the kitchen. He was skinny and balding, his hair narrowing to a peak on his forehead. The lenses of his gold-rimmed eyeglasses were smudged. He didn't stand up to greet them. "You must be Mr. Heron," Dash said.

"This is my husband, Dorn," Valerie said, answering for him.

Mike crossed in front of Dash with his hand extended. Dorn shook it, but looked around Mike to the TV mounted on the wall. Black wires snaked from two speakers crudely hung behind Dorn's head. Maybe his lack of courtesy was due to a problem with his hearing. The football lying in the grass on the screen was twice its actual size. As the camera panned to the players, she caught sight of Julius Robinette, his name across the shoulders of his jersey, and thought again of his hand blessing Emery on Christmas Eve. Emery's surgery should have happened by now, though she'd yet to hear a word about it. She hoped it went well, that Brooke and her husband were making arrangements for how to care for him once he was discharged.

The Falcons were driving. Dash and Mike stood in the living room and watched the snap, the quarterback drop back into the pocket, and the receivers run into their slots. She wanted Julius to tear through the line and grind the QB into the turf, but he got hung up by the left tackle. The pass landed incomplete, and when Dash looked down at Dorn she saw there was a boy in the chair on his other side. He was skinny, like Dorn, with black hair and protuberant teeth, his mouth not quiet set fully inside his skull. A scar ran from his hairline to his neck, and there were burn scars on his forearms. Valerie saw her noticing. "Taden is Landon's foster brother," Valerie said. "He's been with us for a while."

"Hi," Mike said.

Taden didn't respond. The golden retriever came back to Dash, sniffing her knees and crotch. She set her hand on the dog's soft head as its tail flapped in a circle.

"Landon adores Sheba," Valerie said. "It's his job to walk and feed her every morning and night. He also empties the trash and does the dinner dishes. We eat together, as a family."

"What does Taden do?" Dash asked.

"He has other jobs," Dorn said, not moving his eyes from the screen.

"Everyone helps out," Valerie said.

"Where is Landon?" For a moment Dash worried he wasn't there. "Can we see him?"

"He's upstairs," Valerie said. "I wanted to make sure you got to meet all of us."

"We're grateful for that," Mike said. He shifted the bag of clothes to his other hand. "Landon's been minding his manners?"

"We've been working with him," Valerie said, leading them up the narrow, paneled stairs. "We do a lot of exercises focused on boundaries. He's making great strides."

Dash wondered what Valerie and Dorn Heron could possibly do with Landon that she hadn't tried herself. What special training qualified them to better care for him, what set of exercises or encouragements or incantations that, if uttered, could somehow set Landon right? It seemed to Dash part of the dogma of foster care: the belief that your home—by virtue of your willingness to receive an outsider—was by definition better than the home the child came from. Maybe it was true in some cases; hell, in most cases. But not in *their* case.

Both doors at the top of the stairs had alarms. Landon's was on the right.

"Does he spend all day in there?" Dash asked.

"We keep him busy. He's got school during the day, and his treatment program. We go to the YMCA, too, and church."

"What parish do you attend?" Dash asked.

"Oh, we're not Catholic," Valerie said. She let out a small laugh. "Definitely *not* Catholic. We go to Celebration Congregation in Runyan. Landon does the chairs before and after the service. He sets them out and puts them away."

Dash pictured this addled woman and her string-bean husband swaying in the service, their eyes closed and their mouths agape. She didn't like the idea of it, Landon among the holy rollers. The things they might con him into saying or doing. "You've put him to work," she said.

"Part of his program," Valerie said, and opened the door.

Landon sat on the unmade bed with his feet on the floor, his back humped over his knees. His head was enlarged by his headphones. Dash was relieved to see he still had the pair she'd bought him. He glanced up at his parents, briefly, before letting his gaze settle back on the floor. His song wasn't over and Dash knew he couldn't turn off his music until the song ended. All the same, she couldn't help wondering if he was punishing her.

There was wood paneling on the walls and ceiling eaves. For furniture he had a wooden bed frame with a built-in bookshelf at the head, an old dresser with clothes spilling out of the open drawer. There were no typed instructions taped to his wall, no charts of chores and accomplishments with foil stars to mark his progress. A poster of Wisconsin lake fish hung on the wall, and on the slanted ceiling was another poster listing all the names of Jesus in different colors: *Prince of Peace, Lamb of God, Bishop of Souls, I AM.*

Landon removed his headphones.

"Hey," Dash said, and stepped in front of him. "What were you listening to?"

"Backstreet Boys," he said. "*Backstreet's Back.* It sold over five million copies in Europe. It was number one in seven European countries."

She ached to put her arms around him, kiss his hair. "That's good music."

"*Millennium* is the fourth-best-selling album in the United States," Landon said to the carpet.

"Can you look at me, honey?" Dash said. "Can you look me in the eyes when you talk?"

"Some people accuse the Backstreet Boys of lip-syncing, but they don't," Landon said. "They sing with their real voices."

"You sure know a lot about those boys," Mike said from the wall. "You get a chance to play your video game?" He turned to Valerie. "I don't know if you got a computer, but there's a game he likes. *Hadean Eon.*"

"My husband and I considered it," Valerie said. "We concluded the game wasn't in Landon's best interest. It's too violent, and it doesn't promote a worldview in line with our values."

"It's a game," Dash said. "The characters are all prehistoric."

"Evolution is not a worldview we endorse," Valerie said. "We don't want to teach one thing and condone another. A consistent message is better."

Dash set the groceries on the floor and went to the dresser. "His clothes are all a mess."

"I wash them," Valerie said. "It's his responsibility to put them away."

"He doesn't know how," Dash said, indignant. She'd sent a note along with Landon's things and wondered what had happened to it. If Landon or Camille or Valerie herself had found it and thrown it away. "I put his clothes in his drawers in coordinated stacks. Each pile is an outfit, so he knows what to wear every day. It's been our system for years."

"He's learning to take more responsibility," Valerie said. "If you ask me, people don't learn that enough. Everyone wants someone else to handle things for them."

"That's not us," Dash said sharply. "He can do a lot for himself."

Mike set his hand on her shoulder. "Let's get these things unpacked."

Dash knelt and unzipped the duffel. She began transferring clothes to the dresser, pulling out Landon's wadded T-shirts and underwear and folding them neatly before laying them back inside the drawer along with the clothes she'd brought from home. She noticed his Hanover Medical Center fleece had a large red stain near the waist. Next, she unpacked the groceries, the cereal boxes and granola bars, the one-pound bag of peanut M&Ms, the twelve-pack of Mello Yello, Landon's favorite. "We brought you a few treats," she said, shaking the M&Ms.

"We don't allow sugar," Valerie said. Her small eyes were focused and unyielding, her nose more pinched than ever. "Part of Landon's treatment involves resetting his diet. We got rid of as many toxic substances as possible. We use real maple syrup and honey, and none of us drinks caffeine or soda."

"He's never eaten a lot of candy," Dash said. She was still on her knees in front of the dresser. "Only on special occasions."

"It's part of his treatment." Valerie looked at Dash. "We don't allow no pornography, either. It's one of the reasons he doesn't use the computer."

"We didn't bring any of that." Her neck and palms grew hot and she turned her back to Valerie. Gripped the dresser drawer in both hands.

"That was just an experiment," Mike said. "A social worker recommended it."

"Not one that I know," Valerie said.

Dash was glad to see Mike's face tighten, and a part of her wished he'd let Valerie have it. Where did she get off? Mike drew in a long breath, and, for a moment, she thought he would. Instead he turned to Landon and asked, "Say, bud. Who's your favorite Backstreet Boy?"

"Brian Littrell," Landon said. "Brian Littrell had heart surgery in the middle of the Backstreet's Back Tour. He has a son named Baylee."

"He's the one I like," Valerie said, smiling. "He sang the song 'In Christ Alone.'"

Dash checked her watch. They'd only been inside the house for twenty minutes; after weeks of fretting that two hours wouldn't be enough time, an hour and forty minutes seemed a container too large to fill. Landon's bedroom lacked so much as a single chair and she couldn't bear the thought of sitting in the Herons' living room, on their awful microsuede furniture smelling of dog hair and syrup, while Dorn Heron stared blankly at the television.

The bedroom door creaked open and Sheba, the dog, nosed her way inside, sniffing at their knees. She trotted over to Landon. He reached out and stroked the scruff behind her neck. "Sheba helps boys like Landon learn how to interact," Valerie said.

"Maybe we could take her for a walk?" Mike asked.

"Not many places to go," Valerie said. "But she has a ball she likes to chase."

Landon pulled on his stained fleece and followed them down the staircase. At the back door he lifted his lambswool jacket from the hook and shoved his arms down inside. Dash recognized his green-and-yellow cap and deerskin choppers in the basket beside the row of boots; he'd never liked fabrics on his hands or head, and Dash would have let it go had Valerie not been standing there. She held them out to Landon and said, "It's cold out. You'll want these." Landon accepted them without argument or resistance, and Dash wondered whether being in this place, with these people, had robbed her son of his will to assert himself. And whether that was a bad thing.

She and Mike scrambled back into their coats, warmed now by the furnace vent, and followed Landon and the dog out the door. Sheba leapt and wagged her tail at the sight of the ball. Landon held it above his head where she couldn't get it. "Hold on," he said to the dog. "Wait."

The wind had died down and clouds had rolled overhead, their undersides rimmed with lavender and orange. The sky looked bruised, but the air was warmer. Landon led Sheba past the house and heaved the ball over his head, his foot rising into the air as he wound up to throw. The neon orb arced into the sky, a tiny satellite against the clouds, before plunging into the snow. Sheba bolted after it, snow flying up behind her as she crossed the field. The dog returned and dropped the ball into Landon's palm for him to throw again.

This was new behavior, Dash had to admit. Maybe the Herons had a few tricks up their sleeves; maybe being here was good for him. Even if admitting it made her sad.

Dash stepped closer to Mike and burrowed her face in his collar. She smelled his Skin Bracer, the cold air against his neck. Dash saw their car sitting by the house and considered the keys in her husband's pocket. They could be halfway to the county road before Valerie noticed them gone. They could make it across the state line and into the Upper Peninsula within a few hours, Canada by midnight, if they drove flat out. They'd have to get Kasey, and there was the matter of money, so of course the whole enterprise was impossible. But it warmed her to imagine it.

"Come closer, honey," she said. Landon turned and obediently stepped inside the huddle his parents' bodies made. His breath steamed around his face and his nose was red. Sheba sat beside him, one paw lifted from the snow. "Can we go somewhere?" he asked.

"Not this time, bud," Mike said. He lifted his wrist to his mouth and blew down inside the cuff of his glove. "Next time, we'll go have a look around. Get a bite to eat. The new

Cabela's over in Green Bay has an impressive display of animals. We could check that out. Sound okay?"

"When can I go home?"

"We'll have to see how you do here," Mike said.

The question had been circling since the night Camille drove him away. Dash leaned closer, though Mike was the one who asked it. "Why'd you say you were going to kill your sister? Why would you go and say something like that?"

Landon didn't answer. He looked blankly at her, as if the question didn't make sense, and Dash wondered if maybe it didn't. It was possible he didn't have a reason. There was no *why*.

"We talked about doing your private business in your room," Dash said. "With your door closed. I thought we'd agreed on keeping the door closed."

"Kasey's only thirteen," Mike said. His cheeks were flecked with tiny burst capillaries, like he'd been pricked with a needle. "She shouldn't see stuff like that."

"It was her fault," Landon said.

"What did you say?" Mike said. "What did you just say?"

"She's the one."

"You said you were going to hurt her. Whose fault was that, son? You promised to kill her." The tendons in Mike's jaw flexed. "Wasn't it bad enough you had to go to court? Why would you say something like that to your sister?"

Landon made no response, again. His eyes blinked heavily.

"Can you answer me?" Mike said. "After everything that's happened, aren't you even a *little* sorry? Or are you really that stupid?"

"Hey!" Dash said. "That's enough. That's quite enough."

A lone bird crossed overhead, much too late to be moving south. Maybe it was lost or maybe it had found a way to survive the winter on its own. What was it doing here? She'd been asking herself the same question for weeks. How did they get here? All month she'd nursed the belief that everything had been blown out of proportion. After all, Landon hadn't *actually* hurt his sister, or Izzy, when she was there. Threats were just threats, and fears like bad dreams dissolved in daylight.

Now, close enough to touch him, she recalled Kasey on the waterslide, her skinny legs kicking over the edge of the tube, and knew Landon could no longer laze around their house in flannel pajamas or play video games in the basement. He wasn't safe at home, and home wasn't safe with him in it.

"I'm cold," Landon said. "I'm cold and bored."

"You had enough of throwing the ball?" Dash asked.

"*Millennium* and *Black & Blue* both sold more than a million copies their first week," Landon said, Sheba wagging beside him. "The Backstreet Boys are the first group since the Beatles to have back-to-back albums sell more than a million copies in their first week."

"We'll let you get back to it, then," Mike said. He broke the huddle and turned toward the house, his fists rammed down inside his jacket pockets. They stepped inside the vestibule and closed the storm door. Landon rang the bell and Dash reached out to brush the hair over his ears. Valerie opened the door and kitchen smells wafted out, the closed-in odor of a family that wasn't hers. She couldn't go inside again; she couldn't. "Be good until we come back, okay?" Dash leaned in to kiss Landon goodbye but he was already going up the steps. He slid past Valerie Heron and into the house, away from her.

21

Atlantis regarded Brooke with a bemused detachment, surprised but not alarmed to find her beneath the quilt on the couch each morning. The girl sat cross-legged on the carpet in front of the television, a bowl of dry cereal in her lap. When one show ended, the screen split and the credits rolled on the bottom half while a new episode started on top. She watched *SpongeBob* and *The Fairly OddParents* and *Phineas and Ferb,* shows with farting robots and talking blobs of dog shit and Japanese-style characters with enormous eyes that projected streams of colored secretions. Atlantis could watch all day without growing bored, though now and then she'd turn from the TV to appraise Brooke, the spaces between her teeth stained with food.

"Do you need something?" Brooke asked, but it was only something to say. Atlantis refilled her bowl when she wanted more. She used the bathroom by herself. When she grew tired, she wandered to her bedroom and slept.

Brooke considered the amount of food Justus had bought at the drugstore. It was clear he wouldn't be coming back in two days, as he'd promised. The snow had started the night he left, and had been going on and off for three days. There were periods of heavy flakes that looked like torn paper, and times when the snow turned so fine it revealed itself only in the bands of light shining from the back of the house. Soft white powder lay in slender piles along narrowest tree branches and around the rims of the empty terra cotta pots. The birches and pines sagged and small plumes of snow burst like smoke from the upper branches. Each morning Brooke looked out the window and saw the road and driveway unmarred by tracks, and wondered if Justus would be coming at all.

Her second day, she'd tried to let Harper know she was alive, not tied up in a basement or lying in a ditch. The house had a phone jack, but no phone. She punched a text into her cell, *Staying with a friend for a while. I'm sorry,* and held the phone to the ceiling, as if that would help. The battery wore down looking for a signal. She found a charger plugged into the wall and left the phone connected, but whenever she looked at it, no messages had come through. It never made a sound.

If the hospital had taught her anything, it was the art of squandering time. How to open her mind enough to let the minutes and hours and even whole days drain away like sand through her fingers without a thought to how else she might have spent them. That was the trick, to indulge in no other thoughts but the present, to refuse to acknowledge the past or future or places other than *here*. Out the back window, a plastic slide lay on its side in the backyard, already half covered by snow. It reminded her of Ollie's play set in the backyard, but once the flakes piled up enough to cover it, she forgot it was ever there. She peeked inside the bedrooms. Atlantis's room had been painted cotton-candy pink, but hastily. Beneath the bismuth Brooke could see the roller marks of another color, and beneath that, streaks of spray paint. She made out the word Kiloz. The girl's bed was a twin mattress and box spring set atop cinder blocks, her floor littered with clothes, stained underpants twisted inside out, naked Barbies in a mass grave. Justus's bed was a great slab of a mattress covered in a navy sheet, the outline of a body visible in lines of dried sweat. She didn't find a washing machine or a door to a basement. It may have been inside the burnt-out kitchen for all she knew. A third room contained a Pack 'n Play and a half package of diapers, torn open and sitting on the floor. They were the only signs the baby had ever been here. Thinking of Cannon made her think of Emery, and of herself turning away from the ambulance. There is no Emery, she reminded herself. There never was. None of that ever happened.

Atlantis's shows, with their paralyzing barrage of sounds and flashes, could induce a kind of twilight stupor, one she gave over to in the same way that she'd once given over to the monitor in the NICU. She found she could slow her thoughts to the point where she could feel them moving through her brain, like water spilled over parched soil: fanning out in a web, filling the gaps. A rush of odor would fill her nose and then abruptly disappear. Hour by hour, she trawled her mind in search of her vanished daughter, trying to summon back the visitor from her first night. She kept hoping to wander down the right pathway of axons and dendrites and find the lingering brainwaves and electromagnetic fields of her lost children, the remnants of their broken-down cells and half-formed souls. But no matter where she looked, they weren't there. No one was.

She'd lost count of the nights she'd slept there when she heard a soft whimper coming from the hallway. Brooke lay on the sofa and listened for a while. It had been years since she'd heard a child crying from another room. The night was strangely bright, the lumens of the stars dialed up. Behind the hum of the space heater and running faucet, the sky roared like an airplane passing overhead. Outside it was twenty degrees below zero.

Atlantis's voice rose like bubbles through water, bloops and blobs, indecipherable. After a time, they formed a word. *Help.* Brooke turned on the light in the living room, then the hallway, brightening her path. The stench hit her when she opened the door. Atlantis's pillow and bedsheets, her nightgown and bare legs, were covered in vomit. Brooke held her finger to her nose.

"I don't feel good," Atlantis said.

"Can you make it to the bathroom?"

Brooke sat on the toilet lid while she pulled off Atlantis's nightgown and turned it inside out. Vomit clung to the matted ends of her hair. Brooke could see the yellowed crotch of Atlantis's underpants before she pulled them down. She held Atlantis's hands as she stepped inside the tub. The bottle of Suave on the edge of the tub was nearly empty, so Brooke pulled the cap from the bottle and ran it under the faucet, enough to make the tub water bubble.

Atlantis lay back and floated, her hair a kelp bed around her head, her nose and chin above the water line. Brooke noticed the red sores dotting her arms and legs, some scratched to bleeding and allowed to scab over, the flaky skin around her knees. The girl's compact and hairless labia were inflamed, splotched and dark pink. Atlantis shifted in the water, sending a wave lapping against the porcelain. Her face twisted and she reached to grab at her lower back, like an old lady. "Does it hurt back there?" Brooke asked.

Atlantis's hand shot to her crotch. She arched her back and wailed, "Ow, ow, ow!" A ripple of yellow emerged through the cracks of her fingers and dissolved in the graying water. "It hurts to pee?" Brooke asked, at last understanding the problem.

Atlantis nodded, crying too hard to speak.

"I should have told you to change your undies."

Atlantis blinked. Her hair was plastered to her forehead. "It hurts," she said. "It hurts bad."

"Do you have a thermometer?" Brooke asked. "It sort of looks like a pencil, but it's for taking a temperature. Does your dad have one of those?"

Atlantis shook her head. A thermometer would only tell Brooke what she already knew: that Atlantis had a urinary tract infection. She turned on the cold water and pulled the drain stopper to replace some of the hot. The medicine cabinet above the sink contained several bottles of aspirin and Advil that rattled when she shook them, but when she popped the caps the pills inside were a rainbow of colors and shapes and she didn't think she could risk any of them. She wondered where she could go to call for help and how she'd explain herself if she got through. She brought Atlantis a soda, holding the can from the bottom while the little girl took tiny sips. Brooke set the can on the floor beside the tub and held Atlantis's head to help her slide lower into the water. The water was cooler now, enough to bring Atlantis's temperature down. Her teeth and chin began to quiver. "Believe it or not, this will help with the fever," Brooke said. "When we're finished, I'll make you something better to eat."

After days of beating back every memory, Brooke gave in to its pull. The last time she'd been conscripted into the service of a sick child was the week they submitted the paperwork to the foster care agency. Harper rented a cabin on a lake an hour north of Minocqua, to celebrate their new path. They could cross-country ski if they wanted, or sit by the fire and cook and be together. He put his arms around her waist and said it would be like the time they flew the coop to Solberg Lake, only without the gas station bean dip. Brooke said it sounded nice, though she felt annoyed by his optimism, his everything's-going-to-work-out-great faith in the unseen forces of the universe, and she considered, for a moment, telling him how she'd held their daughter in the wind while she waited for the ambulance, simply to bring him down a notch. She hadn't wanted to hurt him, but watching him strap his cross-country skis onto the roof of the car, she realized she could do exactly that. She could hurt him by telling him something he didn't know.

Oliver was supposed to stay with his mom, but the night before they left, Sara called and begged Harper to trade. Her husband was out of town and she'd been hit with the flu; there was no way she could keep up with both kids on her own. Brooke was painting her toenails on the bed, her bare foot propped on a magazine, while Harper paced the bedroom on the phone. "Of course," Harper said. He didn't turn to face Brooke, didn't hold the phone to his thigh to whisper-ask if it was okay. "Of course, we'll take him," he said.

The cabin had two bedrooms. They'd still have plenty of privacy, Harper said. The toes on Brooke's right foot were the same deep red as the negligee she'd packed for the weekend. She'd yet to paint her left. She slid the nail polish brush down inside the bottle and fastened the cap. "The more the merrier," she said.

Ollie was chatty in the car for the first hundred miles, but once they left the interstate and began to weave up the two-lane highway, he closed his eyes and laid his head on the door handle. He held his hand like a catcher's mask across his face. Harper pulled over to check on him and Ollie leapt from the car in his socks to throw up in the snow. "Too many windy roads," Harper said, though they both knew the weekend had turned on them.

Oliver puked all night, first in the toilet and then in his bed. He couldn't hold anything down and was too achy to sleep. He spent Saturday groaning on the couch while they made half-hearted attempts to watch *Ghostbusters* and *Home Alone*. By Saturday night the vomit came in thin green strings that looked like grass and Harper called the pediatrician in Hanover. The doctor offered to write a prescription for Zofran to quell the nausea, but he would have to drive down to Minocqua, nearly an hour away, to pick it up. Harper stacked extra logs on the fire and said he'd be back as soon as he could.

Ollie shivered, his fever spiking. "It's heavy," he said. "It's really heavy."

"What is?" Brooke asked. "What's heavy?"

"Get it off," he said, clutching at the air. "I can't breathe."

She came to the couch and knelt beside him. She touched his forehead, the wet fringe of his hair. "There's nothing there, kiddo. It's the fever."

"I can't breathe."

She slipped her hand beneath his back to prop him against the corner of the sofa. The blankets smelled fluish. Brooke stirred the logs and settled in beside him. Oliver wasn't often sick. A sniffle here, a cough there; it was a rare for a virus to bite him hard enough for him to miss school, let alone send his dad through the snow to a pharmacy. Ollie canted his head back and his mouth fell open. In the firelight his teeth were a monstrous yellow. She patted his thigh through the blanket, less to comfort him than to feel the shape of her resentment. Oliver was the embodiment of the thing she wanted but wasn't hers. Every pregnancy had been, in its way, an attempt to reset the balance, and none had worked. Even the prospect of a foster child couldn't change it. Harper would always belong to Ollie first. She wondered, watching

Oliver's Adam's apple bob in his throat, whether he enjoyed the power he had over Harper, and so over her, or simply believed it was the natural way of things.

They were still sitting together when Harper returned. Ollie's head was on her shoulder and his arm was across her chest. Harper stared down at them, set the medicine and keys on the table, and came toward her. He leaned over the couch arm and kissed her deeply, eagerly, with more passion than she'd felt in a long time. "This is enough, isn't it?" he asked. "Our little family? Don't we have everything we need right here?"

It shamed her, lifting Atlantis out of the water and standing her on the linoleum, that she'd been unable, or unwilling, to agree. Harper and Ollie should have been enough, but they weren't. How long had she'd fought against her own good life.

Brooke helped Atlantis into a clean nightgown and tucked her inside the quilt on the couch. They'd eaten most of the food Justus had bought. The chips had disappeared days ago, so had the cookies and Crunch 'n Munch, the microwavable mac and cheese. They were down to tuna and ramen, a sleeve of spaghetti and a jar of sauce. What she needed, they didn't have: cranberry juice, ginger ale, soda crackers, bananas. The plywood barrier to the kitchen had been screwed in tight to the wall, a bead of caulk added to hold out the cold and the wind. Brooke opened the front and hall closets, pulling out gloves, random sneakers, an oscillating table fan, its white blades caked in a heavy layer of gray dust. In Justus's bedroom closet she found a pair of crusted work boots and a flannel-lined parka. She slid her arms inside the sleeves, cinched the boots as tight as she could, and slipped her phone into her pocket. She opened the front door and stepped outside for the first time in days. The frozen air stung her lungs.

She postholed across the snow to the driveway and came back up again to the side door. Warped by the fire, the frame gave easily. Despite the cold, the room still smelled heady, of burnt wood and paint thinner. Plastic soda bottles and milk gallons lined the floor, melted and misshapen, stained a brownish yellow. The cabinets above the stove and along the wall and ceiling were black with char and the plastic controls of the stove had liquified in their housings. On this side, the plywood barrier was a wall of ice, though farther from the stove the counters were okay and the lower cupboards still contained a pile of cans and jars. Soy sauce, a few boxes of Pasta Roni, several cans of soup. She stuffed as many as she could fit into her pockets and found a large pot to hold the rest. The refrigerator and freezer were bare, except for an open box of Arm and Hammer, which she took with her. She recalled, from her own urinary tract infections as a girl, her mother bringing her glasses of warm water mixed with baking soda to help reduce the acid in her urine and ease the pain. Sometimes her mother stirred in a spoonful of cream of tartar, once used as an antibiotic, and to her surprise, she found a cylinder of it among the tumbled canisters of spices in the cupboard.

She set the pot of food in the snow at the end of the driveway and held her phone to the sky. The sharp sunlight through the trees cast webs of shadow over the snow. The branches creaked and groaned and glittered with crystals. At the end of the driveway, she moved out into the full sun, the cold freezing the lining of her nose and the wells of her eyes, and at the end of the road, she came to the lake, windswept and rippled with hard edges, like the surface of the moon. The horizon throbbed as if on fire. She stepped past the tree line, down a short embankment, and onto the ice. She closed her eyes against the wind, turned her heels, and leaned forward to keep from falling. When she opened her mouth, the wind forced itself down her throat, straight to her lungs, so much air she couldn't breathe it all. She turned so the wind was at her back, and her eyes traveled along the wooded shoreline where in the summer wild phlox and lupine would bloom among the undergrowth, but which now showed only bands of light and dark, ice and earth. The ice under her feet sang and pinged. It seemed incredible to her that Hanover lay only thirty miles to the south and that, in a tiny cove in the lake's corner, the Lake Hanover Edsel, underwater for more than sixty years, rested on a bed of stones. She'd lived almost half her life on the shore of this lake and still it surprised her. Its shifting spectrum of water colors, its remote and wild corners, its ferocious and unyielding beauty.

In her pocket, her phone began buzzing.

Her voicemail was full. Her mother had called several times, and she had messages from the hospital in Madison, Jenny Ramirez, Department of Child Protective Services, all inquiring about her whereabouts. Harper's voice, when she played back the messages, slid from panicked to resigned. She scrolled up to the top of Harper's texts and moved down through the string.

RU OK? Where RU?

Madison said U never made it. Where RU?

What friends? Please call me.

It's OK you didn't go to Madison. I understand it I think. I haven't been much help. If you could just let me know that you're OK. I just want to know.

The last call had come from the house line. From home. She hit call and listened to it ring while she trudged back toward the shelter of the trees, hoping the signal would hold. Ollie's voice was loud when he answered, like he'd been waiting for her to call. Or waiting for some kind of call. "It's Brooke," she said. "Is Dad home?"

"No," he said, but didn't say where Harper had gone.

"You're home alone?"

"There's no school today because of the cold. My grandparents and Aunt Liz are coming over soon." He paused. "You're really hard to hear."

She covered her mouth with her hand. "I'm outside. I haven't had any reception."

"Where are you?" Ollie asked, carefully. "Are you in Madison?"

"No, kiddo, I didn't go down there. But could you tell Dad I called? Tell him nothing bad happened to me. In case he's worried about that."

"He told me that if you called, I should find out where you are."

"I'm nowhere." She turned to look at the lake again. "Really, nowhere."

"He's going to be so mad that I didn't find out where you are."

"You can blame me," she said. She was hungry, suddenly, her stomach pitted. Her hands were going numb and she worried she'd drop the phone. She looked back toward the house and could see Atlantis's pink parka through the trees. Temps this low could send her little body into shock. "Look, I need to go. Tell Dad I called, okay?"

"Okay," Oliver said.

"You're a good boy," Brooke said. She stopped walking and said, "You've been a real trouper. I haven't always been a good stepmom, but I do love you. If we don't see each other for a while, I wanted you to know that."

"Where are you going?"

"I don't know yet. I need to figure out a few things."

"Will you bring me something?" he asked, his voice hopeful. He sounded like he'd already forgotten everything. He only cared about what was to come.

"Sure thing, kiddo. Anything you want."

Atlantis's eyes were wide, as though she'd seen a ghost. Her skin was more sallow in the glaring outdoor light. "Are you feeling sick again?" Brooke asked. She held her hand to the girl's forehead.

"I worried you were running away," Atlantis said. Her small voice was hoarse. "I worried you were leaving me all alone."

"You are my running away," Brooke said. "When I ran away, I came here."

She picked Atlantis up and carried her across the snow toward the house. Atlantis gripped Brooke's neck and her shampooed hair blew across Brooke's face. Back inside, Brooke propped Atlantis in the corner of the couch, with extra cushions behind her back and the quilt around her shoulders. She heated the minestrone in the microwave and fed Atlantis spoons of broth and then, after Atlantis said she was still hungry, bites of softened vegetables. She scrubbed a dish towel with soap in the bathroom sink, turned the water cold, and folded the towel into a rectangle. She laid the towel across Atlantis's forehead. Brooke slid beneath the quilt on the other side of the couch, her feet tucked against Atlantis's hip, and scrolled through the channels until she landed on *Swiss Family Robinson*. "It's like we're having a slumber party," she told Atlantis.

"What's a slumber party?" Atlantis asked.

"It's where friends sleep over at each other's houses. They stay up late watching movies and talking and eating popcorn. I didn't have very many when I was a kid, but they were always fun."

"Can we have one at your house?" Atlantis asked.

"We'll do the next one at my house." Brooke lay with her head against the arm of the sofa, watching the Robinsons build their elaborate treehouse and thinking about Justus's offer to buy her a plane ticket—whether he really meant it and, if he did, where she'd go. A deserted island in the South Pacific sounded nice, a place where she might sleep beneath a palm tree and drink from a coconut. Before Fritz and Ernst could rescue Roberta from the pirates, Atlantis had fallen asleep. Before long, Brooke had, too.

Later that night, that same night, she heard his tires crunch the snow. She saw the headlights flash through the front windows. Atlantis was awake and hungry again, her forehead cooler beneath Brooke's hand. Justus looked worse than when he'd left. His clothes were wrinkled and slept in and he hadn't shaved. The cigarettes hid the stench of his body, though only barely. He regarded Brooke oddly, surprised to still find her there. She wasn't sure whether she wanted to get out of the house or to convince Justus to turn around and leave again. "Atlantis has been sick," she said. "We're low on food. Think we could run to the store?"

"Tomorrow," Justus grumbled. Brooke followed him as he staggered toward the back of the house. In the bathroom, he opened the medicine cabinet and began shaking the pill bottles. He popped the cap off the Advil, peered inside with one eye closed, and set the bottle back on the shelf without replacing the lid. He tried another, opening a bottle of Midol and plunging in a finger. The pills rattled and Justus turned the bottle over and emptied it into his palm. He plucked the two he wanted from the pile and returned the rest to the bottle. He slapped his hand to his mouth and swallowed.

“Let me borrow your truck,” Brooke said as Justus slumped toward the bedroom. “I’ll go to the store and come right back. I could also find a laundromat. Atlantis got sick all over her sheets.”

Justus sat hunched over the bed with his hands on his knees. After a while he lay back with his feet still on the floor. He cocked one eye open and stared at her. “No one drives my truck but me,” he said. He raised his index finger. “No one.”

He closed his eyes and drifted away. Brooke could see the keys bulging inside the kangaroo pocket of his sweatshirt, a small mound on his stomach. She slid her hand inside and he didn’t stir. He lifted a hand to scratch his neck and grinned in his sleep.

22

Jenny Ramirez, leaning against the NICU nurses' station, informed them that Emery Jensen would be coming back. She'd been on the phone with the hospital in Madison for most of the morning. The surgeons had ligated his arterial ductus, placed the trach and G-tube, and cleared a bowel obstruction Dr. Fackelman hadn't warned them about. Emery was pooping better now, his oxygen weaned down to 40 percent with stable vent pressures and no supplemental steroids. Apnea and bradycardia were ongoing issues, and he needed to gain weight, but those could all be managed in Hanover. Eight days after admitting him, the children's hospital was sending him home.

"Fast," Dash said, secretly glad. She'd been tending to the feeder-growers along the windows, babies fretted over by mothers whose faces twisted whenever a lead slipped or the monitor toned. Little more than a glorified babysitter. She plucked a donut from the box on the counter. "I thought Emery would be discharged from Madison. Isn't that what they said?"

"They're turfing him," Jenny said. "They don't want the hassle."

"Sounds like he's through the woods now."

"After the medical problems come the social." Jenny rolled her eyes. "The case manager thinks medical foster care could be in his future. Children's is kind enough to put that matter into our hands."

"How sweet," Dr. Fackelman said. "No word from Mom?"

They'd whispered about it for the last week, the nurses and doctor, on morning rounds and in the corners of the unit, by the filing drawers and the laundry. Brooke wasn't the first mother to disappear. Her empty promises to visit in December had been the first sign, and the most glaring. Her glassed-over eyes and empty expression the night of the transfer was proof of what they'd already known. It was all too familiar, and shameful: a mother abandoning her child when he most needed her. Even if the nurses whispered Opal's name ("And don't forget the first two," Dash had said, "I made molds for them, too"). None of them, they were sure, would have run.

"Every call goes straight to voicemail," Jenny said, shaking her head. "Thankfully their insurance company still answers the phone."

"Going to be a big bill," Dash said. "Though I'm sure they can afford it."

"Enough time in this place can wipe out anyone," Dr. Fackelman said. She turned to Jenny. "I suppose Madison would like us to come get him?"

"At your earliest convenience."

That night a mass of arctic air swept south and stalled over Wisconsin. A polar vortex, the weatherman called it, a hurricane of swirling bitter air, only much, much larger. He used both hands to trace its path across the map. Standing temperatures plummeting into the double digits below zero. In the morning, the thermometer mounted outside Dash's kitchen window read eighteen below zero, and that wasn't factoring the wind.

The ambulance bay was warm, but when Dash pressed her hand to the rear window her skin stuck to the glass. She caught glimpses of barns and bullet-shaped grain silos rising out of the fields, the streaming road crusted with ice. The moon was visible against the blinding sunlight. Dr. Fackelman rode with her eyes closed, complaining of car sickness, but when they crossed beneath Interstate 90 and the traffic thickened, she became more attentive. She craned her neck to see, noting that the mall and its garrison of hotels hadn't been there when she was a student, but the Avenue Club had been and it was nice to see it again. Dr. Fackelman said she'd left Wisconsin for medical school and had stayed away for twenty years. Madison had always been a happy place for her. "I don't come down here enough."

Besides hospital transfers, Dash never came to the capital. Her family was north, or else far away, and it never occurred to her to come down. They had a Chili's in Hanover, and movie theaters, and the lakes were better north of Highway 29. What was there to do in Madison besides watch the Badgers? The ambulance stopped at a red light, and when Dash glanced out the window she saw the corners and sidewalks crowded with young people, the university buildings behind them. A cluster of women waited at the corner in identical black parkas but with bare legs, paper coffee cups held to their noses. "Those girls need pants," Dash said. "Dumbest thing I've ever seen."

Dr. Fackelman leaned forward. "I was like them when I was a student," she said. "I walked everywhere, in all kinds of weather."

"I used to think the winters were worse when I was a kid. In my memory it's always snowing. But this one so far has been a doozy."

"It got cold when I was in college," Dr. Fackelman said. "I remember it being cold. I just didn't care. I was too preoccupied with my future. And finding a boyfriend."

Dash had never been preoccupied that way, with futures and boyfriends, though she'd had good grades in high school. Better, certainly, than her brothers, who spent their time rebuilding motorcycles. School for them was like church: something they couldn't not do but wouldn't have chosen on their own. A few of Dash's teachers had taught every one of her siblings—Marty was a senior when Dash was in kindergarten—and joked that her solid wall of A's was a sign she was adopted. Her chemistry teacher said Stevens Point had good programs and wasn't far, but Madison was famous, and with her grades she had a running shot. There were scholarships for smart girls, he said, though Dash couldn't tell whether or not he thought that was a good thing.

She met Mike the summer before junior year, the night Dash and her sister Dottie drove with Cheryl Hietpas to see *Back to the Future* and then to B&D for burgers. The restaurant had planted a stand of pines and set out picnic tables to keep the riff-raff away from the other customers. Instead of going inside to use the bathroom, the boys peed in the trees. Dash recalled their T-shirted backs among the pines, their shoulders squared and their hands at their waists, so obvious and yet so casual, their outlines phantasmagoric in the summer grapelight. The burgers came wrapped in cardboard boxes that served as little trays you could balance on your knees. Dash was sitting on the tabletop with her feet on the bench, allowing the boys to appraise her legs and pretending to laugh when they teased her and Dottie for looking alike, when a car full of boys pulled into the lot. Three sat up front and three more sat in back. When the door opened she caught the whiff of their cigarettes and beer. One of them she recognized from history, a taciturn boy with a wrestler's build. He came right toward her, not even a glance in Dot's direction. For the first time she felt like she wasn't tied to her sister. She wasn't comparable to anyone at all. By the time he made it to her, she had his name in her mouth.

They'd made a good life together. She never saw college as something she'd given up; she considered herself lucky. Now, with Landon in Papasay, a certain ease had returned to the entire house. Kasey talked too much, but at least she didn't hide. Mike touched Dash's hip at the bathroom sink; he rubbed her earlobes when they lay down beside each other in bed. Yet for the duration of a stoplight it was tempting to imagine a different life. College, maybe even medical school, marriage to a fraternity brother from Waukesha. Any one of those things would have meant more money, which would have been nice, but also different genes. Genes that might have spared Landon. Spared them all.

"I'll bet it's warmer in California," Dash said to Dr. Fackelman.

The doctor rode with her thumbs hooked under the shoulder harness. "A friend sent me their weather report last night, just to rub it in. It's seventy-five and sunny. People are at the beach."

"Why on earth did you ever leave?"

"It was time," she said. "My personal life was in the crapper. I needed to get out."

"Your husband?"

"The thing is, we were never married. We were together for twenty-four years and never tied the knot. Jonathan was an infectious-disease specialist, an AIDS researcher. His parents were sociology professors, and he argued that marriage was a historically corrupt practice. Women traded for farmland and cattle, that sort of thing. He refused to take part in it simply because it had become a custom. Later he maintained marriage equality was the issue, you know, since so many of his patients were gay. When the California

Supreme Court ruled in favor of gay marriage, I said, hey, maybe we should do it. You know, a show of support. But Jonathan said he still didn't want to."

"He said it like that?"

"He was always very candid. I used to love that about him, but that stung. After that, things began to unravel. I could tell he wasn't happy and I wasn't either, but he wouldn't do anything about it. So I finally moved out."

"Good for you," Dash said. "That's when you came here?"

Dr. Fackelman glanced sideways at her, as though weighing whether to continue. She kept her back straight, her head against the padded rest. "That was eighteen months *before* I left. What happened next is pretty much an episode of *General Hospital*. Jonathan was forty-four and handsome, and his career literally involved saving the world. He spent at least six weeks each year in Africa, the whole white guy in the shanty town with a stethoscope around his neck thing. A guy like that can date anyone he likes, whether she's twenty-one or sixty-seven."

"Uh-oh," Dash said.

"Jonathan started dating a nurse practitioner. I was okay with that, at least at first. I mean, at least she wasn't a floor nurse. No offense."

Dash knew what Dr. Fackelman meant. The cliché of a middle-aged doctor shacking up with a nubile young helper. "Bah."

The doctor swallowed. "The night I learned they were engaged, a friend of mine talked me into going out for a drink. I put back a couple of angry chardonnays, too fast, and ended up talking with a group of surgical residents, all hotshot young guys. They figured out I was an attending and started sucking up and buying me drinks. I was half hoping Jonathan would walk in right then and see me surrounded by all those boys. That his years of bullshit would cost him more than they cost me. I didn't realize I'd had too much to drive until I got in my car. I went maybe half a block and pulled over to call a cab. But a cop saw me get into the car. He had me on his dashcam. I ended up with a DUI. That's when I decided to go."

"Why here?" Dash asked. The ambulance's engine strained as it climbed a hill.

"I grew up in Milwaukee. My family had a place on the north side of Lake Hanover. The pretty side, way up north. I learned how to sail and water-ski there. In my memory, Hanover was like summer camp. When the recruiter told me about Dr. Marlowe retiring and the practice in Madison buying him out, I thought Hanover sounded like a great place to hide."

"Do the other nurses know?"

"God, I hope not," Dr. Fackelman said. "My partners in the practice know, but they're down here, so I'm out of sight, out of mind. I went to treatment to save my medical license."

"I won't tell anyone," Dash said. She drew an X across her chest. "You can trust me."

"That's not why I told you," Dr. Fackelman said. She shifted and crossed her legs. Her gold necklace dangled beneath her chin, the charm at the end swinging. "The nurses don't tell me much, so I'm not really in the know, but I've heard some things. I know you've had some problems with your son. Maybe it helps to hear that you're not the only one whose life is fucked up."

Dash felt a bubble expanding inside her blood vessels, as though she were rising up from a great depth. "The last few months, they've been hard." She didn't trust herself to say more.

The ambulance slowed and turned into the children's hospital. Dash began unbuckling her shoulder straps, but

Dr. Fackelman sat still, waiting. Dash leaned forward and the doctor caught her wrist. "You're not as alone as you think you are," she said.

The corridor through the hospital lobby led past an artificial and bygone Wisconsin, façades paneled with red barn siding, a gift shop decorated with a striped awning, a barber pole, and, oddly, a red British telephone booth. There were paw prints on the floor, turtles and fish along the wall. The sink outside the NICU was tiled blue-green and lit with recessed bulbs. Dash felt she didn't belong there, a feeling that often swept over her whenever she entered a hospital other than her own, her scrubs the wrong color, the signs so out of order they might have been in a foreign language, as though only inside her own unit was she actually a nurse, capable of helping anyone.

"I'll bet all their bilirubin lights are new and fancy," Dr. Fackelman said, pressing the buzzer.

The administrative assistant led them into a pod room, large enough to hold six babies at a time. The beds were arranged in a starfish shape against the walls. Dash pushed the portable Isolette they'd brought from Hanover toward the corner, unsure of what to expect. Most babies left alone and unloved either died or turned vegetative, and crossing toward Emery she steeled herself to find him devastated, ashen and sallow, surgically repaired but emptied of animus, of anything that might be called a life. But his eyes were open, his color ruddy and full. He gripped the elbow tube of his tracheotomy the way he'd once gripped the vent, like it was a pacifier.

Dash raised the lid to look closer, opening the snaps on his sleeper to examine the scar from his PDA, a small line of tight sutures beneath his left arm. She inspected the MIC-KEY button covering the opening to the G-tube in his abdomen. His tongue, so long depressed by the endotracheal tube in his throat, lolled over his gums and lips. Dash blew against his face and his eyes fluttered and rolled. The extent of his cognitive impairments wouldn't be known for months, or even years, until certain milestones were missed. Still, he looked good. That he was alive at all—after such a traumatic and early birth, after all the awful labs and terrible blood gases, his failing kidneys and lungs, after three surgeries and more than a week alone in this big unit—was something. Here was a testament to the tenacious persistence of life. The instinct to exist. Dash pressed her stethoscope to Emery's heart and listened to it thump. His belly was soft beneath her fingers.

"Mr. Happy," the nurse said. She was full-figured, with mahogany skin, and wore a thermal top beneath her scrubs. "Always smiling."

"He's been a good boy?" Dash asked.

"We've tried to spend extra time with him since he hasn't had a lot of visitors. Dad's been going back and forth. Mom's MIA."

"Dad's been here?" Dash asked. "Harper?"

"The handsome newsman. Yes, he's been here. Said his wife has been sick, but I don't know if I buy it. If it were my baby in here, wild horses couldn't drag me away."

"Mom's had a rough go."

"We heard about the others," the nurse said, shaking her head. "The NEC baby. These fertility treatments, I tell you. These poor people throw their life savings into having babies when they ought to be listening to what God's trying to tell them. If it doesn't work the old-fashioned way, maybe it wasn't meant to be."

Dash leaned forward again and inhaled the laundered perfume of Emery's sleeper. "But he's here," she said. "He's come through. He's coming through."

The nurse tapped her pencil against the chart. "Social worker talked to your unit about foster care? He's going to need special care for a long time. If you ask me, that's the way to go."

"We didn't ask," Dash said. "But thanks."

Harper was waiting outside the NICU when they arrived in Hanover. He wore dark jeans with orange running shoes, a down parka open over a hooded Packers sweatshirt, like every father or husband who ever roamed the hospital after dark. In fact Dash didn't recognize him until she drew closer, and in the next breath she hoped the woman standing beside was Brooke, that she'd come back. The woman was tall and handsome, her hair streaked with gray, her looks a complement to Harper's. Brooke had told her once, her eyes on the floor, how she and Harper had met, and seeing the woman now led Dash to wonder if there was more to Brooke's absence. If so, she saw the irony in it, and the appeal of dating an older woman. A few months in the NICU will shift your fantasy life from pornographic sex with a college student to falling asleep with a magazine on your chest.

Dash and Dr. Fackelman stopped so Harper and the woman could look inside the incubator. Emery was asleep, his chest and belly rising and falling. Harper and the woman smiled lovingly at each other. "Once we get him settled," Dr. Fackelman said, "you can say a proper hello."

"I don't believe we've met," Dash said to the woman.

"This is Elizabeth," Harper said. "My sister."

"Nice to meet you," Elizabeth said, extending her hand.

Dash held up her gloves. "Sorry," she said.

Harper sat in the glider while the nurse and doctor worked. He watched in silence, his head against the cushion and his jacket and hood bunched beneath his jaw. He hadn't shaved in a few days, Dash noticed, and the skin beneath his eyes sagged. Harper's chest sank, and sitting there he reminded Dash of Mike in the truck, slumped and exhausted, driving away from the Herons'. Harper's sister touched his shoulder and he lifted his head, blinked hard several times in a row. Dash lifted Emery out of his crib, scooping the intubation tubing and leads along with him. Harper turned his hands up, his arms on his thighs and palms open, as if ready to catch a body falling from an upstairs window. The air whooshed through the breathing hose. Emery's body trembled as the nurse slid him into his father's arms. Harper's sister leaned over his shoulder to stroke the baby's fine hair. "He's beautiful, Harp," she said. "Definitely a Jensen."

Harper made a low humming sound, close to a moan, and let his shoulders fall again.

Elizabeth's phone rang. She reached inside her purse, apologizing, and said she'd be right back. Dash opened Emery's sleeper and uncapped the MIC-KEY button to attach the feeding tube. "Don't be afraid of it," she told Harper. "It's way easier than the gavage." She poured the formula into the canister and handed it to Harper. The yellow-white liquid slowly descended through the line. "I can take him back whenever you've had enough. Been a long day."

"More than one day," Harper said. The chair rocked back and forth.

Dash moved around him the way she'd once moved around Brooke, updating the chart, flushing lines, restocking supplies. With Emery in his arms he appeared almost natural, almost up to the task. She felt Harper watching again. "Am I making you upset?" she asked.

"I was thinking I owed you an apology. I behaved badly in the fall."

"Most dads do," she said. "If there's one thing the NICU isn't, it's a man's world."

"I was out of line. I'm sorry about that."

The blanket cascaded over Harper's arm and into his lap. He held his left hand at an awkward angle beneath Emery's head to avoid jostling the breathing tube. "You'll get used to all the junk," she said.

"I'm not sure I can do this," Harper said quietly, staring down at Emery. "I can't take care of him on my own."

"No word from Brooke?"

"She talked to my son, but didn't say where she was. I was hoping she might come here."

"She hasn't called us. You have family around? Your sister?"

"She lives in St. Paul," Harper said. "She has her own family."

"There are options," Dash said, and set her hand on Harper's shoulder. She added—refusing to think of the alarm on Landon's door, the wires snaking across the Herons' ceiling—"We'll figure something out."

Her driver's side door was frozen and her key wouldn't fit inside the lock. Temperatures had continued to drop throughout the day. She got the passenger side open and had to crawl across the center console, her parka twisting around her knees. The car was a tomb of frozen air, and she had to pump the gas several times before the engine bleated weakly to life. It was after eight and she'd traveled more than two hundred and fifty miles. Mike was at Lowe's until eleven, then UPS until morning, and when her phone began ringing in her pocket she was tempted to ignore it. Whatever it was could wait, at least until the morning.

The number on the display belonged to Camille Martin. "I wanted you to know that Landon split from his foster home," the social worker said.

"What?" Dash asked. She turned down the blower on the defrost. "He split?"

"He took off."

"I don't understand."

"Kids do this sometimes. They bolt."

"Not Landon," Dash said. "He hides, but he doesn't run."

"Valerie called me," Camille said. "Landon took the dog out and didn't come back inside. She noticed he was gone when the dog started barking at the door. Has he tried to contact you?"

"I've been at work," Dash said. She pulled her phone away from her ear and looked at it. There were no messages, no missed calls. "It's freezing out."

"Valerie called the police," Camille said. "They're looking."

Her windshield was white with frost, save a small band of clear glass along the bottom, closest to the vents. "I'm going up there."

"You should be at home in case he tries to call you," Camille said. "A lot of foster kids try to go home. Let the police do their jobs."

"They'd better do their jobs," Dash said. She was already at the exit to the parking lot, already looking north. "God help them if they don't."

If she pressed her chin to the steering wheel she could see beneath the frost enough to follow the road. She didn't want to think about Landon getting inside a stranger's car, or the kind of person who would stop for him. Worse was the prospect of him wandering in the cold. She got through to her sister-in-law, Carol, to ask if Kasey could stay the night, then tried to call Mike. Lowe's said he'd clocked out already to go to his other job. She didn't have the number for UPS; information only had the useless 1-800 listing. He wouldn't check his cell until his break.

North of Hanover the highway narrowed, the streetlamps disappeared, and the only light was from her headlights on the faded line in the center of the asphalt. There were few cars on the road, the bait shops and fishing motels and taverns all shuttered. Twice she saw glass eyes—deer eyes—staring out from the trees, and froze, fearing they'd jump in front of her car. She watched for the county road, noting the mileage on the odometer so she wouldn't miss the turnoff. Her lights flashed on the windows at the end of the long gravel drive and Valerie Heron came through the plywood vestibule, her coat zipped to her neck and her hood over her frizzy hair. She stopped in front of the headlights, then came around to the window. "Dorn went to look for him."

The wind through the window was as sharp as a blade. Valerie gritted her teeth and clamped her eyes shut. Dash clenched her eyes until the gust passed. "You're sure he didn't hide?"

"There's only one way back inside the house," Valerie said. "The shed's locked and he's not in the garage. We looked everywhere."

The driveway was illuminated by the house and headlights, angled shadows trampled with footprints and crisscrossing tire tracks. Dash set the brake and went around to the front of the car and bent into the headlight beams. The fields beyond the house were pitch-black, behind winter's curtain. "What was he wearing?" Dash asked. "What did he have on?"

Valerie looked back toward the house. "That fleece of his," she said. "He was only taking Sheba out to pee. I told him to wear his coat, but it's still on the hook."

"Hat and gloves?" Dash asked, though she knew the answer before Valerie shook her head. The picture in her mind was clear now. Now she could see him clearly: his hands jammed inside his pockets, his chin buried inside the collar, his ears gone indigo. Her son alone in the dark and cold was a horror she'd seen for years. She'd seen it on the September afternoon when Landon picked at the lawn while Dash and Mike and Kasey tried to explain him to the neighbors. In her nightmares he was always walking away from her, swallowed by darkness. His ears would freeze first, then the bulb of his nose, his fingers and toes. By the time the cold drove him to seek shelter, it would be too late. He'd either be found now or not at all. Without another word to Valerie Heron, she got back in her car and drove away, back toward town, as fast as she could.

She circled the high school and middle school, wings of the same squat building, and crawled through Papasay's downtown, scanning the windows and streetlamps for clouds of breath, her son's telltale gait. She rolled down the window and called his name, the cold stinging her cheeks and eyes. She studied the faces of the two men smoking outside the Ding-a-Ling tavern, the neon Miller and Pabst signs at their backs. She asked if either of them had seen a boy—a big boy—in a fleece jacket. They shook their heads, and one of them dragged on his cigarette, a pinpointed glow haloed in smoke. "Sorry," the nonsmoking man said, the word clouding his face.

If Landon was holed up in a doghouse or in the back of a garage, she'd never find him. He'd freeze to death trying to stay out of sight. He wouldn't be found until daylight, or later, when someone bothered to investigate what their dog kept going after. Dread waved through her. The first crash was the hardest, the most thunderous, almost enough to make her vomit, but each successive undulation was gentler by small degrees, her body slowly growing used to the idea. Accepting it. She saw Landon in the frigid plywood vestibule before the Herons' door. He might not feel lonely at the end because he didn't feel loneliness, not the way she did.

The road into the town park had been plowed and the boat launch ramp was sheathed in ice. Tire tracks rutted the snow and disappeared at the edge of the light. She put the car in park and got out. The air was so cold and clear, the trees so bare, that she could see the lights of Hanover thirty miles to the south, a garland wreathing the horizon. Footprints in the crusted snow walked away into the darkness. She closed her eyes and saw him again, trudging toward home with his head down. Hypothermia would kill him within the first mile. She cupped her hands around her mouth and yelled: "Landon! Landon!" The void swallowed the sound.

She returned to the car and put it into gear. She angled her tires into the ruts and eased onto the ramp and down onto the ice. She felt the back tires of her car—her heavy, old Chrysler Concorde, all thirty-five hundred pounds of it—leave the ramp and roll onto the ice. She kept the windows down, listening for his voice calling back. She pressed on the brake and tilted her ear into the wind. Something beneath her shifted and heaved. Who knew where the ice grew thin or contained holes left by the ice fishers large enough to trap her wheel? Who could see though such darkness? She shifted into reverse and backed up. Her wheels spun on the iced incline, and her car wouldn't climb the ramp. She let her foot off the brake and rolled forward in neutral until she was flat, then shifted into reverse again and stomped the accelerator.

The Chrysler shot up the ramp, back onto firm ground. The plowed road reappeared in her headlights. She put the car in park, slumped against the steering wheel, and wept.

The Piggly Wiggly's glowing red letters floated against the building's beige façade. Through the front windows she could see the deserted aisles, the rows of boxes and cans and jars, the checkout lines with their numbered towers. The woman behind the customer service counter had metal rings up the lobe of her left ear and a star tattooed at the top of her neck. Her name tag said Raven. Her hair had been dyed an oily black and her scalp was stained beneath her part.

Raven shook her head when Dash explained who she was looking for. She hadn't seen anyone fitting Landon's description, but she hadn't been watching the door. "You got a picture of him?" she asked.

Her ID badge was in her coat pocket. Behind the family picture, she kept Landon's senior portrait, taken last September. All the graduating boys wore tuxedo jackets and bowties. The clothes made Landon look older, more handsome. She slid the photograph from the plastic sleeve and passed it across the counter.

"You can leave it if you want," Raven said. "I can ask the stock boys."

"I only have the one."

"I'll make a copy then." Raven laid the picture face down on the copier's glass and waited while a green light passed beneath it. She took the page from the tray, examined it, threw it away. She adjusted the settings and hit the button again. This time she nodded at the page and brought it to Dash. Landon's picture had been blown up to twice its size, and the resolution was clear. "How about you write his name and your phone number on here and I'll make you some more," Raven said. Dash wrote MISSING in large block letters at the top, her name and number along the bottom. Raven fed the sheet into the copier. Pages accumulated in the tray.

Raven set the stack on the counter and divided it. "I'll keep some up here and you take the rest. I made a hundred."

"Thank you," Dash said. "Thank you very much." A lone cashier leaned against the conveyor belt, thumbing a magazine. "You mind if I look around here a little?"

"Be my guest," Raven said. "But I don't think he's here."

The cashier hadn't seen him, nor had the older lady who came from the back of the bakery when Dash rang the bell. She roamed the aisles, up one and down the other, past the soda and bottles of ketchup and loaves of bread, past the Oreos and Chips Ahoy and M&Ms, touching the foods Landon liked as if they might offer some clue about where he'd gone. It was all she could think of to do. Once she left the store, she'd reenter a world in which her firstborn and only son, born hypoxic and too early and later grown too big, all her hope and sorrow, was gone.

In the cereal aisle a woman and a little girl stared intently at the boxes. The girl wore a pink coat, the color faded and smudged with black along the sleeves, her mittens dangling from a string. The woman's parka was big and shabby, a man's. Dash could smell the stale reek of cigarettes from far away. "Excuse me," she said, the flyers in her hand. The woman turned to face her and Dash saw it was Brooke Jensen.

Brooke stared hard for a moment before speaking. "What are you doing here?"

Dash held out the flyer. "My son is missing. He's in a foster home up here and he ran away. I've been looking for him. I've looked everywhere."

Brooke took the page from Dash's hand. She studied it intently. "Foster home?" Brooke's lips moved softly around the word. "Landon."

"He's had some trouble the last few months," Dash said. "He got into some trouble. So he came up here for a while. He ran away and now he's lost."

Dash saw Brooke fit the pieces together: her black eye, the scar at her throat. "It's awfully cold out," she said.

"His foster home is about two miles from here, if he went through the woods. I'm hoping he came this way and can find somewhere to get warm." Dash licked her index finger and separated two more flyers from the stack. "You'll take these? Call me if you see him?"

"Of course."

"Who's this little lady?" Dash asked. The girl had tucked herself behind Brooke's leg.

"Atlantis," Brooke said. She took a step back and slid a hand inside the pocket of the coat. "I've been staying at her place."

"We've missed you," Dash said. "Emery came back to us today. He looks a lot better."

"Who's Emery?" Atlantis asked, her neck craned.

Brooke ignored the question and looked at Dash.

"He's a little fighter, that one," Dash said, though fighter wasn't a word she ordinarily used. She ordinarily considered the word ridiculous because it implied that babies who died in the NICU died from a failure of will rather than of biology. But it seemed to fit Emery. All by himself he'd found a way to endure. "The surgery closed his PDA and resolved some bowel issues. He's breathing a lot better."

"You've been taking care of him?" Brooke asked.

"Dr. Fackelman and I brought him back from Madison today. His dad was waiting for us at the hospital when we arrived."

"Harper?" Brooke touched her chin.

After a time, Dash said, "No one blames you."

"Yeah, right."

"Well, let's just say we'd be glad to see you come back. Come back and see him." She took the paper from Brooke's hand and reached inside her purse for a pen. She wrote her home number on the bottom of the page, as well as Mike's cell. "If you see Landon, call me, okay? Call any one of these numbers."

Brooke stared at the photograph again, Landon smiling in his bowtie and satin lapels, his eyes not quite centered on the camera's lens. Brooke remembered him. Someone up here knew who he was. *That* he was. The bubbling-up Dash had felt in the ambulance that morning came back to her, along with Dr. Fackelman's words, You're not as alone as you think you are. She was in Papasay and so was Brooke. As she walked away she heard the little girl ask Brooke, "Can we get Cocoa Puffs?"

The credit union marquee said the temperature was minus eighty-eight. The air was so cold the machine couldn't measure it, so it assumed the worst. The heated seats in Justus's truck were warm but still her breath fogged. The electric panel in the dashboard was slow to respond and the radio couldn't lock onto a station. Brooke switched it off and drove in silence, trying to remember the way back. If she could slip the keys back inside Justus's sweatshirt before he woke up, or even on the bed beside his pocket, he'd never know she'd been gone.

She'd bought Children's Motrin for Atlantis, along with cranberry juice and a bottle of gummy vitamins advertised to help with UTIs. After several glasses of Judge Pamela's special home brew of warm water mixed with baking soda and cream of tartar, Atlantis's fever was down and she'd stopped crying when she peed. Along with the meds and treats, Brooke had bought a dozen eggs, a gallon of milk, and a pound of strawberries, so red and plump in their plastic carton they hardly seemed real. Her mouth watered, wanting one. She didn't know what Justus would say when he saw them. She hoped he was too stoned to remember their conversation that evening. If he did, she could tell him she'd walked to the store. If he didn't believe her, well, she'd make up something else.

"I'm cuckoo for Cocoa Puffs," Atlantis said. She held the box between her hands, like a toy. She touched the letters as she sounded out the words. "What's MFG?" she asked.

"Preservatives," Brooke said. "So the cereal won't go stale." She recalled the alphabet soup of acronyms from the NICU. POS, PVL, PDA, TPN, NEC. NEC. It had taken her weeks to discern which abbreviations were good and which were bad, though in the end she'd concluded that anything reduced to a code had to be bad. There was no acronym for healthy. Healthy didn't belong in the hospital.

She hoped Dash found her son, and soon. People didn't last long in temperatures this cold. Stumble away from a party and pass out in the snow on a night like this and you were a goner. She had Dash's flyer folded in her coat pocket, the nurse's phone numbers scrawled beneath the picture of Landon—her boy who'd survived the NICU. Brooke wondered what would happen if she called Dash to ask whether Harper seemed mad or disgusted, or how Emery looked when they brought him back to the unit. Whether her baby was even real.

"Can we go to your house and have a slumber party?" Atlantis asked.

"It's late, kiddo. We need to go to bed. We'll go to my house soon."

At the last stoplight in Papasay, Brooke leaned her head back against the rest and closed her eyes. She was sleepy, and this was a pleasant enough place to be for the moment—the cab of the truck slowly warming, Atlantis jabbering beside her like a talk show. She came back when Atlantis tapped on her arm to tell her the light was green, it was their turn to go, why wasn't she moving? Flecks of ice swirled across the windshield, a blizzard beneath the streetlamps.

Pulled by the house lights, she turned right into the neighborhood of small clapboard houses. She hadn't noticed them before, in the daylight, but now they glowed a deep amber, as if they'd risen out of the snow. A television flickered inside one window, a floor lamp illuminated a sofa and table inside another. Furnace pipes puffed exhaust steam. She drove slowly, admiring the houses. She remembered Halloween night when she and Harper had admired the houses and decorations in their neighborhood. His warm hand and the scent of his jacket lining. Her breast still tender from Opal's suckling. How real it had all felt, how close and how hopeful, her life like an apple she could pluck from a branch. Thirty miles across the ice, her house was still there, its furnace and lights on, Harper and maybe even Oliver inside. Nearer still, just forty-five minutes down the eastern shore, was the hospital, and Emery. Yet she still felt—as she had since the night she followed Justus to his truck—that if she were to try to return, Hanover wouldn't be there. The city and all it contained would have been wiped away. The frozen lake would go on forever.

She saw a figure moving in the darkness. Following the streetlamps but also staying back, avoiding them, trudging through the snowy yards. Brooke steered toward the curb and flicked on the high beams. She saw the ice in his hair. His broad back was navy blue, covered only in a thin fleece. She honked once, softly, just enough to get his attention. He turned into the headlights and she saw the embroidered HMC logo above the heart, the image she'd seen on every lab sheet and name badge, every white coat and scrub top, every cup and mug. That's how she knew, before she even saw his face, that it was him.

23

Atlantis slept like a cat, curled on a chair in the waiting room of the emergency department at Hanover Medical Center. She made a pillow of her small hands folded beneath her cheek. Her soft snore was almost a purr, barely audible in the crowded waiting room. The people around her dozed fitfully, shifting their feet and coughing into their coats, their heads on one another's shoulders. Brooke took comfort in the fact that, in Justus's drooping coat and sagging jeans, she looked like everyone else in the room. No one knew she was here. No one expected her to stay.

She slept a while but woke when she felt a hand on her knee. "You've been out here all this time?" Dash asked, leaning over her.

"How long has it been? What time is it?"

"Almost two," Dash said, looking at her watch. "Not almost. After."

"How's Landon?"

"They've moved him up to the burn unit. That's where they treat frostbite, like it's a burn. My husband's with him." The nurse straightened her back and gazed down at Atlantis. "We can find a more comfortable room than this. Let's take her upstairs."

Brooke cupped her hand over Atlantis's head, but Dash said, "Don't wake her." She slid one hand beneath the girl's head and the other beneath her knees. Atlantis appeared to levitate upward from the chair, floating weightlessly before the nurse spun her and laid the girl's head against her shoulder. Atlantis's small rear end was a ball above Dash's elbow. "Follow me," Dash said.

Brooke listened to the elevator ding for each floor. She watched the red numbers tick by. Of course they were going to three. They came out in a back hallway, at the end of a corridor. The overhead lights flickered on as they moved down the hall, triggered by motion sensors. At the junction Brooke remembered where she was. The NICU was two corridors to the left and through the double doors. She could once again feel her children, living and dead, around her. She waved her hand in front of her face to send them away.

Dash stopped in front of Dr. Fackelman's office and asked Brooke to get the door. She pushed it open and then followed Dash into the lightless space, obeying when Dash told her to leave the light switch alone. Dash lay Atlantis down somewhere before reaching to switch on a floor lamp. The sofa was leather, same as the reclining chair beside it. A small television sat atop a mini fridge. Dash spread a blanket across Atlantis and tucked it beneath her feet.

"The doctor won't mind that we're in here?" Brooke asked.

Dash shook her head. "It's fine, don't worry. What else can I get you?"

"Nothing," Brooke said, fearing Dash might try to talk her into visiting the NICU, as if she could pick up where she left off. As if she had any right to be here. "Maybe you have some cranberry juice? Atlantis has a UTI."

"Should we have a doctor take a look?"

"She's through the worst of it, I think. But some juice wouldn't hurt. That's why we were at the store when we saw you. Buying juice and ibuprofen."

"Does Justus know you're here? Dash asked. "Have you called him?"

"Not yet," Brooke said. "He wasn't exactly present when we left him."

"Might as well wait till morning." Dash touched her elbow. Her fingers were light and warm. "I don't know what would've happened if you hadn't found Landon," she said. "I don't know what would've happened."

Landon had tried to run when Brooke called to him, but his legs had wobbled and he'd fallen over in the snow. He'd been difficult to lift, and Brooke had had to keep saying his name until he'd allowed Brooke to lead him. Beneath the dome light of the truck, she saw his head was bleeding, the blood frozen beside his ear and down his jaw. Landon mumbled, more groans than words, and his hands were swollen and purple, as hard as stone. She'd turned the heat on full blast and had driven him straight to the emergency room in Hanover, calling Dash from the car.

"I was lucky," Brooke said.

"I think it was more than that," Dash said, her grip a little tighter now. "I'd like to say God put you there, on that road, but I don't know anymore what God does. I just know it wasn't random. It wasn't simply luck."

Dash looked down at Atlantis again. "Do you need to call anyone else?"

"Not now," Brooke said, reaching across Atlantis's face to turn off the floor lamp. "Not just yet. Just the cranberry juice, if you have some. I'll sit with her a while."

Falling asleep would mean waking up here, in the same building as Emery, and attempting to sort out what she'd done. And whether to do it again. Justus's truck was in the parking lot. Atlantis was safe and warm; Brooke could be gone before anyone other than Dash knew she'd been here.

She listened to the building, a soft hissing through the walls, very low and faint, like a distant breath. Heat moved through the ducts, and oxygen through a dedicated pipe from the central plant, and inside the pneumatic tubes zoomed blood and medicine, tissue and urine and fecal samples. The hospital's muscles pumped and its lungs breathed, even while it slept, which it never fully did. Only occasionally was she disturbed by someone squeaking past the open door, the corridor lights flashing on as a pair of blue scrubs rushed past, then going dark again a minute later.

Long after she'd lost track of time, she heard the elevator ding. His footsteps at the end of the hall were soft but she knew them. She heard him pause before each door, reading the numbers and the names on the placards. Her heart raced. She sat very still in the dark.

He stopped in the doorway, his silhouette framed by the hallway lights behind him. There was his dark outline, the peak of his shoulders, his distinctive smell. He carried his parka slung over his forearm. He gripped the doorframe. "Brooke?" Harper whispered. "Are you here?"

Atlantis rolled over, burying her face in the couch. "Let's talk in the hall," Brooke said.

Harper wore sweatpants, a hooded sweatshirt. His hair was matted on the side and his cheeks were stubbled. He looked a decade older than Brooke remembered, and for a moment she doubted how long she'd actually been gone.

Harper opened his arms and Brooke, whether by habit or want or some combination of the two, stepped into them. "Are you okay?" he asked.

"I'm okay," she said, conscious of her grimy clothes and cigarette stench.

"I was so worried." He breathed against her scalp. "I was so worried."

"You want to know where I was." She didn't ask it as a question. It wasn't a question.

"I'm mostly glad you're safe. And that you're here." He took a step back. "You said you were at a friend's?"

"Wasn't really a friend. Parent of another NICU baby. He offered me a ride."

"He?"

"Dad of a NICU baby. Atlantis's dad. Nothing happened, other than I stayed at their place for a few days. Longer than a few, I guess."

Harper rolled his bottom lip beneath his top teeth. "I went to the police, but when I showed them your message, they said there's no law against an adult running away. I kept hoping you'd show up in Madison. When you didn't, I started to worry that you'd disappeared in a way you couldn't come back from. Your mom didn't think you'd do something"—he paused to swallow—"*final*, but when I thought about the way you looked the night you left, how I mentioned sending Emery to a facility, I got pretty scared. I almost said something on the air. Julie told me not to, but I almost did it anyway." He ran his hand through his hair and gripped the back of his neck. He blinked twice, the wrinkles deepening around his eyes. "I was out of my mind."

"Ollie told me you went to Madison."

"One of us—" he stopped. "I didn't want him to be there alone. I should have gone with him in the first place."

"I'm sorry."

"You should call your mom," he said. "She'll want to know you're okay."

"Should I do it right now?"

"You can wait till she's awake." Harper drew in another deep breath and let it out. Brooke smelled his anguish leaking away from him. "You came back. That's all I really care about."

He pulled her close again. "Do you want to see him?"

"I don't know if I should. I don't think it would be right."

"Who knows what's right, Brooke?" Her name sounded strange, as though he hadn't said it in a long time. She caught herself: she hadn't *heard* her name in a long time. Atlantis had only called her "you." For more than a week, she hadn't existed. She'd fallen through a hole in time. "I have no idea about what's right and what's not," Harper said. "But Emery's ours, and he's down the hall."

The unit door made her more aware of her clothes. The interior lights were dimmed, and the room smelled of formula and diapers and antibacterial soap. Brooke pushed her sleeves as high as she could and took her time at the sink, bending over to do her face after she finished with her arms. She waited for Harper to dry his hands before going around the corner. Instinct propelled her toward Bed Eight, but Emery wasn't there. "He's over here now," Ting said, coming forward to greet them. "Welcome back."

Emery was in Bed Five, in the corner near the window. He lay in an open crib instead of an enclosed Isolette. The translucent oxygen tubing that once ran to his mouth now lay against his chest and terminated at the fitting in his throat. There were his eyes, their delta of hairfine vessels, his nose. His lips, no longer forced apart by the ET tube, were pursed. His hands were open near his head, at the high point of a snow angel. Brooke studied the wrinkles in his palms for a long moment before she realized they were due to the extra flesh.

"I was going to feed him," Ting said. "Sit down. I'll show you how."

Brooke pointed at Harper. "He'll do it."

"You should," Harper said, frowning. "I was here earlier."

"Not yet," Brooke said. "I want to watch first."

Brooke stood behind the glider as Ting settled Emery into Harper's arms. Ting connected the feeding gavage to the G-tube and filled the syringe with formula. Brooke leaned forward and cupped her hand around Emery's head. She could feel the ventilator vibrate through his skull. She touched his lips, then slid her pinky between his gums. He received it eagerly, clamping his mouth around her finger. She felt the blood swell beneath her nail. Emery had only ever eaten by fatty injection, then by nasal gavage, and now though a surgically implanted tube in his belly. But the instinct to feed, to suck and swallow, was there. The fact of it amazed her.

The syringe empty, Ting disconnected the tube and pulled the curtain closed around them. Neither of them spoke until the window began to gray and the skeletons of the trees in the courtyard emerged in the glass. Brooke whispered to Harper about the night of Emery's transfer, the offer that had prompted her to run, and the house where she had stayed. When Harper asked how she'd found the nurse's boy, she tried to explain about the house lights in the neighborhood but she couldn't seem to get the words right, so she told Harper, as she'd told Dash, that she'd gotten lucky. Dawn came on, bright and cloudless and frigid, the day hardly warmer than the night it had shoved aside. Moisture condensed in the corners of the glass and froze there. Sometime later the curtain slid open and Fran stood on the other side, her hair freshly spiked. The little girl Brooke had left sleeping in the doctor's office was awake and asking for her. Jenny Ramirez also wanted to talk.

Dr. Fackelman waited with Jenny in the conference room. They sat down and Harper took Brooke's hand beneath the table. Beside Jenny's coffee cup was a yellow legal pad, a pen laid diagonally across it. "We were all worried when we heard you hadn't made it to Madison. We're glad you're back."

"Is Atlantis okay?" Brooke asked.

"CPS is with her," Jenny said. "They've been here all morning."

"Because of Landon?"

"That's not something I can discuss," Jenny said. She'd cut her hair since Brooke had last seen her, and bangs now hung across her eyebrows. Her earrings, Brooke noticed, were little Japanese fans. Her necklace had snagged on the collar of her sweater.

"We need to talk now?" Harper interrupted. "It's been a hell of a night."

"Our concerns aren't ones we want to sit on," Dr. Fackelman said.

"You want to know where I went," Brooke said.

"Not so much 'where' as 'why,'" the social worker said. "And whether you intend to stay. We're at a point now when we need to make a decision about Emery's welfare."

Dr. Fackelman frowned. "I'd really like to know how you're feeling. Your state of mind."

"It was my fault," Harper said. "I suggested looking into a long-term care facility for Emery. I told Brooke I didn't think we could care for him."

"It wasn't his fault," Brooke said. She recalled the emptiness she'd felt when she'd touched Emery in the portable Isolette and when she watched the ambulance round the corner. Even now she could recall the impulse to flee with a terrible intensity; even here it called to her. She still had Justus's keys in her pocket. "I'm the one who left him behind."

Harper said, "She's here now, though."

"Unfortunately, that's not enough," Jenny said. She ran her finger along her necklace to free it. "We've had situations like this before. And it wasn't like this happened out of the blue. You've been pretty scarce since November."

Harper set his hands on the table and leaned forward. He'd been as absent from the unit during the fall as she had been, though only now did it occur to Brooke that he'd been going through the same feelings, the same despair, also on his own. "You might recall a few things happening in November," he said. "You might recall our daughter dying in your unit."

"Yes," Dr. Fackelman said sadly.

"You might also recall the two babies who died in September."

"Ruby and Pearl," Brooke echoed. Again Dr. Fackelman nodded.

"You've been through an awful lot," Jenny said. "We know that."

"You have no idea," Harper said, lacing his fingers together. "None whatsoever."

Dr. Fackelman sipped from her coffee. "Emery has significant issues that will affect him in the long term. In addition to his lung disease, he's showing signs of neurological impairment."

"Because of the steroids?" Harper asked.

"It's possible," Dr. Fackelman said. "We did what we needed to do to save his life. Now we have to think about how to care for him. He's going to need full-time care for a while. You weren't wrong to bring up an acute care facility. It's an option you really ought to discuss. Caring for him at home might not be the best choice for your family."

Brooke twisted her wedding ring around on her finger. "I expected more from myself."

"So did we," Jenny said.

Dr. Fackelman reached beyond her coffee, toward the table's center. Her hand was still several feet from Brooke's.

"Emery has several weeks to go before he's ready for discharge. He needs to grow out of his arrhythmias and bradycardias. There's plenty to do. Let's see how it goes."

Atlantis sat cross-legged on the sofa in the Family Room with a Styrofoam bowl of Froot Loops cradled in her palm. Brooke sat in the armchair beside the window, staring through the crosshatched pane at the frozen lake. She held a paper cup of coffee, the liquid so black it looked like oil, the powdered creamer clumping on the surface. For close to an hour, Brooke had tried to explain to the social worker from Child Protective Services how she and Atlantis had ended up together. She told the truth plainly while Maggie Caras wrote and Harper listened: about the night she saw Justus in the parking lot. How he hadn't forced her to come with him, nor hurt her while she stayed at his house. In fact, she'd been alone most of the time. She didn't mention the doctor she'd visited or the prescription she'd filled, but assumed CPS could find out both if they dug hard enough. She deserved whatever consequences came as a result.

Maggie's glasses sat a little crookedly on her face. Unlike Jenny Ramirez, she didn't seem as skeptical about why Brooke left or whether she was fit to mother a child, either her own or someone else's. Maggie pulled her dark curls into her fist and twisted her hair into a knot, then shoved her pen through the bun to hold it in place. She told Brooke she'd done the right thing by getting Atlantis away from Justus's house. "I've been to that house," Maggie said. "We've been involved there for a while. Was there any food in the cupboard?"

"They'd had a kitchen fire," Brooke said. "The kitchen was closed off from the rest of the house. Justus went to the store before he left, so we didn't go hungry."

"Kitchen fire?" Maggie asked. The stud in her tongue clicked against her teeth. "I doubt he was cooking food."

"It smelled bad," Brooke said, recalling the melted plastic bottles on the floor.

Maggie shook her head. The pen jabbed through her hair didn't budge. "He's had so many chances. Too many."

Maggie told Brooke she could wait with Atlantis until Justus arrived. Harper went to the cafeteria and came back with bagels and more coffee. He offered to read with Atlantis, but she was too involved in her show and claimed she didn't like books. Maggie stepped out several times with her phone in her hand to try to get through to Justus, who finally made it to the hospital after three, his boots stomping down the hallway to make himself sound larger and tougher than he really was.

He wore the same work pants and sweatshirt he'd had on the night before, a stocking cap pulled over his head. His boots were gray with snow. Harper stood when he thundered inside the Family Room. Justus glowered at Brooke. "Where's my truck? Where's my fucking truck?"

"It's in the lot," Brooke said, holding out his keys. Justus snatched them from her hand, and she felt Harper flinch behind her. "I'm sorry I took it," she said.

Justus pointed his finger at her. "She stole my truck," he said to Maggie. "You heard her say it. She stole my truck and kidnapped my daughter."

"I heard a different story," Maggie said. She straightened her glasses and didn't seem the slightest bit intimidated. "I heard you invited Brooke to your house and left her stranded there for some time. I also heard that Atlantis has been left alone a lot and that she's not attending school."

"I *told* her she couldn't take my truck," Justus said. "I said it right to her bitch face."

"Hey now," Harper said. He clenched his fist and stepped forward. Justus shuffled backward and turned his shoulder toward Harper. His dingy sweatshirt was much larger than the one Brooke's husband wore, baggy around the shoulders and hanging below his waist. He no longer looked dangerous. He didn't seem dangerous when he came home last night, and he didn't seem dangerous now. Brooke believed she saw him as he really was: a scared man-child who expected the world to turn against him, to dole out pain and disappointment instead of the blessings of ordinariness. All morning she'd struggled to explain to Harper why she'd gone with Justus, but now she felt she understood it better. In the darkness outside the hospital, in the small flame at the end of his hand, she'd recognized her own helplessness. Maybe he'd seen the same thing in her. Maybe that was why he'd offered her the ride.

"Cool it," Maggie said. "Enough of the language. You can take your truck, but not Atlantis. One thing that's been made abundantly clear is that she's not safe with you. She came in with a urinary tract infection."

"That wasn't my fault," Justus said. His eyelids were purple. He looked scared. "I wasn't the one watching her."

"Exactly," Maggie said, her voice matter-of-fact. "You should have been. We've come to your house on several past occasions. We've made every reasonable attempt to help you keep Atlantis at home. But there's no way she's going back to a house where illegal activity is going on. Absolutely no way."

"She stole my truck," Justus said, pointing again at Brooke. "I want to press charges for that. I tried to help her and she stole from me."

Maggie opened her notebook and pulled a card from an inside pocket, which she passed to Justus. "We don't handle criminal complaints. You can take it up with the sheriff. I think the police would be pretty interested in learning more about the cause of your little kitchen fire."

Denny, the young security guard, appeared in the doorway of the Family Room. He stood with his arms crossed, a radio receiver clipped to his shirt and a yellow-handled Taser holstered to his belt. Justus glared. "Looks like Mighty Mouse is here to save the day."

"Want to make sure you find the exit safely," Denny said.

Justus lifted his coat from the back of the chair and shrugged it on. "Don't take any shit, Squirt," he said to Atlantis. He patted the top of her head. "Don't make it easy on anybody. Give 'em hell. You'll be back with me before you know it."

"Okay, Dad," Atlantis said.

The thought of sending Atlantis away with Justus had disturbed Brooke, though she hadn't known it until Maggie had prevented it from happening. A child could not return to that house, with that man, even if Justus was her father. Atlantis needed clean sheets, clean underwear, help brushing her teeth. She needed cooked food and to go to school. Yet Atlantis wouldn't be here had Brooke not turned away from the ambulance a week and a half earlier. All her life seemed a series of small choices made on a whim that radiated ever-larger circles of hurtful consequences. Everyone got caught in her wake. She folded the coat she'd taken from Justus's closet and handed it to him. "This is yours," she said. "I didn't mean to cause you any trouble."

His tongue filled the gap in his teeth. His grin was an arrow aimed at her. "You want trouble? Just wait until I call my lawyer."

Brooke waited until Denny had followed Justus to the elevator and the door had dinged twice—once to arrive and once to leave—until she and Harper and Atlantis and Maggie Caras were the only ones left in the Family Room. Brooke closed the door and turned the television back on for Atlantis before she whispered to Maggie, "What will happen to her? Where will Atlantis go now?"

"Sounds like anywhere is better than where she's been," Harper said.

Maggie motioned them into the corner, near the door. Atlantis sat with her legs crossed and her thumb in her mouth. A cartoon man in a kilt exclaimed, "Holy haggis!" as a runaway jackhammer danced and skittered across a kitchen floor. Atlantis laughed, her teeth still tight around her thumb. A part of Brooke wished she were still beneath the quilt on Justus's sofa, watching *Swiss Family Robinson.*

Maggie turned her back to Atlantis and lowered her voice, so low Brooke could barely hear her over the TV. "We'll find a foster home for her. We have families ready to accept emergency placements at any time."

"What about her mother?" Brooke asked. "Shantel's not her mom. Where's her real mom?"

"Cannon's mom?" Maggie said. "No, she's not Atlantis's mother. Atlantis's mother hasn't had contact in a long time. She no longer has parental rights."

"She's not scared?" Harper asked, nodding toward Atlantis. "She didn't even cry when her dad left her. I'd be out of my gourd."

"This isn't her first time. She was removed two years ago. She went to three foster homes until we found one where she started to settle in. Her dad fought tooth and nail to get her back."

"The lawsuit," Brooke said.

"That's right," Maggie said. "I shouldn't say too much, though I suspect things will be different this time around. If what you're saying is accurate, there's too much evidence of neglect and endangerment. We'll be visiting his house soon. Tomorrow morning, if I can find Atlantis a home."

"It's already near the end of the day," Harper said. "Someone's going to come get that little girl tonight? Like, now?"

"We have families who will come whenever we call. After midnight, if we need them."

Atlantis turned from her show. "I don't want to go with a stranger," she said. "I want to stay with Brooke. She had a slumber party at my house and said we could have the next one at hers."

"How about we find a nice house for you?" Maggie said to the girl. "A comfy bed, all to yourself. Maybe even a bunk bed."

"I want to stay with Brooke," Atlantis said.

"I wish that was how it worked," Maggie said, more to Brooke and Harper than to Atlantis, as if to prevent them from offering to take her. "I wish it were that simple. I can't tell you how many times the nurses here tell me they want to take a baby home, even though they've all seen me enough times to know better."

"After all that's happened, I don't think you'd let me anyway," Brooke said.

"You did a good job looking after her," Maggie said. "That's not the issue. There's a whole licensing process required to become a foster parent. We conduct interviews, do home visits. It takes months. We can't just turn a kid over to anybody with a big heart."

Harper leaned a shoulder against the wall, then stood straight again. His eyes never left Brooke. "We did all that," he said to Maggie, as though he and Brooke had already agreed. As though, in their early morning hours with Emery and in the Family Room with Atlantis, this one thing had been decided. They might not be equipped to care for their own sick child, they might never be able to bring Emery home, but Atlantis they could help, even if only for a short while. She could not be cast out. “This time last year we thought we were going the foster care route,” Harper said. “We finished our licensing not long before we found out Brooke was pregnant.”

“Wait,” Maggie said. “What? You’re serious?”

24

The full extent of the frostbite wouldn't be known for weeks. The burn unit intensivist told them there was a good chance Landon would lose the middle, ring, and pinky fingers on his right hand, the thumb and index finger on his left. His toes were also a concern; so too were the zygomatic arches of his cheeks and the tip of his penis. It was possible Landon had wet his pants during the hours he'd spent in the cold, and the urine had frozen against his skin. The tissues might recover, or they might not. If the skin began to blacken, they'd know.

Landon lay on his back with his bandaged hands elevated. He looked like he was praying or reaching out for help. The morphine would make sure he stayed sleepy for a while. The valleys of his molars were dark with stains, and Dash feared the Herons, in all their chair-stacking holy rolling, had never reminded him to brush. She squeezed a glob of Colgate onto a hospital-issued toothbrush, dipped it in water, and gently worked it over Landon's teeth, her hand cupped around his chin. The same way she'd held his face at the bathroom sink when he was small.

She poured a little water into his mouth. "Don't try to spit it," she said. "Swallow it down."

She wet the bristles of her hairbrush beneath the sink faucet and combed his hair. His heart rate was one thirty, slow but okay; blood pressure was one ten over seventy. She lifted his chin to close his mouth, but as soon as she moved her hand away his jaw fell slack again. He'd be eighteen in five weeks. Whatever decisions they needed to make, they needed to make soon.

"Gangrene isn't a foregone conclusion," the doctor said. He was a bearded, barrel-chested man with a limp caused by hip dysplasia. "We're not going to amputate preemptively." They'd have to wait and see.

It had been a year of waiting and seeing. Of making plans and weighing contingencies and plotting out next steps, and they were out of time. If Landon's fingers or toes needed amputating, he'd have to consent for himself. Once discharged, where would he go? Not home, and God forbid not back to the Herons. What would stop him from running off again? What would happen when the police answered a call from a panicked homeowner about a strange man with yellowed teeth in their yard? If commanded to lie on the ground, to put his hands up, would he do it? It was all Dash thought about. She settled into her chair beside Landon's bed and selfishly wished for the gangrene to overtake Landon's feet so the surgeon would be forced to hobble him.

The nurse who came to exchange Landon's empty IV wore her hair in a topknot with a thin elastic headband, a style popular with younger nurses, except she was at least forty. Dash wondered how long she'd been in the job, whether she'd come to it after flaming out at some other endeavor. Whether she was qualified to care for her boy. The nurse lifted the catheter receptacle from the side of the bed and studied the hash marks. Landon's urine at first had been almost brown but had gradually begun to lighten. At least his kidneys were coming around.

The nurse pushed the buttons on the monitor with her middle finger, glancing at Dash out of the corner of her eye. Watch yourself, sister, Dash thought. The nurse shuffled out of the room, but came right back with a plastic grocery sack. "For you," she said.

"What's this for?"

"Breakfast," the nurse said.

Inside she found a bottle of Mountain Dew and a sandwich wrapped in white paper. "I mean where did it come from?"

"Someone dropped it off for you."

"Who?"

"I didn't see," the nurse said. "Left it at the desk."

"Well, thanks."

"You were awake. I figured you'd be getting hungry."

"I guess I haven't slept in a long time." She couldn't remember when. The night before her trip to Madison? It felt like weeks, months.

"Maybe that should come next," the nurse said. She dimmed the lights and lifted the handle to silence the click of the latch.

The sandwich was an egg and ham but no cheese, on an everything bagel. The dough was warm and soft, and the disc of scrambled egg dissolved in her mouth. She chowed it down without stopping, then opened the soda and took a gigantic swig that made her hiccup. The food weighted her to the chair so heavily she didn't think she could move. The urge to sleep was hard to fight and it almost had her when she heard Mike's voice. She lifted her finger to her lips and Mike hunched his shoulders and stood on his toes. "What are you doing here so early?" she asked. It wasn't even eight o'clock.

"I got a call to come up."

Dash sat up straighter. "Who called you?"

"I forget her name," Mike said. He removed his cap and smoothed down the hair over his ears. "Maybe she didn't tell it to me. Just said I needed to come up for a meeting. About Landon."

"No one told me. Was it Maggie Caras or Camille Martin?"

"None of them." Mike blinked twice. "Sorry. It was early. Kasey's down the hall, in that little room with the TV and all the old magazines."

She debated with herself whether it was Friday or Saturday before deciding to err on the side of caution. "It's a school day, isn't it? She should be in school."

"I'll take her in late."

"I don't want her to get into trouble for skipping school."

"It's okay, Dash. Let's see what we can find out."

She ran Landon's toothbrush under the hot water and used it to brush her own teeth. She didn't have time for a shower, so she washed her face in the sink and ran her wet hands over her hair, then zipped her fleece to her chin to hide whatever she smelled like. She followed Mike to an education room outfitted with a round table and four padded chairs. The only thing that separated it from the rooms where she'd met to talk about Landon with his doctors and social workers, where she met with NICU parents to talk about their own babies, was the number on the door. The hospital was full of rooms for delivering bad news. They were met there by a man in a gray suit beneath a black wool overcoat, his cornflower tie a jolt of color down his chest. He smelled like leather. He said his name was Curt Shafer, from Waterman, Ford, and Sandborn.

"You're from the court?" Mike asked.

"I'm a lawyer, yes," he said. "Your son's case was referred to me."

"Landon can't leave," Dash said. "He has severe frostbite. Not even to go to the courthouse."

"That shouldn't be necessary," Curt Shafer said. He draped his coat over the back of the empty chair and motioned for them to sit. Mike removed his cap and hid it below the table. "I'm thinking we can get everything settled without having to appear before a judge again."

"You're our new public defender?" Mike asked. "What happened to Ms. Wilmar?"

"I'm not a public defender. I'm a family attorney. I specialize in cases like Landon's. Kids with mental health problems."

"I don't understand why you're here," Dash said. She wiped her eyes with the back of her wrist. "If you're not a public defender."

Curt Shafer touched his tie, and Dash could tell he knew more than he was saying. "Your son's case was referred to me. I have been retained."

"Who called you?"

"They've asked to remain anonymous."

"Well, that's great," Mike said. "How much will this run us? Even this little sit-down can't be cheap."

"I should have been clearer," Curt Shafer said. "My fees are being paid by a friend."

"Our anonymous friend," Dash said.

"That's right." He set his briefcase on the table and withdrew a manila folder. He slid a pair of silver reading glasses over his eyes. "I got Landon's file from the public defender's office, and I've spoken with his social workers."

"Maggie or Camille?"

"Both of them, as well as Jennifer Ramirez from the hospital. Tell me if I'm missing something. Landon appeared in Family Court last fall and was removed from the home in January of this year." He looked over the rim of his reading glasses before adding, "He made threats against your life and his sister's."

Read so plainly, the description sounded even more terrible. "He wasn't removed from us," Dash said. "We gave him up. We sent him away."

"We did what we had to do," Mike said. "Before something terrible happened."

"We're lucky we got him back," Dash said, sternly, her eyes locked on her husband. "He nearly froze to death. We're lucky he's alive."

"I'm glad he's okay," Mike said.

"We don't know that he is yet. He could lose his fingers."

"I have more documents to review," Curt Shafer interrupted. "It's clear you've been an advocate for him. You've had him in therapy." He removed his glasses and set them upside down on the table. The knot of his tie was the size of Dash's fist, a silk origami figurine. "I've seen other kids like Landon. Boys and girls from good families, with cognitive impairments that cause them to act in ways beyond their control. You can't tell me in good conscience he'd be better off in jail or shuffled around the system. You ask me, he never should have gone into foster care."

At last someone saw it her way. But she also recognized the subtext, the meaning of the lawyer's scented hands, his leather valise. "Good families" meant families with money, who could afford to make their kids' legal problems go away. Curt Shafer, she could tell, believed in the goodness and righteousness of what he was doing, but his righteousness wasn't free.

He continued, "I'm confident I can get his previous charges dismissed and his record expunged. My real goal is to find him a better place to live. Somewhere closer to you, in Hanover. That way he can take the bus to work."

"Another foster home?" Mike asked.

"I'm thinking a corporate group home will be a better fit," Curt Shafer said. "I know some good ones in the area. Full-time staff who can help with everyday needs."

"Landon's almost eighteen," Dash said. "He'll be considered an adult next month."

"Ah," Curt Shafer said, withdrawing a page from his folder. "That's the good news. His competency evaluation came back. He was declared incompetent."

"That's good news?" Mike asked.

"*Very* good news. He needs a guardian to make decisions on his behalf."

It was all so pragmatic and sensible, this plan put forward by Curt Shafer, Esq., of Waterman, Ford, and Sandborn, that Dash was inclined to resist it out of habit if not distrust. She'd fought for Landon for so long that it was hard to stop, let alone to trust in the assistance of a stranger. Even Mike's efforts she'd been wary of. She was wary of Mike now, nodding beside her with his cap on his knee and his meaty hands knit together. She didn't want a plan. She wanted Landon to stay right where he was, snowed on morphine and immobilized in the one place where she felt capable and in control. In her mind Landon had never stopped being that fragile infant with a blood-swamped brain, kindly old Dr. Marlowe telling her that letting him go would be the more merciful choice. She longed for the time when she'd begged for his life, for a blessing better than death, for the beauty of that single, fundamental want. She'd come to work in the NICU not for the acuity of the care or the skills the job demanded but for the grace that adhered to such tiny human bodies, their souls bursting at the follicles of their gelatinous skin. Every preemie teetered at the edge of life, too small and early to know what they'd be missing if they let go, and it was her job to hold them back. Holding them back—the babies and Landon, the first premature infant she'd ever known—was her life's purpose. The fact that her son's life was becoming one she could not always watch over and guard filled her with an inconsolable sadness. Even though she knew she had no choice.

"We want to pay you," Dash said. "We pay our own bills."

Mike studied the lines in his palm. His fingers moved one at a time, weighing the costs. "Maybe we can work out an installment plan. I'll finish my accounting course at the tech this spring. I'm hoping to find something soon after."

"I've been paid," Curt Shafer said. He held up his hands. "It's been taken care of."

"At least tell me who it was," Dash said. "Was it Lydia Fackelman? Dr. Lydia Fackelman?"

"I can't say. I really can't."

Though of course she already knew. She couldn't imagine anyone else.

The elevator dropped her onto Peds and she engined down the corridors, fobbing her way through one locked door after another, past Maternity and the well-baby nursery, past the delivery and surgical rooms, past the nurses' station, through the heavy doors dividing the NICU from the rest of the floor. She didn't know why she was angry. Maybe it was pride; maybe it was privacy. Nurses were forever prying into one another's lives, treating other people's emotions the same way they treated bodies, with curious, judgmental detachment. Like it wasn't humiliating enough for a nearly grown boy to be catheterized by a stranger, to be wiped clean after voiding his bowels in bed. Nurses gossiped about everything: their sex lives and home lives, how their children failed to live up to expectations, the smells of their husbands' farts. The doctors were no better, despite their fancy cars and big bank accounts. As much as she loved the hospital, she hated people in her business, especially when that business concerned her son. If she could not pay Curt Shafer, she could at least scold Dr. Fackelman—for now she felt certain Dr. Fackelman had hired him—for meddling. Her charity, though well intentioned, wasn't wanted.

She stopped outside the unit. Penny's desk was empty, her light turned off. Through the glass Dash could see the beds along the windows. In the far corner, beyond the mixing table and nurses' station and partially obscured by shadow, she could see a woman's light-brown hair, a statically charged crown illuminated by the winter sunlight. The short, gray-flecked hair of a man beside her. The woman turned and Dash saw that it was Brooke Jensen, which meant that the baby in her arms was Emery. Dash could see the blue and white oxygen tubes snaking from the wall. She was glad Brooke had decided to stay. She again recalled the simple hope the NICU made possible, and for a beat envied Brooke's place in the glider.

She stood long enough to see Dr. Fackelman come into the Jensens' bed space, place her stethoscope inside her ears, and extend the bell to the blankets in Brooke's arms. Dr. Fackelman—Lydia—pulled the earpieces away from her ears and let them close around her neck. The doctor glanced toward the door, and Dash lifted her hand, hoping to beckon her out. Dr. Fackelman, however, didn't see her standing there. Harper was the one who noticed her and held her gaze across the busy room. He nodded, smiling. As though he knew something.

Fran passed by him and he spoke to her. Fran turned and came to the door. She wore a headband similar to Landon's nurse. Maybe it was more than a fad. "What are you doing? You forget your key fob?"

"I'm not on today," Dash said. "Not till Monday."

"Well, don't show your face around here. Place is a zoo."

"New admission?"

"Early this morning. Twenty-six-week twins." Fran turned to look over her shoulder. "You see that you-know-who came back?"

"Good for her."

"Well, of course you know. But it's too little, too late, I think."

"I hope not," Dash said. "I hope that's not the case."

"How's our boy?" Fran asked, her face concerned. "What's the news?"

"We won't know about his hands and toes for several weeks. They're watching his kidneys."

"He'll be okay. He's strong." Fran looked Dash up and down. "Did you eat?"

"A bagel and a Dew arrived for me this morning. Dropped off by elves, apparently."

"Ah, the magic bagel," Fran smiled. "Like manna from heaven." She'd likely been the one to call Mike to tell him to hightail it to the hospital to meet Curt Shafer. Mike should've recognized her voice, but Fran might have disguised it or given Mike a fake name. It was also possible the doctor hadn't hired the lawyer on her own. The nurses could have taken up a collection. Or even that—thinking of Harper's nod, his knowing half-smile—she'd read the situation wrong entirely.

"Thank you," Dash said. "I ate it in two bites."

"It was nothing," Fran said. "You'd do the same for me. For anyone in here." She looked back into the unit again. "Well, maybe not *everyone*."

"Not everyone," Dash said, though right then she couldn't think of a single nurse in the unit, or for that matter, a single person in the entire hospital—from Leif Gunnarson, the president, to Denny, the security guard—she wouldn't bring a hot meal to if they were in her position. All around her, down every corridor, behind every door, people were going through all kinds of things. Everyone could use a cup of kindness. She vowed to make more of an effort.

"What did you come by for?" Fran asked. "Did you need something?"

"Hard to stay away, I guess."

"Girl, not me. Punch my ticket and I am gone."

They were both lying.

Back in the burn unit she felt useless and a little restless. Maybe she *should* change into clean scrubs and clock in for a few hours. Mike could take Kasey home and she'd distract herself by restoring order to things. She was outside the education room, now emptied of Curt Shafer and his leather briefcase, when the elevator dinged. Mike and Kasey came down the hall.

"There you are," Mike said. Kasey was sucking on a large soda, the straw dark with color.

"The orthodontist says soda is bad for your teeth," Dash said.

Kasey shrugged. "I'm sick of milk."

"Let it go, Dash," Mike said. "Given everything else going on."

She smiled apologetically. "Did you get some breakfast? Get something good?"

Kasey nodded and stepped closer to her dad. Dash saw the gesture, and felt it in her throat. She didn't know how to be a mother without Landon, what role she was supposed to fill for a child who didn't need her the way Landon had. Mike had helped Kasey turn a block of pine into a racecar, and build a salt-dough topographical map of Virginia, and fashioned tiny motorized dancers out of copper wire and a battery. Mike had taught her how to ride her bike in the driveway and to shoot a layup; for God's sake, Mike had been the one to take Kasey to the drugstore when she started her period. Mike! From Dash Kasey had required nothing more than food at the end of the day, clean clothes in her drawers, a steady check to pay the bills when her dad's job moved away. For most of Kasey's life—okay, for all of it—Dash had hoped these things were enough and had relied on Mike to make up what she lacked. Starting over with Kasey seemed an impossible project, exhausting beyond measure. She wanted to sit down.

"I was about to check on the boyo," Dash said.

"Should I wait in that room again?" Kasey asked.

"Up to you," Mike said. He thought about it for a second. "Maybe you ought to."

Dash reached her arm around Kasey's shoulder and felt her daughter stiffen beneath her grip. How long would it be before Kasey and Landon would occupy the same room again? Would they ever reclaim anything like a connection? When the day came—God willing years from now—that Kasey was called upon to care for her brother, would she know him well enough to do the job? Dash squeezed the bony knob of Kasey's shoulder and had an appallingly late thought: What about the things that had happened to *her*? The things Kasey had seen, the threats made against her, the fear she'd had to live with. Her adolescence had barely begun and already she'd been subjected to far too much adulthood, and too many adult failings. Dash hoped to God that Kasey could recover, in time and with therapy, and with a mother to support her. A mother to drive her to the appointments, to wait outside the therapist's office while she cried, if she needed to cry, to listen to whatever Kasey had to say. The Three Gorges Dam, tampons versus maxi pads, the Amish churning butter. Whatever it was, Dash could listen. She could at least do that much. She could at least start there.

Dash told Mike to go ahead without her. She'd sit with Kasey for a while. Mike said he'd go down and come back in a little bit. He walked away with his hands in his pockets, his cap perched on his head. Dash opened the door to the education room—the room where she let go of her son in order to save him, so that her family might begin again—and led her daughter inside.

Part Five

25

There was no end to the things she needed to learn. Managing the ventilator made Brooke's neck so hot and sweaty she had to tie up her hair with a pencil. She had to separate the ventilator housing from the cuff, suction the opening, flush the inner cannula, and clean the skin around the flange, all while Emery lay deprived of oxygen, his mouth gaping like a fish in the well of a boat. He cried whenever Dash took her through the steps, and Dash was a pro. The idea that Brooke would have to carry out these tasks herself, alone, made her feel like she'd swallowed a brick.

The crease between her eyebrows grew moist. She tried to step away from the Isolette, but Dash gripped her arm and yanked her back. "You have to work fast." Dash didn't scold; she simply continued. "Suction out the goop but not his air. Too much suction, you'll deflate his lungs."

"How do I know?" Brooke asked. Her hands were shaking.

"Use a three count until you get the feel of it. Pretty soon it's muscle memory."

The feeding tube, thank God, was less complicated. At least Emery could breathe while Brooke gavaged formula through the G-tube. Drawing up the meds—Keppra to prevent seizures, baclofen to help with muscle spasms, vitamin D, albuterol, Atrovent, an H_2 blocker, an antibiotic—would mean tracking the dosages and when they needed to be administered and pushing them through the feeding tube with a syringe. Emery would continue to wear a pulse ox monitor on his foot. Dash unfastened the cuff and held it under Brooke's nose. "When it stinks up his room, you'll know it's time to change it."

"It'd be easier if I could take notes," Brooke said, for the hundredth time.

"A notebook is a crutch you can't let yourself lean on," Dash said. "You have to keep your hands free. You have to know what to do, not stop to look it up. The trick is to make everything a part of your daily routine. Do the same things, in the same order, every day."

Brooke's ankles throbbed from standing too long in one place. She didn't want to walk; she wanted to run. She wanted to excuse herself to the ladies', take the elevator to the lobby, and cross the parking lot to her car. In the past weeks, she'd tried to convince herself that running had been an aberration, a single moment when she'd yielded to a lesser self, but the more she tried to see herself in a better light, the more she understood her weaknesses had been anything but momentary. She was weak, and would daily battle her desire to submit to weakness's pull to run again. She wondered how long she'd last.

"Welcome to forever," she said, glumly.

"Not forever," said Dr. El Sadda, the pulmonologist. Brooke couldn't recall seeing her since October, though Dr. El Sadda said she'd been in the unit every other week, and had seen Emery in Madison, too. Brooke remembered that she was the one who'd been missing, not the doctor.

Dr. El Sadda wore the ends of her hijab tucked inside the collar of her white coat. The bangles on her wrists clinked as she moved her stethoscope around Emery's chest. "Not forever and ever," she said. "For now. For the next several years, but not for his whole life. There's a good chance he'll outgrow the vent. I'll bet a dollar on it."

"Not a big bet."

"Symbolic," the pulmonologist said, blinking. Her eyelashes, Brooke noticed, looked like paintbrushes. "What's the saying in English? A gentleman's wager? We are not men, so I'll say it's because I don't want to go through the trouble of making you pay. Babies aren't the same as adults. They rebound in ways adults cannot. That's their magic power."

Dr. El Sadda slid her hands around Emery's head and ran her thumb across the scar where Dr. Fackelman had placed the arterial line when Emery was hardly an hour old. Dr. El Sadda widened her eyes and smiled. "I didn't have very much faith in him in the beginning, but look at him now. I saw him in Madison and thought, 'This is a baby who wants to live.' My prediction, *inshallah*, is that he will go to kindergarten breathing on his own."

Kindergarten was a horizon so remote Brooke couldn't imagine it. "Will I ever sleep?"

"Most new parents, they don't sleep much."

"You'll have a home nurse to help you for the first few months," Dash said, coming back to the bedside. "You'll get used to it. Right when you get accustomed to things being one way, they'll change."

"If he comes home," Brooke said. The decision had not yet been made. Harper had scheduled appointments with two long-term care facilities, one in Hanover and one in Green Bay. Just to explore the option, he said. Do their due diligence.

Brooke saw the nurse's thoughts drift away. "How is he?" she asked. "How's Landon?'

"We're moving him into his new place on Saturday. A group home the lawyer found for him. He'll live with four other boys close to his age."

"Sounds like a frat house," Dr. Fackelman joked.

"Just no beer, no girls, and a strict bedtime," Dash said. "Not that I'd know a frat house if I fell into one."

Dr. El Sadda had moved over to the twins in Bed Seven. Her silk hijab bowed toward the Isolette as if in prayer. The baby's mother, still panic-stricken, sat in the glider in a yellow bathrobe. Brooke had overheard Dr. Fackelman tell the woman that her babies were both doing quite well, given their gestational ages. Both would survive, though who could say for sure until it happened?

"How do you feel about him going there?" Brooke asked Dash. In spite of all she was learning to do, she didn't know what she wanted. Not yet. "Do you feel okay about it?"

"It's like anything," Dash said. "You deal with it because it's your life." She snapped shut the buttons on Emery's sleeper and wiggled the pacifier in his mouth. "Don't get me wrong. It'll be better than where he was." Dash slid her arm around Brooke's waist, low enough that the other nurses couldn't see her do it. The women's sides pressed together. "I thank God every day that he's alive, thanks to you."

At first Kasey said she didn't want to come. Mike said she didn't have to; no one expected her to be there. There was cold chicken in the fridge and leftover potatoes she could microwave for lunch. They'd only be gone a few hours. Dash said she'd let Georgina Heineman know Kasey would be home alone, in case there were any problems.

Kasey sprawled on the couch with the remote control on her chest while Mike loaded the car. Dash had called the facility director to ask if cookies were okay to bring, if she brought enough for all the residents, and he'd said that would be fine. She waited till the last minute to take the final batch out of the oven, sliding them, still hot and soft, onto the wax paper inside the Rubbermaid and snapping down the lid, hoping to trap in some of the aroma. Landon's room, when she and Mike toured it, had smelled slightly damp, either from a leaky pipe in the walls or the carpet cleaner. Curt Shafer said the facility was among the best in their part of the state. Some of the residents had lived there for years; others had been able to eventually live on their own.

Dash wrapped the Rubbermaid in a dish towel. "I left you a few," she said to Kasey. "Eat lunch first, okay?"

Kasey flicked off the television. "Maybe I'll come."

"You sure?" Dash asked, and Kasey said she was. Kasey slid her feet inside her boots and zipped her down vest beneath her fleece. Ice had begun to drip from the eaves of the roof, hanging from the gutters in long stalactites that shone in the sun.

The group home lay on the south side of Hanover, down a small side street behind the technical college and only a mile from the mall. On the other side of a chain-link fence, truck-driving students were practicing backing the rigs between parallel lines of orange cones. The private drive led to a parking lot surrounded by four brick ranch-style houses and a central commons area, still covered in snow, with both a basketball and a volleyball court and three charcoal grills on steel posts. A lopsided snowman with a cucumber nose slowly melted into the asphalt, a stream of water running toward the grate. The director had spoken of summer cookouts with cornhole games and music, hand-cranked homemade ice cream, square dancing taught by a volunteer. Every week had different activities. Residents weren't allowed to hide away in their rooms; they had to join the community. Dash thought, *This isn't a bad place to be young.*

Landon sat on the far end of the sectional sofa curved along two walls of the living room in House B. Like the other boys beside him—one heavyset and bearded in an oversized T-shirt, another whose broad forehead and drooping round cheeks Dash recognized as the markers of Williams syndrome—he stared at the television with his mouth open. Close one eye and they were just boys, hanging out on a Saturday morning. Dash didn't recognize the show, but she remembered Paul, the house manager. Thick through the chest and gut, with tattoos emerging from his rolled-up sleeves that made his arms look even stronger. Paul shook Mike's hand and offered to help unload the car.

"We can manage," Mike said. He carried a duffel bag on each shoulder and a box in his hands. "We don't have but two trips' worth."

Mike carried the luggage down the hallway toward Landon's room while Dash and Kasey followed behind. Dash carried two sacks of groceries and Kasey toted a laundry basket of folded towels. All three boys looked at her when she stepped into the foyer, watching her cross the room. Even in her vest and fleece, she was still a girl, with hair down her back and small hands, and the boys watched her. Kasey set the basket on the floor and stepped toward the door, and Dash saw she was still afraid. She'd be afraid until she decided she wasn't. When Mike returned, Dash nodded toward her daughter, so her husband could see what was happening. "Come on, Kase," Mike said, setting his hand on her shoulder. Dash watched Kasey exhale. Only with him did she truly feel safe. "We've more stuff to get yet," Mike said, and led her outside.

Landon's room came furnished with a twin mattress, a nightstand, and a dresser. The stale dampness was now mixed with piney disinfectant. Landon's window was gray with silt and the room struck Dash as small and bare and too dark. She told herself to pretend the room was a dorm; she should pretend she was dropping her firstborn off at college, the way other parents did, overcome with disbelief that time, once as inexhaustible as a magician's handkerchief, had run out so quickly. Come Monday, Landon would start the ServSafe Food Handler program at the tech so he could one day get a job in a restaurant.

Dash lifted the latches on the window and slid the pane a few inches to the left, to let in some fresh air. The breeze smelled of diesel from the trucking school, but also of the crocuses beneath the window, and the cold air dragged away the room's closed-up musk. Landon came in and sat on the bare mattress. Dash reached for a hanger, but stopped herself. "Come help me," she said. "It's good for you to learn how to do these sorts of things."

Landon stood and shuffled forward. The scars on his cheeks, where the gangrenous patches had been cut away, were twisted and tight, like melted plastic. He was missing the index finger on his right hand, the ring and pinky on his left, all below the second knuckle. Thankfully, he still had both thumbs and all his toes. His penis, too, had come through, though only Landon could say whether the sensation there had changed. He'd turned compliant in the last few months, since going to the Herons'. If his spirit had been broken, Dash hoped it might at least help him get along in the world.

She offered him a hanger and he took it from her, letting it dangle from his thumb. "Pants you fold in half," she said, showing him. "Like this. Your T-shirts we'll put in the dresser, but your work shirts and polos will look better if you hang them up. I like to button the top button and slide the hook up from underneath. That way your collars don't stretch out. See?"

His hands made the job slower, but by using his thumbs to push the buttons through the holes, he eventually got his clothes onto the hangers and into the closet. Dash set out his underwear and socks and told Landon to find a place for them in his dresser. He put the underwear in the middle drawer, closest to his waist, and the socks on the bottom. Dash no longer organized his clothes into outfits the way she once had. Landon would pick out his own clothes. If they didn't match, it didn't much matter.

Dash opened the cookies, and a small puff of steam rose out of the container, sugary and sweet. The chocolate melted on her tongue. Landon had chocolate in the corners of his mouth. "We brought you a surprise," she said, moving the flat, paper-wrapped rectangle out from behind the bedroom door. Landon tore at the paper, shredding it into confetti, and squealed when he saw the posters, one of *The Golden Lance* and the second of the Backstreet Boys, both in lightweight plastic frames. "Your sister picked these out for you."

Landon clapped. "Sweet!"

Dash had brought Command Strips so she could hang the posters without using a hammer or nails. She asked Landon where he wanted them to go and he pointed to the wall above the dresser and the wall above his bed. She unfolded Landon's sheets and comforter and stretched them across the mattress. With the bed made and a line of clothes spanning the closet rod, the room no longer looked so forlorn and empty. The next time she came, the house would look more familiar. She'd welcome the sight of his dirty clothes on the floor, the dimensions of the laundry basket beneath her arm, the weekly errand during which she'd pretend that Landon's life, or hers, hadn't changed. Eventually—and she knew this already—she'd stop comparing Landon's new life to his old. Eventually, she'd stop pretending.

26

Brooke asked the nurse on Peds if a little girl with cystic fibrosis had been admitted. If not now then maybe recently. The nurse's lips were deeply wrinkled and her teeth were smudged with lipstick. She wasn't allowed to say who was or wasn't on the unit. Brooke held up her wristband. "It's not like I'm a reporter," she said, forgetting for a moment that she was married to one.

The nurse said the law was the law.

"Maybe you could give her a message, if you see her?" Brooke asked.

The nurse absently slid the note beneath her keyboard and went back to whatever she was looking at on her screen. Brooke logged into Facebook and searched through every Ingrid in Hanover, but none of them were her. The only other thing she could think of was to use the bathroom closest to Peds, which took her past the Maternity rooms, all those doors open to new families, other families, mothers so young they looked like children, siblings and grandparents and dads. In one she saw a woman cradling her baby against her naked breast while two male guards from the Department of Corrections stood watch; in another, two men mooned over a newborn in a bassinet while Jenny Ramirez talked to the mother in the bed. Nearly every room was festooned with flowers or balloons or both, and she recalled the way the celebrations had once bothered her. Now she saw them for what they were. Offerings to the gods for their babies' safe passage into the world.

Their lawyer told them that Justus was likely heading back to jail for the unlawful imprisonment charge. Child endangerment and manufacturing narcotics in the presence of a child would surely bump up his sentence. Child Protective Services had been initially skeptical about placing Atlantis with Brooke and Harper, given Brooke's disappearing act, but when no other family could be located, they'd come around. If Justus did indeed end up back in prison, there was a solid chance Brooke and Harper would get to keep Atlantis, though both their lawyer and Maggie Caras thought it best to let Atlantis settle in for several months before anyone started talking about adoption. Brooke felt sorry when she thought of Justus, as though his returning to prison was somehow her fault. She already blamed herself for so many things, so many fallouts and still-smoldering catastrophes, that it was hard not to keep adding to the pile. "She'd be in foster care one way or another," Harper said. "Better that she's with us."

It had taken half a bottle of conditioner to work most of the knots out of Atlantis's hair, and still the hairstylist had had to take off more than six inches to get the rest. Atlantis ended up with a cute pageboy just long enough to pull into a small ponytail. Brooke bought a plastic step stool at Target for Atlantis to stand on while she brushed her teeth. The dentist said Atlantis needed to do a better job brushing, but she didn't have any major problems. Her baby teeth would begin falling out in the next year, so now was the perfect time to develop better habits. Each night Atlantis worked the toothbrush around her mouth long past the point of thoroughness, eager to prove herself, especially when Ollie was there. He hung a sign on his bedroom door that said

NO GIRLS ALLOWED, and several times asked how long Atlantis would be staying—a question Brooke was glad to let Harper answer. Tucking Atlantis into bed, Brooke found the toothpaste and three boxes of cereal stashed beneath her bedframe. Just in case her next foster home didn't have those things, Atlantis explained. Brooke smoothed the little girl's hair away from her forehead. "You're not going to another foster home," she said. "Not if I can help it. You're here now."

Brooke's mother agreed that taking in Atlantis was the right thing to do. "The *only* thing, given her dismal circumstances," Pamela said. "Any child spared the foster system is a good thing. Unless, of course, there's no alternative." About Brooke's absence during Emery's stay in Madison, she said not a word, but a few days later a box arrived containing games and puzzles as well as gift certificates to the movies, Chuck E. Cheese, Merry Maids housecleaning service, and a note in her mother's precisely slanted cursive. "Please let me know when I might visit again. I can't wait to meet your growing family."

The week Atlantis started kindergarten, Brooke took her to Old Navy, where they bought six pairs of jeans and corduroys, as many turtlenecks and T-shirts, three sweatshirts, three nightgowns, heaps of socks and panties, two dresses for fancy occasions, a new winter coat, and a backpack and lunchbox for school. Atlantis said she liked whatever she tried on, and by the end of the afternoon Brooke had concluded that Atlantis had probably never been shopping before or had someone buy her new clothes. To her surprise it was the lunchbox, rose gold with a glittery letter A affixed to the side, that Atlantis cradled in her arms on the way home, opening the zipper and pretending to eat. She wanted to know her teacher's name and what she looked like, whether her classroom would have easels and a computer and a microwave oven, like on *Sid the Science Kid.* "I don't know yet," Brooke said, looking into the rearview mirror. "We'll meet her together."

Atlantis stood before the front door with her lunchbox in her hand so Brooke could take her picture. When they arrived at the school, Atlantis wanted to know exactly where Brooke would meet her that afternoon. "How about by this tree?" Brooke said.

"What if I forget which one it is?" Atlantis asked. "What if I wait by the wrong tree and you never find me?"

"Don't worry, kid," Ollie told her. "I'll find you." The night before, he'd taught Atlantis how to play Uno and told her she could watch TV with him, so long as she didn't talk during the show. "We can wait together," he said.

"I'll be here before the bell rings," Brooke said. "You won't have to wait."

Atlantis jabbed her finger at Brooke's nose. "You be right here," she said, sternly. "Right in this spot."

"I promise," Brooke said.

The next week, Brooke walked by a Peds room and found what she'd been looking for. Anna lay tranquilized with a nebulizer over her mouth and nose and the patchwork sweater clutched in her arms. Brooke knocked on the doorframe as she stepped inside. The chair beside the bed was empty, the bathroom door was open and the light was off. "Hello," Brooke said, though Anna didn't stir. She walked to the end of the hallway, turned and came back, and there she was, coming from the other direction. "I was just about to come looking for you," Ingrid said, opening her arms to embrace her. "One of the nurses said someone had asked for me. I figured it was you."

"Did you get the message I left?"

"Message? What did it say?"

"Just that I was here. If you were, too, I hoped we could have coffee again."

Ingrid craned her neck around the doorway. A thin cloud of mist floated over her daughter's face. "After the day I've had, I need a beer."

They cut across the parking lot, past Seoul Food and toward Wilkie's Tavern, their footprints side by side in the snow. The clouds were low and diaphanous and moisture beaded on Brooke's face. The oak bar at Wilke's was as ornate as a church organ, with fleurs-de-lis in the molding and an expansive mirror behind the glass shelves. Brooke and Ingrid sat facing their own reflections. Brooke's hair had blown sideways and her cheeks were red. Ingrid's eyes teared from the cold. Her eyeliner had started to run. "When I left the message with the nurse," Brooke said, "I realized I didn't know your last name."

"We should exchange numbers," Ingrid said, pulling her phone from her purse. "You've got to be close to going home by now."

"Another few weeks."

The bartender set the beers in front of them, the glasses white with frost. Ingrid sucked at the foam. "There are a lot of things to come, once you leave the hospital," she said. "There's the whole rest of life. I'm guessing you could use the support."

Brooke nodded. "Yes, I could."

Ingrid stared down at her beer with her hands in her lap. "I'm not being honest," she said. "*I* could use the support. Anna's getting sicker and I don't have many friends left from my life before her. Most people don't understand how consuming this whole thing is." She waved her hands as if to say, *this place, this bar,* though Brooke understood what she meant. "It would be nice to talk to someone without having to apologize for bringing up the subject again."

"There's something I should tell you," Brooke said, and Ingrid's eyebrows went up. "Emery went to Madison last month for surgery. I was supposed to go with him, but I didn't. I left him." Ingrid didn't move, so Brooke came out with the rest. Not only Justus and Atlantis but also the doctor she'd visited in Papasay, the stretch of empty weeks before that when she'd visited less and less often until she'd hardly come in at all. It was the first time she'd told the entire story to anyone and it occurred to her that she'd wandered the corridors looking for Ingrid specifically in order to tell it to her. She felt as though she'd pulled a stopper from a sink full of stagnant water.

Ingrid listened without interrupting, then sat quietly. "That *was* you, then," she said after a time. "That day at Sears."

"I didn't know what to say when I saw you."

"You looked bad. I remember thinking that you looked really bad."

"Yes."

"You'd had enough," Ingrid said. "You know you're not supposed to feel that way, so you felt you had to punish yourself." She leaned closer. "Anna spent a few weeks in at the children's hospital in Milwaukee after she was diagnosed. There was a girl on her floor whose mother had tried to drive the two of them into a lake. Not Lake Michigan, some other lake in their neighborhood. The tires went through the ice before the water was deep enough to go under. The mom was over in the other hospital, on the psych unit, while her daughter was in the PICU. All the nurses talked about her like she was batshit, but when they finally let her come visit, I could tell she wasn't. She was exhausted." Ingrid stared at herself in the mirror behind the bottles. "Here's the kicker. At the time, I'd been having the same thoughts myself. For me, it wasn't the lake. It was the garage. With her weak lungs, she'd have gone fast. I used to lie in bed thinking about how it would all play out. Sitting in the back seat with her, the heater and the radio on, kissing her toes until she fell asleep. Then I'd have fallen asleep holding her."

"What about your husband?"

"It took me a while to realize that my little Jonestown fantasy was a sign. Tony has good insurance, and he comes over to visit with her. He couldn't do to the day-to-day. I blame him and I don't. The day-to-day is hard."

"That's the part that scares me the most," Brooke said. "I haven't been much of a stepmother in the last year. Now I'm a foster mom, too. The nurses keep telling me that Emery will need all this attention if we bring him home, and that scares me. I don't want the other kids to suffer. I'm afraid of what I might turn into."

Ingrid sipped from her beer and rolled her lips together. "Sometimes I think about the people who lived in the 1800s. You know, all those Germans and Swedes who came to Wisconsin to farm. They spent most of their time outside, even in the winter. They were peasants, so I suppose they were made of sturdier stuff. Back then, though, if a baby came early, it died. If a baby had CF, it was considered sickly and eventually it died, too. There was a natural order to things. The weak and small didn't make it, like with the farm animals. People accepted it. They tried again."

"Until they died of dysentery," Brooke said. "Or in childbirth."

"Yes, well, there's that. All I'm saying is that things were different without the endless limbo. All the talk of hope." Ingrid pressed her fingers against the sides of her temples. "My God, I am so sick of all the bullshit about hope. 'Hope' this and 'hope' that. It's just a way of kicking the can down the road so that someone else can shell out the bad news. There's a relief to the thing happening, the finality. Which we never seem to get." She looked off again. "Until, I guess, we do get it."

Brooke didn't know much about cystic fibrosis, but judging from the way Ingrid was talking, she guessed Anna's outlook was grim. Was it better to die at four or five than to make it to your twenties, when you finally caught a glimpse of an entire life? Emery could outgrow the ventilator by kindergarten or he could die of pneumonia. They could have Atlantis for three months or three years. Was it worth it to put so much time and energy—so much hope—into such a gamble? Into a life with a glass heart under constant threat of shattering?

"I guess I'm trying to say, I don't fault you," Ingrid said. "Mothers are supposed to be these superheroes endowed with some primal life force that makes us all invincible when it comes to protecting our children. Mama grizzlies. But it's all bullshit, you know? Something to post on Facebook when you're not getting enough attention. Mothers are just people. You're just a person. Everyone has a limit."

"I keep thinking of things I could have done differently," Brooke said.

"If that kind of thinking ever led anywhere, no one would ever have sex in the first place. You've got to think in totally different terms."

Brooke twisted her mouth. "Such as?"

"Such as you'll never look for a parking place again. Fuck the soccer moms in their SUVs."

Week by week, babies were discharged, new infants were admitted, and Emery advanced along the windows. From

Bed Five to Four, Four to Three, Three to Two. Snow fell, a swarm of static that clung to the bricks before melting into long tendrils that dripped down the mortar. Emery ate two ounces, then three, and Dr. Fackelman told Brooke to bring in the stroller. She and Harper needed to practice getting Emery in and out of it, along with the portable ventilator and the monitor, the primary oxygen tank and the backup. They shouldn't go anywhere without a backup.

The double strollers—they'd bought two—had sat in their boxes in the back of the garage since the summer. They'd been purchased in a fit of optimism after their weeks of arguments about whether to reduce the pregnancies, when they believed they'd need room for four babies. The cardboard was speckled with mold, but the strollers inside were encased in plastic. After a good wipe down, Dash suggested that the equipment ride up front so Emery could have the rear seat. Removing the canopy shade over the front seat made it easier to get the ventilator and monitor to fit. The oxygen canisters slid in nicely down below.

Together Brooke and Harper wheeled him through the corridors, through Maternity and Peds, through Med-Surg and the anterooms of the ICU and Oncology. They spent several mornings this way, turning into corners of the hospital they'd never seen before, even after all this time. Strangers were drawn to the stroller, blind to the equipment in the front seat; only once they peered inside did they understand and turn hard on their heels or, worse, pretend not to notice. The elderly volunteers in their blue vests said things like, "How adorable!" despite the terror in their faces. At least they tried to say something nice. All the same, Brooke scowled at anyone who came too close. She was becoming a scowler. But she was also, she knew, recovering an instinct she feared she'd lost.

Strolling together, they talked: about the equipment they'd need, the therapists and specialists they'd likely visit. Emery would have retinal surgery at some point, and the G-tube and tracheostomy were active surgical wounds requiring diligent attention. Muscle spasticity and seizures were both issues they'd need to watch for. Atlantis needed trauma-informed counseling and a tutor to help her catch up in school. Going back to work was impossible, at least in the near term; maybe she could freelance part-time. Ingrid sold Pampered Chef products, so maybe Brooke could do something like that on the side. Slowly they stopped debating the merits of the acute care facility and agreed to bring Emery home. Brooke told herself they could revisit the question of the facility later, while also knowing that once he came home, they'd never give him up.

One Saturday morning while Ollie was with his mom, Brooke allowed Atlantis to push the stroller away from the locked units and down a corridor of meeting rooms, carpeted spaces with tables and chairs, a few larger rooms empty of furniture. Brooke and Harper flanked the stroller on either side, Harper with a hand on Atlantis's shoulder to help her move the weight of their rolling barge. Three abreast, they took up half the hallway. Atlantis pushed with her head down, though she refused to quit when Brooke asked if she needed a break. "If I'm going to be his big sister, I have to do the stroller," Atlantis said. "For when I babysit."

"No babysitters for a while," Brooke said. "Though you're already a great big sister."

She peeked inside to check on Emery, who lay sleeping with his thumb inside his gums.

Harper made a fist and flexed his bicep. "You're strong," he said to Atlantis. "Everyone knows big sisters have to be super strong. So you can teach Em to ride a bike."

Atlantis's eyes filled with tears. "I don't know how to ride a bike!"

"Ollie will teach you," Harper said. "As soon as it's warm out."

Atlantis drew in a long breath. Brooke watched her chest expand inside her sweatshirt, her small belly protruding. Atlantis shook her head, tightened her grip on the stroller handle, and went back to pushing.

They heard singing at the far end of the hallway. They walked toward it, stopping to look inside the open door. A balding man in a flowered aloha shirt played the guitar while two children stood beside him, pantomiming hand gestures. The audience was nearly all children. Fran stood at the front, too, her hands on her knees, and Dr. Fackelman leaned against the wall near the door, the sleeves of her blouse rolled to her elbows. The doctor came toward them. "Do you want to come in?" she asked.

"Somebody's birthday?" Brooke asked.

"NICU reunion," the doctor said. "We invite families back every year."

Atlantis slid between the adults and through the doorway. "Go on, darling," the doctor said, touching the back of her head.

Brooke's gaze followed Atlantis as she stepped between the children seated on the floor, toward an open spot on the carpet. The crowd was several dozen strong, in jeans and sneakers and hooded sweatshirts, baseball caps and stocking caps and braids. Several wore glasses but many did not, and if any of the children needed supplemental oxygen or ate through a G-tube, Brooke couldn't tell from where she stood. "How many were patients in the unit?" she asked.

"There are probably a few siblings scattered in," Dr. Fackleman said. "But most are ours."

"The ones that made it," Harper said. Brooke had been thinking the same thing and was glad he'd been the one to say it.

"Some of these kids were pretty sick," the doctor said. Her eyes closed gently. "The families we see for a week or two, they don't tend to come back. They want to put the NICU behind them as fast as they can. You're looking at a room full of long-termers."

"As long as us?" Brooke wanted to know. "As long as Emery?"

"I'd have to check. If Emery has the record, it's not by much."

They stood in the doorway and listened to the music. The man with the guitar told everyone to stand up, and the kids scrambled to their feet. "Theeeeeere's a dog in school!" he sang, to which the children called back, "Oh, no!"

Brooke recalled the baby—Bruce, *Brucie Smoochie*—who'd visited during their early days in the unit. Had his name not been odd she never would have remembered it. She recalled the Hmong family loading their baby into their green minivan. She scanned the parents standing against the wall but couldn't see either family. She thought of Opal then, who also should have been here but wasn't. Brooke saw her among the children in the room—Opal, as well as Pearl and Ruby, and all the babies she'd conceived and carried for a short while. Their brainwaves and dendritic flashes, their etherized disembodied souls, at last had a place to land.

Beneath the music, she could hear the steady susurration of Emery's ventilator. She could feel the machine's rhythms in the hinge of her jaw, at the back of her throat. She wasn't ready to picture Emery in this room, not yet, and maybe not ever. It was hard to believe such a day would ever come. But among the dancing children, in the center of the young survivors, was Atlantis, twirling in a line with three other girls. Had they all endured the NICU? The needles and the tubing, the vomiting and diarrhea, the drugs that made them drowsy yet unable to truly sleep, their mottled arms rigid with spasms. Did their mothers ever stop touching their chests and abdomens, palming the domes of their skulls, afraid of the trouble lurking inside? Brooke waved away the bad thoughts and instead watched the girls spin faster as the song's tempo increased. When the music stopped, they all four tumbled to the carpet, dizzy and laughing. Atlantis looked toward the doorway. Locking eyes with Brooke, she came running over with her arms spread wide, just as she had after her first day of kindergarten.

27

For six months she'd seen the NICU as a kind of a prison, but suddenly she dreaded the prospect of leaving it. Of being alone with Emery, solely responsible for him, of everything that could go wrong. Dash noticed and told her it was time for her and Harper to spend a night in the hospital with Emery so they could practice caring for him overnight. Jenny Ramirez still checked in with her almost every day, and the other nurses watched her warily, waiting for her to fail. Rooming in, Dash called it, though Brooke knew it really meant a test.

Harper's sister, Elizabeth, offered to drive over from St. Paul to spend the night with the kids. Her daughters would come, too, so Atlantis could have a slumber party with her foster cousins. Jenny Ramirez arranged for Brooke and Harper to have one of the new Maternity suites, with the queen-sized bed and the Jacuzzi tub. The lake beyond the windows was still frozen, though in the slanted evening sun—it was late March now—Brooke could see dark rivulets of water emerging between the cracked slabs. Their boat sat under a tarp in the marina; in another month, if the weather cooperated, it would be time to change the oil and fill the cooling system, scrape and repaint the hull, get it in the water. If they put up the Bimini top and Harper drove slowly, maybe Emery could go for a ride.

Dash wheeled Emery down before report out and talked Brooke and Harper through the monitor and vent controls. "Can you see all these numbers on your computer?" Harper asked. "Are we connected to the unit?"

"Not this machine," Dash said. "But we're right down the hall."

Dash lowered the volume and dimmed the monitor's screen. She put her hands on Brooke's shoulders. "Remember all those hours you spent watching the monitor? You know what you're looking at. Don't be afraid."

Harper found extra pillows in the cupboard and arranged them on the bed so they could sit up and watch TV. Emery slept in a plastic bassinet beside them, the ventilator shushing while they watched a rerun of *Law and Order*. When they were first together, creeping off to hotels and friends' apartments, there inevitably came a time after making love when they were alone together. At first, they'd filled the hours talking, but once Harper said he was going to tell Sara about her, they'd stopped. Each time they made love they were reminded that he hadn't told her yet, and that whatever love they professed for each other was diluted by the fact that it remained a secret. So they watched TV like a married couple, their heads propped and the blankets up to their shoulders. They grew to love *Law and Order* because it was always on somewhere. Such was the comfort of television: it waited for you; it took you in if you let it. Ten years later it took her in again, though when the screen split in half, the credits rolling on the bottom while the next episode started on top, she remembered watching TV with Atlantis, in the little house near the lake. She stroked the hair on Harper's arm, sorry all over again for abandoning him, and grateful he was beside her.

At ten o'clock, Harper changed into flannel pajama bottoms before warming the bottle of formula in the bathroom sink. Brooke set Emery on her lap with his back and head propped. Harper opened his sleeper and connected the feeding tube to the MIC-KEY button. Emery's eyes flashed open and he let his head sink back against Brooke's arm as the liquid sank through the syringe. He squeezed his eyes, bearing down as his face turned red. Harper removed the stopper from a clean syringe, fit the end into the feeding tube, and a moment later came the release of air. "How'd you know how to do that?" Brooke asked.

"The nurses in Madison showed me," Harper said. "Kid's got to burp somehow."

Harper slid his hands beneath Emery's armpits and lifted him from Brooke's lap, bouncing him in the crook of his arm. Emery gripped the elbow of his vent and watched, staring, while Brooke unzipped her overnight bag and withdrew her pajamas. She slid off her jeans and pulled her blouse over her head. She looked up and caught Harper's eyes on her bare legs and underwear, her breasts falling forward in her bra. Her cesarean scar a crimson rope bisecting her abdomen. She'd never wear a bikini again. "Nothing you haven't seen before," she said.

"I've missed it."

Emery's eyes were heavy. Dash had told them to try to keep him awake for a little while after he ate so his food would settle. Harper bounced him, swinging his arms from side to side.

"Are you doing this because you want to?" Brooke asked. "Or because it's the right thing to do?"

Harper sat with his white socks crossed. "I don't know. How about you?"

"I asked you first."

"I suppose they're the same," Harper said. "I *want* to do the right thing. How's that? I want to be someone who does what's right." He laid Emery in the crib, feeding the vent tube through his hands to make sure it wasn't kinked. "I know I wasn't much help these last months. I thought I was helping by staying out of the way, but deep down I knew I was a selfish prick. It all got to be more than I could handle. I'll probably feel guilty about that for a long time. I'd like to feel something better. I'd like to rebalance the scales."

"But do you *want* to?" she asked. The answer, she realized, mattered tremendously. It was the question that had been hanging over them for weeks. Despite the return of what felt like a routine—watching Harper on the news while lying in bed, waking up with him in the morning, breakfast together at the kitchen table after taking Oliver and Atlantis to school—something had lingered between them, an uncloseable distance. She hadn't come all the way home. "All the changes we'll have to make," she said. "Will you be happy?"

Harper crossed his arms, then let them hang at his sides. "I always thought of myself as a happy person. That one way or another, things would be okay if I just stayed positive. I guess I don't think that way anymore, not after Opal. If I think about happiness for too long, I'll start to talk myself out of it. So maybe it's best not to think so much." He pulled off his T-shirt and shoved it down inside his bag. "I can say this much. We've come through a lot and I'm proud of that. Ollie, Atlantis, the home we've made. I didn't expect any of it, but I'm proud of it. I'm proud of Emery, too. He had a thousand chances to quit and he didn't. He just keeps on. Talk about a fighting spirit."

"You think Ollie's okay with everything? He's had a lot thrown at him."

"He told me in the car the other day that he likes Atlantis. Says she's funny. He also told me that his mom said we're crazy for bringing a strange kid into our house, especially with a baby in the hospital. Both sound like wins to me."

"And me?" Brooke asked. "Are you happy with me?"

He stepped closer until his bare chest brushed against her breasts, unencumbered beneath her pajama top. She felt the electrostatic current between them, the frankness of his want flashing from the ether. Even here, of all places. Her own desires weren't so far away. "You and I have quite a history," he said. "I've grown attached to it. I couldn't imagine life without it."

The Wednesday before discharge, Emery's temperature climbed above one hundred, and Dr. Fackelman said they'd better run a short course of antibiotics to be safe. That set them back a week, and they didn't have Oliver again until the weekend. "Can we wait until Saturday?" Harper asked. "A few more days won't kill us, right?"

"Ollie should be there," Brooke agreed, though she spent three days pacing the unit, waiting for Emery's temperature to spike again. Every time she looked at the temperature display on the monitor, she held her breath. On Saturday morning she called the unit at seven thirty. "It's 98.6," Dash said. "Steady as a steamship."

"You're already there?" Brooke asked.

"I switched shifts. I wouldn't miss it."

While the kids ate cereal at the kitchen counter and Harper was in the shower, Brooke unearthed an old calendar from the kitchen drawer. She started on the Saturday before Labor Day and counted forward. Two hundred and three days. Dr. Fackelman told her that when it came to gauging development, height and weight, the ability to walk and talk, a preemies' adjusted age started with discharge. Today was day one.

Oliver and Atlantis watched TV in the Family Room at the hospital while Dash reviewed the discharge instructions. They'd gone through the list twice already, on Thursday and Friday, but she wanted to make sure one more time. Dash had gone down to the pharmacy herself to pick up Emery's medicines; later, they'd refill them at Walgreens. Dash lined up each bottle on the supply cart, reading the label and asking Brooke to confirm it before dropping it in the sack. Emery had follow-up appointments with neurology and pulmonology, the high-risk pediatric specialist. The home nurse would come over later that afternoon. The checklist alone took more than an hour, and Brooke felt the light passing across the window, another day going by.

It was after two when Dr. Fackelman lifted Emery from the crib and cradled him in her elbow so Ting could take a picture. Then one with Dash, one with Ting, and another with all the nurses and Brooke, too, leaning in from the right. The doctor lowered Emery into the stroller and helped buckle him in. "So long, sweet thing," Dr. Fackelman said. "Come back and see us sometime."

They wheeled through the door to the foyer where Harper stood with Ollie and Atlantis. Oliver's hands were red from scrubbing in the Family Room sink, and he stared uncertainly at the hose emerging from Emery's neck, the whir of the ventilator. "Come say hi," Brooke said. "It's okay to touch him."

Ollie didn't know where to set his hands and settled on a cupped palm over Emery's skull. He snatched his hand away when he touched the scar in his fontanel. Atlantis only stared, her eyes saucered. Dash led them toward the elevator. Harper had moved the car around and left it running, to keep it warm. Dash and Ting worked together to transfer Emery from the stroller to his car seat, one on each side of the back seat, their butts sticking out the doors. Harper collapsed the stroller and stowed it in the hatch. Brooke set the discharge paperwork on the dashboard and turned to say one final goodbye.

Brooke and Dash faced each other. The sun glared through the marbled clouds and the holly trees in the parking lot planters were starting to bud with small white flowers. The receding snow had scythed away the mulch in the beds and scoured the green out of the grass; the ice that remained was dirty and granulated. The oozing meltwater looked as black as blood. Brooke could hear birds in the branches. Dash shielded her eyes and said, "I'm on nights for the next few weeks, so if you come to the unit, I guess you won't see me."

Brooke wanted to suggest they meet for coffee or dinner, but she'd never seen a nurse run off for coffee with a former patient, and it seemed awkward to propose with Ting there and Ollie leaning against the car door. She held Dash as tight as she could. "Thank you for everything," she whispered. Dash squeezed her close, her breath at Brooke's neck.

28

Two hundred and three days after Brooke's placenta abrupted and a doctor cut open her uterus to pull Emery into the world, he was going home. Two hundred and three days. If Brooke added up all the times she'd been pregnant, the mornings she'd spent examining her belly in the bathroom mirror, the hours lying awake, imagining this moment, the days numbered in the thousands. Seated behind Harper as he piloted the car through the lot, she could hardly digest that it was occurring. That it was *now*. She watched the portable SAT monitor, addicted to it all over again; if the cool blue wave flowing across the screen were to flatten, she'd have no one to call for help. Atlantis leaned against Brooke's left arm, over the arm of her booster seat, studying the glittered polish on her fingernails. Brooke had painted them the night before. Brooke studied the razored line separating Harper's hair from the pale skin at the back of his neck, his clenched jaw whenever he turned to check his blind spot, his determination to ferry them safely home. He drove slower than the traffic, with the headlights on, like a car in a parade. The cars behind them changed lanes to pass theirs, staring at them as they zoomed by. Harper lifted one hand from the wheel and waved. Brooke told herself, "I'm driving my baby home. We're in the car right now." Here was the grand ceremony she'd once envisioned. She wondered if mothers who left the hospital two days after giving birth ever thought this way. If they had to remind themselves to pay attention.

Oliver turned around in the front seat. "How's he doing?"

"So far so good," Brooke said. Once she was home, she'd feel calmer.

Harper turned onto their street and Brooke saw the balloons tied to the mailbox. The mylar one said *It's a Boy!*, and a gigantic teddy bear, like a prize from a county fair, sat against the front door. "Jerry Stark hinted that Linda was going to string up some decorations," Harper said. "Looks like she went all out."

"Nice of her," Brooke said.

She didn't notice the little white sedan until Harper turned into the driveway. A short-haired woman waited behind the wheel. She got out and walked toward the garage. She wore a black fleece and scrub pants and carried a small bag at her hip, like an overnight guest. Brooke stayed in the back seat with Emery and Atlantis while Harper went to talk to her. She'd wanted so badly to be home, but now that she was, she wished they could keep driving around town for the rest of the day. Her patchwork family, all together for the first time, safe inside the car.

Harper led the nurse to the garage and opened the door. Emery was awake now, blinking at the shapes through the window. "This is Ronnie," Harper said.

The nurse craned her neck inside the back seat. "Hey there," she said. "Let me help you."

Brooke carried Emery in his seat while Nurse Ronnie held the vent, monitor, and pump like a wedding attendant behind a bride. Harper followed with the bag of Emery's sleepers and blankets. The three of them moved in a train through the back door and into the kitchen where Brooke wanted to pause to let the kids come inside and so Emery could take in his new home. But she could see the strain in Ronnie's face, the equipment unwieldy in the nurse's hands, so she kept going, up the stairs to the nursery, where she set the car seat carrier atop the changing table. Ronnie gloved her hands while Brooke unbuckled Emery, then reached in to take over, transferring Emery from the portable to the regular vent, a quick suction of the trach that caused Emery's face to redden. "Pipe down," Ronnie said, much too brusquely. "It's a hard-knock life."

Ronnie was here to ensure Emery's safety. Wasn't that what she feared? Keeping him as safe here as he was in the hospital? Watching Ronnie's sheathed hands, something inside Brooke rose up. This was her house, her child. "Please be gentle," she said. "Be more gentle with him."

Ronnie pulled off her gloves and dropped them in the trash can. "Do you want to get unpacked?" she asked. She moved toward the rocking chair. "I'll be here."

Oliver was at the door, looking in. He'd waited longer than anyone to meet his brother, his own two hundred and three days. His brief encounter outside the NICU an hour ago hardly counted as a proper introduction. "Could you give us a few minutes?" Brooke said to Ronnie, shooing her out.

Twenty-four-hour nursing care turned out to be not quite twenty-four hours. There were gaps: an hour or two in the morning after the night attendant left and before the day nurse came on. The same in the evenings. Ronnie was one of six on rotation, all uniformed in scrubs and fleece jackets, all superficially nice and competent, though it was Ronnie, having first disrupted her homecoming, who seemed the most present, the most invasive. It was Ronnie's voice she most often heard through the walls, Ronnie whose shifts seemed to last the longest. Brooke counted the minutes until

Ronnie left, savoring the prospect of an hour alone, but the moment the nurse's car pulled away, she grew feverish with worry. She sat in Emery's room, fixed on the monitor, watching him sleep, afraid to hold him, afraid to cook dinner or shower or make any move at all. She wished she were back in the NICU, Emery safely connected to oxygen piped in from a central plant, watched over by a team of professionals. Safely contained in his glass box against the wall.

Harper's schedule gave her a reason to stay up at night, when she felt most wired. Her drowsiest periods were the afternoons when the sun was in the trees. She had to force herself to bed when Harper came home, if for nothing else than to foster the illusion that they were a normal couple who went to bed together, whose children slept in the adjacent rooms, even if one of those rooms was occupied only half the time and the other contained a nurse paid to stand watch.

The nurses proved fortuitous in an unexpected way. Their presence lent an element of danger to sex, as though the woman in the next room were a parent who might catch them in the act. As though they were young again, desperate for each other. She and Harper spoke in whispers. They panted into each other's mouths. In the morning Brooke searched the nurses' faces for signs they'd heard them. The possibility that they *had* heard but weren't allowed to say anything made Brooke want to do it again.

She woke up before three and couldn't go back to sleep. She lay listening to Harper breathe and to the faint echo of the ventilator in the other room. Emery had a pulmonology appointment later that morning, speech therapy right after. He'd been home a month. She planned to ask Dr. El Sadda about adjusting the Albuterol because the medication seemed to be making him wheeze. There was a chance the doctor would bring down his oxygen levels or his vent pressures, either of which would be a sign of progress. If, on the other hand, Dr. El Sadda bumped him up, she'd feel crushed. She turned to her side and then onto her stomach, imagining all the worst-case scenarios. What good was sleeping in your own bed if you couldn't actually sleep? It was just another place to worry.

She sat down on the toilet lid with her phone in her hand. Ingrid would answer, but calling in the middle of the night wasn't fair. She opted instead for a text: *Coffee tomorrow afternoon? Could use someone to talk to.* She watched the message go through, and then lingered in the silence, waiting for the pulsing ellipses that said someone was listening. When nothing happened, she called the unit. She recognized Dash's voice the moment she heard it. "It's Brooke," she said.

"What's wrong?" Dash asked. "Is Emery okay?"

"The home nurse is here. I hate it when she's here, but I get more scared when she leaves."

"You're home but you're not back to normal," Dash said.

"There's no more normal. That's the problem."

In the background a monitor sounded, the grinding honk of the pulse oximeter alarm. The sounds of the NICU moved through her, and with them, the old feeling: her wistfulness for the unit's close quarters and plastic smells, its bulletproof enclosure. The comfort of its terrible isolation. "Is everything okay?"

"Probe slipped," Dash said. "Nothing to see here, folks."

"I keep wishing we were back in the unit," Brooke said. "Isn't that nuts?"

"No, Brooke," Dash said. "It's not nuts at all. Just don't forget you're Emery's mother. I was only his nurse. They're different things. I was only ever technical support."

"Hardly."

"Parents aren't personnel. Most moms get that right away because it's an instinct. This place beats your instincts out of you, so now you're doubting everything." Dash paused. "How's that little girl doing?" she asked.

"Atlantis? She's fine. Likes kindergarten. She got invited to a birthday party next month."

"Does she go to bed with clean teeth? Do you kiss her goodnight?"

"Of course."

"See what I mean?" Dash said. "You've got this. One day you'll forget all about the home nurses. You'll forget about us, too."

"Never," Brooke said.

"Maybe not being here," Dash said. "Maybe not the ordeal of it. But our names and faces. We'll become the doctors and nurses who took care of your son. The white coats and the scrubs. It's better that way. Emery won't remember us at all. We'll be a story you'll tell him."

"I keep thinking I won't know what to do when something happens."

"I made sure you knew how to do everything before you went home. I made sure of it. If you can't trust yourself, trust me."

The alarm sounded again. "I should get back," Dash said. "Do you feel any better?"

To her surprise, she did. "Would you mind if I called you again? Another night?"

"Honey," Dash said, "you can call me anytime you want."

She crossed through the darkness to Emery's room, where the night nurse, Charlotte, sat reading *People* magazine, lamplight shining on the glossy pages. "I thought I heard you talking."

"I was on the phone," Brooke said. "I came to say I'm awake. You can go early."

"I'm on till seven," Charlotte said. It was a few minutes after four.

"I couldn't sleep," Brooke said. "I'd like to be with him for a while."

"I'll need to call in," Charlotte said. She slid the magazine into her bag. She was slight and very thin. Her white nurse's shoes looked enormous.

"I won't tell if you don't."

Charlotte hesitated before she nodded. "I'll call the office later." She put on her coat and slid her hands inside her gloves.

The house shifted as the front door opened and closed. In the silence that replaced the clamor of the nurse's exit, Brooke could hear Ollie snoring. She cracked open his door to peek in and found him with his mouth open, his room close with the funk of adolescence. In the next room, Atlantis lay beneath a mound of down and cotton, one small foot peeking out the side. Brooke kissed her fingertips and touched her foster daughter's soft toes.

Emery stared at her through the slats of his crib. His eyes seemed to focus better in dimmer light. Right then they were still. They did not flutter and they did not roll. The pulses in his brain had paused. Emery gazed intently at Brooke, his eye whites opalescent in the moonlight through the window and the reading lamp crooked over the nurse's chair. Brooke slid her hand beneath his back and lifted him, careful to support his neck, the leads, the tubing of the trach. The oxygen saturation probe slipped from his foot, setting off the alarm, and Brooke fumbled to silence it before she broke the spell. Emery gazed up, unfazed. He'd known this noise his entire life; to him there was no alarm, no reason to fear. He knew only the life he'd lived so far. Everything Brooke knew of love and the world, everything about what was possible or inevitable, had been altered by the same span of time. She wasn't prepared for the rest of life, but she'd hadn't been prepared before and somehow she'd made it this far. At least now she could feel the shape and weight of what she didn't know. The monitor glowed its ethereal glow beside the crib. She shifted Emery to her shoulder, his head against her chest and the breathing tubes in the pocket between their two bodies. She held his small diapered bottom in her palm.

On the sidewalk below, a dark figure wrapped in a parka and hat held a dog by a leash. The streetlamps tinted the asphalt and streaks of early light striped through the clouds. Two blocks over, the lake ice was melting. The sturgeon were waking from their long hibernation. Everything buried by snow was resurfacing, every fallen leaf and flower, every shriveled insect and scrap of garbage, every living thing sent under by winter. The dog couldn't get enough of it. It sniffed hungrily at the grass and tree, then lifted its leg while the owner looked up at Brooke's window. Charlotte's reading lamp was still on behind her. Brooke felt exposed, standing there in her T-shirt and pajama bottoms, her hair in a knot, the baby in her arms connected to a machine. She was on display behind another pane of glass. Her scowl pulled her mouth toward her chin and she cupped her hand over Emery's head to shield him from the dog walker's prying eye, his morbid curiosity. But when she caught her reflection in the window, she saw what her neighbor must have seen when he lifted his eyes to her: nothing more than a mother holding a baby in the first hours of the morning.

Author's Note

On a wet, gray afternoon in February 2007, the rain turning to snow as the light faded and the temperature dropped, my wife delivered our second child: a boy, like our first, and, like our first, a surprise. We'd learned of the pregnancy only a few weeks before we moved to Appleton, Wisconsin, where I was to begin teaching at a small liberal arts college. It had been a taxing fall and winter: Wisconsin was darker and colder than any place my wife or I had ever lived, we knew no one in our town, and early ultrasounds of the fetus had shown signs of a lethal genetic anomaly, requiring a series of expensive and invasive tests. The results, thankfully, had come back negative, but on New Year's Eve, my wife started bleeding, and we rushed to the hospital, fearing premature labor. The obstetrician scheduled an induction for a week before our son's due date—despite the difficult road we'd traveled, the baby was healthy, the doctor assured us, and everything would be fine.

When the nurse handed him to us, wrapped in a blanket, rosy and warm, he did seem fine. But when she opened the blanket on the warming table to measure his temperature, weight, and length, she saw that his chest had turned gray, his lips a dull lavender. His five-minute Apgar score, which assesses vital signs, was lower than his one-minute. His skin was pale; his arms and legs had gone floppy, unresponsive to stimuli and his breathing was shallow. My mother-in-law, a veteran pediatric nurse in a major children's hospital, stood over her grandson with her lips pursed. She cooed gently to him and reassured the delivery nurses they were doing a good job, but her face gave away her concern.

Chest X-rays revealed fluid in his lungs. Later tests would warn of an enlarged heart. The snow was falling harder, sticking to the windows and whiting out the cars in the parking lot. The labor and delivery nurses were growing anxious. My wife, who had worked as a medical social worker in the same children's hospital as her mother, recognized the nurses' anxiety for what it was: the baby was too sick to stay in the regional hospital. That evening, a specialized nurse in a blue jumpsuit threaded an intubation tube between our son's vocal cords, connected his lungs to a ventilator, and handed him off to two mustachioed paramedics, who loaded him into a portable incubator and wheeled him through the empty hospital corridors to an ambulance waiting outside. They drove him a half hour south to a hospital with a neonatal intensive care unit, my wife and I following behind. The windshield wipers struggled to stay ahead of the blizzarding snow, and I lost sight of the ambulance halfway through what felt like an interminable journey, driving in silence while my wife, one day postpartum, cradled her stomach and tried not to cry. I'd never been so scared in my life.

After ten days, our son's lungs had recovered enough for him to come home. The heart issue, too, had resolved as his lungs responded to the medication. The day of his discharge, the neonatologist posed for a picture with him before the nurses helped us secure his carrier into the back seat of our car. I was sure I'd feel calmer once we got him home—I'd been fantasizing about his homecoming since the night of his birth.

Instead, I had trouble sleeping. I lay in the dark and listened to his faint exhalations, worried that the baby would spontaneously stop breathing. As the days moved forward and winter melted into spring, the minute-by-minute tick-tock playing in my mind of my son's birth, decline, and hurried admission to the NICU began to collapse into a nebulous dread, one that subsumed even the initial happy memories of his arrival. I felt as if I were watching a city recede in my rearview mirror, all the buildings and parks and freeways merging into a hazy skyline in which the NICU remained the only recognizable structure.

In a stroke of either dumb luck or divine providence, two weeks after our son's discharge from the hospital, my wife accepted a position as a social worker at the NICU in Appleton's Catholic hospital—a different hospital from the one where our son was treated, though it was of similar size, capacity, and level of care, and it served the same northeastern Wisconsin community as ours did. This meant that my wife essentially returned each day to the site of what had been our worst nightmare: the same assembly of ventilators, incubators, monitors, IV pumps, and bilirubin lights that had surrounded our infant son. The prospect of working in such an environment terrified me, but my wife welcomed it. She felt she better understood the agonized worry of the parents in the NICU now that she had endured the same worry herself, and she felt a special bond with the fragile newborns, some weighing barely more than a pound.

It was my wife's responsibility, as the sole social worker for the unit, to ensure that babies would be discharged to safe home environments. She screened parents for postpartum depression and housing insecurity and helped them apply for Medicaid. Most of the babies in her unit—a Level III NICU—survived, which meant that their parents' experiences largely echoed ours: a frightful beginning gradually giving way to a return to normal life. The most acute cases, those requiring surgical interventions, were transferred to Level IV NICUs in Madison or Milwaukee. Rarely, though, a baby would be born too early or too sick to save. On those nights—and the worst tragedies often seemed to occur in the dead of night—my wife would go the distance with the families, talking the parents through the decision to withdraw treatment, then staying in the room while they held their children for the first and final time. Each evening, when she arrived home from work, I plied her with questions. I wanted to know everything she'd seen, everything that had happened. I could envision these stories so clearly, as though they were happening not to strangers but to me.

In June, we attended the wedding of one of my wife's coworkers, a neonatologist. After the ceremony, we accompanied other members of the NICU staff to a local brewpub. I happened to sit beside a nurse who had recently started working in the NICU at Children's Minnesota, where a young couple had given birth a few weeks earlier to sextuplets. They'd been conceived with the help of the fertility drug Follistim, which had caused the mother's ovaries to release multiple eggs in one ovulation cycle. The couple's doctors had urged them to "reduce" the number of fetuses, but the parents, both deeply religious, had refused.

The sextuplets were born at twenty weeks of gestation, a full month shy of their third trimester and only halfway to full term. The heaviest of the six weighed a whopping nineteen ounces, the smallest only eleven. They were among the smallest human beings ever to be born alive, and by the time I sat beside the nurse after the wedding, three of the babies had died. Two more would perish by the end of July, leaving only one survivor: a boy. The birth of the sextuplets, compounded by the subsequent, seemingly endless cascade of losses, had made national news. I watched the reports obsessively, recalling my own terrified days and nights in the NICU when I stood over my son, watching his chest retract and counting his breaths. Some in the media had likened the parents to fanatical crackpots who'd landed in a mess of their own making. But I couldn't do that, not after what my wife and I had been through. That would have felt like a denial, or worse, a betrayal.

The thought of attending to my son's death, which had once seemed so near, could still make me cry. The idea of watching five children perish one by one was too much to comprehend. When I asked the nurse what it had been like, being in the NICU with the family, her eyes welled up. Along with the parents and the other members of the staff, she'd had no choice but to stare down into death's abyss and fathom its depth. Our own abyss had been shallower, and we'd forestalled going over its edge—my son was now four months old, smiling and lifting his head when laid on his belly. I'd yet to entertain the possibility of one day writing about the NICU, but at the brewpub that afternoon I felt I needed to listen, to bear witness to the things the nurse had seen.

The nurse seemed eager to talk, as though she'd been waiting for someone to ask her about the sextuplets. I leaned on my elbow, nursed my beer, and hung on to her every word. By the time we left the brewpub to head to the reception, I knew I'd one day write about the NICU.

I started working on this book in 2012. My wife had worked in the unit for five years by that point. We'd attended holiday parties, retirement send-offs, bowling nights, and summer cookouts, and several members of the staff—including the doctor whose wedding we'd attended—had become close friends. In addition to compiling a long reading list, I contacted the volunteer coordinator at the hospital and offered to do any task, no matter how menial, so long as it was in the NICU. I took a brief orientation class, pledged not to release any medical information relating to the babies or their parents, and was given a name badge and a vest to wear over my shirt.

For six months I folded laundry, restocked supply carts, and answered the phone. I sanitized the equipment and got reacquainted with the noises and smells of the unit, this time without the panic that every blinking light and honking sound meant my son's heart was stopping. Some weeks there would be a frenetic rush of admissions, the doctors working around the clock for several days in a row, and, a week or two later, the unit would empty and the staff would spend the morning gossiping at the nurses' station. During the slower weeks, I reorganized the medical supply closet and assembled brochures into admission packets, which my wife would give out when she met with the families. When things really slowed down, I'd duck into a corner and scribble in my notebook.

I started to see the NICU as occupying a kind of vortex within the larger hospital. The unit was adjacent to Labor and Delivery, the one hospital wing where people routinely went not in sickness but in health and with the expectation that the outcome would always, and only, be good. Babies would tumble into the world, healthy and vernix-coated and attended by video cameras and balloons. The NICU, in contrast, lay behind a locked door, nondescript from the outside, a door most visitors and patients and hospital employees breezed by without bothering, or daring, to look inside. To have a baby rushed from the delivery room or its mother's arms to such a place was to be yanked rudely away from the happy fantasy, like a fish plucked from a stream. And like a gasping trout lying in the hull of a boat, your abiding thought was to re-enter the water from whence you came as soon as possible. I recalled a NICU nurse telling me, as we stood together beside my son's bed years earlier, "People think that being in here is the end of the world. They don't understand that there's a place in the world for sick babies." I still thought about the family of the sextuplets. They still maintained their website and occasionally posted updates: the baby that had survived was nearly the same age as my own son. He had some mild cerebral palsy and retinopathy, both resulting from his extreme prematurity, but he otherwise seemed pretty healthy. Like my son, he played on playgrounds and smiled beside his parents, and now two younger sisters, in their photographs. I couldn't say whether or not the family was happy, but they seemed to have charted a path forward. A baby born halfway through the gestational process had not only survived but had found a place in the world. His was a story of tragedy and endurance and, ultimately, redemption. Precisely the kind of story I wanted to tell.

Acknowledgments

Everything We Could Do would not have been possible without the selfless efforts of many people. The NICU staff at St. Elizabeth Hospital in Appleton, Wisconsin, welcomed my presence and continued to indulge my questions long after my time as a volunteer had come to an end. Thanks, especially, to Kathy Moy-Bye, RN, for helping grease the skids with the staff, to Dr. Kim Seeger Langlais and Dr. Cathy Fakler Azzarello for their on-the-fly lessons in neonatology, and to Julie Coenen, RN, Tracy Adams, RN, and Tracy Heiman, RN, for explaining every procedure, process, and piece of equipment in the NICU. I'm also grateful to Paula Gilson, RN, for allowing me to attend her class on neonatal resuscitation. Joleen Turner welcomed the invitation to talk about caring for an extremely premature and medically compromised baby. My dear friend Julie Janus, MSS, LCSW, talked me through the nitty-gritty of treatment foster care and introduced me to several colleagues, especially Dawn Martin, who shared her experiences as both a foster parent and a mom of an adult son diagnosed with an autism spectrum disorder, and Katie Van Groll, MSW, LCSW, who answered endless rounds of questions regarding the juvenile justice system, family court, and inpatient and outpatient treatment programs for kids with intellectual disabilities. Julie also allowed me to tag along to the home of foster parents Ashly and Gary Balza, who graciously opened their doors and spoke about their efforts to help disadvantaged adolescents. To everyone who goes the distance with the most fragile and vulnerable humans on the planet—you are my heroes.

I'm additionally grateful to *The American Scholar* for printing my essay "Look Back in Wonder" (a portion of which reappears here as the Author's Note) in its spring 2023 issue. Jayne Ross was a perspicacious editor, while the ever-wise Sudip Bose championed the essay from submission to publication and in the process became a true friend. Meanwhile Michael Nye plucked an excerpt from *Story*'s slush pile and gave it a home in the journal. "Heron Lane" appears in *Story* #10. Thanks to the luminous (and numinous) Rev. Spencer Reece for allowing me to use a line from his sublime poem "ICU" for my epigraph.

Dara Hyde, my agent, believed in this novel from the very beginning, read it again and again, and never gave up on it, or on me. She's a better reader, advocate, and representative than I ever could have hoped for, and my gratitude is unending. Thanks, also, to Megan Jauregui Eccles and Taylor Schaefer for their enthusiasm, faith, and intelligent comments. Taylor showed me where I needed to revise, and her words gave me the courage to face the work. Bonnie Nadell added direction and experience from behind the scenes.

A million thank-yous to Parneshia Jones, Marisa Siegel, Courtney Smotherman, Mary Klein, Charlotte Keathley, Maddie Schultz, Kristen Twardowski, and everyone at Northwestern University Press. Marisa providentially handed my manuscript to Megan Stielstra, who saw *exactly* what I was trying to do. What a gift, to land with an editor with such a capacious mind and heart who's also a knockout writer. Megan tended to this book, and me, with mountains of love and care. If you know her, you know exactly what I mean. If you don't, go read her work. You won't regret it.

I wouldn't have made it through the writing, or the publication, of this book without the love and care of more people than I can thank here. A partial list includes Peter Allen, Scott Powley, Margaret Allen, Jeanne Powley, Robert Anthony Siegel, Karen Bender, Erin McGraw, Melanie Rae Thon, Kirsten Sundberg Lunstrum, Tim Spurgin, Jake Frederick, Peter Thomas, Lea Gysan, Angela Vanden Elzen, Rev. Dr. Linda Morgan-Clement, Rev. Patrick Twomey, Rev. Jim Kirk, Sarah Miller, Rebecca Turner, Doug Caruso, and my Crew from the U: Lynn Kilpatrick, Nicole Walker, Matt Batt, Margot Singer, and Steve Tuttle. You all provided perspective, good company, and encouragement when I wanted to quit.

Everything I write, no matter how brief or how long, I write in the hope of making my sons, Galen and Hayden, proud. Given that this book originates in Hayden's frightening birth, my life as a father was never far from my mind while I worked.

Lastly, Katherine McGlynn has made a career of meeting people in their most dire moments. For nearly twenty-five years, she's inspired me with her stories of courage and kindness in the face of illness, injury, and mortality. Her commitment to her work as a medical social worker has taught me the meaning of compassion and has helped me believe that the world is more good than bad. Thank you for sharing your life with me.